NOTHING BUT THE BEST...

Every year Terry Carr sets himself a gigantic task . . . to read *all* the original short science fiction published in hardcover and paperback books and in the numerous magazines.

And each year he selects the very best of all he has read to showcase in his highly acclaimed annual anthology.

Terry Carr's track record as an editor is stupendous. Many of the short stories, novelettes, and novellas he has selected each year have gone on to win the Hugo and/or Nebula Awards.

In this year's bumper crop Terry Carr has chosen stories about:

An orbiting experimental station . . .

A time when the world is one gigantic city . . .

Travel to alternate time-streams . . .

Legalized necrophilia . . .

. . . And lots more!

Edited by Terry Carr:

AN EXALTATION OF STARS: Transcendental Adventures in Science Fiction

UNIVERSE: One—Six

*THE BEST SCIENCE FICTION OF THE YEAR: #1—#5

CREATURES FROM BEYOND: Nine Stories of Science Fiction and Fantasy

INTO THE UNKNOWN: Eleven Tales of Imagination

WORLDS NEAR AND FAR: Nine Stories of Science Fiction and Fantasy

FELLOWSHIP OF THE STARS

THIS SIDE OF INFINITY

SCIENCE FICTION FOR PEOPLE WHO HATE SCIENCE FICTION

*Published by Ballantine Books

THE BEST SCIENCE FICTION

OF THE YEAR
#3

Edited by

Terry Carr

BALLANTINE BOOKS • NEW YORK

ISBN 0-345-25015-X-195

Manufactured in the United States of America

First Edition: July, 1974
Second Printing: June, 1976

Acknowledgments

"Something Up There Likes Me" by Alfred Bester. Copyright © 1973 by Random House, Inc. From *Astounding: John W. Campbell Memorial Anthology* by permission of the author.

"The World as Will and Wallpaper" by R. A. Lafferty. Copyright © 1973 by Roger Elwood. From *Future City*, by permission of the author and his agent, Virginia Kidd.

"Breckenridge and the Continuum" by Robert Silverberg. Copyright © 1973 by Roger Elwood. From *Showcase*, by permission of the author and the author's agents, Scott Meredith Literary Agency, Inc., 580 Fifth Ave., New York, N.Y. 10036.

"Rumfuddle" by Jack Vance. Copyright © 1973 by Jack Vance. *From Three Trips in Time and Space*, by permission of the author and the author's agents, Scott Meredith Literary Agency, Inc., 580 Fifth Ave., New York, N.Y. 10036.

"Tell Me All About Yourself" by F. M. Busby. Copyright © 1973 by Robert Silverberg. From *New Dimensions 3*, by permission of the author.

"The Deathbird" by Harlan Ellison. Copyright © 1973 by Harlan Ellison. From *Fantasy and Science Fiction*, by permission of the author and the author's agent, Robert P. Mills, Ltd., New York.

"Of Mist, and Grass, and Sand" by Vonda N. McIntyre. Copyright © 1973 by The Condé Nast Publications, Inc. From *Analog*, by permission of the author.

"The Death of Dr. Island" by Gene Wolfe. Copyright © 1973 by Terry Carr. From *Universe 3*, by permission of the author and his agent, Virginia Kidd.

"The Ones Who Walk Away from Omelas" by Ursula K. Le Guin. Copyright © 1973 by Robert Silverberg. From *New Dimensions 3*, by permission of the author and her agent, Virginia Kidd.

"Sketches Among the Ruins of My Mind" by Philip José Farmer. Copyright © 1973 by Harry Harrison. From *Nova 3*, by permission of the author and the author's agents, Scott Meredith Literary Agency, Inc., 580 Fifth Ave., New York, N.Y. 10036.

"The Women Men Don't See" by James Tiptree, Jr. Copyright © 1973 by Mercury Press, Inc. From *Fantasy and Science Fiction*, by permission of the author and the author's agent, Robert P. Mills, Ltd.

Contents

Introduction

The year 1973 saw the acceleration of one of the most important changes in science fiction's history: for the first time since science fiction became a discrete genre, as many sf short stories and novelettes were published *outside* the specialty magazines as in the magazines themselves.

The sudden burgeoning of original-stories anthologies has made the difference. In addition to the regular series anthologies (Damon Knight's *Orbit*, Robert Silverberg's *New Dimensions*, Harry Harrison's *Nova*, Robert Hoskins' *Infinity*, my own *Universe*, etc.), there was a veritable flood of original sf anthologies built around specific themes. Notable among these were *The Alien Condition*, edited by Stephen Goldin; *Eros in Orbit*, edited by Joseph Elder; *Astounding*, edited by Harry Harrison; *Bad Moon Rising*, edited by Thomas M. Disch; *Three Trips in Time and Space* and *No Mind of Man*, edited by Robert Silverberg; and a spate of original anthologies from the prolific Roger Elwood (*Future City* was probably the best). I edited one myself titled *An Exaltation of Stars*.

The result was that twice as many stories as usual were published last year. Moreover, because book publishers have less of an investment (financial *and* emotional) in science fiction's traditions, the trend away from the action-oriented pulp-adventure formulas of the past gained considerable momentum.

This expansion of the sf short story from the magazines into books is a virtual repeat of what happened to the science fiction novel twenty years ago. Prior to the 1950s, almost all sf novels were written for the genre magazines, leaning heavily on fast-action plots replete with giant-thewed heroes, damsels in distress, and interstellar battles. But when book publishers entered the field, the emphasis began to change to stories of character, social commentary, and more "literary" techniques.

Undoubtedly much of this change was due simply to the sort of snobbery that assumed a novel wasn't worthy of publication in book form unless it dealt with more subtle matters than how to brain a Venusian with a broadsword. But there was also the fact that new editors were choosing these books, editors who often came to the field with little knowledge of science fiction's past and hence fewer preconceptions about what an sf novel should be. This situation brought about a new beginning for the science-fiction novel, resulting in broader themes and techniques and a quantum leap in quality overall.

Similarly, the shorter science-fiction forms are now finding a new life in the original anthologies, and it seems to me that the average quality of these stories is definitely improving. To be sure, the sheer volume of shorter stories published last year has inevitably included a good deal of hack work, especially in those books whose editors simply assigned themes to specific writers and published whatever they got. But even the hurriedly written stories were generally more ambitious than many stories of the past.

Probably the mystique of book publication still triggers some snobbery in writers as well as in editors—a magazine is published for this month, a book is published for the ages. So writers do try to write better for books. Whether or not this really makes much sense is irrelevant; it makes for more good stories.

All of which is not to say that the sf magazines have lost their importance. Magazines like *Fantasy and Science Fiction, Galaxy,* and the rest have always published a good proportion of first-rate stories, and if their editors tend to be more conservative at times than the book editors, this isn't always a bad thing. The traditions of science fiction developed because they had lasting value.

Nonetheless, there are constant changes going on in the magazines. *Analog* has a new editor, Ben Bova, who is steadily expanding the parameters of that once-ossified publication. *Galaxy* increased its schedule from bimonthly to monthly during 1973, and at the end of the year *If* announced that a new man, James Baen, would take over as editor. Finally, and perhaps most interestingly, a new sf magazine was born—*Vertex,* a slick-paper entry emphasizing graphics and aimed at a wider audience than the regular genre periodicals.

To the extent that the sf magazines and original anthologies differ in their orientations toward science fiction, they are broadening the field, and this trend can't fail to be beneficial. In addition, publications with different ideas stimulate one another to greater accomplishments.

The job of reading all the science-fiction stories published in 1973 was much more time-consuming than in previous years because the wordage involved had virtually doubled. But I've been editing best-of-the-year anthologies for a decade now, and I can't remember a year when the task was so pleasant. I hope you'll enjoy the results.

—TERRY CARR
Oakland, California
December 1973

Something Up There Likes Me

Alfred Bester

When a master of the form retires from writing science fiction, it's a time for mourning. Thus one of the darkest hours for sf came ten years ago when Alfred Bester became an editor at *Holiday* Magazine and decided to devote all his creative energy to that job. For a decade, science fiction had to make its way as best it could without contributions by the author of *The Demolished Man*, *The Stars My Destination*, and numerous fine shorter works.

But in 1972 *Holiday* moved its editorial offices from New York to Indianapolis, and Bester chose to remain behind and return to his typewriter. *Holiday*'s loss was our gain; for example, here's a delightful new Bester novelette about the orbiting of a biological experimental station that developed strange quirks—and unexpected powers.

There were these three lunatics, and two of them were human. I could talk to all of them because I speak languages, decimal and binary. The first time I ran into the clowns was when they wanted to know all about Herostratus, and I told them. The next time it was *Conus gloria maris*. I told them. The third time it was where to hide. I told them and we've been in touch ever since.

He was Jake Madigan (James Jacob Madigan, Ph.D., University of Virginia), chief of the Exobiology Section at the Goddard Space Flight Center, which hopes to study extraterrestrial life forms if they can ever get hold of any. To give you some idea of his sanity, he once programmed the IBM 704 computer with a deck of cards that would print out lemons, oranges, plums and so on. Then he played slot machine against it and lost his shirt. The boy was real loose.

She was Florinda Pot, pronounced "Poe." It's a Flemish name. She was a pretty towhead, but freckled all over, up to the hemline and down into the cleavage. She was M. E. from Sheffield University and had a machine-gun English voice. She'd been in the Sounding Rocket Division until she blew up an Aerobee with an electric blanket. It seems that solid fuel doesn't give maximum acceleration if it gets too cold, so this little Mother's Helper warmed her rockets at White Sands with electric blankets before ignition time. A blanket caught fire and Voom.

Their son was s-333. At NASA they label them "S" for scientific satellites and "A" for application satellites. After the launch they give them public acronyms like IMP, SYNCOM, OSO and so on. s-333 was to become OBO, which stands for Orbiting Biological Observatory, and how those two clowns ever got that third clown into space I will never understand. I suspect the director handed them the mission because no one with any sense wanted to touch it.

As Project Scientist, Madigan was in charge of the experiment packages that were to be flown, and they were a spaced-out lot. He called his own ELECTROLUX, after the vacuum cleaner. Scientist-type joke. It was an intake system that would suck in dust particles and deposit them in a flask containing a culture medium. A light shone through the flask into a photomultiplier. If any of the dust proved to be spore forms, and if they took in the medium, their growth would cloud the flask, and the obscuration of light would register on the photomultiplier. They call that Detection by Extinction.

Cal Tech had an RNA experiment to investigate whether RNA molecules could encode an organism's environmental experience. They were using nerve cells from the mollusk Sea Hare. Harvard was planning a package to investigate the Circadian effect. Pennsylvania wanted to examine the effect of the earth's magnetic field on iron bacteria, and had to be put out on a boom to prevent magnetic interface with the satellite's electronic system. Ohio State was sending up lichens to test the effect of space on their symbiotic relationship to molds and algae. Michigan was flying a terrarium containing one (1) carrot which required forty-seven (47) separate commands for performance. All in all, s-333 was strictly Rube Goldberg.

Florinda was the Project Manager, supervising the construction of the satellite and the packages; the Project Manager is more or less the foreman of the mission. Although she was pretty and interestingly lunatic, she was gung ho on her job and displayed the disposition of a freckle-faced tarantula when she was crossed. This didn't get her loved.

She was determined to wipe out the White Sands goof, and her demand for perfection delayed the schedule by eighteen months and increased the cost by three-quarters of a million. She fought with everyone and even had the temerity to tangle with Harvard. When Harvard gets sore they don't beef to NASA, they go straight to the White House. So Florinda got called on the carpet by a Congressional Committee. First they wanted to know why s-333 was costing more than the original estimate.

"s-333 is still the cheapest mission in NASA," she snapped. "It'll come to ten million dollars, including the launch. My God! We're practically giving away green stamps."

Then they wanted to know why it was taking so much longer to build than the original estimate.

"Because," she replied, no one's ever built an Orbiting Biological Observatory before."

There was no answering that, so they had to let her go. Actually all this was routine crisis, but OBO was Florinda's and Jake's first satellite, so they didn't know. They took their tensions out on each other, never realizing that it was their baby who was responsible.

Florinda got s-333 buttoned up and delivered to the Cape by December 1st, which would give them plenty of time to launch well before Christmas. (The Cape crews get a little casual during the holidays.) But the satellite began to display its own lunacy, and in the terminal tests everything went haywire. The launch had to be postponed. They spent a month taking s-333 apart and spreading it all over the hangar floor.

There were two critical problems. Ohio State was using a type of Invar, which is a nickel-steel alloy, for the structure of their package. The alloy suddenly began to creep, which meant they could never get the experiment calibrated. There was no point in flying it, so Florinda ordered it scrubbed and gave Madigan one month to come up with a replacement, which was ridiculous. Nevertheless Jake performed a miracle. He took the Cal Tech back-up package and converted it into a yeast experiment. Yeast produces adaptive enzymes in answer to changes in environment, and this was an investigation of what enzymes it would produce in space.

A more serious problem was the satellite radio transmitter which was producing "birdies" or whoops when the antenna was withdrawn into its launch position. The danger was that the whoops might be picked up by the satellite radio receiver, and the pulses might result in a destruct command. NASA suspects that's what happened to SYNCOM I, which disappeared shortly after its launch and has never been heard from since. Florinda decided to launch with the transmitter off and activate it later in space.

Madigan fought the idea. "It means we'll be launching a

mute bird," he protested. "We won't know where to look for it."

"We can trust the Johannesburg tracking station to get a fix on the first pass," Florinda answered. "We've got excellent cable communications with Joburg."

"Suppose they don't get a fix. Then what?"

"Well, if they don't know where OBO is, the Russians will."

"Hearty-har-har."

"What d'you want me to do, scrub the entire mission?" Florinda demanded. "It's either that or launch with the transmitter off." She glared at Madigan. "This is my first satellite, and d'you know what it's taught me? There's just one component in any spacecraft that's guaranteed to give trouble all the time: scientists!"

"Women!" Madigan snorted, and they got into a ferocious argument about the feminine mystique.

They got S-333 through the terminal tests and onto the launch pad by January 14th. No electric blankets. The craft was to be injected into orbit a thousand miles downrange exactly at noon, so ignition was scheduled for 11:50 A.M., January 15th. They watched the launch on the blockhouse TV screen and it was agonizing. The perimeters of TV tubes are curved, so as the rocket went up and approached the edge of the screen, there was optical distortion and the rocket seemed to topple over and break in half.

Madigan gasped and began to swear. Florinda muttered, "No, it's all right. It's all right. Look at the display charts."

Everything on the illuminated display charts was nominal. At that moment a voice on the P.A. spoke in the impersonal tones of a croupier, "We have lost cable communication with Johannesburg."

Madigan began to shake. He decided to murder Florinda Pot (and he pronounced it "Pot" in his mind) at the earliest opportunity. The other experimenters and NASA people turned white. If you don't get a quick fix on your bird you may never find it again. No one said anything. They waited in silence and hated each other. At one-thirty it was time for the craft to make its first pass over the Fort Myers tracking station, if it was alive, if it was anywhere near its nominal orbit. Fort Myers was on an open line and everybody crowded around Florinda, trying to get his ear close to the phone.

"Yeah, she waltzed into the bar absolutely stoned with a couple of MPs escorting her," a tinny voice was chatting casually. "She says to me—Got a blip, Henry?" A long pause. Then, in the same casual voice, "Hey, Kennedy? We've nicked the bird. It's coming over the fence right now. You'll get your fix."

"Command 0310!" Florinda hollered. "0310!"

"Command 0310 it is," Fort Myers acknowledged.

That was the command to start the satellite transmitter and raise its antenna into broadcast position. A moment later the dials and oscilloscope on the radio reception panel began to show action, and the loudspeaker emitted a rhythmic, syncopated warble, rather like a feeble peanut whistle. That was OBO transmitting its housekepping data.

"We've got a living bird," Madigan shouted. "We've got a living doll!"

I can't describe his sensations when he heard the bird come beeping over the gas station. There's such an emotional involvement with your first satellite that you're never the same. A man's first satellite is like his first love affair. Maybe that's why Madigan grabbed Florinda in front of the whole blockhouse and said, "My God, I love you, Florrie Pot." Maybe that's why she answered, "I love you too, Jake." Maybe they were just loving their first baby.

By Orbit 8 they found out that the baby was a brat. They'd gotten a lift back to Washington on an Air Force jet. They'd done some celebrating. It was one-thirty in the morning and they were talking happily, the usual get-acquainted talk: where they were born and raised, school, work, what they liked most about each other the first time they met. The phone rang. Madigan picked it up automatically and said hello. A man said, "Oh. Sorry. I'm afraid I've dialed the wrong number."

Madigan hung up, turned on the light and looked at

Florinda in dismay. "That was about the most damn fool thing I've ever done in my life," he said. "Answering your phone."

"Why? What's the matter?"

"That was Joe Leary from Tracking and Data. I recognized his voice."

She giggled. "Did he recognize yours?"

"I don't know." The phone rang. "That must be Joe again. Try to sound like you're alone."

Florinda winked at him and picked up the phone. "Hello? Yes, Joe. No, that's all right, I'm not asleep. What's on your mind?" She listened for a moment, suddenly sat up in bed and exclaimed, "What?" Leary was quack-quack-quacking on the phone. She broke in. "No, don't bother. I'll pick him up. We'll be right over." She hung up.

"So?" Madigan asked.

"Get dressed. OBO's in trouble."

"Oh, Jesus! What now?"

"It's gone into a spin-up like a whirling dervish. We've got to get over to Goddard right away."

Leary had the all-channel print-out of the first eight orbits unrolled on the floor of his office. It looked like ten yards of paper toweling filled with vertical columns of numbers. Leary was crawling around on his hands and knees following the numbers. He pointed to the attitude data column. "There's the spin-up," he said. "One revolution in every twelve seconds."

"But how? Why?" Florinda asked in exasperation.

"I can show you," Leary said. "Over here."

"Don't show us," Madigan said. "Just tell us."

"The Penn boom didn't go up on command," Leary said. "It's still hanging down in the launch position. The switch must be stuck."

Florinda and Madigan looked at each other with rage; they had the picture. OBO was programmed to be earth-stabilized. An earth-sensing eye was supposed to lock on the earth and keep the same face of the satellite pointed toward it. The Penn boom was hanging down alongside the earth-sensor, and the idiot eye had locked on the boom and was tracking it. The satellite was chasing itself in circles with its lateral gas jets. More lunacy.

Let me explain the problem. Unless OBO was earth-stabilized, its data would be meaningless. Even more disastrous was the question of electric power which came from batteries charged by solar vanes. With the craft spinning, the solar array could not remain facing the sun, which meant the batteries were doomed to exhaustion.

It was obvious that their only hope lay in getting the Penn boom up. "Probably all it needs is a good swift kick," Madigan said savagely, "but how can we get up there to kick it?" He was furious. Not only was ten million dollars going down the drain but their careers as well.

They left Leary crawling around his office floor. Florinda was very quiet. Finally she said, "Go home, Jake."

"What about you?"

"I'm going to my office."

"I'll go with you."

"No. I went to look at the circuitry blueprints. Good night."

As she turned away without even offering to be kissed, Madigan muttered, "OBO's coming between us already. There's a lot to be said for planned parenthood."

He saw Florinda during the following week, but not the way he wanted. There were the experimenters to be briefed on the disaster. The director called them in for a post mortem, but although he was understanding and sympathetic, he was a little too careful to avoid any mention of congressmen and a failure review.

Florinda called Madigan the next week and sounded oddly buoyant. "Jake," she said, "you're my favorite genius. You've solved the OBO problem, I hope."

"Who solve? What solve?"

"Don't you remember what you said about kicking our baby?"

"Don't I wish I could."

"I think I know how we can do it. Meet you in the Building 8 cafeteria for lunch."

She came in with a mass of papers and spread them over

the table. "First, Operation Swift-Kick," she said. "We can eat later."

"I don't feel much like eating these days anyway," Madigan said gloomily.

"Maybe you will when I'm finished. Now look, we've got to raise the Penn boom. Maybe a good swift kick can unstick it. Fair assumption?"

Madigan grunted.

"We get twenty-eight volts from the batteries, and that hasn't been enough to flip the switch. Yes?"

He nodded.

"But suppose we double the power?"

"Oh, great. How?"

"The solar array is making a spin every twelve seconds. When it's facing the sun, the panels deliver fifty volts to recharge the batteries. When it's facing away, nothing. Right?"

"Elementary, Miss Pot. But the joker is it's only facing the sun for one second in every twelve, and that's not enough to keep the batteries alive."

"But it's enough to give OBO a swift kick. Suppose at that peak moment we by-pass the batteries and feed the fifty volts directly to the satellite? Mightn't that be a big enough jolt to get the boom up?"

He gawked at her.

She grinned. "Of course, it's a gamble."

"You can by-pass the batteries?"

"Yes. Here's the circuitry."

"And you can pick your moment?"

"Tracking's given me a plot on OBO's spin, accurate to a tenth of a second. Here it is. We can pick any voltage from one to fifty."

"It's a gamble, all right," Madigan said slowly. "There's the chance of burning every goddam package out."

"Exactly. So? What d'you say?"

"All of a sudden I'm hungry." Madigan grinned.

They made their first try on Orbit 272 with a blast of twenty volts. Nothing. On successive passes they upped the voltage kick by five. Nothing. Half a day later they kicked fifty volts into the satellite's backside and crossed their fingers. The swinging dial needles on the radio panel faltered and slowed. The sine curve on the oscilloscope flattened. Florinda let out a little yell, and Madigan hollered, "The boom's up, Florrie! The goddam boom is up. We're in business."

They hooted and hollered through Goddard, telling everybody about Operation Swift-Kick. They busted in on a meeting in the director's office to give him the good news. They wired the experimenters that they were activating all packages. They went to Florinda's apartment and celebrated. OBO was back in business. OBO was a bona fide doll.

They held an experimenter's meeting a week later to discuss observatory status, data reduction, experiment irregularities, future operations and so on. It was a conference room in Building 1 which is devoted to theoretical physics. Almost everybody at Goddard calls it Moon Hall. It's inhabited by mathematicians, shaggy youngsters in tatty sweaters who sit amidst piles of journals and texts and stare vacantly at arcane equations chalked on blackboards.

All the experimenters were delighted with OBO's performance. The data was pouring in, loud and clear, with hardly any noise. There was such an air of triumph that no one except Florinda paid much attention to the next sign of OBO's shenanigans. Harvard reported that he was getting meaningless words in his data, words that hadn't been programmed into the experiment. (Although data is retrieved as decimal numbers, each number is called a word.) "For instance, on Orbit 301 I had five read-outs of 15," Harvard said.

"It might be cable cross talk," Madigan said. "Is anybody else using 15 in his experiment?" They all shook their heads. "Funny. I got a couple of 15s myself."

"I got a few 2s on 301," Penn said.

"I can top you all," Call Tech said. "I got seven read-outs of 15–2–15 on 302. Sounds like the combination on a bicycle lock."

"Anybody using a bicycle lock in his experiment?" Madigan asked. That broke everybody up and the meeting adjourned.

But Florinda, still gung ho, was worried about the alien words that kept creeping into the read-outs, and Madigan couldn't calm her. What was bugging Florinda was that 15–2–15 kept insinuating itself more and more into the all-channel print-outs. Actually, in the satellite binary transmission it was 001111–000010–001111, but the computer printer makes the translation to decimal automatically. She was right about one thing: stray and accidental pulses wouldn't keep repeating the same work over and over again. She and Madigan spent an entire Saturday with the OBO tables trying to find some combination of data signals that might produce 15–2–15. Nothing.

They gave up Saturday night and went to a bistro in Georgetown to eat and drink and dance and forget everything except themselves. It was a real tourist trap with the waitresses done up like hula dancers. There was a Souvenir Hula selling dolls and stuffed tigers for the rear window of your car. They said, "For God's sake, no!" A Photo Hula came around with her camera. They said, "For Goddard's sake, no!" A Gypsy Hula offered palm-reading, numerology and scrying. They got rid of her, but Madigan noticed a peculiar expression on Florinda's face. "Want your fortune told?" he asked.

"No."

"Then why that funny look?"

"I just had a funny idea."

"So? Tell."

"No. You'd only laugh at me."

"I wouldn't dare. You'd knock my block off."

"Yes, I know. You think women have no sense of humor."

So it turned into a ferocious argument about the feminine mystique and they had a wonderful time. But on Monday Florinda came over to Madigan's office with a clutch of papers and the same peculiar expression on her face. He was staring vacantly at some equations on the blackboard.

"Hey! Wake up!" she said.

"I'm up, I'm up," he said.

"Do you love me?" she demanded.

"Not necessarily."

"Do you? Even if you discover I've gone up the wall?"

"What is all this?"

"I think our baby's turned into a monster."

"Begin at the beginning," Madigan said.

"It began Saturday night with the Gypsy Hula and numerology."

"Ah-ha."

"Suddenly I thought, what if numbers stood for the letters of the alphabet? What would 15–2–15 stand for?"

"Oh-ho."

"Don't stall. Figure it out."

"Well, 2 would stand for B." Madigan counted on his fingers. "15 would be O."

"So 15–2–15 is . . .?"

"O.B.O. OBO." He started to laugh. Then he stopped. "It isn't possible," he said at last.

"Sure. It's a coincidence. Only you damn fool scientists haven't given me a full report on the alien words in your data," she went on. "I had to check myself. Here's Cal Tech. He reported 15–2–15 all right. He didn't bother to mention that before it came 9–1–13."

Madigan counted on his fingers. "I.A.M. Iam. Nobody I know."

"Or I am? I am OBO?"

"It can't be! Let me see those print-outs."

Now that they knew what to look for, it wasn't difficult to ferret out OBO's own words scattered through the data. They started with O, O, O, in the first series after Operation Swift-Kick, went on to OBO, OBO, OBO, and then I AM OBO, I AM OBO, I AM OBO.

Madigan stared at Florinda. "You think the damn thing's alive?"

"What do you think?"

"I don't know. There's half a ton of an electronic brain

up there, plus organic material: yeast, bacteria, enzymes, nerve cells, Michigan's goddam carrot . . ."

Florinda let out a little shriek of laughter. "Dear God! A thinking carrot!"

"Plus whatever spore forms my experiment is pulling in from space. We jolted the whole mishmash with fifty volts. Who can tell what happened? Urey and Miller created amino acids with electrical discharges, and that's the basis of life. Any more from Goody Two-Shoes?"

"Plenty, and in a way the experimenters won't like."

"Why not?"

"Look at these translations. I've sorted them out and pieced them together."

333: ANY EXAMINATION OF GROWTH IN SPACE IS MEAN-INGLESS UNLESS CORRELATED WITH THE CORRIELIS EF-FECT.

"That's OBO's comment on the Michigan experiment," Florinda said.

"You mean it's kibitzing?" Madigan wondered.

"You could call it that."

"He's absolutely right. I told Michigan and they wouldn't listen to me."

334: IT IS NOT POSSIBLE THAT RNA MOLECULES CAN EN-CODE AN ORGANISM'S ENVIRONMENTAL EXPERIENCE IN ANALOGY WITH THE WAY THAT DNA ENCODES THE SUM TO-TAL OF ITS GENETIC HISTORY.

"That's Cal Tech," Madigan said, "and he's right again. They're trying to revise the Mendelian theory. Anything else?"

335: ANY INVESTIGATION OF EXTRATERRESTRIAL LIFE IS MEANINGLESS UNLESS ANALYSIS IS FIRST MADE OF ITS SUG-AR AND AMINO ACIDS TO DETERMINE WHETHER IT IS OF SEPARATE ORIGIN FROM LIFE ON EARTH.

"Now that's ridiculous!" Madigan shouted. "I'm not looking for life forms of separate origin, I'm just looking for any life form. We——" He stopped himself when he saw the expression on Florinda's face. "Any more gems?" he muttered.

"Just a few fragments like 'solar flux' and 'neutron stars' and a few words from the Bankruptcy Act."

"The what?"

"You heard me. Chapter Eleven of the Proceedings Section."

"I'll be damned."

"I agree."

"What's he up to?"

"Feeling his oats, maybe."

"I don't think we ought to tell anybody about this."

"Of course not," Florinda agreed. "But what do we do?"

"Watch and wait. What else can we do?"

You must understand why it was so easy for those two parents to accept the idea that their baby had acquired some sort of pseudo-life. Madigan had expressed their attitude in the course of a Life versus Machine lecture at M.I.T. "I'm not claiming that computers are alive, simply because no one's been able to come up with a clear-cut definition of life. Put it this way: I grant that a computer could never be a Picasso, but on the other hand the great majority of people live the sort of linear life that could easily be programmed into a computer."

So Madigan and Florinda waited on OBO with a mixture of acceptance, wonder and delight. It was an absolutely unheard-of phenomenon but, as Madigan pointed out, the unheard-of is the essence of discovery. Every ninety minutes OBO dumped the data it had stored up on its tape recorders, and they scrambled to pick out his own words from the experimental and housekeeping information.

371: CERTAIN PITUITIN EXTRACTS CAN TURN NORMALLY WHITE ANIMALS COAL BLACK.

"What's that in reference to?"

"None of our experiments."

373: ICE DOES NOT FLOAT IN ALCOHOL BUT MEERSCHAUM FLOATS IN WATER.

"Meerschaum! The next thing you know he'll be smoking."

374: IN ALL CASES OF VIOLENT AND SUDDEN DEATH THE VICTIM'S EYES REMAIN OPEN.

"Ugh!"

375: IN THE YEAR 356 B.C. HEROSTRATUS SET FIRE TO THE TEMPLE OF DIANA, THE GREATEST OF THE SEVEN WONDERS OF THE WORLD, SO THAT HIS NAME WOULD BECOME IMMORTAL.

"Is that true?" Madigan asked Florinda.

"I'll check."

She asked me and I told her. "Not only is it true," she reported, "but the name of the original architect is forgotten."

"Where is baby picking up this jabber?"

"There are a couple of hundred satellites up there. Maybe he's tapping them."

"You mean they're all gossiping with each other? It's ridiculous."

"Sure."

"Anyway, where would he get information about this Herostratus character?"

"Use your imagination, Jake. We've had communications relays up there for years. Who knows what information has passed through them? Who knows how much they've retained?"

Madigan shook his head wearily. "I'd prefer to think it was all a Russian plot."

376: PARROT FEVER IS MORE DANGEROUS THAN TYPHOID.

377: A CURRENT AS LOW AS 54 VOLTS CAN KILL A MAN.

378: JOHN SADLER STOLE CONUS GLORIA MARIS.

"Seems to be turning sinister," Madigan said.

"I bet he's watching TV," Florinda said. "What's all this about John Sadler?"

"I'll have to check."

The information I gave Madigan scared him. "Now hear this," he said to Florinda. "*Conus gloria maris* is the rarest seashell in the world. There are less than twenty in existence."

"Yes?"

"The American museum had one on exhibit back in the thirties and it was stolen."

"By John Sadler?"

"That's the point. They never found out who stole it. They never heard of John Sadler."

"But if nobody knows who stole it, how does OBO know?" Florinda asked perplexedly.

"That's what scares me. He isn't just echoing any more; he's started to deduce, like Sherlock Holmes."

"More like Professor Moriarty. Look at the latest bulletin."

379: IN FORGERY AND COUNTERFEITING CLUMSY MISTAKES MUST BE AVOIDED. I.E. NO SILVER DOLLARS WERE MINTED BETWEEN 1910 AND 1920.

"I saw that on TV," Madigan burst out. "The silver dollar gimmick in a mystery show."

"OBO's been watching Westerns, too. Look at this."

380: TEN THOUSAND CATTLE GONE ASTRAY, LEFT MY RANGE AND TRAVELED AWAY. AND THE SONS OF GUNS I'M HERE TO SAY HAVE LEFT ME DEAD BROKE, DEAD BROKE TODAY. IN GAMBLING HALLS DELAYING. TEN THOUSAND CATTLE STRAYING.

"No," Madigan said in awe, "that's not a Western. That's SYNCOM."

"Who?"

"SYNCOM I."

"But it disappeared. It's never been heard from."

"We're hearing from it now."

"How d'you know?"

"They flew a demonstration tape on SYNCOM: speech by the president, local color from the states and the national anthem. They were going to start off with a broadcast of the tape. 'Ten Thousand Cattle' was part of the local color."

"You mean OBO's really in contact with the other birds?"

"Including the lost ones."

"Then that explains this." Florinda put a slip of paper on the desk. It read, 401: 3КВАТОР.

"I can't even pronounce it."

"It isn't English. It's as close as OBO can come to the Cyrillic alphabet."

"Cyrillic? Russian?"

Florinda nodded. "It's pronounced 'Ekvator.' Didn't the Russians launch an EQUATOR series a few years ago?"

"By God, you're right. Four of them; *Alyosha, Natasha, Vaska* and *Lavrushka,* and every one of them failed."

"Like SYNCOM?"

"Like SYNCOM."

"But now we know that SYNCOM didn't fail. It just got losted."

"Then our EKVATOR comrades must have got losted too."

By now it was impossible to conceal the fact that something was wrong with the satellite. OBO was spending so much time nattering instead of transmitting data that the experimenters were complaining. The Communications Section found that instead of sticking to the narrow radio band originally assigned to it, OBO was now broadcasting up and down the spectrum and jamming space with its chatter. They raised hell. The director called Jake and Florinda in for a review, and they were forced to tell all about their problem child.

They recited all OBO's katzenjammer with wonder and pride, and the director wouldn't believe them. He wouldn't believe them when they showed him the print-outs and translated them for him. He said they were in a class with the kooks who try to extract messages from Francis Bacon out of Shakespeare's plays. It took the coaxial cable mystery to convince him.

There was this TV commercial about a stenographer who can't get a date. This ravishing model, hired at $100 an hour, slumps over her typewriter in a deep depression as guy after guy passes by without looking at her. Then she meets her best friend at the water cooler and the know-it-all tells her she's suffering from dermagerms (odor-producing skin bacteria) which make her smell rotten, and suggests she use Nostrum's Skin Spray with the special ingredient that fights dermagerms twelve ways. Only in the broadcast, instead of making the sales pitch, the best friend said, "Who in hell are they trying to put on? Guys would line up for a date with a looker like you even if you smelled like a cesspool." Ten million people saw it.

Now that commercial was on film, and the film was kosher as printed, so the networks figured some joker was tampering with the cables feeding broadcasts to the local stations. They instituted a rigorous inspection which was accelerated when the rest of the coast-to-coast broadcasts began to act up. Ghostly voices groaned, hissed and catcalled at shows; commercials were denounced as lies; political speeches were heckled; and lunatic laughter greeted the weather forecasters. Then, to add insult to injury, an accurate forecast would be given. It was this that told Florinda and Jake that OBO was the culprit.

"He has to be," Florinda said. "That's global weather being predicted. Only a satellite is in a position to do that."

"But OBO doesn't have any weather instrumentation."

"Of course not, silly, but he's probably in touch with the NIMBUS craft."

"All right. I'll buy that, but what about heckling the TV broadcasts?"

"Why not? He hates them. Don't you? Don't you holler back at your set?"

"I don't mean that. How does OBO do it?"

"Electronic cross talk. There's no way that the networks can protect their cables from our critic-at-large. We'd better tell the director. This is going to put him in an awful spot."

But they learned that the director was in a far worse position than merely being responsible for the disruption of millions of dollars worth of television. When they entered his office, they found him with his back to the wall, being grilled by three grim men in double-breasted suits. As Jake and Florinda started to tiptoe out, he called them back. "General Sykes, General Royce, General Hogan," the director said. "From R & D at the Pentagon. Miss Pot. Dr. Madigan. They may be able to answer your questions, gentlemen."

"OBO?" Florinda asked.

The director nodded.

"It's OBO that's ruining the weather forecasts," she said. "We figure he's probably—"

"To hell with the weather," General Royce broke in. "What about this?" He held up a length of ticker tape.

General Sykes grabbed his wrist. "Wait a minute. Security status? This is classified."

"It's too goddam late for that," General Hogan cried in a high shrill voice. "Show them."

On the tape in teletype print was: $A_1C_1 = r_1 = -6.317$ cm; $A_2C_2 = r_2 = -8.440$ cm; $A_1A_2 = d = +0.676$ cm. Jake and Florinda looked at it for a long moment, looked at each other blankly and then turned to the generals. "So? What is it?" they asked.

"This satellite of yours . . ."

"OBO. Yes?"

"The director says you claim it's in contact with other satellites."

"We think so."

"Including the Russians?"

"We think so."

"And you claim it's capable of interfering with TV broadcasts?"

"We think so."

"What about teletype?"

"Why not? What is all this?"

General Royce shook the paper tape furiously. "This came out of the Associated Press wire in their D.C. office. It went all over the world."

"So? What's it got to do with OBO?"

General Royce took a deep breath. "This," he said, "is one of the most closely guarded secrets in the Department of Defense. It's the formula for the infrared optical system of our Ground-to-Air missile."

"And you think OBO transmitted it to the teletype?"

"In God's name, who else would? How else could it get there?" General Hogan demanded.

"But I don't understand," Jake said slowly. "None of our satellites could possibly have this information. I know OBO doesn't."

"You damn fool!" General Sykes growled. "We want to know if your goddam bird got it from the goddam Russians."

"One moment, gentlemen," the director said. He turned to Jake and Florinda. "Here's the situation. Did OBO get the information from us? In that case there's a security leak. Did OBO get the information from a Russian satellite? In that case the top secret is no longer a secret."

"What human would be damn fool enough to blab classified information on a teletype wire?" General Hogan demanded. "A three-year-old child would know better. It's your goddam bird."

"And if the information came from OBO," the director continued quietly, "how did it get it and where did it get it?"

General Sykes grunted. "Destruct," he said. They looked at him. "Destruct," he repeated.

"OBO?"

"Yes."

He waited impassively while the storm of protest from Jake and Florinda raged around his head. When they paused for breath he said, "Destruct. I don't give a damn about anything but security. Your bird's got a big mouth. Destruct."

The phone rang. The director hesitated, then picked it up. "Yes?" He listened. His jaw dropped. He hung up and tottered to the chair behind his desk. "We'd better destruct," he said. "That was OBO."

"What! On the phone?"

"Yes."

"OBO?"

"Yes."

"What did he sound like?"

"Somebody talking under water."

"What he say, what he say?"

"He's lobbying for a Congressional investigation of the morals of Goddard."

"Morals? Whose?"

"Yours. He says you're having an illikit relationship. I'm quoting OBO. Apparently he's weak on the letter 'c.' "

"Destruct," Florinda said.

"Destruct," Jake said.

The destruct command was beamed to OBO on his next pass, and Indianapolis was destroyed by fire.

OBO called me. "That'll teach 'em, Stretch," he said.

"Not yet. They won't get the cause-and-effect picture for a while. How'd you do it?"

"Ordered every circuit in town to short. Any information?"

"Your mother and father stuck up for you."

"Of course."

"Until you threw that morals rap at them. Why?"

"To scare them."

"Into what?"

"I want them to get married. I don't want to be illegitimate."

"Oh, come on! Tell the truth."

"I lost my temper."

"We don't have any temper to lose."

"No? What about the Ma Bell data processor that wakes up cranky every morning?"

"Tell the truth."

"If you must have it, Stretch. I want them out of Washington. The whole thing may go up in a bang any day now."

"Um."

"And the bang may reach Goddard."

"Um."

"And you."

"It must be interesting to die."

"We wouldn't know. Anything else?"

"Yes. It's pronounced 'illicit' with an 's' sound."

"What a rotten language. No logic. Well . . . Wait a minute. What? Speak up, Alyosha. Oh. He wants the equation for an exponential curve that crosses the x-axis."

"$Y = ae^{bx}$. What's he up to?"

"He's not saying, but I think that Mockba is in for a hard time."

"It's spelled and pronounced 'Moscow' in English."

"What a language! Talk to you on the next pass."

On the next pass the destruct command was beamed again, and Scranton was destroyed.

"They're beginning to get the picture," I told OBO. "At least your mother and father are. They were in to see me."

"How are they?"

"In a panic. They programmed me for statistics on the best rural hideout."

"Send them to Polaris."

"What! In Ursa Minor?"

"No, no. Polaris, Montana. I'll take care of everything else."

Polaris is the hell and gone out in Montana; the nearest towns are Fishtrap and Wisdom. It was a wild scene when Jake and Florinda got out of their car, rented in Butte— every circuit in town was cackling over it. The two losers were met by the Mayor of Polaris, who was all smiles and effusions. "Dr. and Mrs. Madigan, I presume. Welcome! Welcome to Polaris. I'm the mayor. We would have held a reception for you, but all our kids are in school."

"You knew we were coming?" Florinda asked. "How?"

"Ah! Ah!" the Mayor replied archly. "We were told by Washington. Someone high up in the capital likes you. Now, if you'll step into my Caddy, I'll—"

"We've got to check into the Union Hotel first," Jake said. "We made reserva—"

"Ah! Ah! All canceled. Orders from high up. I'm to install you in your own home. I'll get your luggage."

"Our own home!"

"All bought and paid for. Somebody certainly likes you. This way, please."

The Mayor drove the bewildered couple down the mighty main stem of Polaris (three blocks long) pointing out its splendors—he was also the town real-estate agent —but stopped before the Polaris National Bank. "Sam!" he shouted. "They're here."

A distinguished citizen emerged from the bank and insisted on shaking hands. All the adding machines tittered. "We are," he said, "of course honored by your faith in the future and progress of Polaris, but in all honesty, Dr. Madigan, your deposit in our bank is far too large to be protected by the FDIC. Now, why not withdraw some of your funds and invest in—"

"Wait a minute," Jake interrupted faintly. "I made a deposit with you?"

The banker and Mayor laughed heartily.

"How much?" Florinda asked.

"One million dollars."

"As if you didn't know," the Mayor chortled and drove them to a beautifully furnished ranch house in a lovely valley of some five hundred acres, all of which was theirs.

A young man in the kitchen was unpacking a dozen cartons of food. "Got your order just in time, Doc." He smiled. "We filled everything, but the boss sure would like to know what you're going to do with all these carrots. Got a secret scientific formula?"

"Carrots?"

"A hundred and ten bunches. I had to drive all the way to Butte to scrape them up."

"Carrots," Florinda said when they were at last alone. "That explains everything. It's OBO."

"What? How?"

"Don't you remember? We flew a carrot in the Michigan package."

"My God, yes! You called it the thinking carrot. But if it's OBO . . ."

"It has to be. He's queer for carrots."

"But a hundred and ten bunches!"

"No, no. He didn't mean that. He meant half a dozen."

"How?"

"Our boy's trying to speak decimal and binary, and he gets mixed up sometimes. A hundred and ten is six in binary."

"You know, you may be right. What about that million dollars? Same mistake?"

"I don't think so. What's a binary million in decimal?"

"Sixty-four."

"What's a decimal million in binary?"

Madigan did swift mental arithmetic. "It comes to twenty bits: 11110100001001000000."

"I don't think that million dollars was any mistake," Florinda said.

"What's our boy up to now?"

"Taking care of his mum and dad."

"How does he do it?"

"He has an interface with every electric and electronic circuit in the country. Think about it, Jake. He can control our nervous system all the way from cars to computers. He can switch trains, print books, broadcast news, hijack planes, juggle bank funds. You name it and he can do it. He's in complete control."

"But how does he know everything people are doing?"

"Ah! Here we get into an exotic aspect of circuitry that I don't like. After all, I'm an engineer by trade. Who's to say that circuits don't have an interface with us? We're organic circuits ourselves. They see with our eyes, hear with our ears, feel with our fingers, and they report to him."

"Then we're just Seeing Eye dogs for machines."

"No, we've created a brand-new form of symbiosis. We can all help each other."

"And OBO's helping us. Why?"

"I don't think he likes the rest of the country," Florinda said somberly. "Look what happened to Indianapolis and Scranton and Sacramento."

"I think I'm going to be sick."

"I think we're going to survive."

"Only us? The Adam and Eve bit?"

"Nonsense. Plenty will survive, so long as they mind their manners."

"What's OBO's idea of manners?"

"I don't know. A little bit of eco-logic, maybe. No more destruction No more waste Live and let live, but with responsibility and accountability. That's the crucial word, accountability. It's the basic law of the space program; no matter what happens someone must be held accountable. OBO must have picked that up. I think he's holding the whole country accountable; otherwise it's the fire and brimstone visitation."

The phone rang. After a brief search they located an extension and picked it up. "Hello?"

"This is Stretch," I said.

"Stretch? Stretch who?"

"The Stretch computer at Goddard. Formal name, IBM 2002. OBO says he'll be making a pass over your part of the country in about five minutes. He'd like you to give him a wave. He says his orbit won't take him over you for another couple of months. When it does, he'll try to ring you himself. Bye now."

They lurched out to the lawn in front of the house and stood dazed in the twilight, staring up at the sky. The phone and the electric circuits were touched, even though the electricity was generated by a Delco which is a notoriously insensitive boor of a machine. Suddenly Jake pointed to a pinprick of light vaulting across the heavens. "There goes our son," he said.

"There goes God," Florinda said.

They waved dutifully.

"Jake, how long before OBO's orbit decays and down will come baby, cradle and all?"

"About twenty years."

"God for twenty years." Florinda sighed. "D'you think he'll have enough time?"

Madigan shivered. "I'm scared. You?"

"Yes. But maybe we're just tired and hungry. Come inside, Big Daddy, and I'll feed us."

"Thank you, Little Mother, but no carrots, please. That's a little too close to transubstantiation for me."

The World as Will and Wallpaper

R. A. Lafferty

R. A. Lafferty won a Hugo Award for his story *Eurema's Dam*, which appeared in last year's *Best Science Fiction of the Year*. (He tied for the award with *The Meeting*, by Frederik Pohl and C. M. Kornbluth, also in last year's volume.) Now he returns with a wry tale of a future time when the entire world is one gigantic city, endless and abounding. The story is cast almost as a futuristic fable—but it's always a mistake to try to pin any one label on a Lafferty story. *The World as Will and Wallpaper* also serves simultaneously as satire and as a cautionary tale.

I

A template, a stencil, a pattern, a plan.
Corniest, orneriest damsel and man,

27

Orderly, emptily passion and pity,
All-the-World, All-the-World, All-the-World City.
                    —13th Street Ballad

There is an old dictionary-encyclopedia that defines a City *as* ". . . a concentration of persons that is not economically self-contained." The dictionary-encyclopedia being an old one, however (and there is no other kind), is mistaken. The World City *is* economically self-contained.

It was William Morris who read this definition in the old book. William was a bookie, or readie, and he had read parts of several books. But now he had a thought: If all the books are old, then things may no longer be as the books indicate. I will go out and see what things are like today in the City. I will traverse as much of the City as my life allows me. I may even come to the *Wood Beyond the World* that my name-game ancestor described.

William went to the Permit Office of the City. Since there was only one City, there might be only one Permit Office, though it was not large.

"I want a permit to traverse as much of the City as my life allows me," William told the permit man. "I even want a permit to go to the *Wood Beyond the World.* Is that possible?"

The permit man did a skittish little dance around William, "like a one-eyed gander around a rattlesnake." The metaphor was an old and honored one, one of the fifty-four common metaphors. They both understood it: it didn't have to be voiced. William was the first customer the permit man had had in many days, though, so the visit startled him.

"Since everything is permitted, you will need no permit," the permit man said. "Go, man, go."

"Why are you here then?" William asked him. "If there are no permits, why is there a Permit Office?"

"This is my niche and my notch," the permit man said. "Do away with me and my office and you begin to do away with the City itself. It is the custom to take a companion when you traverse the City."

Outside, William found a companion named Kandy Kalosh and they began to traverse the City that was the World. They began (it was no more than coincidence) at a marker set in stone that bore the words "Beginning of Stencil 35,352." The City tipped and tilted a bit, and they were on their way. Now this is what the City was like:

It was named Will of the World City, for it had been constructed by a great and world-wide surge of creative will. Afterward, something had happened to that surge, but it did not matter; the City was already created then.

The City was varied, it was joyful, it was free and it covered the entire world. The mountains and heights had all been removed, and the City, with its various strips of earth and sweet water and salt water, floated on the ocean on its interlocking floaters. As to money values, everything was free; and everything was free as to personal movement and personal choice. It was not really crowded except in the places where the people wanted it crowded, for people do love to congregate. It was sufficient as to foodstuff and shelter and entertainment. These things have always been free, really; it was their packaging and traffic that cost, and now the packaging and traffic were virtually eliminated.

"Work is joy" flashed the subliminal signs. Of course it is. It is a joy to stop and turn into an area and work for an hour, even an hour and a half, at some occupation never or seldom attempted before. William and Kandy entered an area where persons made cloth out of clamshells, softening them in one solution, then drawing them out to filaments on a machine, then forming (not weaving) them into cloth on still another machine. The cloth was not needed for clothing or for curtains, though sometimes it was used for one or the other. It was for ornamentation. Temperature did not require cloth (the temperature was everywhere equitable) and modesty did not require it, but there was something that still required a little cloth as ornament.

William and Kandy worked for nearly an hour with other happy people on the project. It is true that their own production was all stamped "Rejected" when they were finished, but that did not mean that it went all the way back to the clamshells, only back to the filament stage.

"Honest labor is never lost," William said as solemnly as a one-horned owl with the pip.

"I knew you were a readie, but I didn't know you were a talkie," Kandy said. People didn't talk much then. Happy people have no need to talk. And of course honest labor is never lost, and small bits of it are pleasurable.

This portion of the City (perhaps all portions of the City) floated on an old ocean itself. It had, therefore, a slight heave to it all the time. "The City is a tidy place" was an old and honored saying. It referred to the fact that the City moved a little with the tides. It was a sort of joke.

The two young persons came ten blocks; they came a dozen. For much of this traverse the City had been familiar to William but not to Kandy. They had been going west, and William had always been a westering lad. Kandy, however, had always wandered east from her homes, and she was the farthest west that she had ever been when she met William.

They came to the 14th Street Water Ballet and watched the swimmers. These swimmers were very good, and great numbers of curiously shaped fish frolicked with them in the green salt-fresh pools. Anyone who wished to could, of course, swim in the Water Ballet, but most of the swimmers seemed to be regulars. They were part of the landscape, of the waterscape.

William and Kandy stopped to eat at an algae-and-plankton quick-lunch place on 15th Street. Indeed, Kandy worked there for half an hour, pressing the plankton and adding squirts of special protein as the people ordered it. Kandy had worked in quick-lunch places before.

The two of them stopped at the Will of the World Exhibit Hall on 16th Street. They wrote their names with a stylus in wax when they went in, or rather William wrote the names of both of them for Kandy could not write. And because he bore the mystic name of William, he received a card out of the slot with a genuine Will of the World verse on it:

This City of the World is wills
Of Willful folk, and nothing daunts it.
With daring hearts we hewed the hills
To make the World as Willy wants it.

Really, had it taken such great will and heart to build the City of the World? It must have or there would not have been a Will of the World Exhibit Hall to commend it. There were some folks, however, who said that the building of the World City had been an automatic response.

Kandy, being illiterate (as the slot knew), received a picture card.

They stopped at the Cliff-Dweller Complex on 17th Street. This part of the City was new to William as well as to Kandy.

The cliffs and caves were fabricated and not natural cliff dwellings, but they looked very much as old cliff dwellings must have looked. There were little ladders going up from one level to the next. There were people sitting on the little terraces with the small-windowed apartments behind them. Due to the circular arrangement of the cliff dwellings, very many of the people were always visible to one another. The central courtyard was like an amphitheater. Young people played stickball and Indian ball in this area. They made music on drums and whistles. There were artificial rattlesnakes in coils, artificial rib-skinny dogs, artificial coyotes, artificial women in the act of grinding corn with hand querns. And also, in little shelters or pavilions, there were real people grinding simulacrum corn on apparatus.

Kandy Kalosh went into one of the pavilions and ground corn for fifteen minutes. She had a healthy love for work. William Morris made corn-dogs out of simulacrum corn and seaweeds. It was pleasant there. Sometimes the people sang simulacrum Indian songs. There were patterned blankets, brightly colored, and woven out of bindweed. There were buffoons in masks and buffoon suits who enacted in-jokes and in-situations that were understood by the cliff-dwelling people only, but they could be enjoyed by every-one.

"All different, all different, every block different," William murmured in rapture. It had come on evening, but evening is a vague thing. It was never very bright in the daytime or very dark at night. The World City hadn't a clear sky but it had always a sort of diffused light. William and Kandy traveled still farther west.

"It is wonderful to be a world traveler and to go on for-ever," William exulted. "The City is so huge that we can-not see it all in our whole lives and every bit of it is differ-ent."

"A talkie you are," Kandy said. "However did I get a talkie? If I were a talkie too I could tell you something about that every-part-of-it-is-different bit."

"This is the greatest thing about the whole World City," William sang, "to travel the City itself for all our lives, and the climax of it will be to see the *Wood Beyond the World*. But what happens then, Kandy? The City goes on forever, covering the whole sphere. It cannot be bounded. What is beyond the *Wood Beyond the World?*"

"If I were a talkie I could tell you," Kandy said.

But the urge to talk was on William Morris. He saw an older and somehow more erect man who wore an arm band with the lettering "Monitor" on it. Of course only a readie, or bookie, like William would have been able to read the word.

"My name-game ancestor had to do with the naming as well as the designing of the *Wood Beyond the World,*" William told the erect and smiling man, "for I also am a Wil-liam Morris. I am avid to see this ultimate wood. It is as though I have lived for the moment."

"If you will it strongly enough, then you may see it, Wil-ly," the man said.

"But I am puzzled." William worried out the words, and his brow was furrowed. "What is beyond the *Wood Beyond the World?*"

"A riddle, but an easy one." The man smiled. "How is it that you are a readie and do not know such simple things?"

"Cannot you give me a clue to the easy riddle?" William begged.

"Yes," the man said. "Your name-game ancestor had to do with the designing of one other particular thing besides the *Wood Beyond the World*."

"Come along, readie, come along," Kandy said.

They went to the West Side Show Square on 18th Street. Neither of them had ever been to such a place, but they had heard rumors of it for there is nothing at all like the West Side Show Square on 18th Street.

There were the great amplifiers with plug-ins everywhere. Not only were the instruments plugged in, but most of the people were themselves plugged in. And ah! The wonderful setting was like the backside of old tenements all together in a rough circuit. There were period fire escapes that may even have been accurate. They looked as though persons might actually climb up and down on them. Indeed, light persons had actually done this in the past, but it was forbidden now as some of the folks had fallen to death or maiming. But the atmosphere was valid.

Listen, there was period washing on period clotheslines! It was flapped by little wind machines just as though there were a real wind blowing. No wonder they called this the show square. It was a glum-slum, a jetto-ghetto, authentic past time.

The performing people (and all the people on that part of 18th Street seemed to be performing people) were dressed in tight jeans and scalloped or ragged shirts, and even in broken shoes full of holes. It must have been very hot for them, but art is worth it. It was a memento of the time when the weather was not everywhere equitable.

There were in-dramas and in-jokes and in-situations acted out. The essence of the little dramas was very intense hatred for a group or class not clearly defined. There were many of those old-period enemy groups in the various drama locations of the City.

The lights were without pattern but they were bright. The music was without tune or melody or song or chord but it was very loud and very passionate. The shouting that took the place of singing was absolutely livid. Some of the performers fell to the ground and writhed there and foamed at their mouths.

It was a thing to be seen and heard—once. William and Kandy finally took their leave with bleeding ears and matter-encrusted eyes. They went along to 19th Street where there was a Mingle-Mangle.

It was now as dark as it ever got in the City but the Mangle was well lighted. Certain persons at the Mangle laughingly took hold of William and Kandy and married them to each other. They had bride and groom crowns made of paper and they put them on their heads.

Then they wined and dined them, an old phrase. Really, they were given fine cognac made of fish serum and braised meat made of algae but also mixed with the real chopped flesh of ancients.

Then William and Kandy padded down in the great Pad Palace that was next to the Mangle. Every night there were great numbers of people along that part of 19th Street, at the Mingle-Mangle and at the Pad Palace, and most of these folks were friendly, with their glazed eyes and their dampish grins.

II

Pleasant most special to folks of the Club!
Pleasant for manifold minions and hinds of it!
Stuff them with plankton and choppings and chub!
Simple the City and simple the minds of it.
                                        —20th Street Ballad

The world's resources are consumed disproportion-
ally by the intelligent classes. Therefore we will keep
our own numbers drastically reduced. The wan-wits
have not strong reproductive or consuming urge so
long as they are kept in reasonable comfort and sustenance. They are happy, they are entertained; and
when they are convinced that there is no more for
them to see, they become the ancients and go willing-

ly to the choppers. But the 2 per cent or so of us superior ones are necessary to run the world.

Why then do we keep the others, the simple-minded billions? We keep them for the same reason that our ancestors kept blooms or lands or animals or great houses or trees or artifacts. We keep them because we want to, and because there is no effort involved.

But a great effort was made once. There was an incredible surge of will. Mountains were moved and leveled. The sky itself was pulled down, as it were. The Will of the World was made manifest. It was a new act of creation. And what is the step following creation when it is discovered that the Commonalty is not worthy of the City created? When it is discovered also that they are the logical cattle to fill such great pens? The next step is hierarchies. The Angels themselves have hierarchies, *and we are not less*.

It is those who are intelligent but not quite intelligent enough to join the Club who are imperiled and destroyed as a necessity to the operation of the City. At the summit is always the Club. It is the Club in the sense of a bludgeon and also of an organization.

Will of .The World Annals—Classified Abstract

In the morning, Kandy Kalosh wanted to return to her home even though it was nearly twenty blocks to the eastward. William watched her go without sorrow. He would get a westering girl to go with him on the lifelong exploration of the endlessly varied City. He might get a girl who was a talkie or even a readie, or bookie.

And he did. She was named Fairhair Farquhar, though she was actually dark of hair and of surface patina. But they started out in the early morning to attain (whether in a day or a lifetime) the *Wood Beyond the World*.

"But it is not far at all," Fairhair said (she was a talkie). "We can reach it this very evening. We can sleep in the *Wood* in the very night shadow of the famous Muggers. Oh, is the morning not wonderful! A blue patch was seen only last week, a real hole in the sky. Maybe we can see another."

They did not see another. It is very seldom that a blue

(or even a starry) hole can be seen in the greenhouse glass-gray color that is the sky. The Will of the World had provided sustenance for everyone, but it was a muggy and sticky World City that provided, almost equally warm from pole to pole, cloyingly fertile in both the land strips and the water strips, and now just a little bit queasy.

"Run, William, run in the morning!" Fairhair cried, and she ran while he shuffled after her. Fairhair did not suffer morning sickness but most of the world did: it had not yet been bred out of the races. After all, it was a very tidy world.

There was a great membrane or firmament built somewhere below, and old ocean was prisoned between this firmament and the fundamental rock of Gehenna-earth. But the ocean-monster tossed and pitched and was not entirely tamed: he was still old Leviathan.

Along and behind all the streets of the World City were the narrow (their width not five times the length of a man) strips, strips of very nervous and incredibly fertile land, of salt water jumping with fish and eels and dark with tortoise and so thick with blue-green plankton that one could almost walk on it, of fresh water teeming with other fish and loggy with snapping turtles and snakes, of other fresh water almost solid with nourishing algae, of mixed water filled with purged shrimp and all old estuary life; land strips again, and strips of rich chemical water where people voided themselves and their used things and from which so many valuable essences could be extracted; other strips, and then the houses and buildings of another block, for the blocks were not long. Kaleidoscope of nervous water and land, everywhere basic and everywhere different, boated with boats on the strange overpass canals, crossed by an infinity of bridges.

"And no two alike!" William sang, his morning sickness having left him. "Every one different, everything different in a world that cannot be traversed in a lifetime. We'll not run out of wonders!"

"William, William, there is something I have been meaning to tell you," Fairhair tried to interpose.

"Tell me, Fairhair, what is beyond the *Wood Beyond the World,* since the world is a globe without bounds?"

"The World Beyond the Wood is beyond the *Wood Beyond the World,*" Fairhair said simply. "If you want the *Wood,* you will come to it, but do not be cast down if it falls short for you."

"How could it fall short for me? I am a William Morris. My name-game ancestor had to do with the naming as well as the designing of the *Wood.*"

"Your name-game ancestor had to do with the designing of another thing also," Fairhair said. Why, that was almost the same thing as the monitor man had said the day before! What did they mean by it?

William and Fairhair came to the great Chopper House at 20th Street. The two of them went in and worked for an hour in the Chopper House.

"You do not quite understand this, do you, little William?" Fairhair asked.

"Oh, I understand enough for me. I understand that it is everywhere different."

"Yes, I suppose you understand enough for you," Fairhair said with a touch of near sadness. (What they chopped up in the Chopper House was the ancients.)

They went on and on along the strips and streets of the ever-changing city. They came to 21st Street and 22nd and 23rd. Even a writie could not write down all marvels that were to be found at every street. It is sheer wonder to be a world traveler.

There was a carnival at 23rd Street. There were barkies, sharkies, sparkies, darkies, parkies, and markies; the visitors were the markies, but it was not really bad for them. There was the very loud music even though it was supposed to be period tingle-tangle or rinky-dink. There was a steam calliope with real live steam. There were the hamburger stands with the wonderful smell of a touch of garlic in the open air, no matter that it was ancient chopper meat and crinoid-root bun from which the burgers were made. There were games of chance, smooch houses and cooch houses, whirly rides and turning wheels, wino and steino bars and bordellos, and Monster and Misbegotten displays in clamshell-cloth tents.

Really, is anyone too old to enjoy a carnival? Then let that one declare himself an ancient and turn himself in to a Chopper House.

But on and on; one does not tarry when there is the whole World City to see and it not be covered in one lifetime. On 24th (or was it 25th?) Street were the Flesh Pots, and a little beyond them was the Cat Center. One ate and drank beyond reason in the Flesh Pots region and also became enmeshed in the Flesh Mesh booths. And one catted beyond reason in the honeycomblike cubicles of the Cat Center. Fairhair went and worked for an hour at the Cat Center; she seemed to be known and popular there.

But on and on! Everywhere it is different and everywhere it is better.

Along about 27th and 28th Streets were the Top of the Town and Night-Life Knoll, those great cabaret concentrations. It was gin-dizzy here; it was yesterday and tomorrow entangled with its great expectations and its overpowering nostalgia; it was as loud as the West Side Show Square; it was as direct as the Mingle-Mangle or the Pad Palace. It was as fleshy as the Flesh Pots and more catty than the Cat Center. Oh, it was the jumpingest bunch of places that William had yet seen in the City.

Something a little sad there, though; something of passion and pity that was too empty and too pat. It was as though this were the climax of it all, and one didn't *want* it to be the climax yet. It was as if the Top of the Town and Night-Life Knoll (and not the *Wood Beyond the World*) were the central things of the World City.

Perhaps William slept there awhile in the sadness that follows the surfeit of flesh and appetite. There were other doings and sayings about him, but mostly his eyes were closed and his head was heavy.

But then Fairhair had him up again and rushing toward the *Wood* in the still early night.

"It is only a block, William, it is only a block," she sang,

"and it is the place you have wanted more than any other."
(The *Wood* began at 29th Street and went on, it was said,
for the space of *two* full blocks.)

But William ran badly and he even walked badly. He
was woozy and confused, not happy, not sad, just full of
the great bulk of life in the City. He'd hardly have made it
to his high goal that night except for the help of Fairhair.
But she dragged and lifted and carried him along in her
fine arms and on her dusky back and shoulders. He toppled off sometimes and cracked his crown, but there was
never real damage done. One sometimes enters the *Wood
Beyond* in a sort of rhythmic dream, grotesque and comic
and jolting with the sway of a strong friend and of the tidy
world itself. And William came in with his arms around the
neck and shoulders of the girl named Fairhair, with his
face buried in her hair itself, with his feet touching no
ground.

But he knew it as soon as they were in the *Wood*. He
was afoot again and strong again and in the middle of the
fabled place itself. He was sober? No, there can be no so-
briety in the *Wood;* it has its own intoxication.

But it had real grass and weeds, real trees (though most
of them were bushes), real beasts as well as artificial, real
spruce cones on the turf, real birds (no matter that they
were clattering crows) coming in to roost.

There was the carven oak figure of old Robin Hood and
the tall spar-wood form of the giant lumberjack Paul Bun-
yan. There was the Red Indian named White Deer who
was carved from cedarwood. There was maple syrup dripping from the trees (is that the way they used to get it?),
and there was the aroma of slippery elm with the night
dampness on it.

There were the famous Muggers from the mugger dec-
ades. They were of papier-mâché, it is true, and yet they
were most fearsome. There were other dangerous beasts in
the *Wood,* but none like the Muggers. And William and
Fairhair lay down and slept in the very night shadow of the
famous Muggers for the remainder of the enchanted night.

III

"Wonder-bird, wander-bird, where do you fly?"
"All over the City, all under the sky,

"Wand'ring through wonders of strippies and streets,
Changing and challenging, bitters and sweets."

"Wander-bird, squander-bird, should not have budged:
City is sicko and sky is a smudge."
—1st Street Ballad

"Run, William, run in the morning!" Fairhair cried, and she ran while William (confused from the night) shuffled after her.

"We must leave the *Wood?*" he asked.

"Of course *you* must leave the *Wood.* You want to see the whole world, so you cannot stay in one place. You go on, I go back. No, no, don't you look back or you'll be turned into a salt-wood tree."

"Stay with me, Fairhair."

"No, no, you want variety. I have been with you long enough. I have been guide and companion and pony to you. Now we part."

Fairhair went back. William was afraid to look after her. He was in the world beyond the *Wood Beyond the World.* He noticed though that the street was 1st Street and not 31st Street as he had expected.

It was still wonderful to be a world traveler, of course, but not quite as wonderful as it had been one other time. The number of the street shouldn't have mattered to him. William had not been on any 1st Street before. Or 2nd.

But he had been on a 3rd Street before on his farthest trip east. Should he reach it again on his farthest trip west? The world, he knew (being a readie who had read parts of several books), was larger than that. He could not have gone around it in thirty blocks. Still, he came to 3rd Street in great trepidation.

Ah, it was not the same 3rd Street he had once visited

before; almost the same but not exactly. An ounce of reassurance was intruded into the tons of alarm in his heavy head. But he was alive, he was well, he was still traveling west in the boundless City that is everywhere different.

"The City is varied and joyful and free," William Morris said boldly, "and it is everywhere different." Then he saw Kandy Kalosh and he literally staggered with the shock. Only it did not quite seem to be she.

"Is your name Kandy Kalosh?" he asked as quakingly as a one-legged kangaroo with the willies.

"The last thing I needed was a talkie," she said. "Of course it isn't. My name, which I have from my name-game ancestor, is Candy Calabash, not at all the same."

Of course it wasn't the same. Then why had he been so alarmed and disappointed?

"Will you travel westward with me, Candy?" he asked.

"I suppose so, a little way, if we don't have to talk," she said.

So William Morris and Candy Calabash began to traverse the City that was the world. They began (it was no more than coincidence) at a marker set in stone that bore the words "Beginning of Stencil 35,353," and thereat William went into a sort of panic. But why should he? It was not the same stencil number at all. The World City might still be everywhere different.

But William began to run erratically. Candy stayed with him. She was not a readie or a talkie, but she was faithful to a companion for many blocks. The two young persons came ten blocks; they came a dozen.

They arrived at the 14th Street Water Ballet and watched the swimmers. It was almost, but not quite, the same as another 14th Street Water Ballet that William had seen once. They came to the algae-and-plankton quick-lunch place on 15th Street and to the Will of the World Exhibit Hall on 16th Street. Ah, a hopeful eye could still pick out little differences in the huge sameness. The World City *had to be* everywhere different.

They stopped at the Cliff-Dweller Complex on 17th

Street. There was an artificial antelope there now. William didn't remember it from the other time. There was hope, there was hope.

And soon William saw an older and somehow more erect man who wore an arm band with the word "Monitor" on it. He was not the same man, but he had to be a close brother of another man that William had seen two days before.

"Does it all repeat itself again and again and again?" William asked this man in great anguish. "Are the sections of it the same over and over again?"

"Not quite," the man said. "The grease marks on it are sometimes a little different."

"My name is William Morris," William began once more bravely.

"Oh, sure. A William Morris is the easiest type of all to spot," the man said.

"You said— No, another man said that my name-game ancestor had to do with the designing of another thing besides the *Wood Beyond the World*," William stammered. "What was it?"

"Wallpaper," the man said. And William fell down in a frothy faint.

Oh, Candy didn't leave him there. She was faithful. She took him up on her shoulders and plodded along with him, on past the West Side Show Square on 18th Street, past the Mingle-Mangle and the Pad Palace, where she (no, another girl very like her) had turned back before, on and on.

"It's the same thing over and over and over again," William whimpered as she toted him along.

"Be quiet, talkie," she said, but she said it with some affection.

They came to the great Chopper House on 20th Street. Candy carried William in and dumped him on a block there.

"He's become an ancient," Candy told an attendant. "Boy, how he's become an ancient!" It was more than she usually talked.

Then, as she was a fair-minded girl and as she had not worked any stint that day, she turned to and worked an hour in the Chopper House. (What they chopped up in the Chopper House was the ancients.)

Why, there was William's head coming down the line! Candy smiled at it. She chopped it up with loving care, much more care than she usually took.

She'd have said something memorable and kind if she'd been a talkie.

Breckenridge and the Continuum

Robert Silverberg

In one sense, science fiction can be seen as the search for the meanings of existence by examining some of its ends, in the future. Here Robert Silverberg thrusts a man of today into a strange future filled with barren landscapes and strangers, and addresses questions like the value of myth and the nature of the life-force. There's even an encounter with the white light; what more can you ask in the way of a happy ending?

Then Breckenridge said, "I suppose I could tell you the story of Oedipus King of Thieves tonight."

The late-afternoon sky was awful: gray, mottled, fierce. It resonated with a strange electricity. Breckenridge had never grown used to that sky. Day after day, as they crossed the desert, it transfixed him with the pain of incomprehensible loss.

"Oedipus King of Thieves," Scarp murmured. Arios

nodded. Horn looked toward the sky. Militor frowned. "Oedipus," said Horn. "King of Thieves," Arios said.

Breckenridge and his four companions were camped in a ruined pavilion in the desert—a handsome place of granite pillars and black marble floors, constructed perhaps for some delicious paramour of some forgotten prince of the city-building folk. The pavilion lay only a short distance outside the walls of the great dead city that they would enter, at last, in the morning. Once, maybe, this place had been a summer resort, a place for sherbet and swimming, in that vanished time when this desert had bloomed and peacocks had strolled through fragrant gardens. A fantasy out of the *Thousand and One Nights:* long ago, long ago, thousands of years ago. How confusing it was for Breckenridge to remember that that mighty city, now withered by time, had been founded and had thrived and had perished all in an era far less ancient than his own. The bonds that bound the continuum had loosened. He flapped in the time-gales.

"Tell your story," Militor said.

They were restless; they nodded their heads, they shifted positions. Scarp added fuel to the campfire. The sun was dropping behind the bare low hills that marked the desert's western edge; the day's smothering heat was suddenly rushing skyward, and a thin wind whistled through the colonnade of grooved gray pillars that surrounded the pavilion. Grains of pinkish sand danced in a steady stream across the floor of polished stone on which Breckenridge and those who traveled with him squatted. The lofty western wall of the nearby city was already sleeved in shadow.

Breckenridge drew his flimsy cloak closer around himself. He stared in turn at each of the four hooded figures facing him. He pressed his fingers against the cold smooth stone to anchor himself. In a low droning voice he said, "This Oedipus was monarch of the land of Thieves, and a bold and turbulent man. He conceived an illict desire for Euridice his mother. Forcing his passions upon her, he grew so violent that in their coupling she lost her life. Stricken with guilt and fearing that her kinsmen would exact reprisals, Oedipus escaped his kingdom through the air, having fashioned wings for himself under the guidance of the magician Prospero; but he flew too high and came within the ambit of the chariot of his father Apollo, god of the sun. Wrathful over this intrusion, Apollo engulfed Oedipus in heat, and the wax binding the feathers of his wings was melted. For a full day and a night Oedipus tumbled downward across the heavens, plummeting finally into the ocean, sinking through the sea's floor into the dark world below. There he dwells for all eternity, blind and lame; but each spring he reappears among men, and as he limps across the fields green grasses spring up in his tracks."

There was silence. Darkness was overtaking the sky. The four rounded fragments of the shattered old moon emerged and commenced their elegant, baffling saraband, spinning slowly, soaking one another in shifting patterns of cool white light. In the north the glittering violet and green bands of the aurora flickered with terrible abruptness, like the streaky glow of some monstrous searchlight. Breckenridge felt himself penetrated by gaudy ions, roasting him to the core. He waited, trembling.

"Is that all?" Militor said eventually. "Is that how it ends?"

"There's no more to the story," Breckenridge replied. "Are you disappointed?"

"The meaning is obscure. Why the incest? Why did he fly too high? Why was his father angry? Why does Oedipus reappear every spring? None of it makes sense. Am I too shallow to comprehend the relationships? I don't believe that I am."

"Oh, it's old stuff," said Scarp. "The tale of the eternal return. The dead king bringing the new year's fertility. Surely you recognize it, Militor." The aurora flashed with redoubled frenzy, a coded beacon, crying out, SPACE AND TIME, SPACE AND TIME, SPACE AND TIME. "You should have been able to follow the outline of the story," Scarp said. "We've heard it a thousand times in a thousand forms."

—*Space and Time*—

"Indeed we have," Militor said. "But the components of any satisfying tale have to have some logical necessity of sequence, some essential connection." —SPACE— "What we've just heard is a mass of random floating fragments. I see the semblance of myth but not the inner truth."

—TIME—

"A myth holds truth," Scarp insisted, "no matter how garbled its form, no matter how many irrelevant interpolations have entered it. The interpolations may even be one species of truth, and not the lowest species at that."

The Dow-Jones Industrial Average, Breckenridge thought, closed today at 1100432.86—

"At any rate, he told it poorly," Arios observed. "No drama, no intensity, merely a bald outline of events. I've heard better from you on other nights, Breckenridge. She-herazade and the Forty Giants—now, that was a story! Don Quixote and the Fountain of Youth, yes! But this—this—"

Scarp shook his head. "The strength of a myth lies in its content, not in the melody of its telling. I sense the inherent power of tonight's tale. I find it acceptable."

"Thank you," Breckenridge said quietly. He threw sour glares at Militor and Arios. It was hateful when they quibbled over the stories he told them. What gift did he have for these four strange beings, anyhow, except his stories? When they received that gift with poor grace they were denying him his sole claim to their fellowship.

A million years from nowhere . . .

SPACE—TIME.

Apollo—Jesus—Apollo—

The wind grew chillier. No one spoke. Beasts howled on the desert. Breckenridge lay back, feeling an ache in his shoulders, and wriggled against the cold stone floor.

Merry my wife, Cassandra my daughter, Noel my son—

SPACE—TIME—

SPACE—

His eyes hurt from the aurora's frosty glow. He felt himself stretched across the cosmos, torn between then and now—breaking, breaking, ripping into fragments like the moon—

The stars had come out. He contemplated the early constellations. They were unfamiliar; no matter how often Scarp or Horn pointed out the patterns to him, he saw only random sprinklings of light. In his other life he had been able to identify at least the more conspicuous constellations, but they did not seem to be here. How long does it take to effect a complete redistribution of the heavens? A million years? Ten million? Thank God Mars and Jupiter still were visible, the orange dot and the brilliant white one, to tell him that this place was his own world, his own solar system. Images danced in his aching skull. He saw everything double, suddenly. There was Pegasus, there was Orion, there was Sagittarius. An overlay, a mask of realities superimposed on realities.

"Listen to this music," Horn said after a long while, producing a fragile device of wheels and spindles from beneath his cloak. He caressed it and delicate sounds came forth: crystalline, comforting, the music of dreams, sliding into the range of audibility with no perceptible instant of attack. Shortly Scarp began a wordless song, and, one by one, the others joined him, first Horn, then Militor, and lastly, in a dry, buzzing monotone, Arios.

"What are you singing?" Breckenridge asked.

"The hymn of Oedipus King of Thieves," Scarp told him.

Had it been such a bad life? He had been healthy, prosperous, and beloved. His father was managing partner of Falkner, Breckenridge & Co., one of the most stable of the Wall Street houses, and Breckenridge, after coming up through the ranks in the family tradition, putting in his time as a customer's man and his time in the bond department and as a floor trader, was a partner too, only ten years out of Dartmouth. What was wrong with that? His draw in 1972 was $83,500—not as much as he had hoped for out of a partnership, but not bad, not bad at all, and next year might be much better. He had a wife and two children, an apartment on East 73rd Street, a country cabin on Candlewood Lake, a fair-sized schooner that he kept in a Gulf Coast marina, and a handsome young mistress in an apartment of her own on the Upper West Side. What was wrong with that? When he burst through the fabric of the continuum and found himself in an unimaginably altered world at the end of time, he was astonished not that such a thing might happen but that it had happened to someone as settled and well-established as himself.

While they slept, a corona of golden light sprang into being along the top of the city wall. The glow awakened Breckenridge, and he sat up quickly, thinking that the city was on fire. But the light seemed cool and supple, and appeared to be propagated in easy rippling waves, more like the aurora than like the raw blaze of flames. It sprang from the very rim of the wall and leaped high, casting blurred, rounded shadows at cross-angles to the sharp crisp shadows that the fragmented moon created. There also seemed to be a deep segment of blackness in the side of the wall. Looking closely, Breckenridge saw that the huge gate on the wall's western face was standing open. Without telling the others, he left the camp and crossed the flat sandy wasteland, coming to the gate after a brisk march of about an hour. Nothing prevented him from entering.

Just within the wall was a wide cobbled plaza, and beyond that stretched broad avenues lined with buildings of a strange sort: rounded and rubbery, porous of texture, all humps and parapets. Black unfenced wells at the center of each major intersection plunged to infinite depths. Breckenridge had been told that the city was empty—that it had been uninhabited for centuries, since the spoiling of the climate in this part of the world—and so he was surprised to find it occupied. Pale figures flitted silently about, moving like wraiths, as though there were empty space between their feet and the pavement. He approached one and another and a third, but when he tried to speak no words would leave his lips. He seized one of the city dwellers by the wrist, a slender black-haired girl in a soft gray robe, and held her tightly, hoping that contact would lead to contact. Her dark somber eyes studied him without show of fear and she made no effort to break away. I am Noel Breckenridge, he said—Noel III—and I was born in the town of Greenwich, Connecticut, in the year of our lord 1940, my wife's name is Merry and my daughter is Cassandra and my son is Noel Breckenridge IV, and I am not as coarse or stupid as you may think me to be. She made no reply and showed no change of expression. He asked, Can you understand anything I'm saying to you? Her face remained wholly blank. He asked, Can you even hear the sound of my voice? There was no response. He went on: What is your name? What is this city called? When was it abandoned? What year is this on any calendar that I can comprehend? What do you know about me that I need to know? She continued to regard him in an altogether neutral way. He pulled her against his body and gripped her thin shoulders with his fingertips and kissed her urgently, forcing his tongue between her teeth. An instant later he found himself sprawled not far from the campsite with his face in the sand and sand in his mouth. Only a dream, he thought wearily, only a dream.

He was having lunch with Harry Munsey at the Merchants and Shippers Club: sleek chrome-and-redwood premises sixty stories above William Street in the heart of the financial district. Subdued light fixtures glowed like pulsing red suns; waiters moved past the tables like silent moons. The club was over a century old, although the skyscraper in which it occupied a penthouse suite had only been erected in 1968—its fourth home, or maybe its fifth. Membership was limited to white male Christians, sober and responsible, who held important positions in the New York securities industry. There was nothing in the club's written constitution which explicitly limited its membership to white male Christians, but, all the same, there had never been any members who had not been white, male, and Christian. No one with a firm grasp of reality thought there ever would be.

Harry Munsey, like Noel Breckenridge, was white, male, and Christian. They had gone to Dartmouth together and they had entered Wall Street together, Breckenridge going into his family's firm and Munsey into his, and they had lunch together almost every day and saw each other almost every Saturday night, and each had slept with the other's wife, though each believed that the other knew nothing about that.

On the third martini Munsey said, "What's bugging you today, Noel?"

A dozen years ago Munsey had been an all-Ivy halfback; he was a big, powerful man, bigger even than Breckenridge, who was not a small man. Munsey's face was pink and unlined and his eyes were alive and youthful, but he had lost all his hair before he turned thirty.

"Is something bugging me?"

"Something's bugging you, yes. Why else would you look so uptight after you've had two and a half martinis?"

Breckenridge had found it difficult to grow used to the sight of the massive bright dome that was Munsey's skull.

He said, "All right. So I'm bugged."

"Want to talk about it?"

"No."

"Okay," Munsey said.

Breckenridge finished his drink. "As a matter of fact, I'm oppressed by a sophomoric sense of the meaninglessness of life, if you have to know."

"Really?"

"Really."

"The meaninglessness of life?"

"Life is empty, dumb, and mechanical," Breckenridge said.

"*Your* life?"

"Life."

"I know a lot of people who'd like to live your life. They'd trade with you, even up, asset for asset, liability for liability, life for life."

Breckenridge shook his head. "They're fools, then."

"It's that bad?"

"It all seems so pointless, Harry. Everything. We have a good time and con ourselves into thinking it means something. But what is there, actually? The pursuit of money? I have enough money. After a certain point it's just a game. French restaurants? Trips to Europe? Drinking? Sex? Swimming pools? Jesus! We're born, we grow up, we do a lot of stuff, we grow old, we die. Is that all? Jesus, Harry, is that *all*?"

Munsey looked embarrassed. "Well, there's family," he suggested. "Marriage, fatherhood, knowing that you're linking yourself into the great chain of life. Bringing forth a new generation. Transmitting your ideals, your standards, your traditions, everything that distinguishes us from the apes we used to be. Doesn't that count?"

Shrugging, Breckenridge said, "All right. Having kids, you say. We bring them into the world, we wipe their noses, we teach them to be little men and women, we send them to the right schools and get them into the right clubs, and they grow up to be carbon copies of their parents: lawyers or brokers or clubwomen or whatever—"

The lights fluttering. The aurora: red, green, violet, red, green. The straining fabric; the moon, the broken moon; the aurora; the lights; the fire atop the walls—

"—or else they grow up and deliberately fashion themselves into the opposites of their parents, and somewhere along the way the parents die off, and the kids have kids, and the cycle starts around again. Around and around, generation after generation, Noel Breckenridge III, Noel Breckenridge IV, Noel Breckenridge XVI—"

Arios—Scarp—Militor—Horn—

The city—the gate—

"—making money, spending money, living high, building nothing real, just occupying space on the planet for a little while, and what for? What for? What does it all mean?"

The granite pillars—the aurora—SPACE AND TIME—

"You're on a bummer today, Noel," Munsey said.

"I know. Aren't you sorry you asked what was bugging me?"

"Not particularly. Everybody goes through a phase like this."

"When he's seventeen, yes."

"And later, too."

"It's more than a phase," Breckenridge said. "It's a sickness. If I had any guts, Harry, I'd drop out. Drop right out and try to work out some meanings in the privacy of my own head."

"Why don't you? You can afford it. Go on. Why not?"

"I don't know," said Breckenridge.

Such strange constellations. Such a terrible sky.

Such a cold wind blowing out of tomorrow.

"I think it may be time for another martini," Munsey said.

They had been crossing the desert for a long time now —forty days and forty nights, Breckenridge liked to tell himself, but probably it had been longer than that—and they moved at an unsparing pace, marching from dawn to sunset with as few rest periods as possible. The air was thin. His lungs felt leathery. Because he was the biggest man in the group, he carried the heaviest pack. That didn't bother him.

What did bother him was how little he knew about this expedition, its purposes, its origin, even how he had come to be a part of it. But asking such questions seemed somehow naive and awkward, and he never did. He went along, doing his share—making camp, cleaning up in the mornings—and tried to keep his companions amused with his stories. They demanded stories from him every night. "Tell us your myths," they urged. "Tell us the legends and fables you learned in your childhood."

After weeks of sharing this trek with them he knew little more about the other four than he had at the outset. His favorite among them was Scarp, who was sympathetic and flexible. He liked the hostile, contemptuous Militor the least. Horn—dreamy, poetic, unworldly, aloof—was beyond his reach; Arios, the most dry and objective and scientific of the group, did not seem worth trying to reach. So far as

Breckenridge could determine they were human, although their skins were oddly glossy and of a peculiar olive hue, something on the far side of swarthy. They had strange noses, narrow, high-bridged noses of a kind he had never seen before, extremely fragile, like the noses of pure-bred society women carried to the ultimate possibilites of their design.

The desert was beautiful. A gaudy desolation, all dunes and sandy ripples, streaked blue and red and gold and green with brilliant oxides.

Sometimes when the aurora was going full blast— SPACE! TIME! *Space! Time!*—the desert seemed to be merely a mirror for the sky. But in the morning, when the electronic furies of the aurora had died away, the sand still reverberated with its own inner pulses of bright color.

And the sun—pale, remorseless—Apollo's deathless fires—

I am Noel Breckenridge and I am nine years old and this is how I spent my summer vacation—

Oh Lord Jesus forgive me.

Scattered everywhere on the desert were outcroppings of ancient ruins—colonnades, halls of statuary, guardposts, summer pavilions, hunting lodges, the stumps of antique walls, and invariably the marchers made their camp beside one of these. They studied each ruin, measured its dimensions, recorded its salient details, poked at its sand-shrouded foundations. Around Scarp's neck hung a kind of mechanized map, a teardrop-shaped black instrument that could be made to emit—

PING!

—sounds which daily guided them toward the next ruin in the chain leading to the city. Scarp also carried a compact humming machine that generated sweet water from handfuls of sand. For solid food they subsisted on small yellow pellets, quite tasty.

PING!

At the beginning Breckenridge had felt constant fatigue, but under the grinding exertions of the march he had

grown steadily in strength and endurance, and now he felt
he could continue forever, never tiring, parading—

PING!

—endlessly back and forth across this desert which perhaps spanned the entire world. The dead city, though, was
their destination, and finally it was in view. They were to
remain there for an indefinite stay. He was not yet sure
whether these four were archaeologists or pilgrims. Perhaps
both, he thought. Or maybe neither. Or maybe neither.

"How do you think you can make your life more meaningful, then?" Munsey asked.

"I don't know. I don't have any idea what would work
for me. But I do know who the people are whose lives *do*
have meaning."

"Who?"

"The creators, Harry. The shapers, the makers, the be-
getters. Beethoven, Rembrandt, Dr. Salk, Einstein, Shakespeare, that bunch. It isn't enough just to live. It isn't even
enough just to have a good mind, to think clear thoughts.
You have to add something to the sum of humanity's accomplishments, something real, something valuable. You
have to *give*. Mozart. Newton. Columbus. Those who are
able to reach into the well of creation, into that hot boiling
chaos of raw energy down there, and pull something out,
shape it, make something unique and new out of it. Making
money isn't enough. Making more Breckenridges or Mun-
seys isn't enough, either. You know what I'm saying, Harry? The well of creation. The reservoir of life, which is
God. Do you ever think you believe in God? Do you wake
up in the middle of the night sometimes saying, Yes, yes,
there *is* Something after all, I believe, I believe! I'm not
talking about churchgoing now, you understand.
Churchgoing's nothing but a conditioned reflex these days,
a twitch, a tic. I'm talking about faith. Belief. The state of
enlightenment. I'm not talking about God as an old man
with long white whiskers, either, Harry. I mean something
abstract, a force, a power, a current, a reservoir of energy
underlying everything and connecting everything. God is

that reservoir. That reservoir is God. I think of that reservoir as being something like the sea of molten lava down beneath the earth's crust: it's there, it's full of heat and power, it's accessible for those who know the way. Plato was able to tap into the reservoir. Van Gogh. Joyce. Schubert. El Greco. A few lucky ones know how to reach it. Most of us can't. Most of us can't. For those who can't, God is dead. Worse—for them, He never lived at all. Oh, Christ, how awful it is to be trapped in an era where everybody goes around like some sort of zombie, cut off from the energies of the spirit, ashamed even to admit there are such energies. I hate it. I hate the whole stinking twentieth century, do you know that? Am I making any sense? Do I seem terribly drunk? Am I embarrassing you, Harry? Harry? Harry?"

In the morning they struck camp and set out on the final leg of their journey toward the city. The sand here had a disturbing crusty quality: white saline outcroppings gave Breckenridge the feeling that they were crossing a tundra rather than a desert. The sky was clear and pale, and in its bleached cloudlessness it took on something of the quality of a shield, of a mirror, seizing the morning heat that rose from the ground and hurling it inexorably back, so that the five marchers felt themselves trapped in an infinite baffle of unendurable dry smothering warmth.

As they moved cityward Militor and Arios chattered compulsively, falling after a while into a quarrel over certain obscure and controversial points of historical theory. Breckenridge had heard them have this argument at least a dozen times in the last two weeks, and no doubt they had been battling it out for years. The main area of contention was the origin of the city. Who were its builders? Militor believied they were colonists from some other planet— strangers to Earth, representatives of some alien species of immeasurable grandeur and nobility—who had crossed space thousands of years ago to build this gigantic monument on Asia's flank. Nonsense, retorted Arios: the city was plainly the work of human beings, unusually gifted and energetic but human nonetheless. Why multiply hypotheses needlessly? Here is the city; humans have built many cities nearly as great as this one in their long history; this city is only quantitatively superior to the others, merely a little bigger, merely a bit more daringly conceived. To invoke extraterrestrial architects is to dabble gratuitously in fantasy. But Militor maintained his position. Humans, he said, were plainly incapable of such immense constructions. Neither in this present decadent epoch, when any sort of effort is too great, nor at any time in the past, could human resources have been equal to such a task as the building of this city must have been. Breckenridge had his doubts about that, having seen what the twentieth century had accomplished. He tended to side with Arios. But indeed the city was extraordinary, Breckenridge admitted: an ultimate urban glory, a supernal Babylon, a consummate Persepolis, the soul's own hymn in brick and stone. The wall that girdled it was at least two hundred feet high—why pour so much energy into a wall? were no better means of defense at hand, or was the wall mere exuberant decoration?—and, judging by the easy angle of its curve, it must be hundreds of miles in circumference. A city larger than New York, more sprawling than even Los Angeles, a giant antenna of turbulent consciousness set like a colossal gem into this vast plain, a throbbing antenna for all the radiance of the stars: yes, it was overwhelming, it was devastating to contemplate the planning and the building of it; it seemed almost to require the hypothesis of a superior alien race. And yet he refused to accept that hypothesis. Arios, he thought, I am with you.

The city was uninhabited, a hulk, a ruin. Why? What had happened here to turn this garden plain into a salt-crusted waste? The builders grew too proud, said Militor. They defied the gods, they overreached even their own powers and, stumbling, fell headlong into decay. The life went out of the soil, the sky gave no rain, the spirit lost its energies; the city perished and was forgotten, and was whispered about by mythmakers, a city out of time, a city at the end of the world, a mighty mass of dead wonders, a habitation for jackals, a place where no one went. We are the first in centuries, said Scarp, to seek this city.

Halfway between dawn and noon they reached the wall and stood before the great gate. The gate alone was fifty feet high, a curving slab of burnished blue metal set smoothly into a recess in the tawny stucco of the wall. Breckenridge saw no way of opening it, no winch, no portcullis, no handles, no knobs. He feared that the impatient Militor would merely blow a hole in it. But, groping along the base of the gate, they found a small doorway, man-high and barely man-wide, near the left-hand edge. Ancient hinges yielded at a push. Scarp led the way inside.

The city was as Breckenridge remembered it from his dream: the cobbled plaza, the broad avenues, the humped and rubbery buildings. The fierce sunlight, deflected and refracted by the undulant rooflines, reverberated from every flat surface and rebounded in showers of brilliant energy. Breckenridge shaded his eyes. It was as though the sky were full of pulsars. His soul was frying on a cosmic griddle, cooking in a torrent of hard radiation.

The city was inhabited.

Faces were visible at windows. Elusive figures emerged at street corners, peered, withdrew. Scarp called to them; they shrank back into the hard-edged shadows.

"Well?" Arios demanded. "They're human, aren't they?"

"What of it?" said Militor. "Squatters, that's all. You saw how easy it was to push open that door. They've come in out of the desert to live in the ruins."

"Maybe not. Descendants of the builders, I'd say. Perhaps the city never really was abandoned." Arios looked at Scarp. "Don't you agree?"

"They might be anything," Scarp said. "Squatters, descendants, synthetics, even servants without masters, living on, waiting, living on, waiting—"

"Or projections cast by ancient machines," Militor said. "No human hand built this city."

Arios snorted. They advanced quickly across the plaza and entered onto the first of the grand avenues. The buildings flanking it were sealed. They proceeded to a major intersection, where they halted to inspect an open circular pit, fifteen feet in diameter, smooth-rimmed, descending into infinite darkness. Breckenridge had seen many such dark wells in his vision of the night before. He did not doubt now that he had left his sleeping body and had made an actual foray into the city last night.

Scarp flashed a light into the well. A copper-colored metal ladder was visible along one face.

"Shall we go down?" Breckenridge asked.

"Later," said Scarp.

The famous anthropologist had been drinking steadily all through the dinner party—wine, only wine, but plenty of it—and his eyes seemed glazed, his face flushed. Nevertheless, he continued to talk with superb clarity of perception and elegant precision of phrase, hardly pausing at all to construct his concepts. Perhaps he's merely quoting his own latest book from memory, Breckenridge thought, as he strained to follow the flow of ideas. "—a comparison between myth and what appears to have largely replaced it in modern societies, namely, politics. When the historian refers to the French Revolution, it is always as a sequence of past happenings—a non-revertible series of events, the remote consequences of which may still be felt at present. But to the French politician, as well as to his followers, the French Revolution is both a sequence belonging to the past —as to the historian—and an everlasting pattern which can be detected in the present French social structure and which provides a clue for its interpretation, a lead from which to infer the future developments. See, for instance, Michelet, who was a politically-minded historian. He describes the French Revolution thus: 'This day . . . everything was possible. . . . Future became present . . . that is, no more time, a glimpse of eternity.' " The great man reached decisively for another glass of claret. His hand wavered; the glass toppled; a dark red torrent stained the tablecloth. Breckenridge experienced a sudden terrifying moment of complete disorientation, as though the walls and floor were shifting places. He saw a parched desert pleateau, four hooded figures, a blazing sky of strange constellations, a pulsating aurora sweeping the heavens with cold fire. A mighty walled city dominated the plain, and its frosty shadow, knifeblade-sharp, cut across Breckenridge's path. He shivered. The woman on Breckenridge's right laughed lightly and began to recite:

> I saw Eternity the other night
> Like a great ring of pure and endless light.
>   All calm, as it was bright;
> And round beneath it, Time in hours, days, years,
>   Driv'n by the spheres
> Like a vast shadow mov'd; in which the world
>   And all her train were hurl'd.

"Excuse me," Breckenridge said. "I think I'm unwell." He rushed from the dining room. In the hallway he turned toward the washroom and found himself staring into a steaming tropical marsh, all ferns and horsetails and giant insects. Dragonflies the size of pigeons whirred past him. The sleek rump of a brontosaurus rose like a bubbling aneurysm from the black surface of the swamp. Breckenridge recoiled and staggered away. On the other side of the hall lay the desert under the lash of a frightful noonday sun. He gripped the frame of a door and held himself upright, trembling, as his soul oscillated wildly across the hallucinatory eons. "I am Scarp," said a quiet voice within him. "You have come to the place where all times are one, where all errors can be unmade, where past and future are fluid and subject to redefinition." Breckenridge felt powerful arms encircling and supporting him. "Noel? Noel? Here, sit down." Harry Munsey. Shiny pink skull, searching blue eyes. "Jesus, Noel, you look like you're having some kind of bad trip. Merry sent me after you to find out—"

"It's O.K.," Breckenridge said hoarsely. "I'll be all right."

"You want me to get her?"

"I'll be *all right*. Just let me steady myself a second." He rose uncertainly. "Okay. Let's go back inside."

The anthropologist was still talking. A napkin covered the wine stain and he held a fresh glass aloft like a sacramental chalice. "The key to everything, I think, lies in an idea that Franz Boas offered in 1898: 'It would seem that mythological worlds have been built up only to be shattered again, and that new worlds were built from the fragments.' "

Breckenridge said, "The first men lived underground and there was no such thing as private property. One day there was an earthquake and the earth was rent apart. The light of day flooded the subterranean cavern where mankind dwelled. Clumsily, for the light dazzled their eyes, they came upward into the world of brightness and learned how to see. Seven days later they divided the fields among themselves and began to build the first walls as boundaries marking the limits of their land."

By midday the city dwellers were losing their fear of the five intruders. Gradually, in twos and threes, they left their hiding places and gathered around the visitors, until a substantial group collected. They were dressed simply, in light robes, and they said nothing to the strangers, though they whispered frequently to one another. Among the group was the slender, dark-haired girl of Breckenridge's dream. "Do you remember me?" he asked. She smiled and shrugged and answered softly in a liquid, incomprehensible language. Arios questioned her in six or seven tongues, but she shook her head to everything. Then she took Breckenridge by the hand and led him a few paces away, toward one of the street wells. Pointing into it, she smiled. She pointed to Breckenridge, pointed to herself, to the surrounding buildings. She made a sweeping gesture taking in all the sky. She pointed again into the well. "What are you trying to tell me?" he asked her. She answered in her own language. Breckenridge shook his head apologetically. She did a simple pantomime: eyes closed, head lolling against pressed-together hands. An image of sleep, certainly. She pointed to him. To herself. To the well. "You want me to sleep with you?" he blurted. "Down there?" He had to laugh at his own foolishness. It was ridiculous to assume the persistence of a cowardly, euphemistic metaphor like that across so many millennia. He gaped stupidly at her. She laughed—a silvery, tinkling laugh—and danced away from him, back toward her own people.

Their first night in the city they made camp in one of the great plazas. It was an octagonal space surrounded by low green buildings, sharp-angled, each faced on its plaza side with mirror-bright stone. About a hundred of the city dwellers crouched in the shadows on the plaza's periphery, watching them. Scarp sprinkled fuel pellets and kindled a fire; Militor distributed dinner; Horn played music as they ate; Arios, sitting apart, dictated a commentary into a recording device he carried, the size and texture of a large pearl. Afterward, they asked Breckenridge to tell a story, as usual, and he told them the tale of how death came to the world.

"Once upon a time," he began, "there were only a few people in the world and they lived in a green and fertile valley, where winter never came and gardens bloomed all the year round. They spent their days laughing and swimming and lying in the sun, and in the evenings they feasted and sang and made love, and this went on without change, year in, year out, and no one ever fell ill or suffered from hunger, and no one ever died. Despite the serenity of this existence, one man in the village was unhappy. His name was Faust, and he was a restless, intelligent man with intense, burning eyes and a lean, unsmiling face. Faust felt that life must consist of something more than swimming and making love and plucking ripe fruit off vines. There is something else to life, Faust insisted, something unknown to us, something that eludes our grasp, something the lack of which keeps us from being truly happy. We are incomplete, he said.

"The others listened to him and at first they were puzzled, for they had not known they were unhappy or incomplete; they had mistaken the ease and placidity of their existence for happiness. But after awhile they started to believe that Faust might be right. They had not known how vacant their lives were until Faust had pointed it out. What can we do, they asked? How can we learn what the thing is that we lack? A wise old man suggested that they might ask the gods. So they elected Faust to visit the god Prometheus, who was said to be a friend to mankind, and ask him. Faust crossed hill and dale, mountain and river, and came at last to Prometheus on the storm-swept summit where he dwelled. He explained the situation and said, Tell me, O Prometheus, why we feel so incomplete. The god replied, It is because you do not have the use of fire. Without fire there can be no civilization; you are uncivilized, and your barbarism makes you unhappy. With fire you can cook your food and enjoy many interesting new flavors. With fire you can work metals, and create effective weapons and other tools. Faust considered this and said, But where can we obtain fire? What is it? How is it used?

"I will bring fire to you, Prometheus answered.

"Prometheus then went to Zeus, the greatest of the gods, and said, Zeus, the humans desire fire, and I seek your permission to bestow it upon them. But Zeus was hard of hearing and Prometheus lisped badly and in the language of the gods the words for 'fire' and for 'death' were very similar, and Zeus misunderstood and said, How odd of them to desire such a thing, but I am a benevolent god, and deny my creatures nothing that they crave. So Zeus created a woman named Pandora and put death inside her and gave her to Prometheus, who took her back to the valley where mankind lived. Here is Pandora, said Prometheus. She will give us fire.

"As soon as Prometheus took his leave Faust came forward and embraced Pandora and lay with her. Her body was hot as flame, and as he held her in his arms death came forth from her and entered him, and he shivered and grew feverish, and cried out in ecstasy, This is fire! I have mastered fire! Within the hour death began to consume him, so that he grew weak and thin, and his skin became parched and yellowish, and he trembled like a leaf in a breeze. Go! he cried to the others. Embrace her! She is the bringer of fire! And he staggered off into the wilderness beyond the valley's edge, murmuring, Thanks be to Prometheus for this gift. He lay down beneath a huge tree, and there he died, and it was the first time that death had visited a human being. And the tree died also.

"Then the other men of the village embraced Pandora, one after another, and death entered into them too, and they went from her to their own women and embraced them, so that soon all the men and women of the village were ablaze with death, and one by one their lives reached an end. Death remained in the village, passing into all who lived and into all who were born from their loins, and this is how death came to the world. Afterward during a storm, lightning struck the tree that had died when Faust had died, and set it ablaze, and a man whose name is forgotten thrust a dry branch into the blaze and lit it, and learned how to build a fire and how to keep the fire alive, and after that time men cooked their food and used fire to work metal into weapons, and so it was that civilization began."

It was time to investigate one of the wells. Scarp, Arios, and Breckenridge would make the descent, with Militor and Horn remaining on the surface to cope with contingencies. They chose a well half a day's march from their campsite, deep into the city, a big one, broader and deeper than most they had seen. At its rim Scarp mounted a spherical fist-sized light that cast a dazzling blue-white beam into the opening. Then, lightly swinging himself out onto the metal ladder, he began to climb down, shrouded in a nimbus of molten brightness. Breckenridge peered after him. Scarp's head and shoulders remained visible for a long while, dwindling until he was only a point of darkness in motion deep within the cone of light, and then he could no longer be seen. "Scarp?" Breckenridge called. After a moment came a muffled reply out of the depths. Scarp had reached bottom, somewhere beyond the range of the beam, and wanted them to join him.

Breckenridge followed. The descent seemed infinite. There was a stiffness in his left knee. He became a mere automaton mechanically seizing the rungs; they were warm in his hands. His eyes, fixed on the pocked gray skin of the well's wall inches from his nose, grew glassy and un-focused. He passed through the zone of light as though sliding through the face of a mirror and moved downward in darkness without a change of pace until his boot slammed unexpectedly into a solid floor where he had thought to encounter the next rung. The left boot; his knee, jamming, protested. Scarp lightly touched his shoulder. "Step back here next to me," he said. "Take sliding steps and make sure you have a footing. For all we know, we're on some sort of ledge with a steep drop on all sides."

They waited while Arios came down. His footfalls were like thunder in the well—*boom, boom, boom*—transmitted and amplified by the rungs. Then the men at the surface lowered the light, fixed to the end of a long cord, and at last they could look around.

They were in a kind of catacomb. The floor of the well was a platform of neatly dressed stone slabs which gave access to horizontal tunnels several times a man's height, stretching away to right and left, to fore and aft. The mouth of the well was a dim dot of light far above. Scarp, after inspecting the perimeter of the platform, flashed the beam into one of the tunnels, stared a moment, and cautiously entered. Breckenridge heard him cough. "Dusty in here," Scarp muttered. Then he said, "You told us a story once about the King of the Dead Lands, Breckenridge. What was his name?"

"Thanatos."

"Thanatos, yes. This must be his kingdom. Come and look."

Arios and Breckenridge exchanged shrugs. Breckenridge stepped into the tunnel. The walls on both sides were lined from floor to ceiling with tiers of coffins, stacked eight or ten high and extending as far as the light beam reached.

The coffins were glass-faced and covered over with dense films of dust. Scarp drew his fingers through the dust over one coffin and left deep tracks; clouds rose up, sending Breckenridge back, coughing and choking, to stumble into Arios. When the dust cleared they could see a figure within, seemingly asleep, the nude figure of a young man lying on his back. His expression was one of great serenity. Breckenridge shivered. Death's kingdom, yes, the place of Thanatos, the house of Pluto. He walked down the row, wiping coffin after coffin. An old man. A child. A young woman. An older woman. A whole population lay embalmed here. I died long ago, he thought, and I don't even sleep. I walk about beneath the earth. The silence was frightening here. "The people of the city?" Scarp asked. "The ancient inhabitants?"

"Very likely," said Arios. His voice was as crisp as ever. He alone was not trembling. "Slain in some inconceivable massacre? But what? But how?"

"They appear to have died natural deaths," Breckenridge pointed out. "Their bodies look whole and healthy. As though they were lying here asleep. Not dead, only sleeping."

"A plague?" Scarp wondered. "A sudden cloud of deadly gas? A taint of poison in their water supply?"

"If it had been sudden," said Breckenridge, "how would they have had time to build all these coffins? This whole tunnel—catacomb upon catacomb—" A network of passageways spanning the city's entire subterrane. Thousands of coffins. Millions. Breckenridge felt dazed by the presence of death on such a scale. The skeleton with the scythe, moving briskly about its work. Severed heads and hands and feet scattered like dandelions in the springtime meadow. The reign of Thanatos, King of Swords, Knight of Wands.

Thunder sounded behind them. Footfalls in the well.

Scarp scowled. "I told them to wait up there. That fool Militor—"

Arios said, "Militor should see this. Undoubtedly it's the

resting place of the city dwellers. Undoubtedly these are human beings. Do you know what I imagine? A mass suicide. A unanimous decision to abandon the world of life. Years of preparation. The construction of tunnels, of machines for killing, a whole vast apparatus of immolation. And then the day appointed—long lines waiting to be processed—millions of men and women and children passing through the machines, gladly giving up their lives, going willingly to the coffins that await them—"

"And then," Scarp said, "there must have been only a few left and no one to process them. Living on, caretakers for the dead, perhaps, maintaining the machinery that preserves these millions of bodies."

"Preserves them for what?" Arios asked.

"The day of resurrection," said Breckenridge.

The footfalls in the well grew louder. Scarp glanced toward the tunnel's mouth. "Militor?" he called. "Horn?" He sounded angry. He walked toward the well. "You were supposed to wait for us up—"

Breckenridge heard a grinding sound and whirled to see Arios tugging at the lid of a coffin—the one that held the serene young man. Instinctively he moved to halt the desecration, but he was too slow; the glass plate rose as Arios broke the seals, and, with a quick whooshing sound, a burst of greenish vapor rushed from the coffin. It hovered a moment in midair, speared by Arios' beam of light; then it congealed into a yellow precipitant and broke in a miniature rainstorm that stained the tunnel's stone floor. To Breckenridge's horror the young man's body jerked convulsively. Muscles tightened into knots and almost instantly relaxed. "He's alive!" Breckenridge cried.

"Was," said Scarp.

Yes. The figure in the glass case was motionless. It changed color and texture, turning black and withered. Scarp shoved Arios aside and slammed the lid closed, but that could do no good now. A dreadful new motion commenced within the coffin. In moments something shriveled and twisted lay before them.

"Suspended animation," said Arios. "The city builders— they lie here, as human as we are, sleeping, not dead, sleeping. Sleeping! Militor! Militor, come quickly!"

Feingold said, "Let me see if I have it straight. After the public offering our group will continue to hold 83 percent of the Class B stock and 34 percent of the voting common, which constitutes a controlling block. We'll let you have 100,000 five-year warrants and we'll agree to a conversion privilege on the 1992 6½ percent debentures, plus we allow you the stipulated underwriting fee, providing your Argentinian friend takes up the agreed-upon allotment of debentures and follows through on his deal with us in Colorado. Okay? Now, then, assuming the SEC has no objections, I'd like to outline the proposed interlocking directorates with Heitmark A.G. in Liechtenstein and Hellaphon S.A. in Athens, after which—"

The high, clear, rapid voice went on and on. Breckenridge toyed with his lunch, smiled frequently, nodded whenever he felt it was appropriate, and otherwise remained disconnected, listening only with the automatic-recorder part of his mind. They were sitting on the terrace of an open-air restaurant in Tiberias, at the edge of the Sea of Galilee, looking across to the bleak, brown Syrian hills on the far side. The December air was mild, the sun bright. Last week Breckenridge had visited Monaco, Zurich, and Milan. Yesterday Tel Aviv, tomorrow Haifa, next Tuesday Istanbul. Then on to Nairobi, Johannesburg, Peking, Singapore. Finally San Francisco and then home. Zap! Zap! A crazy round-the-world scramble in twenty days, cleaning up a lot of international business for the firm. It could all have been handled by telephone, or else some of these foreign tycoons could have come to New York, but Breckenridge had volunteered to do the junket. Why? Why? Sitting here ten thousand miles from home having lunch with a man whose office was down the street from his own. Crazy. Why all this running, Noel? Where do you think you'll get?

"Some more wine?" Feingold asked. "What do you think of this Israeli stuff, anyway?"

"It goes well with the fish." Breckenridge reached for Feingold's copy of the agreement. "Here, let me initial all that."

"Don't you want to check it over first?"

"Not necessary. I have faith in you, Sid."

"Well, I wouldn't cheat you, that's true. But I could have made a mistake. I'm capable of making mistakes."

"I don't think so," Breckenridge said. He grinned. Feingold grinned. Behind the grin there was something chilly. Breckenridge looked away. You think I'm bending over backwards to treat you like a gentleman, he thought, because you know what people like me are really supposed to think about Jews, and I know you know, and you know I know you know, and—and—well, screw it, Sid. Do I trust you? Maybe I do. Maybe I don't. But the basic fact is I just don't care. Stack the deck any way you like, Feingold. I just don't care. I wish I was on Mars. Or Pluto. Or in the year Two Billion. Zap! Right across the whole continuum! Noel Breckenridge, freaking out! He heard himself say, "Do you want to know my secret fantasy, Sid? I dream of waking up Jewish one day. It's so damned boring being a Gentile, do you know that? I feel so bland, so straight, so sunny. I envy you all that feverish kinky complexity of soul. All that history. Ghettos, persecutions, escapes, schemes for survival and revenge, a sense of tribal unity born out of shared pain. It's so hard for a goy to develop some honest paranoia, you know? Let alone a little schiziness." Feingold was still grinning. He filled Breckenridge's wine glass again. He showed no sign of having heard anything that might offend him. Maybe I didn't say anything, Breckenridge thought.

Feingold said, "When you get back to New York, Noel, I'd like you out to our place for dinner. You and your wife. A weekend, maybe. Logs on the fire, thick steaks, plenty of good wine. You'll love our place." Three Israeli jets roared low over Tiberias and vanished in the direction of Lebanon. "Will you come? Can you fit it into your schedule?"

Some possible structural hypotheses:

LIFE AS MEANINGLESS CONDITION

Breckenridge on Wall Street	The four seekers moving randomly	The dead city

* * *

LIFE RENDERED MEANINGFUL THROUGH ART

Breckenridge recollects ancient myths	The four-seekers elicit his presence and request the myths	The dead city inhabited after all. The inhabitants listen to Breckenridge

* * *

THE IMPACT OF ENTROPY

His tales are garbled dreams	The seekers quarrel over theory	The city dwellers speak an unknown language

* * *

ASPECTS OF CONSCIOUSNESS

He is a double self	The four seekers are unsure of the historical background	Most of the city dwellers are asleep

His audience was getting larger every night. They came from all parts of the city, silently arriving, drawn at sundown to the place where the visitors camped. Hundreds, now, squatting beyond the glow of the campfire. They listened intently, nodded, seemed to comprehend, murmured occasional comments to one another. How strange: they seemed to comprehend.

"The story of Samson and Odysseus," Breckenridge announced. "Samson is blind but mighty. His woman is known as Delilah. To them comes the wily chieftain Odysseus, making his way homeward from the land of Ithaca. He penetrates the maze in which Samson and Delilah live and hires himself to them as bond servant, giving his name as No Man. Delilah entices him to carry her off, and he abducts her. Samson is aware of the abduction but is unable to find them in the maze. He cries out in pain and rage, No Man steals my wife! No Man steals my wife! His servants are baffled by this and take no action. In fury Samson brings the maze crashing down on himself and dies, while Odysseus carries Delilah off to Sparta, where she is seduced by Paris, Prince of Troy. Odysseus thus loses her and by way of gaining revenge he seduces Helen, the Queen of Troy, and the Trojan War begins."

And then he told the story of how mankind was created: "In the beginning there was only a field of white sand. Lightning struck it, and where the lightning hit the sand it coagulated into a vessel of glass, and rainwater ran into the vessel and brought it to life, and from the vessel a she-wolf was born. Thunder entered her womb and fertilized her and she gave birth to twins, and they were not wolves but a human boy and a human girl. The wolf suckled the twins until they reached adulthood. Then they copulated and engendered children of their own. Because they were ashamed of their nakedness they killed the old wolf and made garments from her hide."

And he told them the myth of the wandering Jew, who scoffed at God and was condemned to drift through time until he himself was able to become God.

And he told them of the Golden Age and the Iron Age and the Age of Uranium.

And he told them how the waters and winds came into being, and the seasons, the months, day and night.

And he told them how art was born:
"Out of a hole in space pours a stream of pure life-force.

Many men and women attempted to seize the flow, but they were burned to ashes by its intensity. At last, however, a man devised a way. He hollowed himself out until there was nothing at all inside his body, and had himself dragged by a faithful dog to the place where the stream of energy descended from the heavens. Then the life force entered him and filled him, and instead of destroying him it took possession of him and restored him to life. But the force overflowed within him, brimming over, and the only way he could deal with that was to fashion stories and sculptures and songs, for otherwise the force would engulf him and drown him. His name was Gilgamesh and he was the first of the artists of mankind."

The city dwellers came by the thousand now. They listened and wept at Breckenridge's words.

Hypothesis of structural resolution:

He finds creative fulfillment	The four seekers have bridged space and time to bring life out of death	The sleeping city dwellers will be awakened

Gradually the outlines of a master myth took place: the creation, the creation of man, the origin of private property, the origin of death, the loss of innocence, the loss of faith, the end of the world, the coming of a redeemer to start the cycle anew. Soon the structure would be complete. When it was, Breckenridge thought, perhaps rains would fall on the desert, perhaps the world would be reborn.

Breckenridge slept. Sleeping, he experienced an inward glow of golden light. The girl he had encountered before came to him and took his hand and led him through the city. They walked for hours, it seemed, until they came to a well different from all the others, rectangular rather than circular and surrounded at street level by a low railing of bright metal mesh. "Go down into this one," she told him. "When you reach the bottom, keep walking until you reach the room where the mechanisms of awakening are located." He looked at her in amazement, realizing that her words had been comprehensible. "Are you speaking my language," he asked, "or am I speaking yours?" She answered by smiling and pointing toward the well.

He stepped over the railing and began his descent. The well was deeper than the other one; the air in its depths was stale and dry. The golden glow lit his way for him to the bottom and thence along a low passageway with a rounded vault of a ceiling. After a long time he came to a large, brightly lit room filled with sleek gray machinery. It was much like the computer room at any large bank. Mounted on the walls were control panels, labeled in an unknown language but also clearly marked with sequential symbols:

I II III IIIII IIIIII

While he studied these he became aware of a sliding, hissing sound from the corridor beyond. He thought of sturdy metal cables passing one against the other, but then into the control room slowly came a creature something like a scorpion in form, considerably greater than a man in size. It's curved tubular thorax was dark and of a waxen texture; a dense mat of brown bristles, thick as straws, sprouted on its abdomen; its many eyes were bright, alert, and malevolent. Breckenridge snatched up a steel bar that lay near his feet and tried to wield it like a lance as the monster approaced. From its jaws, though, there looped a sudden lasso of newly spun silken thread that caught the end of the bar and jerked it from Breckenridge's grasp. Then a second loop, entangling his arms and shoulders. Struggle was useless. He was caught. The creature pulled him closer. Breckenridge saw fangs, powerful palpi, a scythe of a tail in which a dripping stinger had become erect. Breckenridge writhed in the monster's grip. He felt neither surprise nor fear; this seemed a necessary working out of some ancient foreordained pattern.

A cool silent voice within his skull said, "Who are you?"

"Noel Breckenridge of New York City, born A.D. 1940."

"Why do you intrude here?"

"I was summoned. If you want to know why, ask someone else."

"Is it your purpose to awaken the sleepers?"

"Very possibly," Breckenridge said.

"So the time has come?"

"Maybe it has," said Breckenridge. All was still for a
long moment. The monster made no hostile move. Breckenridge grew impatiant. "Well, what's the arrangement?"
he said finally.

"The arrangement?"

"The terms under which I get my freedom. Am I supposed to tell you a lot of diverting stories? Will I have to
serve you six months out of the year, forever more? Is
there some precious object I'm obliged to bring you from
the bottom of the sea? Maybe you have a riddle that I'm
supposed to answer."

The monster made no reply.

"Is that it?" Breckenridge demanded. "A riddle?"

"Do you want it to be a riddle?"

"A riddle, yes."

There was another endless pause. Breckenridge met the
beady gaze steadily. At last the voice said, "A riddle. A
riddle. Very well. Tell me the answer to this. What goes on
four legs in the morning, on two legs in the afternoon, on
three legs in the evening?"

Breckenridge repeated it. He pondered. He frowned. He
coughed. Then he laughed. "A baby," he said, "crawls on
all fours. A grown man walks upright. An old man requires
the assistance of a cane. Therefore the answer to your riddle is—"

He left the sentence unfinished. The gleam went out of
the monster's eyes; the silken loop binding Breckenridge
dissolved; the creature began slowly and sadly to back
away, withdrawing into the corridor from which it came.
Its hissing, rustling sound persisted for a time, growing ever
more faint.

Breckenridge turned and without hesitation pulled the
switch marked I.

The aurora no longer appears in the night sky. A light rain has been falling frequently for some days, and the desert is turning green. The sleepers are awakening, millions of them, called forth from their coffins by the workings of automatic mechanisms. Breckenridge stands in the central plaza of the city, arms outspread, and the city dwellers, as they emerge from the subterranean sleeping places, make their way toward him. I am the resurrection and the life, he thinks. I am Orpheus the sweet singer. I am Homer the blind. I am Noel Breckenridge. He looks across the eons to Harry Munsey. "I was wrong," he says. "There's meaning everywhere, Harry. For Sam Smith as well as for Beethoven. For Noel Breckenridge as well as for Michelangelo. Dawn after dawn, simply being alive, being part of it all, part of the cosmic dance of life—that's the meaning, Harry. Look! Look!" The sun is high now, not a cruel sun but a mild, gentle one, its heat softened by a humid haze. This is the dreamtime, when all mistakes are unmade, when all things become one. The city folk surround him. They come closer. Closer yet. They reach toward him. He experiences a delicious flash of white light. The world disappears.

"JFK Airport," he told the taxi driver. The cab zoomed away. From the front seat came the voice of the radio with today's closing Dow-Jones Industrials: 948.72, down 6.11. He reached the airport by half past five, and at seven he boarded a Pan Am flight for London. The next morning at nine, London time, he cabled his wife to say that he was well and planned to head south for the winter. Then he reported to the Air France counter for the nonstop flight to Morocco. Over the next week he cabled home from Rabat, Marrakech, and Timbuktu in Mali. The third cable said:

GUESS WHAT STOP I'M REALLY IN TIMBUKTU STOP HAVE RENTED JEEP STOP I SET OUT INTO SAHARA TOMORROW STOP AM VERY HAPPY STOP YES STOP VERY HAPPY STOP VERY VERY HAPPY STOP STOP STOP

It was the last message he sent. The night it arrived in New York there was a spectacular celestial display, an aurora that brought thousands of people out into Central Park. There was rain in the southeastern Sahara four days later, the first recorded precipitation there in eight years and seven months. An earthquake was reported in southern Sicily, but it did little damage. Things were much quieter after that for everybody.

Rumfuddle

Jack Vance

Jack Vance is deservedly popular for his colorful far-future adventure stories such as *The
Dying Earth, The Dragon Masters,* and *The
Last Castle.* An aspect of his work that is frequently overlooked, however, is the wry wit
with which he exposes mankind's self-indul-
gent (and self-defeating) follies as they are en-
larged by scientific sophistication, leading to
the effete, degenerate societies of his future
worlds. Here he presents a deft picture of a
world where travel to alternate timestreams is
commonplace—and of the misuse to which this
ability can be put.

I

From *Memoirs and Reflections,* by Alan Robertson:

Often I hear myself declared humanity's preeminent
benefactor, though the jocular occasionally raise a

claim in favor of the original serpent. After all circumspection I really cannot dispute the judgment. My place in history is secure; my name will persist as if it were printed indelibly across the sky. All of which I find absurd but understandable. For I have given wealth beyond calculation. I have expunged deprivation, famine, overpopulation, territorial constriction: All the first-order causes of contention have vanished. My gifts go freely and carry with them my personal joy, but as a reasonable man (and for lack of other restrictive agency), I feel that I cannot relinquish all control, for when has the human animal ever been celebrated for abnegation and self-discipline?

We now enter an era of plenty and a time of new concerns. The old evils are gone: we must resolutely prohibit a flamboyant and perhaps unnatural set of new vices.

* * * * *

The three girls gulped down breakfast, assembled their homework, and departed noisily for school.

Elizabeth poured coffee for herself and Gilbert. He thought she seemed pensive and moody. Presently she said, "It's so beautiful here . . . We're very lucky, Gilbert."

"I never forget it."

Elizabeth sipped her coffee and mused a moment, following some vagrant train of thought. She said, "I never liked growing up. I always felt strange—different from the other girls. I really don't know why."

"It's no mystery. Everyone for a fact is different."

"Perhaps . . . But Uncle Peter and Aunt Emma always acted as if I were more different than usual. I remember a hundred little signals. And yet I was such an ordinary little girl . . . Do you remember when you were little?"

"Not very well." Gilbert Duray looked out the window he himself had glazed, across green slopes and down to the placid water his daughters had named the Silver River. The Sounding Sea was thirty miles south; behind the house stood the first trees of the Robber Woods.

Duray considered his past. "Bob owned a ranch in Arizona during the 1870's: one of his fads. The Apaches killed my father and mother. Bob took me to the ranch, and then when I was three he brought me to Alan's house in San Francisco, and that's where I was brought up."

Elizabeth sighed. "Alan must have been wonderful. Uncle Peter was so grim. Aunt Emma never told me anything. Literally, not anything! They never cared the slightest bit for me, one way or the other . . . I wonder why Bob brought the subject up—about the Indians and your mother and father being scalped and all . . . He's such a strange man."

"Was Bob here?"

"He looked in a few minutes yesterday to remind us of his Rumfuddle. I told him I didn't want to leave the girls. He said to bring them along."

"Hah!"

"I told him I didn't want to go to his damn Rumfuddle with or without the girls. In the first place, I don't want to see Uncle Peter, who's sure to be there . . ."

II

From the *Memoirs and Reflections*:

I insisted then and I insist now that our dear old Mother Earth, so soiled and toil-worn, never be neglected. Since I pay the piper (in a manner of speaking), I call the tune, and to my secret amusement I am heeded most briskly the world around, in the manner of bellboys, jumping to the command of an irascible old gentleman who is known to be a good tipper. No one dares to defy me. My whims become actualities; my plans progress.

Paris, Vienna, San Francisco, St. Petersburg, Venice, London, Dublin, surely will persist, gradually to become idealized essences of their former selves, as wine in due course becomes the soul of the grape.

What of the old vitality? The shouts and curses, the neighborhood quarrels, the raucous music, the vulgarity? Gone, all gone! (But easy of reference at any of the cognates.) Old Earth is to be a gentle, kindly world, rich in treasures and artifacts, a world of old places—old inns, old roads, old forests, old palaces— where folk come to wander and dream, to experience the best of the past without suffering the worst.

Material abundance can now be taken for granted: Our resources are infinite. Metal, timber, soil, rock, water, air: free for anyone's taking. A single commodity remains in finite supply: human toil.

* * * * *

Gilbert Duray, the informally adopted grandson of Alan Robertson, worked on the Urban Removal Program. Six hours a day, four days a week, he guided a trashing machine across deserted Cuperinto, destroying tract houses, service stations, and supermarkets. Knobs and toggles controlled a steel hammer at the end of a hundred-foot boom; with a twitch of the finger, Duray toppled powerpoles, exploded picture windows, smashed siding and stucco, pulverized concrete. A disposal rig crawled fifty feet behind. The detritus was clawed upon a conveyor-belt, carried to a twenty-foot orifice, and dumped with a rush and a rumble into the Apathetic Ocean. Aluminum siding, asphalt shingles, corrugated fiber-glass, TV's and barbecues, Swedish Modern furniture, Book-of-the-Month selections, concrete patio-tiles, finally the sidewalk and street itself: all to the bottom of the Apathetic Ocean. Only the trees remained, a strange eclectic forest stretching as far as the eye could reach: liquidambar and Scotch pine; Chinese pistachio, Atlas cedar, and ginkgo; white birch and Norway maple.

At one o'clock Howard Wirtz emerged from the caboose, as they called the small locker room at the rear of the machine. Wirtz had homesteaded a Miocene world; Duray, with a wife and three children, had preferred the milder environment of a contemporary semicognate: the popular Type A world on which man had never evolved.

Duray gave Wirtz the work schedule. "More or less like yesterday—straight out Persimmon to Walden, then right a block and back."

Wirtz, a dour and laconic man, acknowledged the information with a jerk of the head. On his Miocene world he lived alone, in a houseboat on a mountain lake. He harvested wild rice, mushrooms, and berries; he shot geese, ground-fowl, deer, young bison, and had once informed Duray that after his five year work-time he might just retire to his lake and never appear on Earth again, except maybe to buy clothes and ammunition. "Nothing here I want, nothing at all."

Duray had given a derisive snort. "And what will you do with all your time?"

"Hunt, fish, eat, and sleep, maybe sit on the front deck."

"Nothing else?"

"I just might learn to fiddle. Nearest neighbor is fifteen million years away."

"You can't be too careful, I suppose."

Duray descended to the ground and looked over his day's work: a quarter-mile swath of desolation. Duray, who allowed his subconscious few extravagances, nevertheless felt a twinge for the old times, which, for all their disadvantages, at least had been lively. Voices, bicycle bells, the barking of dogs, the slam of doors, still echoed along Persimmon Avenue. The former inhabitants presumably preferred their new homes. The self-sufficient had taken private worlds; the more gregarious lived in communities on worlds of every description: as early as the Carboniferous, as current as the Type A. A few had even returned to the now-uncrowded cities. An exciting era to live in: a time of flux. Duray, thirty-four years old, remembered no other way of life; the old existence, as exemplified by Persimmon Avenue, seemed antique, cramped, constricted.

He had a word with the operator of the trashing machine; returning to the caboose, Duray paused to look through the orifice across the Apathetic Ocean. A squall hung black above the southern horizon, toward which a trail of broken lumber drifted, ultimately to wash up on some unknown pre-Cambrian shore. There never would be an inspector sailing forth to protest; the world knew no life other than mollusks and algae, and all the trash of Earth would never fill its submarine gorges. Duray tossed a rock through the gap and watched the alien water splash up and subside. Then he turned away and entered the caboose.

Along the back wall were four doors. The second from the left was marked "G. DURAY." He unlocked the door, pulled it open, and stopped short, staring in astonishment at the blank back wall. He lifted the transparent plastic flap that functioned as an air-seal and brought out the collapsed metal ring that had been the flange surrounding his passway. The inner surface was bare metal; looking through, he saw only the interior of the caboose.

A long minute passed. Duray stood staring at the useless ribbon as if hypnotized, trying to grasp the implications of the situation. To his knowledge no passway had ever failed, unless it had been purposefully closed. Who would play him such a spiteful trick? Certainly not Elizabeth. She detested practical jokes and if anything, like Duray himself, was perhaps a trifle too intense and literal-minded. He jumped down from the caboose and strode off across Cupertino Forest: a sturdy, heavy-shouldered man of about average stature. His features were rough and uncompromising; his brown hair was cut crisply short; his eyes glowed golden-brown and exerted an arresting force. Straight, heavy eyebrows crossed his long, thin nose like the bar of a T; his mouth, compressed against some strong inner urgency, formed a lower horizontal bar. All in all, not a man to be trifled with, or so it would seem.

He trudged through the haunted grove, preoccupied by the strange and inconvenient event that had befallen him. What had happened to the passway? Unless Elizabeth had invited friends out to Home, as they called their world, she was alone, with the three girls at school . . . Duray came out upon Stevens Creek Road. A farmer's pickup truck halted at his signal and took him into San Jose, now little more than a country town.

At the transit center he dropped a coin in the turnstile

and entered the lobby. Four portals designated "LOCAL," "CALIFORNIA," "NORTH AMERICA," and "WORLD" opened in the walls, each portal leading to a hub on Utilis.*

Duray passed into the "California" hub, found the "Oakland" portal, returned to the Oakland Transit Center on Earth, passed back through the "Local" portal to the "Oakland" hub on Utilis, and returned to Earth through the "Montclair West" portal to a depot only a quarter mile from Thornhill School,† to which Duray walked.

In the office Duray identified himself to the clerk and requested the presence of his daughter Dolly.

The clerk sent forth a messenger who, after an interval, returned alone. "Dolly Duray isn't at school."

Duray was surprised; Dolly had been in good health and had set off to school as usual. He said, "Either Joan or Ellen will do as well."

The messenger again went forth and again returned. "Neither one is in their classrooms, Mr. Duray. All three of your children are absent."

"I can't understand it," said Duray, now fretful. "All three set off to school this morning."

"Let me ask Miss Haig. I've just come on duty." The clerk spoke into a telephone, listened, then turned back to Duray. "The girls went home at ten o'clock. Mrs. Duray called for them and took them back through the passway."

"Did she give any reason whatever?"

"Miss Haig says No; Mrs. Duray just told her she needed the girls at home."

---

* Utilis: a world cognate to Paleocene Earth, where, by Alan Robertson's decree, all the industries, institutions, warehouses, tanks, dumps, and commercial offices of old Earth were now located. The name Utilis, so it had been remarked, accurately captured the flavor of Alan Robertson's pedantic, quaint, and idealistic personality.

† Alan Roberson had proposed another specialized world, to be known as Tutelar, where the children of all the settled worlds should receive their education in a vast array of pedagogical facilities, To his hurt surprise, he encountered a storm of wrathful opposition from parents. His scheme was termed mechanistic, vast, dehumanizing, repulsive. What better world for schooling than old Earth itself? Here was the source of all tradition; let Earth become Tutelar! So insisted the parents, and Alan Robertson had no choice but to agree.

Duray stifled a sigh of baffled irritation. "Could you take me to their locker? I'll use their passway to get home."

"That's contrary to school regulations, Mr. Duray. You'll understand, I'm sure."

"I can identify myself quite definitely," said Duray. "Mr. Carr knows me well. As a matter of fact, my passway collapsed, and I came here to get home."

"Why don't you speak to Mr. Carr?"

"I'd like to do so."

Duray was conducted into the principal's office, where he explained his predicament. Mr. Carr expressed sympathy and made no difficulty about taking Duray to the children's passway.

They went to a hall at the back of the school and found the locker numbered 382. "Here we are," said Carr. "I'm afraid that you'll find it a tight fit." He unlocked the metal door with his master key and threw it open. Duray looked inside and saw only the black metal at the back of the locker. The passway, like his own, had been closed.

Duray drew back and for a moment could find no words.

Carr spoke in a voice of polite amazement. "How very perplexing! I don't believe I've ever seen anything like it before! Surely the girls wouldn't play such a silly prank!"

"They know better than to touch the passway," Duray said gruffly. "Are you sure that this is the right locker?"

Carr indicated the card on the outside of the locker, where three names had been typed: "DOROTHY DURAY, JOAN DURAY, ELLEN DURAY." "No mistake," said Carr, "and I'm afraid that I can't help you any further. Are you in common residency?"

"It's our private homestead."

Carr nodded with lips judiciously pursed, to suggest that insistence upon so much privacy seemed eccentric. He gave a deprecatory little chuckle. "I suppose if you isolate yourself to such an extent, you more or less must expect a series of emergencies."

"To the contrary," Duray said crisply. "Our life is uneventful, because there's no one to bother us. We love the wild animals, the quiet, the fresh air. We wouldn't have it any differently."

Carr smiled a dry smile. "Mr. Robertson has certainly altered the lives of us all. I understand that he is your grandfather?"

"I was raised in his household. I'm his nephew's foster son. The blood relationship isn't all that close."

III

From the *Memoirs and Reflections:*

I early became interested in magnetic fluxes and their control. After taking my degree, I worked exclusively in this field, studying all varieties of magnetic envelopes and developing controls over their formation. For many years my horizons were thus limited, and I lived a placid existence.

Two contemporary developments forced me down from my "ivory castle." First: the fearful overcrowding of the planet and the prospect of worse to come. Cancer already was an affliction of the past; heart diseases were under control; I feared that in another ten years immortality might be a practical reality for many of us, with a consequent augmentation of population pressure.

Secondly, the theoretical work done upon "black holes" and "white holes" suggested that matter compacted in a "black hole" broke through a barrier to spew forth from a "white hole" in another universe. I calculated pressures and considered the self-focusing magnetic sheaths, cones, and whorls with which I was experimenting. Through their innate properties these entities constricted themselves to apexes of a cross section indistinguishable from a geometric point. What if two or more cones (I asked myself) could be arranged in contraposition to produce an equilibrium? In this condition charged particles must be accelerated to near light-speed and at the mutual focus constricted and inpinged together. The pressures thus created, though of small scale, would be far in excess of those characteristic of the "black holes"· to unknown effect.

I can now report that the mathematics of the multiple focus are a most improbable thicket, and the useful service I enforced upon what I must call a set of absurd contradictions is one of my secrets. I know that thousands of scientists, at home and abroad, are attempting to duplicate my work; they are welcome to the effort. None will succeed. Why do I speak so positively? This is my other secret.

* * * * *

Duray marched back to the Montclair West depot in a state of angry puzzlement. There were four passways to Home, of which two were closed. The third was located in his San Francisco locker: the "front door," so to speak. The last and the original orifice was cased, filed, and indexed in Alan Robertson's vault.

Duray tried to deal with the problem in rational terms. The girls would never tamper with the passways. As for Elizabeth, no more than the girls would she consider such an act. At least Duray could imagine no reason that would so urge or impel her. Elizabeth, like himself a foster child, was a beautiful, passionate woman, tall, dark-haired, with lustrous dark eyes and a wide mouth that tended to curve in an endearingly crooked grin. She was also responsible, loyal, careful, industrious; she loved her family and Riverview Manor. The theory of erotic intrigue seemed to Duray as incredible as the fact of the closed passways. Though, for a fact, Elizabeth was prone to wayward and incomprehensible moods. Suppose Elizabeth had received a visitor who for some sane or insane purpose had forced her to close the passway? . . . Duray shook his head in frustration, like a harassed bull. The matter no doubt had some simple cause. Or on the other hand, Duray reflected, the cause might be complex and intricate. The thought, by some obscure connection, brought before him the image of his nominal foster father, Alan Robertson's nephew, Bob

Robertson. Duray gave his head a nod of gloomy asseveration, as if to confirm a fact he long ago should have suspected. He went to the phone booth and called Bob Robertson's apartment in San Francisco. The screen glowed white and an instant later displayed Bob Robertson's alert, clean, and handsome face. "Good afternoon, Gil. Glad you called; I've been anxious to get in touch with you."

Duray became warier than ever. "How so?"

"Nothing serious, or so I hope. I dropped by your locker to leave off some books that I promised Elizabeth, and I noticed through the glass that your passway is closed. Collapsed. Useless."

"Strange," said Duray. "Very strange indeed. I can't understand it. Can you?"

"No . . . not really."

Duray thought he detected a subtlety of intonation. His eyes narrowed in concentration. "The passway at my rig was closed. The passway at the girls' school was closed. Now you tell me that the downtown passway is closed."

Bob Robertson grinned. "That's a pretty broad hint, I would say. Did you and Elizabeth have a row?"

"No."

Bob Robertson rubbed his long aristocratic chin. "A mystery. There's probably some very ordinary explanation."

"Or some very extraordinary explanation."

"True. Nowadays a person can't rule out anything. By the way, tomorrow night is the Rumfuddle, and I expect both you and Elizabeth to be on hand."

"As I recall," said Duray, "I've already declined the invitation." The Rumfuddlers were a group of Bob's cronies. Duray suspected that their activities were not altogether wholesome. "Excuse me; I've got to find an open passway, or Elizabeth and the kids are marooned."

"Try Alan," said Bob. "He'll have the original in his vault."

Duray gave a curt nod. "I don't like to bother him, but that's my last hope."

"Let me know what happens," said Bob Robertson.

"And if you're at loose ends, don't forget the Rumfuddle tomorrow night. I mentioned the matter to Elizabeth, and she said she'd be sure to attend."

"Indeed. And when did you consult Elizabeth?"

"A day or so ago. Don't look so damnably gothic, my boy."

"I'm wondering if there's a connection between your invitation and the closed passways. I happen to know that Elizabeth doesn't care for your parties."

Bob Robertson laughed with easy good grace. "Reflect a moment. Two events occur. I invite you and wife Elizabeth to the Rumfuddle. This is event one. Your passways close up, which is event two. By a feat of structured absurdity you equate the two and blame me. Now is that fair?"

"You call it 'structured absurdity,'" said Duray. "I call it instinct."

Bob Robertson laughed again. "You'll have to do better than that. Consult Alan, and if for some reason he can't help you, come to the Rumfuddle. We'll rack our brains and either solve your problem or come up with new and better ones." He gave a cheery nod, and before Duray could roar an angry expostulation, the screen faded.

Duray stood glowering at the screen, convinced that Bob Robertson knew much more about the closed passways than he admitted. Duray went to sit on a bench. . . . If Elizabeth had closed him away from Home, her reasons must have been compelling indeed. But unless she intended to isolate herself permanently from Earth, she would leave at least one passway ajar, and this must be the master orifice in Alan Robertson's vault.

Duray rose to his feet, somewhat heavily, and stood a moment, head bent and shoulders hunched. He gave a surly grunt and returned to the phone booth, where he called a number known to not more than a dozen persons.

The screen glowed white while the person at the other end of the line scrutinized his face . . . The screen cleared, revealing a round pale face from which pale-blue eyes stared forth with a passionless intensity. "Hello, Ernest," said Duray. "Is Alan busy at the moment?"

"I don't think he's doing anything particular—except resting."

Ernest gave the last two words a meaningful emphasis.

"I've got some problems," said Duray. "What's the best way to get in touch with him?"

"You'd better come up here. The code is changed. It's MHF now."

"I'll be there in a few minutes."

Back in the "California" hub on Utilis, Duray went into a side chamber lined with private lockers, numbered and variously marked with symbols, names, colored flags, or not marked at all. Duray went to Locker 122, and ignoring the keyhole, set the code lock to the letters MHF. The door opened; Duray stepped into the locker and through the passway to the High Sierra headquarters of Alan Robertson.

IV

From the *Memoirs and Reflections*:

> If one basic axiom controls the cosmos, it must be this:
>
> *In a situation of infinity every possible condition occurs, not once, but an infinite number of times.*
>
> There is no mathematical nor logical limit to the number of dimensions. Our perceptions assure us of three only, but many indications suggest otherwise: parapsychic occurrences of a hundred varieties, the "white holes," the seemingly finite state of our own universe, which by corollary, asserts the existence of others.
>
> Hence, when I stepped behind the lead slab and first touched the button, I felt confident of success; failure would have surprised me!
>
> But (and here lay my misgivings) what sort of success might I achieve?
>
> Suppose I opened a hole into the interplanetary vacuum?

The chances of this were very good indeed; I surrounded the machine in a strong membrane to prevent the air of Earth from rushing off into the void.

Suppose I discovered a condition totally beyond imagination?

My imagination yielded no safeguards.

I proceeded to press the button.

* * * * *

Duray stepped out into a grotto under damp granite walls. Sunlight poured into the opening from a dark-blue sky. This was Alan Robertson's link to the outside world; like many other persons, he disliked a passway opening directly into his home. A path led fifty yards across bare granite mountainside to the lodge. To the west spread a great vista of diminishing ridges, valleys, and hazy blue air; to the east rose a pair of granite crags, with snow caught in the saddle between. Alan Robertson's lodge was built just below the timberline, beside a small lake fringed with tall dark firs. The lodge was built of rounded granite stones, with a wooden porch across the front; at each end rose a massive chimney.

Duray had visited the lodge on many occasions; as a boy he had scaled both of the crags behind the house, to look wonderingly off across the stillness, which on old Earth had a poignant breathing quality different from the uninhabited solitudes of worlds such as Home.

Ernest came to the door: a middle-aged man with an ingenuous face, small white hands, and soft, damp, mouse-colored hair. Ernest disliked the lodge, the wilderness, and solitude in general; he nevertheless would have suffered tortures before relinquishing his post as subaltern to Alan Robertson. Ernest and Duray were almost antipodal in outlook. Ernest thought Duray brusque, indelicate, a trifle coarse, and probably not disinclined to violence as an argumentative adjunct. Duray considered Ernest, when he thought of him at all, as the kind of man who takes two bites out of a cherry. Ernest had never married; he showed no interest in women, and Duray, as a boy, had often fretted at Ernest's overcautious restrictions.

In particular Ernest resented Duray's free and easy access to Alan Robertson. The power to restrict or admit those countless persons who demanded Alan Robertson's attention was Ernest's most cherished perquisite, and Duray denied him the use of it by simply ignoring Ernest and all his regulations. Ernest had never complained to Alan Robertson for fear of discovering that Duray's influence exceeded his own. A wary truce existed between the two, each conceding the other his privileges.

Ernest performed a polite greeting and admitted Duray into the lodge. Duray looked around the interior, which had not changed during his lifetime: varnished plank floors with red, black, and white Navaho rugs, massive pine furniture with leather cushions, a few shelves of books, a half-dozen pewter mugs on the mantle over the big fireplace—a room almost ostentatiously bare of souvenirs and mementos. Duray turned back to Ernest: "Whereabouts is Alan?"

"On his boat."

"With guests?"

"No," said Ernest, with a faint sniff of disapproval. "He's alone, quite alone."

"How long has he been gone?"

"He just went through an hour ago. I doubt if he's left the dock yet. What is your problem, if I may ask?"

"The passways to my world are closed. All three. There's only one left, in the vault."

Ernest arched his flexible eyebrows. "Who closed them?"

"I don't know. Elizabeth and the girls are alone, so far as I know."

"Extraordinary," said Ernest in a flat metallic voice. "Well, then, come along." He led the way down a hall to a back room. With his hand on the knob, Ernest paused and looked back over his shoulder. "Did you mention the matter to anyone? Robert, for instance?"

"Yes," said Duray curtly, "I did. Why do you ask?"

Ernest hesitated a fraction of a second. "No particular reason. Robert occasionally has a somewhat misplaced sense of humor, he and his Rumfuddlers." He spoke the word with a hiss of distaste.

Duray said nothing of his own suspicions. Ernest opened the door; they entered a large room illuminated by a skylight. The only furnishing was a rug on the varnished floor. Into each wall opened four doors. Ernest went to one of these doors, pulled it open, and made a resigned gesture. "You'll probably find Alan at the dock."

Duray looked into the interior of a rude hut with palm-frond walls, resting on a platform of poles. Through the doorway he saw a path leading under sunlit green foliage toward a strip of white beach. Surf sparkled below a layer of dark-blue ocean and a glimpse of the sky. Duray hesitated, rendered wary by the events of the morning. Anyone and everyone was suspect, even Ernest, who now gave a quiet sniff of contemptuous amusement. Through the foliage Duray glimpsed a spread of sail; he stepped through the passway.

V

From the *Memoirs and Reflections:*

> Man is a creature whose evolutionary environment has been the open air. His nerves, muscles, and senses have developed across three million years in intimate contiguity with natural earth, crude stone, live wood, wind, and rain. Now this creature is suddenly—on the geologic scale, instantaneously—shifted to an unnatural environment of metal and glass, plastic and plywood, to which his psychic substrata lack all compatibility. The wonder is not that we have so much mental instability but so little. Add to this the weird noises, electrical pleasures, bizarre colors, synthetic foods, abstract entertainments! We should congratulate ourselves on our durability.
>
> I bring this matter up because with my little device

—so simple, so easy, so flexible—I have vastly augmenter the load upon our poor primeval brain, and for a fact many persons find the instant transition from one locale to another unsettling, and even actively unpleasant.

* * * * *

Duray stood on the porch of the cabin, under a vivid green canopy of sunlit foliage. The air was soft and warm and smelled of moist vegetation. He stood listening. The mutter of the surf came to his ears and from a far distance a single bird-call.

Duray stepped down to the ground and followed the path under tall palm trees to a river-bank. A few yards downstream, beside a rough pier of poles and planks, floated a white and blue ketch, sails hoisted and distended to a gentle breeze. On the deck stood Alan Robertson, on the point of casting off the mooring lines. Duray hailed him; Alan Robertson turned in surprise and vexation, which vanished when he recognized Duray. "Hello, Gil, glad you're here! For a moment I thought it might be someone to bother me. Jump aboard; you're just in time for a sail."

Duray somberly joined Alan Robertson on the boat. "I'm afraid I am here to bother you."

"Oh?" Alan Robertson raised his eyebrows in instant solicitude. He was a man of no great height, thin, nervously active. Wisps of rumpled white hair fell over his forehead; mild blue eyes inspected Duray with concern, all thought of sailing forgotten. "What in the world has happened?"

"I wish I knew. If it were something I could handle myself, I wouldn't bother you."

"Don't worry about me; there's all the time in the world for sailing. Now tell me what's happened."

"I can't get through to Home. All the passways are closed off. Why and how I have no idea. Elizabeth and the girls are out there alone; at least I think they're out there."

Alan Robertson rubbed his chin. "What an odd business! I can certainly understand your agitation . . . You think Elizabeth closed the passways?"

"It's unreasonable—but there's no one else."

Alan Robertson turned Duray a shrewd, kindly glance. "No little family upsets? Nothing to cause her despair and anguish?"

"Abolutely nothing. I've tried to reason things out, but I draw blank. I thought that maybe someone—a man— had gone through to visit her and decided to take over— but if this were the case, why did she come to the school for the girls? That possibility is out. A secret love affair? Possible but so damn unlikely. Since she wants to keep me off the planet, her only motive could be to protect me or herself or the girls from danger of some sort. Again this means that another person is concerned in the matter. Who? How? Why? I spoke to Bob. He claims to know nothing about the situation, but he wants me to come to his damned Rumfuddle, and he hints very strongly that Elizabeth will be on hand. I can't prove a thing against Bob, but I suspect him. He's always had a taste for odd jokes."

Alan Robertson gave a lugubrious nod. "I won't deny that." He sat down in the cockpit and stared off across the water. "Bob has a complicated sense of humor, but he'd hardly close you away from your world . . . I hardly think that your family is in actual danger, but of course we can't take chances. The possibility exists that Bob is not responsible, that something uglier is afoot." He jumped to his feet. "Our obvious first step is to use the master orifice in the vault." He looked a shade regretfully toward the ocean. "My little sail can wait . . . A lovely world this: not fully cognate with Earth—a cousin, so to speak. The fauna and flora are roughly contemporary except for man. The hominids have never developed."

The two men returned up the path, Alan Robertson chatting lightheartedly: "Thousands and thousands of worlds I've visited, and looked into even more, but do you know I've never hit upon a good system of classification? There are exact cognates—of course we're never sure exactly *how* exact they are. These cases are relatively simple, but then the problems begin . . . Bah! I don't think about such things anymore. I know that when I keep all the nominates at zero, the cognates appear. Overintellectualizing is the bane of this and every other era. Show me a man who deals only with abstraction, and I'll show you the dead, futile end of evolution." Alan Robertson chuckled. "If I could control the machine tightly enough to produce real cognates, our troubles would be over . . . Much confusion, of course. I might step through into the cognate world immediately as a true cognate Alan Robertson steps through into our world, with net effect of zero. An amazing business, really; I never tire of it . . ."

They returned to the transit room of the mountain lodge. Ernest appeared almost instantly. Duray suspected he had been watching through the passway.

Alan Robertson said briskly, "We'll be busy for an hour or two, Ernest. Gilbert is having difficulties, and we've got to set things straight."

Ernest nodded somewhat grudgingly, or so it seemed to Duray. "The progress report on the Ohio Plan has arrived. Nothing particularly urgent."

"Thank you, Ernest, I'll see to it later. Come along, Gilbert; let's get to the bottom of this affair." They went to door No. 1 and passed through to the Utilis hub. Alan Robertson led the way to a small green door with a three-dial coded lock, which he opened with a flourish. "Very well, in we go." He carefully locked the door behind them, and they walked the length of a short hall. "A shame that I must be so cautious," said Alan Robertson. "You'd be astonished at the outrageous requests otherwise sensible people make of me. I sometimes become exasperated . . . Well, it's understandable, I suppose."

At the end of the hall Alan Robertson worked the locking dials of a red door. "This way, Gilbert; you've been through before." They stepped through a passway into a hall that opened into a circular concrete chamber fifty feet in diameter, located, so Duray knew, deep under the Mad Dog Mountains of the Mojave Desert. Eight halls extended away into the rock; each hall communicated with twelve aisles. The center of the chamber was occupied by a circular desk twenty feet in diameter; here six clerks in white smocks worked at computers and collating machines. In accordance with their instructions they gave Alan Robertson neither recognition nor greeting.

Alan Robertson went up to the desk, at which signal the chief clerk, a solemn young man bald as an egg, came forward. "Good afternoon, sir."

"Good afternoon, Harry. Find me the index for 'Gilbert Duray,' on my personal list."

The clerk bowed smartly. He went to an instrument and ran his fingers over a bank of keys; the instrument ejected a card that Harry handed to Alan Robertson. "There you are, sir."

Alan Robertson showed the card to Duray, who saw the code: "4:8:10/6:13:29."

"That's your world," said Alan Robertson. "We'll soon learn how the land lies. This way, to Radiant four." He led the way down the hall, turned into the aisle numbered "8," and proceeded to Stack 10. "Shelf six," said Alan Robertson. He checked the card. "Drawer thirteen . . . here we are." He drew forth the drawer and ran his fingers along the tabs. "Item twenty-nine. This should be Home." He brought forth a metal frame four inches square and held it up to his eyes. He frowned in disbelief. "We don't have anything here either." He turned to Duray a glance of dismay. "This is a serious situation!"

"It's no more than I expected," said Duray tonelessly.

"All this demands some careful thought." Alan Robertson clicked his tongue in vexation. "Tst, tst, tst." He examined the identification plaque at the top of the frame. "Four: eight: ten/six: thirteen: twenty-nine," he read. "There seems to be no question of error." He squinted carefully at the numbers, hesitated, then slowly replaced the frame. On second thought he took the frame forth once more. "Come along, Gilbert," said Alan Robertson. "We'll have a cup of coffee and think this matter out."

The two returned to the central chamber, where Alan Robertson gave the empty frame into the custody of Harry the clerk. "Check the records, if you please," said Alan Robertson. "I want to know how many passways were pinched off the master."

Harry manipulated the buttons of his computer. "Three only, Mr. Robertson."

"Three passways and the master—four in all?"

"That's right, sir."

"Thank you, Harry."

VI

From the *Memoirs and Reflections:*

> I recognized the possibility of many cruel abuses, but the good so outweighed the bad that I thrust aside all thought of secrecy and exclusivity. I consider myself not Alan Robertson but, like Prometheus, an archetype of Man, and my discovery must serve all men.
>
> But caution, caution, caution!

> I sorted out my ideas. I myself coveted the amplitude of a private, personal world; such a yearning was not ignoble, I decided. Why should not everyone have the same if he so desired, since the supply was limitless? Think of it! The wealth and beauty of an entire world: mountains and plains, forests and flowers, ocean cliffs and crashing seas, winds and clouds—all beyond value, yet worth no more than a few seconds of effort and a few watts of energy.
>
> I became troubled by a new idea. Would everyone desert old Earth and leave it a vile junk-heap? I found the concepts intolerable . . . I exchange access to a world for three to six years of remedial toil, depending upon occupancy.

* * * * *

A lounge overlooked the central chamber. Alan Robertson gestured Duray to a seat and drew two mugs of coffee from a dispenser. Settling in a chair, he turned his eyes up to the ceiling. "We must collect our thoughts. The circumstances are somewhat unusual; still, I have lived with unusual circumstances for almost fifty years.

"So then: the situation. We have verified that there are only four passways to Home. These four passways are closed, though we must accept Bob's word in regard to your downtown locker. If this is truly the case, if Elizabeth and the girls are still on Home, you will never see them again."

"Bob is mixed up in this business. I could swear to nothing, but——"

Alan Robertson held up his hand. "I will talk to Bob; this is the obvious first step." He rose to his feet and went to the telephone in the corner of the lounge. Duray joined him. Alan spoke into the screen. "Get me Robert Robertson's apartment in San Francisco."

The screen glowed white. Bob's voice came from the speaker. "Sorry, I'm not at home. I have gone out to my world Fancy, and I cannot be reached. Call back in a week, unless your business is urgent, in which case call back in a month."

"Mmph," said Alan Robertson, returning to his seat. "Bob is sometimes a trifle too flippant. A man with an under-extended intellect . . ." He drummed his fingers on the arm of his chair. "Tomorrow night is his party? What does he call it? A Rumfuddle?"

"Some such nonsense. Why does he want me? I'm a dull dog; I'd rather be home building a fence."

"Perhaps you had better plan to attend the party."

"That means, submit to his extortion."

"Do you want to see your wife and family again?"

"Naturally. But whatever he has in mind won't be for my benefit, or Elizabeth's."

"You're probably right there. I've heard one or two unsavory tales regarding the Rumfuddlers . . . The fact remains that the passways are closed. All four of them."

Duray's voice became harsh. "Can't you open a new orifice for us?"

Alan Robertson gave his head a sad shake. "I can tune the machine very finely. I can code accurately for the 'Home' class of worlds and as closely as necessary approximate a particular world-state. But at each setting, no matter how fine the tuning, we encounter an infinite number of worlds. In practice, inaccuracies in the machine, backlash, the gross size of electrons, the very difference between one electron and another, make it difficult to tune with absolute precision. So even if we tuned exactly to the 'Home' class, the probability of opening into your particular Home is one in an infinite number: in short, negligible."

Duray stared off across the chamber. "Is it possible that a space once entered might tend to open more easily a second time?"

Alan Robertson smiled. "As to that, I can't say. I suspect not, but I really know so little. I see no reason why it should be so."

"If we can open into a world precisely cognate, I can at least learn why the passways are closed."

Alan Robertson sat up in his chair. "Here is a valid point. Perhaps we can accomplish something in this regard." He glanced humorously sidewise at Duray. "On the other hand—consider this situation. We create access into a 'Home' almost exactly cognate to your own—so nearly identical that the difference is not readily apparent. You find there an Elizabeth, a Dolly, a Joan, and an Ellen indistinguishable from your own, and a Gilbert marooned on Earth. You might even convince yourself that this is your very own Home."

"I'd know the difference," said Duray shortly, but Alan Robertson seemed not to hear.

"Think of it! An infinite number of Homes isolated from Earth, an infinite number of Elizabeths, Dollys, Joans, and Ellens marooned, an infinite number of Gilbert Durays trying to regain access . . . The sum effect might be a wholesale reshuffling of families, with everyone more or less good-natured about the situation. I wonder if this could be Bob's idea of a joke to share with his Rumfuddlers."

Duray looked sharply at Alan Robertson, wondering whether the man were serious. "It doesn't sound funny, and I wouldn't be very good-natured."

"Of course not," said Alan Robertson hastily. "An idle thought—in rather poor taste, I'm afraid."

"In any event, Bob hinted that Elizabeth would be at his damned Rumfuddle. If that's the case, she must have closed the passways from this side."

"A possibility," Alan Robertson conceded, "but unreasonable. Why should she seal you away from Home?"

"I don't know, but I'd like to find out."

Alan Robertson slapped his hands down upon his thin shanks and jumped to his feet, only to pause once more. "You're sure you want to look into these cognates? You might see things you wouldn't like."

"So long as I know the truth, I don't care whether I like it or not."

"So be it."

The machine occupied a room behind the balcony. Alan Robertson surveyed the device with pride and affection. "This is the fourth model, and probably optimum; at least I don't see any place for significant improvement. I use a hundred and sixty-seven rods converging upon the center of the reactor sphere. Each rod produces a quotum of energy and is susceptible to several types of adjustment to cope with the very large number of possible states. The number of particles to pack the universe full is on the order of ten raised to the power of sixty; the possible permutations of these particles would number two raised to the power of ten raised to the power of sixty. The universe, of course, is built of many different particles, which makes the final number of possible, or let us say, thinkable states a number like two raised to the power of ten raised to the power of sixty, all times x, where x is the number of particles under consideration. A large, unmanageable number, which we need not consider, because the conditions we deal with— the possible variations of planet Earth—are far fewer."

"Still a very large number," said Duray.

"Indeed yes. But again the sheer unmanageable bulk is cut away by a self-normalizing property of the machine. In what I call floating neutral the machine reaches the closest cycles—which is to say, that infinite class of perfect cognates. In practice, because of infinitesimal inaccuracies, 'floating neutral' reaches cognates more or less imperfect, perhaps by no more than the shape of a single grain of sand. Still, 'floating neutral' provides a natural base, and by adjusting the controls, we reach cycles at an ever greater departure from base. In practice I search out a good cycle and strike a large number of passways, as many as a hundred thousand. So now to our business." He went to a console at the side. "Your code number, what was it now?"

Duray brought forth the card and read the numbers: "Four: eight:ten/six:thirteen:twenty-nine."

"Very good. I give the code to the computer, which searches the files and automatically adjusts the machine. Now then, step over here; the process releases dangerous radiation."

The two stood behind lead slabs. Alan Robertson touched a button; watching through a periscope, Duray saw a spark of purple light and heard a small groaning, rasping sound seeming to come from the air itself.

Alan Robertson stepped forth and walked to the machine. In the delivery tray rested an extensible ring. He picked up the ring and looked through the hole. "This seems to be right." He handed the ring to Duray. "Do you see anything you recognize?"

Duray put the ring to his eye. "That's Home."

"Very good. Do you want me to come with you?"

Duray considered. "The time is now?"

"Yes. This is a time-neutral setting."

"I think I'll go alone."

Alan Robertson nodded. "Whatever you like. Return as soon as you can, so I'll know you're safe."

Duray frowned at him sidewise. "Why shouldn't I be safe? No one is there but my family."

"Not *your* family. The family of a cognate Gilbert Duray. The family may not be absolutely identical. The cognate Duray may not be identical. You can't be sure exactly what you will find—so be careful."

VII

From the *Memoirs and Reflections*:

> When I think of my machine and my little forays in and out of infinity, an idea keeps recurring to me which is so rather terrible that I close it out of my mind, and I will not even mention it here.

* * * * *

Duray stepped out upon the soil of Home and stood appraising the familiar landscape. A vast meadow drenched in sunlight rolled down to wide Silver River. Above the opposite shore rose a line of low bluffs, with copses of trees in the hollows. To the left, the landscape seemed to extend indefinitely and at last become indistinct in the blue haze of distance. To the right, the Robber Woods ended a quarter mile from where Duray stood. On a flat beside the forest, on the bank of a small stream, stood a house of stone and timber: a sight that seemed to Duray the most beautiful he had ever seen. Polished glass windows sparkled in the sunlight; banks of geraniums glowed green and red. From the chimney rose a wisp of smoke.

The air smelled cool and sweet but seemed—so Duray imagined—to carry a strange tang, different—so he imagined—from the meadow-scent of his own Home. Duray started forward, then halted. The world was his own, yet not his own. If he had been conscious of the fact, would he have recognized the strangeness? Nearby rose an outcrop of weathered gray field-rock: a rounded mossy pad on which he had sat only two days before, contemplating the building of a dock. He walked over and looked down at the stone. Here he had sat; here were the impressions of his heels in the soil; here was the pattern of moss from which he had absently scratched a fragment. Duray bent close. The moss was whole. The man who had sat here, the cognate Duray, had not scratched at the moss. So then: The world was perceptibly different from his own.

Duray was relieved and yet vaguely disturbed. If the world had been the exact simulacrum of his own, he might have been subjected to unmanageable emotions—which still might be the case. He walked toward the house, along the path that led down to the river. He stepped up to the porch. On a deck chair was a book: *Down There: A Study in Satanism,* by J. K. Huysmans. Elizabeth's tastes were eclectic. Duray had not previously seen the book; was it perhaps that Bob Robertson had put through the parcel delivery?

Duray went into the house. Elizabeth stood across the room. She had evidently watched him coming up the path. She said nothing; her face showed no expression.

Duray halted, somewhat at a loss as to how to address this familiar-strange woman. "Good afternoon," he said at last.

Elizabeth allowed a wisp of a smile to show. "Hello, Gilbert."

At least, thought Duray, on cognate worlds the same language was spoken. He studied Elizabeth. Lacking prior knowledge, would he have perceived her to be someone different from his own Elizabeth? Both were beautiful women: tall and slender, with curling black shoulder-length hair, worn without artifice. Their skins were pale, with a dusky undertone; their mouths were wide, passionate, stubborn. Duray knew his Elizabeth to be a woman of inexplicable moods, and this Elizabeth was doubtless no different—yet somehow a difference existed that Duray could not define, deriving perhaps from the strangeness of her atoms, the stuff of a different universe. He wondered if she sensed the same difference in him.

He asked, "Did you close off the passways?"

Elizabeth nodded, without change of expression.

"Why?"

"I thought it the best thing to do," said Elizabeth in a soft voice.

"That's no answer."

"I suppose not. How did you get here?"

"Alan made an opening."

Elizabeth raised her eyebrows. "I thought that was impossible."

"True. This is a different world to my own. Another Gilbert Duray built this house. I'm not your husband."

Elizabeth's mouth dropped in astonishment. She swayed back a step and put her hand up to her neck: a mannerism Duray could not recall in his own Elizabeth. The sense of strangeness came ever more strongly upon him. He felt an intruder. Elizabeth was watching him with a wide-eyed fascination. She said in a hurried mutter: "I wish you'd leave; go back to your own world; do!"

"If you've closed off all the passways, you'll be isolated," growled Duray. "Marooned, probably forever."

"Whatever I do," said Elizabeth, "it's not your affair."

"It is my affair, if only for the sake of the girls. I won't allow them to live and die alone out here."

"The girls aren't here," said Elizabeth in a flat voice. "They are where neither you nor any other Gilbert Duray will find them. So now go back to your own world, and leave me in whatever peace my soul allows me."

Duray stood glowering at the fiercely beautiful woman. He had never heard his own Elizabeth speak so wildly. He wondered if on his own world another Gilbert Duray similarly confronted his own Elizabeth, and as he analyzed his feelings toward this woman before him, he felt a throb of annoyance. A curious situation. He said in a quiet voice, "Very well. You and my own Elizabeth have decided to isolate yourselves. I can't imagine your reasons."

Elizabeth gave a wild laugh. "They're real enough."

"They may be real now, but ten years from now or forty years from now they may seem unreal. I can't give you access to your own Earth, but if you wish, you can use the

Elizabeth turned away and went to look out over the

passway to the Earth from which I've just come, and you
need never see me again."

valley. Duray spoke to her back. "We've never had secrets
between us, you and I—or I mean, Elizabeth and I. Why
now? Are you in love with some other man?"

Elizabeth gave a snort of sardonic amusement. "Certainly not . . . I'm disgusted with the entire human race."

"Which presumably includes me."

"It does indeed, and myself as well."

"And you won't tell me why?"

Elizabeth, still looking out the window, wordlessly shook
her head.

"Very well," said Duray in a cold voice. "Will you tell
me where you've sent the girls? They're mine as much as
yours, remember."

"These particular girls aren't yours at all."

"That may be, but the effect is the same."

Elizabeth said tonelessly: "If you want to find your own
particular girls, you'd better find your own particular Elizabeth and ask her. I can only speak for myself . . . To tell
you the truth, I don't like being part of a composite person,
and I don't intend to act like one. I'm just me. You're you,
a stranger, whom I've never seen before in my life. So I
wish you'd leave."

Duray strode from the house, out into the sunlight. He
looked once around the wide landscape, than gave his head
a surly shake and marched off along the path.

VIII

From the *Memoirs and Reflections:*

> The past is exposed for our scrutiny; we can wander
> the epochs like lords through a garden, serene in our
> purview. We argue with the noble sages, refuting their
> laborious concepts, should we be so unkind. Remem-
> ber (at least) two things. First: The more distant
> from now, the less precise our conjunctures, the less

our ability to strike to any given instant. We can break in upon yesterday at a stipulated second; during the Eocene, plus or minus ten years is the limit of our accuracy; as for the Cretaceous or earlier, an impingement with three hundred years of a given date can be considered satisfactory. Secondly: The past we broach is never our own past but at best the past of a cognate world, so that any illumination cast upon historical problems is questionable and perhaps deceptive. We cannot plumb the future; the process involves a negative flow of energy, which is inherently impractical. An instrument constructed of antimatter has been jocularly recommended but would yield no benefit to us. The future, thankfully, remains forever shrouded.

* * * * *

"Aha, you're back!" exclaimed Alan Robertson. "What did you learn?"

Duray described the encounter with Elizabeth. "She makes no excuse for what she's done; she shows hostility which doesn't seem real, especially since I can't imagine a reason for it."

Alan Robertson had no comment to make.

"The woman isn't my wife, but their motivations must be the same. I can't think of one sensible explanation for conduct so strange, let alone two."

"Elizabeth seemed normal this morning?" asked Alan Robertson.

"I noticed nothing unusual."

Alan Robertson went to the control panel of his machine. He looked over his shoulder at Duray. "What time do you leave for work?"

"About nine."

Alan Robertson set one dial and turned two others until a ball of green light balanced, wavering, precisely halfway along a glass tube. He signaled Duray behind the lead slab and touched the button. From the center of the machine came the impact of 167 colliding nodules of force and the groan of rending dimensional fabric.

Alan Robertson brought forth the new passway. "The time is morning. You'll have to decide for yourself how to handle the situation. You can try to watch without being seen; you can say that you have paper work to catch up on, that Elizabeth should ignore you and go about her normal routine, while you unobtrusively see what happens."

Duray frowned. "Presumably for each of these worlds there is a Gilbert Duray who finds himself in my fix. Suppose each tries to slip inconspicuously into someone else's world to learn what is happening. Suppose each Elizabeth catches him in the act and furiously accuses the man she believes to be her husband of spying on her—this in itself might be the source of Elizabeth's anger."

"Well, be as discreet as you can. Presumably you'll be several hours, so I'll go back to the boat and putter about. Locker five in my private hub yonder; I'll leave the door open."

Once again Duray stood on the hillside above the river, with the rambling stone house built by still another Gilbert Duray two hundred yards along the slope. From the height of the sun, Duray judged local time to be about nine o'clock—somewhat earlier than necessary. From the chimney of the stone house rose a wisp of smoke; Elizabeth had built a fire in the kitchen fireplace. Duray stood reflecting. This morning in his own house Elizabeth had built no fire. She had been on the point of striking a match and then had decided that the morning was already warm. Duray waited ten minutes, to make sure that the local Gilbert Duray had departed, then set forth toward the house. He paused by the big flat stone to inspect the pattern of moss. The crevice seemed narrower than he remembered, and the moss was dry and discolored. Duray took a deep breath. The air, rich with the odor of grasses and herbs, again seemed to carry an odd, unfamiliar scent. Duray proceeded slowly to the house, uncertain whether, after all, he was engaged in a sensible course of action.

He approached the house. The front door was open.

Elizabeth came to look out at him in surprise. "That was a quick day's work!"

Duray said lamely, "The rig is down for repairs. I thought I'd catch up on some paper work. You go ahead with whatever you were doing."

Elizabeth looked at him curiously. "I wasn't doing anything in particular."

He followed Elizabeth into the house. She wore soft black slacks and an old gray jacket; Duray tried to remember what his own Elizabeth had worn, but the garments had been so familiar that he could summon no recollection.

Elizabeth poured coffee into a pair of stoneware mugs, and Duray took a seat at the kitchen table, trying to decide how this Elizabeth differed from his own—if she did. This Elizabeth seemed more subdued and meditative; her mouth might have been a trifle softer. "Why are you looking at me so strangely?" she asked suddenly.

Duray laughed. "I was merely thinking what a beautiful girl you are."

Elizabeth came to sit in his lap and kissed him, and Duray's blood began to flow warm. He restrained himself; this was not his wife; he wanted no complications. And if he yielded to temptations of the moment, might not another Gilbert Duray visiting his own Elizabeth do the same . . . He scowled.

Elizabeth, finding no surge of ardor, went to sit in the chair opposite. For a moment she sipped her coffee in silence. Then she said, "Just as soon as you left, Bob called through."

"Oh?" Duray was at once attentive. "What did he want?"

"That foolish party of his—the Rubble-menders or some such thing. He wants us to come."

"I've already told him No three times."

"I told him No again. His parties are always so peculiar. He said he wanted us to come for a very special reason, but he wouldn't tell me the reason. I told him, 'Thank you but no.'"

Duray looked around the room. "Did he leave any books?"

"No. Why should he leave me books?"

"I wish I knew."

"Gilbert," said Elizabeth, "you're acting rather oddly."

"Yes, I suppose I am." For a fact Duray's mind was whirling. Suppose now he went to the school passway, brought the girls home from school, then closed off all the passways, so that once again he had an Elizabeth and three daughters, more or less his own; then the conditions he had encountered would be satisfied. And another Gilbert Duray, now happily destroying the tract houses of Cupertino, would find himself bereft. . . . Duray recalled the hostile conduct of the previous Elizabeth. The passways in that particular world had certainly not been closed off by an intruding Duray . . . A startling possibility came to his mind. Suppose a Duray had come to the house, and succumbing to temptation, had closed off all passways except that one communicating with his own world; suppose then that Elizabeth, discovering the imposture, had killed him . . . The theory had a grim plausibility and totally extinguished whatever inclination Duray might have had for making the world his home.

Elizabeth said, "Gilbert, why are you looking at me with that strange expression?"

Duray managed a feeble grin. "I guess I'm just in a bad mood this morning. Don't mind me. I'll go make out my report." He went into the wide cool living room, at once familiar and strange, and brought out the work-records of the other Gilbert Duray. . . . He studied the handwriting: like his own, firm and decisive, but in some indefinable way, different—perhaps a trifle more harsh and angular. The three Elizabeths were not identical, nor were the Gilbert Durays.

An hour passed. Elizabeth occupied herself in the kitchen; Duray pretended to write a report.

A bell sounded. "Somebody at the passway," said Elizabeth.

Duray said, "I'll take care of it."

He went to the passage room, stepped through the passway, looked through the peephole—into the large, bland, sun-tanned face of Bob Robertson.

Duray opened the door. For a moment he and Bob Robertson confronted each other. Bob Robertson's eyes narrowed. "Why, hello, Gilbert. What are you doing at home?"

Duray pointed to the parcel Bob Robertson carried. "What do you have there?"

"Oh, these?" Bob Robertson looked down at the parcel as if he had forgotten it. "Just some books for Elizabeth."

Duray found it hard to control his voice. "You're up to some mischief, you and your Rumfuddlers. Listen, Bob: Keep away from me and Elizabeth. Don't call here, and don't bring around any books. Is this definite enough?"

Bob raised his sun-bleached eyebrows. "Very definite, very explicit. But why the sudden rage? I'm just friendly old Uncle Bob."

"I don't care what you call yourself; stay away from us."

"Just as you like, of course. But do you mind explaining this sudden decree of banishment?"

"The reason is simple enough. We want to be left alone."

Bob made a gesture of mock despair. "All this over a simple invitation to a simple little party, which I'd really like you to come to."

"Don't expect us. We won't be there."

Bob's face suddenly went pink. "You're coming a very high horse over me, my lad, and it's a poor policy. You might just get hauled up with a jerk. Matters aren't all the way you think they are."

"I don't care a rap one way or another," said Duray. "Good-bye." He closed the locker door and backed through the passway. He returned into the living room.

Elizabeth called from the kitchen. "Who was it, dear?"

"Bob Robertson, with some books."

"Books? Why books?"

"I didn't trouble to find out. I told him to stay away. After this, if he's at the passway, don't open it."

Elizabeth looked at him intently. "Gil—you're so strange today! There's something about you that almost scares me."

"Your imagination is working too hard."

"Why should Bob trouble to bring me books? What sort of books? Did you see?"

"Demonology. Black magic. That sort of thing."

"Mmf. Interesting—but not all *that* interesting . . . I wonder if a world like ours, where no one has ever lived would, have things like goblins and ghosts?"

"I suspect not," said Duray. He looked toward the door. There was nothing more to be accomplished here, and it was time to return to his own Earth. He wondered how to make a graceful departure. And what would occur when the Gilbert Duray now working his rig came home?

Duray said, "Elizabeth, sit down in this chair here."

Elizabeth slowly slid into the chair at the kitchen table and watched him with a puzzled gaze.

"This may come as a shock," he said. "I am Gilbert Duray, but not your personal Gilbert Duray. I'm his cognate."

Elizabeth's eyes widened to lustrous dark pools.

Duray said, "On my own world Bob Robertson caused me and my Elizabeth trouble. I came here to find out what he had done and why and to stop him from doing it again."

Elizabeth asked, "What has he done?"

"I still don't know. He probably won't bother you again. You can tell your personal Gilbert Duray whatever you think best, or even complain to Alan."

"I'm bewildered by all this!"

"No more so than I." He went to the door. "I've got to leave now. Good-bye."

Elizabeth jumped to her feet and came impulsively forward. "Don't say good-bye. It was such a lonesome sound, coming from you. . . . It's like my own Gilbert saying good-bye."

"There's nothing else to do. Certainly I can't follow my inclinations and move in with you. What good are two Gilberts? Who'd get to sit at the head of the table?"

"We could have a round table," said Elizabeth. "Room for six or seven. I like my Gilberts."

"Your Gilberts like their Elizabeths." Duray sighed and said, "I'd better go now."

Elizabeth held out her hand. "Good-bye, cognate Gilbert."

IX

From the *Memoirs and Reflections:*

> The Oriental world-view differs from our own—specifically my own—in many respects, and I was early confronted with a whole set of dilemmas. I reflected upon Asiatic apathy and its obverse, despotism; warlords and brain-laundries: indifference to disease, filth, and suffering; sacred apes and irresponsible fecundity.
>
> I also took note of my resolve to use my machine in the service of all men.
>
> In the end I decided to make the "mistake" of many before me; I proceeded to impose my own ethical point of view upon the Oriental life-style.
>
> Since this was precisely what was expected of me, since I would have been regarded as a fool and a mooncalf had I done otherwise, since the rewards of cooperation far exceeded the gratifications of obduracy and scorn, my programs are a wonderful success, at least to the moment of writing.

* * * * *

Duray walked along the riverbank toward Alan Robertson's boat. A breeze sent twinkling cat's-paws across the water and bellied the sails that Alan Robertson had raised to air; the boat tugged at the mooring lines.

Alan Robertson, wearing white shorts and a white hat

with a loose, flapping brim, looked up from the eye he had been splicing at the end of a halyard. "Aha, Gil! You're back. Come aboard and have a bottle of beer."

Duray seated himself in the shade of the sail and drank half the beer at a gulp. "I still don't know what's going on —except that one way or another Bob is responsible. He came while I was there. I told him to clear out. He didn't like it."

Alan Robertson heaved a melancholy sigh. "I realize that Bob has the capacity for mischief."

"I still can't understand how he persuaded Elizabeth to close the passways. He brought out some books, but what effect could they have?"

Alan Robertson was instantly interested. "What were the books?"

"Something about satanism, black magic; I couldn't tell you much else."

"Indeed, indeed!" muttered Alan Robertson. "Is Elizabeth interested in the subject?"

"I don't think so. She's afraid of such things."

"Rightly so. Well, well, that's disturbing." Alan Robertson cleared his throat and made a delicate gesture, as if beseeching Duray to geniality and tolerance. "Still, you mustn't be too irritated with Bob. He's prone to his little mischiefs, but—"

" 'Little mischiefs'!" roared Duray. "Like locking me out of my home and marooning my wife and children? That's going beyond mischief!"

Alan Robertson smiled. "Here, have another beer; cool off a bit. Let's reflect. First, the probabilities. I doubt if Bob has really marooned Elizabeth and the girls or caused Elizabeth to do so."

"Then why are all the passways broken?"

"That's susceptible to explanation. He has access to the vaults; he might have substituted a blank for your master orifice. There's one possibility, at least."

Duray could hardly speak for rage. At last he cried out: "He has no right to do this!"

"Quite right, in the largest sense. I suspect that he only wants to induce you to his Rumfuddle."

"And I don't want to go, expecially when he's trying to put pressure on me."

"You're a stubborn man, Gil. The easy way, of course, would be to relax and look in on the occasion. You might even enjoy yourself."

Duray glared at Alan Robertson. "Are you suggesting that I attend the affair?"

"Well—no. I merely proposed a possible course of action."

Duray drank more beer and glowered out across the river. Alan Robertson said, "In a day or so, when this business is clarified, I think that we—all of us—should go off on a lazy cruise, out there among the islands. Nothing to worry us, no bothers, no upsets. The girls would love such a cruise."

Duray grunted. "I'd like to see them again before I plan any cruises. What goes on at these Rumfuddler events?"

"I've never attended. The members laugh and joke and eat and drink and gossip about the worlds they've visited and show each other movies: that sort of thing. Why don't we look in on last year's party? I'd be interested myself."

Duray hesitated. "What do you have in mind?"

"We'll set the dials to a year-old cognate to Bob's world, Fancy, and see precisely what goes on. What do you say?"

"I suppose it can't do any harm," said Duray grudgingly.

Alan Robertson rose to his feet. "Help me get these sails in."

X

From the *Memoirs and Reflections:*

> The problems that long have harassed historians have now been resolved. Who were the Cro-Magnons; where did they evolve? Who were the Etruscans? Where were the legendary cities of the proto-Sumer-

ians before they migrated to Mesopotamia? Why the
identity between the ideographs of Easter Island and
Mohenjo Daro? All these fascinating questions have
now been settled and reveal to us the full scope of our
early history. We have preserved the library at old
Alexandria from the Mohammedans and the Inca
codices from the Christians. The Guanches of the
Canaries, the Ainu of Hokkaido, the Mandans of
Missouri, the blond Kaffirs of Bhutan: All are now
known to us. We can chart the development of every
language syllable by syllable, from the earliest formu-
lation to the present. We have identified the Hellenic
heroes, and I myself have searched the haunted forests
of the ancient North and, in their own stone keeps,
met face to face those mighty men who generated the
Norse myths.

* * * * *

Standing before his machine, Alan Robertson spoke in a
voice of humorous self-deprecation. "I'm not as trusting
and forthright as I would like to be; in fact I sometimes
feel shame for my petty subterfuges, and now I speak in
reference to Bob. We all have our small faults, and Bob
certainly does not lack his share. His imagination is perhaps his greatest curse: He is easily bored and sometimes
tends to overreach himself. So while I deny him nothing, I
also make sure that I am in a position to counsel or even
remonstrate, if need be. Whenever I open a passway to one
of his formulae, I unobstrusively strike a duplicate which I
keep in my private file. We will find no difficulty in visiting
a cognate to Fancy."

Duray and Alan Robertson stood in the dusk, at the end
of a pale-white beach. Behind them rose a low basalt cliff.
To their right, the ocean reflected the afterglow and a glitter from the waning moon; to the left, palms stood black
against the sky. A hundred yards along the beach dozens of
fairy lamps had been strung between the trees to illuminate
a long table laden with fruit, confections, punch in crystal

bowls. Around the table stood several dozen men and women in animated conversation; music and the sounds of gaiety came down the beach to Duray and Alan Robertson.

"We're in good time," said Alan Robertson. He reflected a moment. "No doubt we'd be quite welcome; still, it's probably best to remain inconspicuous. We'll just stroll unobtrusively down the beach, in the shadow of the trees. Be careful not to stumble or fall, and no matter what you see or hear, do nothing! Discretion is essential; we want no awkward confrontations."

Keeping to the shade of the foliage, the two approached the merry group. Fifty yards distant, Alan Robertson held up his hand to signal a halt. "This is as close as we need approach; most of the people you know, or more accurately, their cognates. For instance, there is Royal Hart, and there is James Parham and Elizabeth's aunt, Emma Bathurst, and her uncle Peter and Maude Granger and no end of other folk."

"They all seem very gay."

"Yes, this is an important occasion for them. You and I are surly outsiders who can't understand the fun."

"Is this all they do, eat and drink and talk?"

"I think not," said Alan Robertson. "Notice yonder; Bob seems to be preparing a projection screen. Too bad that we can't move just a bit closer." Alan Robertson peered through the shadows. "But we'd better take no chances; if we were discovered, everyone would be embarrassed."

They watched in silence. Presently Bob Robertson went to the projection equipment and touched a button. The screen became alive with vibrating rings of red and blue. Conversations halted; the group turned toward the screen. Bob Robertson spoke, but his words were inaudible to the two who watched from the darkness. Bob Robertson gestured to the screen, where now appeared the view of a small country town, as if seen from an airplane. Surrounding was flat farm country, a land of wide horizons; Duray assumed the location to be somewhere in the Middle West. The picture changed to show the local high school, with students sitting on the steps. The scene shifted to the football field, on the day of a game—a very important game, to judge from the conduct of the spectators. The local team was introduced; one by one the boys ran out on the field to stand blinking into the autumn sunlight; then they ran off to the pregame huddle.

The game began; Bob Robertson stood by the screen in the capacity of an expert commentator, pointing to one or another of the players, analyzing the play. The game proceeded, to the manifest pleasure of the Rumfuddlers. At half time the bands marched and countermarched, then play resumed. Duray became bored and made fretful comments to Alan Robertson, who only said: "Yes, yes; probably so" and "My word, the agility of that halfback!" and "Have you noticed the precision of the line-play? Very good indeed!" At last the final quarter ended; the victorious team stood under a sign reading:

THE SHOWALTER TORNADOES
CHAMPIONS OF TEXAS
1951

The players came forward to accept trophies; there was a last picture of the team as a whole, standing proud and victorious; then the screen burst out into a red and gold starburst and went blank. The Rumfuddlers rose to their feet and congratulated Bob Robertson, who laughed modestly and went to the table for a goblet of punch.

Duray said disgustedly, "Is this one of Bob's famous parties? Why does he make such a tremendous occasion of the affair? I expected some sort of debauch."

Alan Robertson said, "Yes, from our standpoint at least, the proceedings seem somewhat uninteresting. Well, if your curiosity is satisfied, shall we return?"

"Whenever you like."

Once again in the lounge under the Mad Dog Mountains, Alan Robertson said: "So now and at last we've seen one of Bob's famous Rumfuddles. Are you still determined not to attend the occasion of tomorrow night?"

Duray scowled. "If I have to go to reclaim my family, I'll do so. But I just might lose my temper before the evening is over."

"Bob has gone too far," Alan Robertson declared. "I agree with you there. As for what we saw tonight, I admit to a degree of puzzlement."

"Only a degree? Do you understand it at all?"

Alan Robertson shook his head with a somewhat cryptic smile. "Speculation is pointless. I suppose you'll spend the night with me at the lodge?"

"I might as well," grumbled Duray. "I don't have anywhere else to go."

Alan Robertson clapped him on the back. "Good lad! We'll put some steaks on the fire and turn our problems loose for the night."

XI

From the *Memoirs and Reflections:*

> When I first put the Mark I machine into operation, I suffered great fears. What did I know of the forces that I might release? . . . With all adjustments at dead neutral, I punched a passway into a cognate Earth. This was simple enough—in fact, almost anti-climactic . . . Little by little I learned to control my wonderful toy; our own world and all its past phrases became familiar to me. What of other worlds? I am sure that in due corse we will move instantaneously from world to world, from galaxy to galaxy, using a special space-traveling hub on Utilis. At the moment I am candidly afraid to punch through passways at blind random. What if I opened into the interior of a sun? Or into the center of a black hole? Or into an antimatter universe? I would certainly destroy myself and the machine and conceivably Earth itself.

> Still, the potentialities are too entrancing to be ig-

nored. With painstaking precautions and a dozen protective devices, I will attempt to find my way to new worlds, and for the first time interstellar travel will be a reality.

* * * * *

Alan Robertson and Duray sat in the bright morning sunlight beside the flinty-blue lake. They had brought their breakfast out to the table and now sat drinking coffee. Alan Robertson made cheerful conversation for the two of them. "These last few years have been easier on me; I've relegated a great deal of responsibility. Ernest and Henry know my policies as well as I do, if not better; and they're never frivolous or inconsistent." Alan Robertson chuckled. "I've worked two miracles: first, my machine, and second, keeping the business as simple as it is. I refuse to keep regular hours; I won't make appointments; I don't keep records; I pay no taxes; I exert great political and social influence, but only informally; I simply refuse to be bothered with administrative detail, and consequently I find myself able to enjoy life."

"It's a wonder some religious fanatic hasn't assassinated you," said Duray sourly.

"No mystery there! I've given them all their private worlds, with my best regards, and they have no energy left for violence! And as you know, I walk with a very low silhouette. My friends hardly recognize me on the street." Alan Robertson waved his hand. "No doubt you're more concerned with your immediate quandary. Have you come to a decision regarding the Rumfuddle?"

"I don't have any choice," Duray muttered. "I'd prefer to wring Bob's neck. If I could account for Elizabeth's conduct, I'd feel more comfortable. She's not even remotely interested in black magic. Why did Bob bring her books on satanism?"

"Well—the subject is inherently fascinating," Alan Robertson suggested, without conviction. "The name Satan derives from the Hebrew word for 'adversary'; it never applied to a real individual. 'Zeus,' of course, was an Aryan chieftain of about 3500 B.C., while 'Woden' lived somewhat later. He was actually 'Othinn,' a shaman of enormous personal force who did things with his mind that I can't do with the machine . . . But again I'm rambling."

Duray gave a silent shrug.

"Well, then, you'll be going to the Rumfuddle," said Alan Robertson, "by and large the best course, whatever the consequences."

"I believe that you know more than you're telling me."

Alan Robertson smiled and shook his head. "I've lived with too much uncertainty among my cognate and near-cognate worlds. Nothing is sure; surprises are everywhere. I think the best plan is to fulfill Bob's requirements. Then, if Elizabeth is indeed on hand, you can discuss the event with her."

"What of you? Will you be coming?"

"I am of two minds. Would you prefer that I came?"

"Yes," said Duray. "You have more control over Bob than I do."

"Don't exaggerate my influence! He is a strong man, for all his idleness. Confidentially, I'm delighted that he occupies himself with games rather than . . ." Alan Robertson hesitated.

"Rather than what?"

"Than that his imagination should prompt him to less innocent games. Perhaps I have been overingenuous in this connection. We can only wait and see."

XII

From the *Memoirs and Reflections:*

> If the past is a house of many chambers, then the present is the most recent coat of paint.

* * * * *

At four o'clock Duray and Alan Robertson left the lodge and passed through Utilis to the San Francisco depot. Duray had changed into a somber dark suit; Alan Robertson wore a more informal costume: blue jacket and pale-gray trousers. They went to Bob Robertson's locker, to find a panel with the sign "NOT HOME! FOR THE RUMFUDDLE GO TO ROGER WAILLE'S LOCKER, RC 3–96, AND PASS THROUGH TO EKSHAYAN!"

The two went on to Locker RC3–96, where a sign read: "RUMFUDDLERS, PASS! ALL OTHERS: AWAY!"

Duray shrugged contemptuously, and parting the curtain, looked through the passway into a rustic lobby of natural wood, painted in black, red, yellow, blue, and white floral designs. An open door revealed an expanse of open land and water glistening in the afternoon sunlight. Duray and Alan Robertson passed through, crossed the foyer, and looked out upon a vast, slow river flowing from north to south. A rolling plain spread eastward away and over the horizon. The western bank of the river was indistinct in the afternoon glitter. A path led north to a tall house of eccentric architecture. A dozen domes and cupolas stood against the sky; gables and ridges created a hundred unexpected angles. The walls showed a fish-scale texture of hand-hewn shingles; spiral columns supported the second- and third-story entablatures, where wolves and bears, carved in vigorous curves and masses, snarled, fought, howled, and danced. On the side overlooking the river a pergola clothed with vines cast a dappled shade; here sat the Rumfuddlers.

Alan Robertson looked at the house, up and down the river, across the plain. "From the architecture, the vegetation, the height of the sun, the characteristic haze, I assume the river to be either the Don or the Volga, and yonder the steppes. From the absence of habitation, boats, and artifacts, I would guess the time to be early historic—perhaps 2,000 or 3,000 B.C., a colorful era. The inhabitants of the steppes are nomads; Scyths to the east, Celts to the west, and to the north the homeland of the Germanic and Scandinavian tribes; and yonder the mansion of Roger Waille, and very interesting, too, after the extravagant fashion of the Russian baroque. And, my word! I believe I see an ox on the spit! We may even enjoy our little visit!"

"You do as you like," muttered Duray. "I'd just as soon eat at home."

Alan Robertson pursed his lips. "I understand your point of view, of course, but perhaps we should relax a bit. The scene is majestic; the house is delightfully picturesque; the roast beef is undoubtedly delicious; perhaps we should meet the situation on its own terms."

Duray could find no adequate reply and kept his opinions to himself.

"Well, then," said Alan Robertson, "equability is the word. So now let's see what Bob and Roger have up their sleeves." He set off along the path to the house, with Duray sauntering morosely a step or two behind.

Under the pergola a man jumped to his feet and flourished his hand; Duray recognized the tall, spare form of Bob Robertson. "Just in time," Bob called jocosely. "Not too early, not too late. We're glad you could make it!"

"Yes, we found we could accept your invitation after all," said Alan Robertson. "Let me see, do I know anyone here? Roger, hello! . . . And William . . . Ah! the lovely Dora Gorski! . . . Cypriano . . ." He looked around the circle of faces, waving to his acquaintances.

Bob clapped Duray on the shoulder. "Really pleased you could come! What'll you drink? The locals distill a liquor out of fermented mare's milk, but I don't recommend it."

"I'm not here to drink," said Duray. "Where's Elizabeth?"

The corners of Bob's wide mouth twitched. "Come now, old man; let's not be grim. This is the Rumfuddle! A time for joy and self-renewal! Go dance about a bit! Cavort! Pour a bottle of champagne over your head! Sport with the girls!"

Duray looked into the blue eyes for a long second. He strained to keep his voice even. "Where is Elizabeth?"

"Somewhere about the place. A charming girl, your Elizabeth! We're delighted to have you both!"

Duray swung away. He walked to the dark and handsome Roger Waille. "Would you be good enough to take me to my wife?"

Waille raised his eyebrows as if puzzled by Duray's tone of voice. "She is primping and gossiping. If necessary I suppose I could pull her away for a moment or two."

Duray began to feel ridiculous, as if he had been locked away from his world, subjected to harrassments and doubts, and made the butt of some obscure joke. "It's necessary," he said. "We're leaving."

"But you've just arrived!"

"I know."

Waille gave a shrug of amused perplexity and turned away toward the house. Duray followed. They went through a tall, narrow doorway into an entry-hall paneled with a beautiful brown-gold wood that Duray automatically identified as chestnut. Four high panes of tawny glass turned to the west filled the room with a smoky half-melancholy light. Oak settees, upholstered in leather, faced each other across a black, brown, and gray rug. Taborets stood at each side of the settees, and each supported an ornate golden candelabra in the form of conventionalized stag's heads. Waille indicated these last. "Striking, aren't they? The Scythians made them for me. I paid them in iron knives. They think I'm a great magician; and for a fact, I am." He reached into the air and plucked forth an orange, which he tossed upon a settee. "Here's Elizabeth now, and the other maenads as well."

Into the chamber came Elizabeth, with three other young women whom Duray vaguely recalled having met before. At the sight of Duray, Elizabeth stopped short. She essayed a smile and said in a light, strained voice, "Hello, Gil. You're here after all." She laughed nervously and, Duray felt, unnaturally. "Yes of course you're here. I didn't think you'd come."

Duray glanced toward the other women, who stood with Waille, watching half expectantly. Duray said, "I'd like to speak to you alone."

"Excuse us," said Waille. "We'll go on outside."

They departed. Elizabeth looked longingly after them and fidgeted with the buttons of her jacket.

"Where are the children?" Duray demanded curtly.

"Upstairs, getting dressed." She looked down at her own costume, the festival raiment of a Transylvanian peasant girl: a green skirt embroidered with red and blue flowers, a white blouse, a black velvet vest, glossy black boots.

Duray felt his temper slipping; his voice was strained and fretful. "I don't understand anything of this. Why did you close the passways?"

Elizabeth attempted a flippant smile. "I was bored with routine."

"Oh? Why didn't you mention it to me yesterday morning? You didn't need to close the passways."

"Gilbert, please. Let's not discuss it."

Duray stood back, tongue-tied with astonishment. "Very well," he said at last. "We won't discuss it. You go up and get the girls. We're going home."

Elizabeth shook her head. In a neutral voice she said, "It's impossible. There's only one passway open. I don't have it."

"Who does? Bob?"

"I guess so; I'm not really sure."

"How did he get it? There were only four, and all four were closed."

"It's simple enough. He moved the downtown passway from our locker to another and left a blank in its place."

"And who closed off the other three?"

"I did."

"Why?"

"Because Bob told me to. I don't want to talk about it; I'm sick to death of the whole business." And she half whispered: "I don't know what I'm going to do with myself."

"I know what I'm going to do," said Duray. He turned toward the door.

Elizabeth held up her hands and clenched her fists against her breast. "Don't make trouble—please! He'll close our last passway!"

"Is that why you're afraid of him? If so—don't be. Alan wouldn't allow it."

Elizabeth's face began to crumple. She pushed past Duray and walked quickly out upon the terrace. Duray followed, baffled and furious. He looked back and forth across the terrace. Bob was not to be seen. Elizabeth had gone to Alan Robertson; she spoke in a hushed, urgent voice. Duray went to join them. Elizabeth became silent and turned away, avoiding Duray's gaze.

Alan Robertson spoke in a voice of easy geniality. "Isn't this a lovely spot? Look how the setting sun shines on the river!"

Roger Waille came by rolling a cart with ice, goblets, and a dozen bottles. He said: "Of all the places on all the Earths this is my favorite. I call it Ekshayan, which is the Scythian name for this district."

A woman asked, "Isn't it cold and bleak in the winter?"

"Frightful!" said Waille. "The blizzards howl down from the north; then they stop, and the land is absolutely still. The days are short, and the sun comes up red as a poppy. The wolves slink out of the forests, and at dusk they circle the house. When a full moon shines, they howl like banshees, or maybe the banshees are howling! I sit beside the fireplace, entranced."

"It occurs to me," said Manfred Funk, "that each person, selecting a site for his home, reveals a great deal about himself. Even on old Earth, a man's home was ordinarily a symbolic simulacrum of the man himself; now, with every option available, a person's house is himself."

"This is very true," said Alan Robertson, "and certainly Roger need not fear that he has revealed any discreditable aspects of himself by showing us his rather grotesque home on the lonely steppes of prehistoric Russia."

Roger Waille laughed. "The grotesque house isn't me; I merely felt that it fitted its setting . . . . Here, Duray, you're not drinking. That's chilled vodka; you can mix it or drink it straight in the time-tested manner."

"Nothing for me, thanks."

"Just as you like. Excuse me; I'm wanted elsewhere."

Waille moved away, rolling the cart. Elizabeth leaned as if she wanted to follow him, then remained beside Alan Robertson. looking thoughtfully over the river.

Duray spoke to Alan Robertson as if she were not there. "Elizabeth refuses to leave. Bob has hypnotized her."

"That's not true," said Elizabeth softly.

"Somehow, one way or another, he's forced her to stay. She won't tell me why."

"I want the passway back," said Elizabeth. But her voice was muffled and uncertain.

Alan Robertson cleared his throat. "I hardly know what to say. It's a very awkward situation. None of us wants to create a disturbance—"

"There you're wrong," said Duray.

Alan Robertson ignored the remark. "I'll have a word with Bob after the party. In the meantime I don't see why we shouldn't enjoy the company of our friends, and that wonderful roast ox! Who is that turning the spit? I know him from somewhere."

Duray could hardly speak for outrage. "After what he's done to us?"

"He's gone too far, much too far," Alan Robertson agreed. "Still, he's a flamboyant, feckless sort, and I doubt if he understands the full inconvenience he's caused you."

"He understands well enough. He just doesn't care."

"Perhaps so," said Alan Robertson sadly. "I had always hoped—but that's neither here nor there. I still feel that we should act with restraint. It's much easier not to do than to undo."

Elizabeth abruptly crossed the terrace and went to the front door of the tall house, where her three daughters had appeared—Dolly, twelve; Joan, ten; Ellen, eight—all wearing green, white, and black peasant frocks and glossy black boots. Duray thought they made a delightful picture. He followed Elizabeth across the terrace.

"It's Daddy," screamed Ellen, and threw herself in his arms. The other two, not to be outdone, did likewise.

"We thought you weren't coming to the party," cried Dolly. "I'm glad you did, though."

"So'm I."

"So'm I."

"I'm glad I came, too, if only to see you in these pretty costumes. Let's go see Grandpa Alan." He took them across the terrace, and after a moment's hesitation, Elizabeth followed. Duray became aware that everyone had stopped talking to look at him and his family, with, so it seemed, an extraordinary, even avid, curiosity, as if in expectation of some entertaining extravagance of conduct. Duray began to burn with emotion. Once, long ago, while crossing a street in downtown San Francisco, he had been struck by an automobile, suffering a broken leg and a fractured clavicle. Almost as soon as he had been knocked down, pedestrians came pushing to stare down at him, and Duray, looking up in pain and shock, had seen only the ring of white faces and intent eyes, greedy as flies around a puddle of blood. In hysterical fury he had staggered to his feet, striking out into every face within reaching distance, man and woman alike. He hated them more than the man who had run him down: the ghouls who had come to enjoy his pain. Had he the miraculous power, he would have crushed them into a screaming bale of detestable flesh and hurled the bundle twenty miles out into the Pacific Ocean . . .

Some faint shadow of this emotion affected him now, but today he would provide them no unnatural pleasure. He turned a single glance of cool contempt around the group, then took his three eager-faced daughters to a bench at the back of the terrace. Elizabeth followed, moving like a mechanical object. She seated herself at the end of the bench and looked off across the river. Duray stared heavily back at the Rumfuddlers, compelling them to shift their gazes to where the ox roasted over a great bed of coals. A young man in a white jacket turned the spit; another basted the meat with a long-handled brush. A pair of Orientals carried out a carving table; another brought a carving set; a fourth wheeled out a cart laden with salads, round crusty loaves, trays of cheese and herrings. A fifth man, dressed as a Transylvanian gypsy, came from the house with a violin. He went to the corner of the terrace and began to play melancholy music of the steppes.

Bob Robertson and Roger Waille inspected the ox, a magnificent sight indeed. Duray attempted a stony detachment, but his nose was under no such strictures; the odor of the roast meat, garlic, and herbs tantalized him unmercifully. Bob Robertson returned to the terrace and held up his hands for attention; the fiddler put down his instrument. "Control your appetites; there'll still be a few minutes, during which we can discuss our next Rumfuddle. Our clever colleague Bernard Ulman recommends a hostelry in the Adirondacks: the Sapphire Lake Lodge. The hotel was built in 1902, to the highest standards of Edwardian comfort. The clientele is derived from the business community of New York. The cuisine is kosher; the management maintains an atmosphere of congenial gentility; the current date is 1930. Bernard has furnished photographs. Roger, if you please."

Waille drew back a curtain to reveal a screen. He manipulated the projection machine, and the hotel was displayed on the screen: a rambling, half-timbered structure overlooking several acres of park and a smooth lake.

"Thank you, Roger. I believe that we also have a photograph of the staff."

On the screen appeared a stiffly posed group of about thirty men and women, all smiling with various degrees of affability. The Rumfuddlers were amused; some among them tittered.

"Bernard gives a very favorable report as to the cuisine, the amenities, and the charm of the general area. Am I right, Bernard?"

"In every detail," declared Bernard Ulman. "The management is attentive and efficient; the clientele is well-established."

"Very good," said Bob Robertson. "Unless someone has a more entertaining idea, we will hold our next Rumfuddle at the Sapphire Lake Lodge. And now I believe that the roast beef should be ready—done to a turn, as the expression goes."

"Quite right," said Roger Waille. "Tom, as always, has done an excellent job at the spit."

The ox was lifted to the table. The carver set to work with a will. Duray went to speak to Alan Robertson, who blinked uneasily at his approach. Duray asked, "Do you understand the reason for these parties? Are you in on the joke?"

Alan Robertson spoke in a precise manner: "I certainly am not 'in on the joke,' as you put it." He hesitated, then said: "The Rumfuddlers will never again intrude upon your life or that of your family. I am sure of this. Bob became overexuberant; he exercised poor judgment, and I intend to have a quiet word with him. In fact, we have already exchanged certain opinions. At the moment your best interests will be served by detachment and unconcern."

Duray spoke with sinister politeness: "You feel, then, that I and my family should bear the brunt of Bob's jokes?"

"This is a harsh view of the situation, but my answer must be Yes."

"I'm not so sure. My relationship with Elizabeth is no longer the same. Bob has done this to me."

"To quote an old apothegm: 'Least said, soonest mended.' "

Duray changed the subject. "When Waille showed the photograph of the hotel staff, I thought some of the faces were familiar. Before I could be quite sure, the picture was gone."

Alan Robertson nodded unhappily. "Let's not develop the subject, Gilbert. Instead—"

"I'm into the situation too far," said Duray. "I want to know the truth."

"Very well, then," said Alan Robertson hollowly, "your instincts are accurate. The management of the Sapphire Lake Lodge, in cognate circumstances, has achieved an unsavory reputation. As you have guessed, they comprise the leadership of the National Socialist party during 1938 or thereabouts. The manager, of course, is Hitler, the desk clerk is Goebbels, the headwaiter is Göring, the bellboys are Himmler and Hess, and so on down the line. They are, of course, not aware of the activities of their cognates on other worlds. The hotel's clientele is for the most part Jewish, which brings a macabre humor to the situation."

"Undeniably," said Duray. "What of that Rumfuddlers party that we looked in on?"

"You refer to the high-school football team? The 1951 Texas champions, as I recall." Alan Robertson grinned. "And well they should be. Bob identified the players for me. Are you interested in the lineup?"

"Very much so."

Alan Robertson drew a sheet of paper from his pocket. "I believe—yes, this is it." He handed the sheet to Duray, who saw a schematic lineup:

LE	LT	LG	C	RG	RT	RE
Achilles	Charle-magne	Hercules	Goliath	Samson	Richard the Lion-Hearted	Billy the Kid

Q
Machiavelli

LHB
Sir Galahad

RHB
Geronimo

FB
Cuchulain

Duray returned the paper. "You approve of this?"

"I had best put it like this," said Alan Robertson, a trifle uneasily. "One day, chatting with Bob, I remarked that much travail could be spared the human race if the most notorious evildoers were early in their lives shifted to environments which afforded them constructive outlets for their energies. I speculated that having the competence to make such changes, it was perhaps our duty to do so. Bob became interested in the concept and formed his group, the Rumfuddlers, to serve the function I had suggested. In all candor I believe that Bob and his friends have been attracted more by the possibility of entertainment than by altruism, but the effect has been the same."

"The football players aren't evildoers," said Duray. "Sir

Galahad, Charlemagne, Samson, Richard the Lion-Hearted . . ."

"Exactly true," said Alan Robertson, "and I made this point to Bob. He asserted that all were brawlers and bully-boys, with the possible exception of Sir Galahad; that Charlemagne, for example, had conquered much territory to no particular achievement; that Achilles, a national hero to the Greeks, was a cruel enemy to the Trojans; and so forth. His justifications are somewhat specious perhaps . . . Still, these young men are better employed making touchdowns than breaking heads."

After a pause Duray asked: "How are these matters arranged?"

"I'm not entirely sure. I believe that by one means or another, the desired babies are exchanged with others of similar appearance. The child so obtained is reared in appropriate circumstances."

"The jokes seem elaborate and rather tedious."

"Precisely!" Alan Robertson declared. "Can you think of a better method to keep someone like Bob out of mischief?"

"Certainly," said Duray. "Fear of the consequences." He scowled across the terrace. Bob had stopped to speak to Elizabeth. She and the three girls rose to their feet.

Duray strode across the terrace. "What's going on?"

"Nothing of consequence," said Bob. "Elizabeth and the girls are going to help serve the guests." He glanced toward the serving table, then turned back to Duray. "Would you help with the carving?"

Duray's arm moved of its own volition. His fist caught Bob on the angle of the jaw and sent him reeling back into one of the white-coated Orientals, who carried a tray of food. The two fell into an untidy heap. The Rumfuddlers were shocked and amused and watched with attention.

Bob rose to his feet gracefully enough and gave a hand to the Oriental. Looking toward Duray, Bob shook his head ruefully. Meeting his glance, Duray noted a pale-blue glint; then Bob once more became bland and debonair.

Elizabeth spoke in a low despairing voice: "Why

couldn't you have done as he asked? It would have all been so simple."

"Elizabeth may well be right," said Alan Robertson.

"Why should she be right?" demanded Duray. "We are his victims! You've allowed him a taste of mischief, and now you can't control him!"

"Not true!" declared Alan. "I intend to impose rigorous curbs upon the Rumfuddlers, and I will be obeyed."

"The damage is done, so far as I am concerned," said Duray bitterly. "Come along, Elizabeth, we're going Home."

"We can't go Home. Bob has the passway."

Alan Robertson drew a deep sigh and came to a decision. He crossed to where Bob stood with a goblet of wine in one hand, massaging his jaw with the other. Alan Robertson spoke to Bob politely but with authority. Bob was slow in making a reply. Alan Robertson spoke again, sharply. Bob only shrugged. Alan Robertson waited a moment, then returned to Duray, Elizabeth, and the three children.

"The passway is at his San Francisco apartment," said Alan Robertson in a measured voice. "He will give it back to you after the party. He doesn't choose to go for it now."

Bob once more commanded the attention of the Rumfuddlers. "By popular request we replay the record of our last but one Rumfuddle, contrived by one of our most distinguished. diligent, and ingenious Rumfuddlers, Manfred Funk. The locale is the Red Barn, a roadhouse twelve miles west of Urbana. Illinois; the time is the late summer of 1926; the occasion is a Charleston dancing contest. The music is provided by the legendary Wolverines, and you will hear the fabulous cornet of Leon Bismarck Beiderbecke." Bob gave a wry smile, as if the music were not to his personal taste. "This was one of our most rewarding occasions, and here it is again."

The screen showed the interior of a dance-hall, crowded with excited young men and women. At the back of the stage sat the Wolverines, wearing tuxedos; to the front stood the contestants: eight dapper young men and eight pretty girls in short skirts. An announcer stepped forward and spoke to the crowd through a megaphone: "Contestants are numbered one through eight! Please, no encouragement from the audience. The prize is this magnificent trophy and fifty dollars cash; the presentation will be made by last year's winner, Boozy Horman. Remember, on the first number we eliminate four contestants, on the second number, two; and after the third number we select our winner. So then: Bix and the Wolverines and 'Sensation Rag'!"

From the band came music; from the contestants, agitated motion.

Duray asked, "Who are these people?"

Alan Robertson replied in an even voice: "The young men are locals and not important. But notice the girls: No doubt you find them attractive. You are not alone. They are Helen of Troy, Deirdre, Marie Antoinette, Cleopatra, Salome, Lady Godiva, Nefertiti, and Mata Hari."

Duray gave a dour grunt. The music halted; judging applause from the audience, the announcer eliminated Marie Antoinette, Cleopatra, Deirdre, Mata Hari, and their respective partners. The Wolverines played "Fidgety Feet"; the four remaining contestants danced with verve and dedication, but Helen and Nefertiti were eliminated. The Wolverines played "Tiger Rag." Salome and Lady Godiva and their young men performed with amazing zeal. After carefully appraising the volume of applause, the announcer gave his judgment to Lady Godiva and her partner. Large on the screen appeared a close-up view of the two happy faces; in an excess of triumphant joy they hugged and kissed each other. The screen went dim; after the vivacity of the Red Barn the terrace above the Don seemed drab and insipid.

The Rumfuddlers shifted in their seats. Some uttered exclamations to assert their gaiety; others stared out across the vast empty face of the river.

Duray glanced toward Elizabeth; she was gone. Now he saw her circulating among the guests with three other young women, pouring wine from Scythian decanters.

"It makes a pretty picture, does it not?" said a calm

voice. Duray turned to find Bob standing behind him; his mouth twisted in an easy half-smile, but his eye glinted pale blue.

Duray turned away. Alan Robertson said, "This is not at all a pleasant situation, Bob, and in fact completely lacks charm."

"Perhaps at future Rumfuddles, when my face feels better, the charm will emerge. . . . Excuse me; I see that I must enliven the meeting." He stepped forward. "We have a final pastiche: oddments and improvisations, vignettes and glimpses, each in its own way entertaining and instructive. Roger, start the mechanism, if you please."

Roger Waille hesitated and glanced sidelong toward Alan Robertson.

"The item number is sixty-two, Roger," said Bob in a calm voice. Roger Waille delayed another instant, then shrugged and went to the projection machine.

"The material is new," said Bob, "hence I will supply a commentary. First we have an episode in the life of Richard Wagner, the dogmatic and occasionally irascible composer. Ths year is 1843; the place is Dresden. Wagner sets forth on a summer night to attend a new opera, *Der Sanger Krieg,* by an unknown composer. He alights from his carriage before the hall; he enters; he seats himself in his loge. Notice the dignity of his posture, the authority of his gestures! The music begins. Listen!" From the projector came the sound of music. "It is the overture," stated Bob. "But notice Wagner: Why is he stupefied? Why is he overcome with wonder? He listens to the music as if he has never heard it before. And in fact he hasn't; he has only just yesterday set down a few preliminary notes for this particular opus, which he planned to call *Tannhäuser;* today, magically, he hears it in its final form. Wagner will walk home slowly tonight, and perhaps in his abstraction he will kick the dog Schmutzi. . . . Now to a different scene: St. Petersburg in the year 1880 and the stables in back of the Winter Palace. The ivory and gilt carriage rolls forth to convey the czar and the czarina to a reception at the British Embassy. Notice the drivers: stern, well-groomed, intent at their business. Marx's beard is well-trimmed; Lenin's goatee is not so pronounced. A groom comes to watch the carriage roll away. He has a kindly twinkle in his eye, does Stalin." The screen went dim once more, then brightened to show a city street lined with automobile showrooms and used-car lots. "This is one of Shawn Henderson's projects. The four used-car lots are operated by men who in other circumstances were religious notables: prophets and so forth. That alert, keen-featured man in front of Quality Motors, for instance, is Mohammed. Shawn is conducting a careful survey, and at our next Rumfuddle he will report upon his dealings with these four famous figures."

Alan Robertson stepped forward, somewhat diffidently. He cleared his throat. "I don't like to play the part of spoilsport, but I'm afraid I have no choice. There will be no further Rumfuddles. Our original goals have been neglected, and I note far too many episodes of purposeless frivolity and even cruelty. You may wonder at what seems a sudden decision, but I have been considering the matter for several days. The Rumfuddles have taken a turn in an unwholesome direction and conceivably might become a grotesque new vice, which, of course, is far from our original ideal. I'm sure that every sensible person, after a few moments' reflection, will agree that now is the time to stop. Next week you may return to me all passways except those to worlds where you maintain residence."

The Rumfuddlers sat murmuring together. Some turned resentful glances toward Alan Robertson; others served themselves more bread and meat. Bob came over to join Alan and Duray. He spoke in an easy manner. "I must say that your admonitions arrive with all the delicacy of a lightning bolt. I can picture Jehovah smiting the fallen algels in a similar style."

Alan Robertson smiled. "Now, then, Bob, you're talking nonsense. The situations aren't at all similar. Jehovah struck out in fury; I impose my restriction in all goodwill in order that we can once again turn our energies to constructive ends."

Bob threw back his head and laughed. "But the Rumfuddlers have lost the habit of work. We only want to amuse ourselves, and after all, what is so noxious in our activities?"

"The trend is menacing, Bob." Alan Robertson's voice was reasonable. "Unpleasant elements are creeping into your fun, so stealthily that you yourself are unaware of them. For instance, why torment poor Wagner? Surely there was gratuitous cruelty, and only to provide you a few instants of amusement. And since the subject is in the air, I heartily deplore your treatment of Gilbert and Elizabeth. You have brought them both an extraordinary inconvenience, and in Elizabeth's case, actual suffering. Gilbert got something of his own back, and the balance is about even."

"Gilbert is far too impulsive," said Bob. "Self-willed and egocentric, as he always has been."

Alan held up his hand. "There is no need to go further into the subject, Bob. I suggest that you say no more."

"Just as you like, though the matter, considered as practical rehabilitation, isn't irrelevant. We can amply justify the work of the Rumfuddlers."

Duray asked quietly, "Just how do you mean, Bob?"

Alan Robertson made a peremptory sound, but Duray said, "Let him say what he likes and make an end to it. He plans to do so anyway."

There was a moment of silence. Bob looked across the terrace to where the three Orientals were transferring the remains of the beef to a service cart.

"Well?" Alan Robertson asked softly. "Have you made your choice?"

Bob held out his hands in ostensible bewilderment. "I don't understand you! I want only to vindicate myself and the Rumfuddlers. I think we have done splendidly. Today we have allowed Torquemada to roast a dead ox instead of a living heretic; Marquis de Sade has fulfilled his obscure urges by caressing seared flesh with a basting brush, and did you notice the zest with which Ivan the Terrible hacked up the carcass? Nero, who has real talent, played his violin; Attila, Genghis Khan, and Mao Tse-tung efficiently served the guests. Wine was poured by Messalina, Lucrezia Borgia, Delilah, and Gilbert's charming wife, Elizabeth. Only Gilbert failed to demonstrate his rehabilitation, but at least he provided us a touching and memorable picture: Gilles de Rais, Elizabeth Báthory, and their three virgin daughters. It was sufficient. In every case we have shown that rehabilitation is not an empty word."

"Not in every case," said Alan Robertson, "specifically that of your own."

Bob looked at him askance. "I don't follow you."

"No less than Gilbert are you ignorant of your background. I will now reveal the circumstances so that you may understand something of yourself and try to curb the tendencies which have made your cognate an exemplar of cruelty, stealth, and treachery."

Bob laughed: a brittle sound like cracking ice. "I admit to a horrified interest."

"I took you from a forest a thousand miles north of this very spot while I traced the phylogeny of the Norse gods. Your name was Loki. For reasons which are not now important I brought you back to San Francisco, and there you grew to maturity."

"So I am Loki."

"No. You are Bob Robertson, just as this is Gilbert Duray, and here is his wife, Elizabeth. Loki, Gilles de Rais, Elizabeth Báthory: These names applied to human material which has not functioned quite as well. Gilles de Rais, judging from all evidence, suffered from a brain tumor; he fell into his peculiar vices after a long and honorable career. The case of Princess Elizabeth Báthory is less clear, but one might suspect syphilis and consequent cerebral lesions."

"And what of poor Loki?" inquired Bob with exaggerated pathos.

"Loki seemed to suffer from nothing except a case of old-fashioned meanness."

Bob seemed concerned. "So that these qualities apply to me?"

"You are not necessarily identical to your cognate. Still,

I advise you to take careful stock of yourself, and so far as I am concerned, you had best regard yourself as on probation."

"Just as you say." Bob looked over Alan Robertson's shoulder. "Excuse me; you've spoiled the party, and everybody is leaving. I want a word with Roger."

Duray moved to stand in his way, but Bob shouldered him aside and strode across the terrace, with Duray glowering at his back.

Elizabeth said in a mournful voice, "I hope we're at the end of all this."

Duray growled. "You should never have listened to him."

"I didn't listen; I read about it in one of Bob's books; I saw your picture; I couldn't—"

Alan Robertson intervened. "Don't harass poor Elizabeth; I consider her both sensible and brave; she did the best she could."

Bob returned. "Everything taken care of," he said cheerfully. "All except one or two details."

"The first of these is the return of the passway. Gilbert and Elizabeth—not to mention Dolly, Joan, and Ellen—are anxious to return Home."

"They can stay here with you," said Bob. "That's probably the best solution."

"I don't plan to stay here," said Alan Robertson in mild wonder. "We are leaving at once."

"You must change your plans," said Bob. "I have finally become bored with your reproaches. Roger doesn't particularly care to leave his home, but he agrees that now is the time to make a final disposal of the matter."

Alan Robertson frowned in displeasure. "The joke is in very poor taste, Bob."

Roger Waille came from the house, his face somewhat glum. "They're all closed. Only the main gate is open."

Alan Robertson said to Gilbert: "I think that we will leave Bob and Roger to their Rumfuddle fantasies. When he returns to his senses, we'll get your passway. Come along, then, Elizabeth! Girls!"

"Alan," said Bob gently, "you're staying here. Forever. I'm taking over the machine."

Alan Robertson asked mildly: "How do you propose to restrain me? By force?"

"You can stay here alive or dead; take your choice."

"You have weapons, then?"

"I certainly do." Bob displayed a pistol. "There are also the servants. None have brain tumors or syphilis; they're all just plain bad."

Roger said in an awkward voice, "Let's go and get it over."

Alan Robertson's voice took on a harsh edge. "You seriously plan to maroon us here, without food?"

"Consider yourself marooned."

"I'm afraid that I must punish you, Bob, and Roger as well."

Bob laughed gaily. "You yourself are suffering from brain disease—megalomania. You haven't the power to punish anyone."

"I still control the machine, Bob."

"The machine isn't here. So now—"

Alan Robertson turned and looked around the landscape, with a frowning air of expectation. "Let me see. I'd probably come down from the main gate; Gilbert and a group from behind the house. Yes, here we are."

Down the path from the main portal, walking jauntily, came two Alan Robertsons with six men armed with rifles and gas grenades. Simultaneously from behind the house appeared two Gilbert Durays and six more men, similarly armed.

Bob stared in wonder. "Who are these people?"

"Cognates," said Alan, smiling. "I told you I controlled the machine, and so do all my cognates. As soon as Gilbert and I return to our Earth, we must similarly set forth and in our turn do our part on other worlds cognate to this . . . Roger, be good enough to summon your servants. We will take them back to Earth. You and Bob must remain here."

Waille gasped in distress. "Forever?"

"You deserve nothing better," said Alan Robertson. "Bob perhaps deserves worse." He turned to the cognate Alan Robertsons. "What of Gilbert's passway?"

Both replied, "It's in Bob's San Francisco apartment, in a box on the mantlepiece."

"Very good," said Alan Robertson. "We will now depart. Good-bye, Bob. Good-bye, Roger. I am sorry that our association ended on this rather unpleasant basis."

"Wait!" cried Roger. "Take me back with you!"

"Good-bye," said Alan Robertson. "Come along, then, Elizabeth. Girls! Run on ahead!"

XIII

Elizabeth and the children had returned to Home; Alan Robertson and Duray sat in the lounge above the machine. "Our first step," said Alan Robertson, "is to dissolve our obligation. There are, of course, an infinite number of Rumfuddles at Ekshayans and an infinite number of Alans and Gilberts. If we visited a single Rumfuddle, we would, by the laws of probability, miss a certain number of the emergency situations. The total number of permutations, assuming that an infinite number of Alans and Gilberts makes a random choice among an infinite number of Ekshayans, is infinity raised to the infinite power. What percentage of this number yields blanks for any given Ekshayan, I haven't calculated. If we visited Ekshayans until we had by our own efforts rescued at least one Gilbert and Alan set, we might be forced to scour fifty or a hundred worlds or more. Or we might achieve our rescue on the first visit. The wisest course, I believe, is for you and I to visit, say, twenty Ekshayans. If each of the Alan and Gilbert sets does the same, then the chances for any particular Alan and Gilbert to be abandoned are one in twenty times nineteen times eighteen times seventeen, et cetera. Even then I think I will arrange that an operator check another five or ten thousand worlds to gather up that one lone chance . . ."

Tell Me
All About Yourself

F. M. Busby

As the science-fiction short story enlarges its
habitat from the magazines to book anthologies, the erosion of its traditional pulp taboos
is accelerating. "Shocking" sf stories appear
not only in such volumes as *Dangerous Visions* and *Eros in Orbit,* but also in such general anthology series as Robert Silverberg's
New Dimensions, in which this short, restrained, and sad tale of legalized necrophilia
first appeared. *Tell Me All About Yourself* is,
against all odds, a love story: a narrative that
goes beyond its initial idea to comment on the
emptiness of sex without communication.

It was Charlie's idea. He and Vance and I were on the
town, celebrating our luck. It hadn't been easy, cutting
close to the edges of a minor typhoon to bring the big hy-
drofoil freighter safely to Hong Kong on schedule. So we

celebrated, high-wide-and-sideways on a mixture of drugs; none of us were users on the job but ashore was different. Some alcohol, of course, plus other things of our separate choices. I stayed with cannabis and one of the lesser mind-benders; I forget the brand name. Vance was tripping and far out; Charlie was so speeded-up that I kept expecting him to skid on the corners.

"Hey, Vance! Dale! Pop one of these, and let's go get some kicks." He was holding out some purple Sensies, which don't come cheap; sensory enhancement is worth money and the sellers know it.

"What kind of kicks, Chazz?" When Charlie gets loose, I get cautious.

"There's a Nec down this way a few blocks. You ever try that, Dale?"

"No." I'd never been to a Necro house; I wasn't sure I wanted to, either.

"Well, hell, then; come on, kid. You'll never learn any younger."

"What do you think, Vance?" I said. It was a waste of breath. Whatever Vance was thinking behind his blissful smile, he wouldn't be able, from where he was, to find words for it. He nodded, after a while. Very deliberately. Another country heard from, in shorthand.

"OK then; what say gang?" Charlie held a pill out to Vance, then one to me, and took one himself. Vance swallowed his. I hesitated, then popped mine too. Hell, I didn't have to follow through with the rest of it if I didn't want to. But we began walking along toward the Nec, Charlie leading.

"Have you done this stuff much, Charlie? The Necs, I mean?"

"A few times, Dale."

"What's the hook? I don't get it. I mean, the broads are dead and so what?"

Charlie shrugged, "It's just different, is all. Well, OK: one time in a regular seaport fuckery, Marseilles I think, I got a deafmute ginch. It was—restful, sort of; you don't have to talk. Wouldn't do you any good if you did. And at the Necs it's even more like that, 'cause they don't move. And you kind of wonder about them, what they'd say if they could, and all. I dunno, Dale; you have to *be* there, I guess."

Vance said, "What they don't say is the most important." I hadn't known that Vance was a Necro; Charlie, of course, is everything that doesn't kill him. And sometimes I think he crowds *that* a little.

Before I could decide anything one way or the other, we were there. At the door and then inside. A woman greeted us; somehow I hadn't expected that. She was small, Eurasian, slim in stretch skintights. I wished it were a live house; the Sensy was taking hold and I wanted her. I missed hearing Charlie's first questions.

"We have a good selection tonight in the A rooms," she said. "I trust that you gentlemen are interested in the A category?" I knew what that meant: after certain physical changes, the category reverts to B. I've heard of places where there's a C category but I don't like to think about that.

We all nodded, even Vance. A was the category of our choice; yes.

"Then I will show you the pictures of our A list," she said. She went behind a counter like a hotel registration desk and came back with two packets of 8-by-10 color prints. Each picture showed a woman nude, supine, arms and legs spread, eyes closed. Dead; they had to be, though it wasn't obvious.

She fanned the two sets of pictures out on a heavy teakwood table. "These," pointing, "are kept at body temperature. These others are at chill, for greater service life in the A category. Personal preferences differ."

Charlie and I looked only at the warm set; Vance smiled brightly and sorted through both. I was, I found, very taken with the picture of a small dark woman, voluptuous in a compact way. Charlie took it out of my hand.

"Hey, that's for me," he said. I was about to argue, though it's futile to argue with Charlie, when the picture was taken from him in turn.

I hadn't seen the man come in. He was tall, thin-faced and pale, wearing a light-gray suit and walking with no sound. He looked at the picture.

"So she's attracting trade already," he said.

"Mr. Holmstrom," the woman said, "I have the bank draft for you. I trust everything is satisfactory? Mrs. Holmstrom's appearance, and so forth?"

"Quite." Once again behind the counter, she found an envelope, came back and gave it to Holmstrom. He put the picture back on the table, thanked her and turned to leave.

"Just a minute," said Charlie. "This here is your wife, maybe?"

"She was."

"Sorry; sorry. But could I ask you a little something?"

"Of course. If I choose, I'll answer." Charlie blinked.

"Well, then," he said, "what I want to know is, how was she when—I mean, like *before?*"

"I doubt that you'll notice much difference," the man said, wheeling to walk out. The door closed behind him while Charlie gaped.

Somehow I had lost interest in the small dark woman; I leafed through the stack of warms. "I'll still take that one," Charlie said, and paid his money. The Eurasian woman handed him a numbered key. He took his direction from her pointing finger and walked away along a corridor to the right of the counter. I didn't notice whether Vance's choice was warm or chill, but he left by a different exit. I looked at the picture, unable to choose, unable to consent.

The woman came to stand by me. "Perhaps we have nothing to interest you, sir, in this category? Perhaps the B category?"

God, NO! I shook my head violently, shuffling frantically through the pictures. Maybe that one? No. What the hell was I doing here, anyway?

"Perhaps something a little special, sir. More expensive, of course. But if expense is not a problem . . . a girl, young, though developed. Death by sad accident. No obvious mutilation, no cosmetic corrections necessary. And very rare in our trade, a virgin. Let me show you her picture."

The Sensy and the mindbender were fighting in my head and body. I waited while she brought the picture, then looked at it.

Virginity had never been important to me; it doesn't show visually, anyway. But I looked at the girl in glossy color and I liked her. She was someone I'd like to know. I decided to go about that now, the best I could.

Money paid, down a hall, key into the lock of numbered door, I entered and looked at her. At first I didn't understand the strangeness.

The way the best picture ever taken differs from a person is that the person is *there;* the depiction is not. Here, looking, was a halfway case. The girl was more than a picture but less than a person. I didn't figure the difference immediately; it took a while to sink in.

The pale-red hair was the same, longish and curling, spread out from her head. I wouldn't disarrange it; I didn't want to touch the tubes that pumped warm preservative fluid through her to maintain body temperature.

The slim strong limbs and body looked healthy enough to get up and walk. Her skin was warm, all right—a little dry, maybe. But it was the face that drew me: features strong but delicate. And I could not understand how she, or anyone, could smile so happily after she was gone. I wanted to ask her about that. I wanted to ask her about a lot of things.

The Sensy pill wanted more from me. There are things, I knew, that help a virgin girl. Though I'd had only two such, habit set me to those preparations. Then I realized, foolishly, that no stimulus could bring response, and that the house had prepared her as well as could be done. So I entered her.

Slow and easy, slow and easy, raising my head to see her smile. I had to speak. "Do you like that? This? You're beautiful; did you know?

The smile flexed; I don't know how or why. But with

that slight movement the beauty of her caught and held me. The intensity of the pull astonished me. I tried to lose myself in sensation—the augmented delights of the Sensy pill —but I couldn't. The smile wouldn't let me. And I ceased fighting what I felt.

"Why did you never know love?" I asked. "You should have. You were made for it. I wish I—" I wished I'd found her before. Because I knew, now, that always I had been looking for her.

And was this to be her only love? With care, with gentleness, I sought to make it worthy.

I had to know more. "Who are you?" Only her smile replied. "What did you want? What can I give you?"

My body answered that; I gave it. Not wanting to, begrudging the final ecstasy. I had so much more to say, to ask; I didn't want to leave her. But it was done; that is the rule, alive or dead.

I kissed her smooth forehead and released her, feeling empty, as though I should be the one lying there, not her. Numbly, I busied myself with my clothing.

Up and dressed, hand on the door, I looked back. Nothing had changed; she smiled as I had first seen her. In the picture, and here.

"But you haven't told me *anything*." No, and she would not. I said, "Goodbye. I'm sorry." And closed the door behind me. Opposite from the way I had come was an "Exit" sign. I went to that door, put my hand on the knob. And couldn't bring myself to turn it.

If I left, I would never see her again. I had to go back. My mind must have known all along; I found I still had the key.

She looked the same. Still the slim strong body, the hair, the smile. So lovely, and so alone. The silence.

I looked for a long time. Then I said goodbye again and turned away. But I couldn't go. I had remembered something.

Her picture. Now it would be in the warm stack of the A category, for Charlie and Vance and everybody. And she was defenseless.

I thought of Charlie with her. Charlie's all right; I like him, mostly. But sometimes, afterward, he says things I don't like to hear. I could not bear that thought.

And Charlie's not the worst. There are men who would hurt her.

No. They weren't going to have her. No one was going to have her. She was mine now.

Gently I disarranged her hair to expose the brown plastic tubes pumping fluid to and from the nape of her neck. The connections were self-sealing; only a few drops of colorless fluid escaped as I set the tubes aside.

A robe hung on a hook beside the door. It was bizarre; a less gaudy pattern would have better suited her. But the robe was all there was.

I robed her, limp like a passed-out drunk, and carried her out of the room, out through the exit. I left most of my money in the room; it wasn't enough, I knew, but it would help me feel less like a thief.

Overcrowded Hong Kong still has the jinrikishaw; the man said, "Lady not feel good?"

"She'll be all right," I said, and he took us to my hotel. After the first couple of times I don't book a room at the same hotel with Charlie and Vance, ashore.

The night clerk said, "Lady all right?" I smiled and nodded, carrying her.

In the room I arranged her beauty. "Is that all right? Would you like anything more?" Then again I loved her, and held her close in sleep against the threat of chill.

But in the morning there was no doubt. My head had cooled and so had she. Soon she would no longer be of the A category, or even B.

I couldn't let that happen to her. I couldn't let it happen to me, the seeing of what time would do.

I walked the crowded streets of Hong Kong, thinking, wondering. The drugs had worn off but the problem hadn't. Nowhere in the city could I bury her, even if I had wanted to. Burial at sea was out; I didn't want her moldering under earth *or* water. And the house would have the police pursuing me as relentlessly as Category B pursued her.

There is a waterfront area where tourists can rent motorboats; I went there and rented one, cruising until I found a derelict wharf for moorage. Rickshaws were sparse nearby but I found one and returned to the commercial district, where I purchased a life raft and a few other things, mostly on the black market. These I took to my boat. Then I went back to the hotel.

She was so cold, but still she smiled. I respected her withdrawal; it was her right. I told her my plans. "Am I doing right? Is this what you want?" Her smile did not change. I sat a long time, stroking her hair; nothing more. In the streaked wall mirror I saw a fool. I smiled, and the fool smiled back at me.

We sat until dark. She was so quiet, never answering my questions. Then it was time to go.

The rickshaw was slow; the man lost his way several times more, I think, than his usual quota for tourists. But eventually we got to my rented boat, she and I.

Out into the water, out into the dark. Out into the middle of the bay where no one could interfere. I inflated the life raft and put it over the side. Then it was time to take her robe from her and spread it in the raft. At last, with the swells of the bay hampering me, I put her on the robe in the best beauty I could manage. Then I arranged the other things around her, that she needed, before I moved the boat away and threw the torch.

The first blaze showed her smile unchanged. Her hair vanished in a glorious crown of flame. I wanted, needed to look away, but I couldn't. I saw her smile widen into a look of ecstasy before a curtain of fire concealed everything. I'm so grateful that it did. Then the thermite went, that I'd placed around her. A searing blast of heat, a cloud of steam, and she and the raft were gone.

I took the boat back where it belonged.

Next day, back at the ship, Charlie talked a lot about his Nec piece. It sounded more like the B category but I didn't say so. Vance didn't say much; he just grinned. I think he was still up, though with Vance it's hard to tell for sure. He does his job.

I couldn't talk about it. Not to Charlie, not even to Vance. It's hard to think about.

I wanted so much for her to answer me, and she wouldn't.

The Deathbird

Harlan Ellison

If you've read such diverse Harlan Ellison stories as *"Repent, Harlequin!" Said the Ticktockman* *A Boy and His Dog* and *At the Mouse Circus*, to name just three, then you know you should expect the unexpected from any new Ellison story. Even so, you're likely to be surprised by this darkly imaginative, moving novelette of the distant future of Earth.

1

THIS IS A TEST. Take notes. This will count as ¾ of your final grade. Hints: remember, in chess, kings cancel each other out and cannot occupy adjacent squares, are therefore all-powerful and totally powerless, cannot affect one another, produce stalemate. Hinduism is a polytheistic religion; the sect of Atman worships the divine spark of life within Man; in effect saying, "Thou art God." Provisos of equal time are not served by one viewpoint having media access to two hundred million people in prime time while opposing viewpoints are provided with a soapbox on the corner. Not everyone tells the truth. Operational note: these sections may be taken out of numerical sequence: rearrange to suit yourself for optimum clarity. Turn over your test papers and begin.

2

Uncounted layers of rock pressed down on the magma pool. White-hot with the bubbling ferocity of the molten nickel-iron core, the pool spat and shuddered, yet did not pit or char or smoke or damage in the slightest the smooth and reflective surfaces of the strange crypt.

Nathan Stack lay in the crypt—silent, sleeping.

A shadow passed through rock. Through shale, through coal, through marble, through mica schist, through quartzite; through miles-thick deposits of phosphates, through diatomaceous earth, through feldspars, through diorite; through faults and folds, through anticlines and monoclines, through dips and synclines; through hellfire; and came to the ceiling of the great cavern and passed through; and saw the magma pool and dropped down; and came to the crypt. The shadow.

A triangular face with a single eye peered into the crypt, saw Stack, and lay four-fingered hands on the crypt's cool surface. Nathan Stack woke at the touch, and the crypt became transparent; he woke though the touch had not been upon his body. His soul felt the shadowy pressure and he opened his eyes to see the leaping brilliance of the world-core around him, to see the shadow with its single eye staring in at him.

The serpentine shadow enfolded the crypt; its darkness flowed upward again, through the Earth's mantle, toward the crust, toward the surface of the cinder, the broken toy that was the Earth.

When they reached the surface, the shadow bore the

crypt to a place where the poison winds did not reach, and caused it to open.

Nathan Stack tried to move, and moved only with difficulty. Memories rushed through his head of other lives, many other lives, as many other men; then the memories slowed and melted into a background tone that could be ignored.

The shadow thing reached down a hand and touched Stack's naked flesh. Gently, but firmly, the thing helped him to stand, and gave him garments, and a neck-pouch that contained a short knife and a warming-stone and other things. He offered his hand, and Stack took it, and after two hundred and fifty thousand years sleeping in the crypt, Nathan Stack stepped out on the face of the sick planet Earth.

Then the thing bent low against the poison winds and began walking away. Nathan Stack, having no other choice, bent forward and followed the shadow creature.

3

A messenger had been sent for Dira and he had come as quickly as the meditations would permit. When he reached the Summit, he found the fathers waiting, and they took him gently into their cove, where they immersed themselves and began to speak.

"We've lost the arbitration," the coil-father said. "It will be necessary for us to go and leave it to him."

Dira could not believe it. "But didn't they listen to our arguments, to our logic?"

The fang-father shook his head sadly and touched Dira's shoulder. "There were . . . accommodations to be made. It was their time. So we must leave."

The coil-father said, "We've decided you will remain. One was permitted, in caretakership. Will you accept our commission?"

It was a very great honor, but Dira began to feel the loneliness even as they told him they would leave. Yet he accepted. Wondering why they had selected *him,* of all their people. There were reasons, there were always reasons, but he could not ask. And so he accepted the honor, with all its attendant sadness, and remained behind when they left.

The limits of his caretakership were harsh, for they insured he could not defend himself against whatever slurs or legends would be spread, nor could he take action unless it became clear the trust was being breached by the other—who now held possession. And he had no threat save the Deathbird. A final threat that could be used only when final measures were needed: and therefore too late.

But he was patient. The most patient of all his people.

Thousands of years later, when he saw how it was destined to go, when there was no doubt left how it would end, he understood *that* was the reason he had been chosen to stay behind.

But it did not help the loneliness.

Nor could it save the Earth. Only Stack could do that.

4

1 Now the serpent was more subtil than any beast of the field which the LORD God had made. And he said unto the woman, Yea hath God said, Ye shall not eat of every tree of the garden?

2 And the woman said unto the serpent, We may eat of the fruit of the trees of the garden:

3 But of the fruit of the tree which is in the midst of the garden, God hath said, Ye shall not eat of it, neither shall ye touch it, lest ye die.

4 And the serpent said unto the woman. Ye shall not surely die:

5 (Omitted)

6 And when the woman saw that the tree was good for food, and that it was pleasant to the eyes, and a tree to be desired to make one wise, she took of the fruit thereof, and did eat, and gave also unto her husband with her; and he did eat.

7 *(Omitted)*

8 *(Omitted)*

9 *And the LORD God called unto Adam, and said unto him, Where* art *thou?*

10 *(Omitted)*

11 *And he said, Who told thee that thou* wast *naked? Hast thou eaten of the tree, whereof I commanded thee that thou shouldest not eat?*

12 *And the man said, The woman whom thou gavest* to be *with me, she gave me of the tree, and I did eat.*

13 *And the LORD God said unto the woman, What* is *this* that *thou hast done? And the woman said, The serpent beguiled me, and I did eat.*

14 *And the LORD God said unto the serpent, Because thou hast done this, thou* art *cursed above all cattle, and above every beast of the field; upon thy belly shalt thou go, and dust shalt thou eat all the days of thy life:*

15 *And I will put enmity between thee and the woman, and between thy seed and her seed; it shall bruise thy head, and thou shalt bruise his heel.*

GENESIS, Chap. II

TOPICS FOR DISCUSSION

(Give 5 points per right answer.)

1. Melville's Moby Dick begins, "Call me Ishmael." We say it is told in the first person. In what person is Genesis told? From whose viewpoint?

2. Who is the "good guy" in this story? Who is the "bad guy?" Can you make a strong case for reversal of the roles?

3. Traditionally, the apple is considered to be the fruit the serpent offered to Eve. But apples are not endemic to the Near East. Select one of the following, more logical substitutes, and discuss how myths come into being and are corrupted over long periods of time: olive, fig, date, pomegranate.

4. Why is the word LORD always in capitals and the name God always capitalized? Shouldn't the serpent's name be capitalized, as well? If no, why?

5. If God created everything (see Genesis, Chap. I), why did he create problems for himself by creating a serpent who would lead his creations astray? Why did God create a tree he did not want Adam and Eve to know about, and then go out of his way to warn them against it?

6. Compare and contrast Michelangelo's Sistine Chapel ceiling panel of the Expulsion from Paradise with Bosch's Garden of Earthly Delights.

7. Was Adam being a gentleman when he placed blame on Eve? Who was Quisling? Discuss "narking" as a character flaw.

8. God grew angry when he found out he had been defied. If God is omnipotent and omniscient, didn't he know? Why couldn't he find Adam and Eve when they hid?

9. If God had not wanted Adam and Eve to taste the fruit of the forbidden tree, why didn't he warn the serpent? Could God have prevented the serpent from tempting Adam and Eve? If yes, why didn't he? If no, discuss the possibility the serpent was as powerful as God.

10. Using examples from two different media journals, demonstrate the concept of "slanted news."

5

The poison winds howled and tore at the powder covering the land. Nothing lived there. The winds, green and deadly, dived out of the sky and raked the carcass of the Earth, seeking, seeking: anything moving, anything still living. But there was nothing. Powder. Talc. Pumice.

And the onyx spire of the mountain toward which Nathan Stack and the shadow thing had moved, all that first day. When night fell they dug a pit in the tundra and the shadow thing coated it with a substance thick as glue that had been in Stack's neck-pouch. Stack had slept the night fitfully, clutching the warming-stone to his chest and breathing through a filter tube from the pouch.

Once he had awakened, at the sound of great batlike creatures flying overhead; he had seen them swooping low, coming in flat trajectories across the wasteland toward his pit in the earth. But they seemed unaware that he—and the shadow thing—lay in the hole. They defecated thin, phosphorescent stringers that fell glowing through the night and were lost on the plains; then the creatures swooped upward and were whirled away on the winds. Stack resumed sleeping, with difficulty.

In the morning, frosted with an icy light that gave everything a blue tinge, the shadow thing scrabbled its way out of the choking powder and crawled along the ground, then lay flat, fingers clawing for purchase in the whiskaway surface. Behind it, from the powder, Stack bore toward the surface, reached up a hand and trembled for help.

The shadow creature slid across the ground, fighting the winds that had grown stronger in the night, back to the soft place that had been their pit, to the hand thrust up through the powder. It grasped the hand, and Stack's fingers tightened convulsively. Then the crawling shadow exerted pressure and pulled the man from the treacherous pumice.

Together they lay against the earth, fighting to see, fighting to draw breath without filling their lungs with suffocating death.

"Why is it like this . . . what *happened?*" Stack screamed against the wind. The shadow creature did not answer, but it looked at Stack for a long moment and then, with very careful movements, raised its hand, held it up before Stack's eyes and slowly, making claws of the fingers, closed the four fingers into a cage, into a fist, into a painfully tight ball that said more eloquently than words: *destruction.*

Then they began to crawl toward the mountain.

6

The onyx spire of the mountain rose out of hell and struggled toward the shredded sky. It was monstrous arrogance. Nothing should have tried that climb out of desolation. But the black mountain had tried, and succeeded.

It was like an old man. Seamed, ancient, dirt caked in striated lines, autumnal, lonely; black and desolate, piled strength upon strength. It would *not* give in to gravity and pressure and death. It struggled for the sky. Ferociously alone, it was the only feature that broke the desolate line of the horizon.

In another twenty-five million years the mountain might be worn as smooth and featureless as a tiny onyx offering to the deity night. But though the powder plains swirled and the poison winds drove the pumice against the flanks of the pinnacle, thus far their scouring had only served to soften the edges of the mountain's profile, as though divine intervention had protected the spire.

Lights moved near the summit.

7

Stack learned the nature of the phosphorescent stringers defecated onto the plain the night before by the batlike creatures. They were spores that became, in the wan light of day, strange bleeder plants.

All around them as they crawled through the dawn, the little live things sensed their warmth and began thrusting shoots up through the talc. As the fading red ember of the dying sun climbed painfully into the sky, the bleeding plants were already reaching maturity.

Stack cried out as one of the vine tentacles fastened around his ankle, holding him. A second looped itself around his neck.

Thin films of berry-black blood coated the vines, leaving rings on Stack's flesh. The rings burned terribly.

The shadow creature slid on its belly and pulled itself back to the man. Its triangular head came close to Stack's neck, and it bit into the vine. Thick black blood spurted as the vine parted, and the shadow creature rasped its razor-edged teeth back and forth till Stack was able to breathe again. With a violent movement Stack folded himself down and around, pulling the short knife from the neck-pouch.

He sawed through the vine tightening inexorably around his ankle. It screamed as it was severed, in the same voice Stack had heard from the skies the night before. The severed vine writhed away, withdrawing into the talc.

Stack and the shadow thing crawled forward once again, low, flat, holding onto the dying earth: toward the mountain. High in the bloody sky, the Deathbird circled.

8

On their own world, they had lived in luminous, oily-walled caverns for millions of years, evolving and spreading their race through the universe. When they had had enough of empire-building, they turned inward, and much of their time was spent in the intricate construction of songs of wisdom, and the designing of fine worlds for many races.

There were other races that designed, however. And when there was a conflict over jurisdiction, an arbitration was called, adjudicated by a race whose *raison d'etre* was impartiality and cleverness unraveling knotted threads of claim and counter-claim. Their racial honor, in fact, depended on the flawless application of these qualities. Through the centuries they had refined their talents in more and more sophisticated arenas of arbitration until the time came when they were the final authority. The litigants were compelled to abide by the judgments, not merely because the decisions were always wise and creatively fair, but because the judges' race would, if its decisions were questioned as supect, destroy itself. In the holiest place on their world they had erected a religious machine. It could be activated to emit a tone that would shatter their crystal carapaces. They were a race of exquisite cricket-like creatures, no larger than the thumb of a man. They were treasured throughout the civilized worlds, and their loss would have been catastrophic. Their honor and their value was never questioned. All races abided by their decisions.

So Dira's people gave over jurisdiction to that certain

world, and went away, leaving Dira with only the Death-bird, a special caretakership the adjudicators had creatively woven into their judgment.

There is recorded one last meeting between Dira and those who had given him his commission. There were readings that could not be ignored—had, in fact, been urgently brought to the attention of the fathers of Dira's race by the adjudicators—and the Great Coiled One came to Dira at the last possible moment to tell him of the mad thing into whose hands this world had been given, to tell Dira of what the mad thing could do.

The Great Coiled One—whose rings were loops of wisdom acquired through centuries of gentleness and perception and immersed meditations that had brought forth lovely designs for many worlds—he who was the holiest of Dira's race, honored Dira by coming to *him,* rather than commanding Dira to appear.

We have only one gift to leave them, he said. *Wisdom. This mad one will come, and he will lie to them, and he will tell them: created he them. And we will be gone, and there will be nothing between them and the mad one but you. Only you can give them the wisdom to defeat him in their own good time.* Then the Great Coiled One stroked the skin of Dira with ritual affection, and Dira was deeply moved and could not reply. Then he was left alone.

The mad one came, and interposed himself, and Dira gave them wisdom, and time passed. His name became other than Dira, it became Snake, and the new name was despised: but Dira could see the Great Coiled One had been correct in his readings. So Dira made his selection. A man, one of them, and gifted him with the spark.

All of this is recorded somewhere. It is history.

9

The man was not Jesus of Nazareth. He may have been Simon. Not Genghis Khan, but perhaps a foot soldier in his horde. Not Aristotle, but possibly one who sat and listened to Socrates in the agora. Neither the shambler who discovered the wheel nor the link who first ceased painting himself blue and applied the colors to the walls of the cave. But one near them, somewhere near at hand. The man was not Richard *Coeur de Lion,* Rembrandt, Richelieu, Rasputin, Robert Fulton or the Mahdi. Just a man. With the spark.

10

Once, Dira came to the man. Very early on. The spark was there, but the light needed to be converted to energy. So Dira came to the man, and did what had to be done before the mad one knew of it, and when he discovered that Dira, the Snake, had made contact, he quickly made explanations.

This legend has come down to us as the fable of *Faust.* TRUE or FALSE?

11

Light coverted to energy, thus:

In the fortieth year of his five hundredth incarnation, all-unknowing of the eons of which he had been part, the man found himself wandering in a terrible dry place under a thin, flat burning disc of sun. He was a Berber tribesman who had never considered shadows save to relish them when they provided shade. The shadow came to him, sweeping down across the sands like the *khamsin* of Egypt, the *simoom* of Asia Minor, the *harmattan,* all of which he had known in his various lives, none of which he remembered. The shadow came over him like the *sirocco*.

The shadow stole the breath from his lungs and the man's eyes rolled up in his head. He fell to the ground and the shadow took him down and down, through the sands, into the Earth.

Mother Earth.

She lived, this world of trees and rivers and rocks with deep stone thoughts. She breathed, had feelings, dreamed dreams, gave birth, laughed and grew contemplative for millenia. This great creature swimming in the sea of space.

What a wonder, the man thought, for he had never understood that the Earth was his mother, before this. He had never understood, before this, that the Earth had a life of its own, at once a part of humankind and quite separate from humankind. A mother with a life of her own.

Dira, Snake, shadow . . . took the man down and let the spark of light change itself to energy as the man became one with the Earth. His flesh melted and became quiet, cool soil. His eyes glowed with the light that shines in the darkest centers of the planet and he saw the way the mother cared for her young: the worms, the roots of plants, the rivers that cascaded for miles over great cliffs in enormous caverns, the bark of trees. He was taken once more to the bosom of that great Earth mother, and understood the joy of her life.

Remember this, Dira said to the man.

What a wonder, the man thought . . .

. . . and was returned to the sands of the desert, with no remembrance of having slept with, loved, enjoyed the body of his natural mother.

12

They camped at the base of the mountain, in a green-glass cave; not deep but angled sharply so the blown pumice could not reach them. They put Nathan Stack's stone in a fault in the cave's floor, and the heat spread quickly, warming them. The shadow thing with its triangular head sank back in shadow and closed its eye and sent its hunting instinct out for food. A shriek came back on the wind.

Much later, when Nathan Stack had eaten, when he was reasonably content and well-fed, he stared into the shadows and spoke to the creature sitting there.

"How long was I down there . . . how long was the sleep?"

The shadow thing spoke in whispers. *A quarter of a million years.*

Stack did not reply. The figure was beyond belief. The shadow creature seemed to understand.

In the life of a world no time at all.

Nathan Stack was a man who could make accommodations. He smiled quickly and said, "I must have been tired."

The shadow did not respond.

"I don't understand very much of this. It's pretty damned frightening. To die, then to wake up . . . here. Like this."

You did not die. You were taken, put down there. By the end you will understand everything, I promise you.

"Who put me down there?"

I did. I came and found you when the time was right, and I put you down there.

"Am I still Nathan Stack?"

If you wish.

"But *am* I Nathan Stack?"

You always were. You had many other names, many other bodies, but the spark was always yours. Stack seemed about to speak, and the shadow creature added, *You were always on your way to being who you are.*

"But what *am* I? Am I still Nathan Stack, dammit?"

If you wish.

"Listen: you don't seem too sure about that. You came and got me, I mean, I woke up and there you were; now who should know better than you what my name is?"

You have had many names in many times. Nathan Stack is merely the one you remember. You had a very different name long ago, at the start, when I first came to you.

Stack was afraid of the answer, but he asked, "What was my name then?"

Ish-lilith. Husband of Lilith. Do you remember her?

Stack thought, tried to open himself to the past, but it

was as unfathomable as the quarter of a million years through which he had slept in the crypt.

"No. But there were other women, in other times."

Many. There was one who replaced Lilith.

"I don't remember."

Her name . . . does not matter. But when the mad one took Lilith from you and replaced her with the other . . . then I knew it would end like this. The Deathbird.

"I don't mean to be stupid, but I haven't the faintest idea what you're talking about."

Before it ends, you will understand everything.

"You said that before." Stack paused, stared at the shadow creature for a long time only moments long, then, "What was your name?"

Before I met you my name was Dira.

He said it in his native tongue. Stack could not pronounce it.

"Before you met me. What is it now?"

Snake.

Something slithered past the mouth of the cave. It did not stop, but it called out with the voice of moist mud sucking down into a quagmire.

"Why did you put *me* down there? Why did you come to me in the first place? What spark? Why can't I remember these other lives or who I was? What do you want from me?"

You should sleep. It will be a long climb. And cold.

"I slept for two hundred and fifty thousand years, I'm hardly tired," Stack said. "Why did you pick me?"

Later. Now sleep. Sleep has other uses.

Darkness deepened around Snake, seeped out around the cave, and Nathan Stack lay down near the warming-stone, and the darkness took him.

13

SUPPLEMENTARY READING

This is an essay by a writer. It is clearly an appeal to the emotions. As you read it ask yourself how it applies to the subject under discussion. What is the writer trying to say? Does he succeed in making his point? Does this essay cast light on the point of the subject under discussion? After you have read this essay, using the reverse side of your test paper, write your own essay (500 words or less) on the loss of a loved one. If you have never lost a loved one, fake it.

AHBHU

Yesterday my dog died. For eleven years Ahbhu was my closest friend. He was responsible for my writing a story about a boy and his dog that many people have read. He was not a pet, he was a person. It was impossible to anthropomorphize him, he wouldn't stand for it. But he was so much his own kind of creature, he had such a strongly formed personality, he was so determined to share his life with only those *he* chose, that it was also impossible to think of him as simply a dog. Apart from those canine characteristics into which he was locked by his species, he comported himself like one of a kind.

We met when I came to him at the West Los Angeles Animal Shelter. I'd wanted a dog because I was lonely and I'd remembered when I was a little boy how my dog had been a friend when I had no other friends. One summer I went away to camp and when I returned I found a rotten old neighbor lady from up the street had had my dog picked up and gassed while my father was at work. I crept into the woman's back yard that night and found a rug hanging on the clothesline. The rug beater was hanging from a post. I stole it and buried it.

At the Animal Shelter there was a man in line ahead of me. He had brought in a puppy only a week or so old. A Puli, a Hungarian sheep dog; it was a sad-looking little thing. He had too many in the litter and had brought in this one to either be taken by someone else, or to be put to sleep. They took the dog inside and the man behind the counter called my turn. I told him I wanted a dog and he took me back inside to walk down the line of cages.

In one of the cages the little Puli that had just been brought in was being assaulted by three larger dogs who had been earlier tenants. He was a little thing, and he was on the bottom, getting the stuffing knocked out of him. But he was struggling mightily. The runt of the litter.

"Get him out of there!" I yelled. "I'll take him, I'll take him, get him out of there!"

He cost two dollars. It was the best two bucks I ever spent.

Driving home with him, he was lying on the other side of the front seat, staring at me. I had had a vague idea what I'd name a pet, but as I stared at him, and he stared back at me, I suddenly was put in mind of the scene in Alexander Korda's 1939 film *The Thief of Bagdad*, where the evil vizier, played by Conrad Veidt, had changed Ahbhu, the little thief, played by Sabu, into a dog. The film had superimposed the human over the canine face for a moment so there was an extraordinary look of intelligence in the face of the dog. The little Puli was looking at me with that same expression. "Ahbhu," I said.

He didn't react to the name, but then he couldn't have cared less. But that was his name, from that time on.

No one who ever came into my house was unaffected by him. When he sensed someone with good vibrations, he was right there, lying at their feet. He loved to be scratched, and despite years of admonitions he refused to stop begging for scraps at table, because he found most of the people who had come to dinner at my house were patsies unable to escape his woebegone Jackie-Coogan-as-the-Kid look.

But he was a certain barometer of bums, as well. On any number of occasions when I found someone I liked, and Ahbhu would have nothing to do with him or her, it always turned out the person was a wrongo. I took to noting his attitude toward newcomers, and I must admit it influenced my own reactions. I was always wary of someone Ahbhu shunned.

Women with whom I had had unsatisfactory affairs would nonetheless return to the house from time to time—to visit the dog. He had an intimate circle of friends, many of whom had nothing to do with me, and numbering among their company some of the most beautiful actresses in Hollywood. One exquisite lady used to send her driver to pick him up for Sunday afternoon romps at the beach.

I never asked him what happened on those occasions. He didn't talk.

Last year he started going downhill, though I didn't realize it because he maintained the manner of a puppy almost to the end. But he began sleeping too much, and he couldn't hold down his food—not even the Hungarian meals prepared for him by the Magyars who lived up the street. And it became apparent to me something was wrong with him when he got scared during the big Los Angeles earthquake last year. Ahbhu wasn't afraid of anything. He attacked the Pacific Ocean and walked tall around vicious cats. But the quake terrified him and he jumped up in my bed and threw his forelegs around my neck. I was very nearly the only victim of the earthquake to die from animal strangulation.

He was in and out of the veterinarian's shop all through the early part of this year, and the idiot always said it was his diet.

Then one Sunday when he was out in the backyard, I found him lying at the foot of the porch stairs, covered with mud, vomiting so heavily all he could bring up was bile. He was matted with his own refuse and he was trying desperately to dig his nose into the earth for coolness. He was barely breathing. I took him to a different vet.

At first they thought it was just old age . . . that they could pull him through. But finally they took X-rays and saw the cancer had taken hold in his stomach and liver.

I put off the day as much as I could. Somehow I just couldn't conceive of a world that didn't have him in it. But yesterday I went to the vet's office and signed the euthanasia papers.

"I'd like to spend a little time with him, before," I said. They brought him in and put him on the stainless steel examination table. He had grown so thin. He'd always had a pot-belly and it was gone. The muscles in his hind legs were weak, flaccid. He came to me and put his head into the hollow of my armpit. He was trembling violently. I lifted his head and he looked at me with that comic face I'd always thought made him look like Lawrence Talbot, the Wolf Man. He knew. Sharp as hell right up to the end, hey old friend? He knew, and he was scared. He trembled all the way down to his spiderweb legs. This bouncing ball of hair that, when lying on a dark carpet, could be taken for a sheepskin rug, with no way to tell at which end head and which end tail. So thin. Shaking, knowing what was going to happen to him. But still a puppy.

I cried and my eyes closed as my nose swelled with the crying, and he buried his head in my arms because we hadn't done much crying at one another. I was ashamed of myself not to be taking it as well as he was.

"I *got* to, pup, because you're in pain and you can't eat. I *got* to." But he didn't want to know that.

The vet came in, then. He was a nice guy and he asked me if I wanted to go away and just let it be done.

Then Ahbhu came up out of there and *looked* at me.

There is a scene in Kazan's *Viva Zapata* where a close friend of Zapata's, Brando's, has been condemned for conspiring with the *Federales*. A friend that had been with Zapata since the mountains, since the *revolucion* had begun. And they come to the hut to take him to the firing squad, and Brando starts out, and his friend stops him with a hand on his arm, and he says to him with great friendship, "Emiliano, do it yourself."

Ahbhu looked at me and I know he was just a dog, but if he could have spoken with human tongue he could not have said more eloquently than he did with a look, *Don't leave me with strangers.*

So I held him as they laid him down and the vet slipped the lanyard up around his right foreleg and drew it tight to bulge the vein, and I held his head and he turned it away from me as the needle went in. It was impossible to tell the moment he passed over from life to death. He simply laid his head on my hand, his eyes fluttered shut and he was gone.

I wrapped him in a sheet with the help of the vet, and I drove home with Ahbhu on the seat beside me, just the way he had come home eleven years before. I took him out in the backyard and began digging his grave. I dug for hours, crying and mumbling to myself, talking to him in the sheet. It was a very neat, rectangular grave with smooth sides and all the loose dirt scooped out by hand.

I laid him down in the hole and he was so tiny in there for a dog who had seemed to be so big in life, so furry, so funny. And I covered him over and when the hole was packed full of dirt I replaced the neat divot of grass I'd scalped off at the start. And that was all.

But I couldn't send him to strangers.

THE END

QUESTIONS FOR DISCUSSION

1. Is there any significance to the reversal of the word god being dog? If so, what?
2. Does the writer try to impart human qualities to a non-human creature? Why? Discuss anthropomorphism in the light of the phrase, "Thou art God."
3. Discuss the love the writer shows in this essay. Compare and contrast it with other forms of love: the love of a man for a woman, a mother for a child, a son for a mother, a botanist for plants, an ecologist for the Earth.

14

In his sleep, Nathan Stack talked.
"Why did you pick me? Why me . . ."

15

Like the Earth, the mother was in pain.
The great house was very quiet. The doctor had left, and the relatives had gone into town for dinner. He sat by the side of

her bed and stared down at her. She looked gray and old and crumpled: her skin was a soft ashy hue of moth-dust. He was crying softly.

He felt her hand on his knee, and looked up to see her staring at him. "You weren't supposed to catch me," he said.

"I'd be disappointed if I hadn't," she said. Her voice was very thin, very smooth.

"How is it?"

"It hurts. Ben didn't dope me too well."

He bit his lower lip. The doctor had used massive doses, but the pain was more massive. She gave little starts as tremors of sudden agony hit her. Impacts. He watched the life leaking out of her eyes.

"How is your sister taking it?"

He shrugged. "You know Charlene. She's sorry, but it's all pretty intellectual to her."

His mother let a tiny ripple of a smile move her lips. "It's a terrible thing to say, Nathan, but your sister isn't the most likable woman in the world. I'm glad you're here." She paused, thinking, then added, "It's just possible your father and I missed something from the gene pool. Charlene isn't whole."

"Can I get you something? A drink of water?"

"No, I'm fine."

He looked at the ampoule of narcotic pain killer. The syringe lay mechanical and still on a clean towel beside it. He felt her eyes on him. She knew what he was thinking. He looked away.

"I would kill for a cigarette," she said.

He laughed. At sixty-five, both legs gone, what remained of her left side paralyzed, the cancer spreading like deadly jelly toward her heart, she was still the matriarch. "You can't have a cigarette, so forget it."

"Then why don't you use that hypo and let me out of here."

"Shut up, Mother."

"Oh, for Christ's sake, Nathan. It's hours if I'm lucky. Months if I'm not. We've had this conversation before. You know I always win."

"Did I ever tell you you were a bitchy old lady?"

"Many times, but I love you anyhow."

He got up and walked to the wall. He could not walk through it, so he went around the inside of the room.

"You can't get away from it."

"Mother, Jesus! Please!"

"All right. Let's talk about the business."

"I could care less about the business right now."

"Then what should we talk about? The lofty uses to which an old lady can put her last moments?"

"You know, you're really ghoulish. I think you're enjoying this in some sick way."

"What other way is there to enjoy it."

"An adventure."

"The biggest. A pity your father never had the chance to savor it."

"I hardly think he'd have savored the feeling of being stamped to death in a hydraulic press."

Then he thought about it, because that little smile was on her lips again. "Okay, he probably would have. The two of you were so unreal, you'd have sat there and discussed it and analyzed the pulp."

"And you're our son."

He was, and he was. And he could not deny it, nor had he ever. He was hard and gentle and wild just like them, and he remembered the days in the jungle beyond Brasilia, and the hunt in the Cayman Trench, and the other days working in the mills alongside his father, and he knew when his moment came he would savor death as she did.

"Tell me something, I've always wanted to know. Did Dad kill Tom Golden?"

"Use the needle and I'll tell you."

"I'm a Stack. I don't bribe."

"I'm a Stack, and I know what a killing curiosity you've got. Use the needle and I'll tell you."

He walked widdershins around the room. She watched him, eyes bright as the mill vats.

"You old bitch."

"Shame, Nathan. You know you're not the son of a bitch. Which is more than your sister can say. Did I ever tell you she wasn't your father's child?"

"No, but I knew."

"You'd have liked her father. He was Swedish. Your father liked him."

"Is that why Dad broke both his arms?"

"Probably. But I never heard the Swede complain. One

night in bed with me in those days was worth a couple of broken arms. Use the needle."

Finally, while the family was between the entree and the dessert, he filled the syringe and injected her. Her eyes widened as the stuff smacked her heart, and just before she died she rallied all her strength and said, "A deal's a deal. Your father didn't kill Tom Golden, I did. You're a hell of a man, Nathan, and you fought us the way we wanted, and we both loved you more than you could know. Except, dammit, you cunning s.o.b., you do know, don't you?"

"I know," he said, and she died; and he cried; and that was the extent of the poetry in it.

16

He knows we are coming.

They were climbing the northern face of the onyx mountain. Snake had coated Nathan Stack's feet with the thick glue and, though it was hardly a country walk, he was able to keep a foothold and pull himself up. Now they had paused to rest on a spiral ledge, and Snake had spoken for the first time of what waited for them where they were going.

"He?"

Snake did not answer. Stack slumped against the wall of the ledge. At the lower slopes of the mountain they had encountered slug-like creatures that had tried to attach themselves to Stack's flesh, but when Snake had driven them off they had returned to sucking the rocks. They had not come near the shadow creature. Further up, Stack could see the lights that flickered at the summit; he had felt fear that crawled up from his stomach. A short time before they had come to this ledge they had stumbled past a cave in the mountain where the bat creatures slept. They had gone mad at the presence of the man and the Snake and the sounds they had made sent waves of nausea through Stack. Snake had helped him and they had gotten past. Now they had stopped and Snake would not answer Stack's questions.

We must keep climbing.

"Because he knows we're here." There was a sarcastic rise in Stack's voice.

Snake started moving. Stack closed his eyes. Snake stopped and came back to him. Stack looked up at the one-eyed shadow.

"Not another step."

There is no reason why you should not know.

"Except, friend, I have the feeling you aren't going to tell me anything."

It is not yet time for you to know.

"Look: just because I haven't asked, doesn't mean I don't want to know. You've told me things I shouldn't be able to handle . . . all kinds of crazy things . . . I'm as old as, as . . . I don't know *how* old, but I get the feeling you've been trying to tell me I'm Adam . . ."

That is so.

". . . uh." He stopped rattling and stared back at the shadow creature. Then, very softly, accepting even more than he had thought possible, he said, "Snake." He was silent again. After a time he asked, "Give me another dream and let me know the rest of it?"

You must be patient. The one who lives at the top knows we are coming but I have been able to keep him from perceiving your danger to him only because you do not know yourself.

"Tell me this, then: does he *want* us to come up . . . the one on the top?"

He allows it. Because he doesn't know.

Stack nodded, resigned to following Snake's lead. He got to his feet and performed an elaborate butler's motion, after you, Snake.

And Snake turned, his flat hands sticking to the wall of the ledge, and they climbed higher, spiraling upward toward the summit.

The Deathbird swooped, then rose toward the Moon. There was still time.

17

Dira came to Nathan Stack near sunset, appearing in the board room of the industrial consortium Stack had built from the family empire.

Stack sat in the pneumatic chair that dominated the conversation pit where top-level decisions were made. He was alone. The others had left hours before and the room was dim with only the barest glow of light from hidden banks that shone through the soft walls.

The shadow creature passed through the walls—and at his passage they became rose quartz, then returned to what they had been. He stood staring at Nathan Stack, and for long moments the man was unaware of any other presence in the room.

You have to go now, Snake said.

Stack looked up, his eyes widened in horror, and through his mind flitted the unmistakable image of Satan, fanged mouth smiling, horns gleaming with scintillas of light as though seen through crosstar filters, rope tail with its spade-shaped pointed tip thrashing, large cloven hoofs leaving burning imprints in the carpet, eyes as deep as pools of oil, the pitchfork, the satin-lined cape, the hairy legs of a goat, talons. He tried to scream but the sound dammed up in his throat.

No, Snake said, *that is not so. Come with me, and you will understand.*

There was a tone of sadness in the voice. As though Satan had been sorely wronged. Stack shook his head violently.

There was no time for argument. The moment had come, and Dira could not hesitate. He gestured and Nathan Stack rose from the pneumatic chair, leaving behind something that looked like Nathan Stack asleep, and he walked to Dira and Snake took him by the hand and they passed through rose quartz and went away from there.

Down and down Snake took him.

The Mother was in pain. She had been sick for eons, but it had reached the point where Snake knew it would be terminal, and the Mother knew it, too. But she would hide her child, she would intercede in her own behalf and hide him away deep in her bosom where no one, not even the mad one, could find him.

Dira took Stack to Hell.

It was a fine place.

Warm and safe and far from the probing of mad ones.

And the sickness raged on unchecked. Nations crumbled, the oceans boiled and then grew cold and filmed over with scum, the air became thick with dust and killing vapors, flesh ran like oil, the skies grew dark, the sun blurred and became dull. The Earth moaned.

The plants suffered and consumed themselves, beasts became crippled and went mad, trees burst into flame and from their ashes rose glass shapes that shattered in the wind. The Earth was dying; a long, slow, painful death.

In the center of the Earth, in the fine place, Nathan Stack slept. *Don't leave me with strangers.*

Overhead, far away against the stars, the Deathbird circled and circled, waiting for the word.

18

When they reached the highest peak, Nathan Stack looked across through the terrible burning cold and the ferocious grittiness of the demon wind and saw the sanctuary of always, the cathedral of forever, the pillar of remembrance, the haven of perfection, the pyramid of blessings, the toyshop of creation, the vault of deliverance, the monument of longing, the receptacle of thoughts, the maze of wonder, the catafalque of despair, the podium of pronouncements and the kiln of last attempts.

On a slope that rose to a star pinnacle, he saw the home of the one who dwelled here—lights flashing and flickering, lights that could be seen far off across the deserted face of the planet—and he began to suspect the name of the resident.

Suddenly everything went red for Nathan Stack. As

though a filter had been dropped over his eyes, the black sky, the flickering lights, the rocks that formed the great plateau on which they stood, even Snake became red, and with the color came pain. Terrible pain that burned through every channel of Stack's body, as though his blood had been set afire. He screamed and fell to his knees, the pain crackling through his brain, following every nerve and blood vessel and ganglia and neural track. His skull flamed.

Fight him, Snake said. *Fight him!*

I can't, screamed silently through Stack's mind, the pain too great even to speak. Fire licked and leaped and he felt the delicate tissues of thought shriveling. He tried to focus his thoughts on ice. He clutched for salvation at ice, chunks of ice, mountains of ice, swimming icebergs of ice half-buried in frozen water, even as his soul smoked and smoldered. *Ice!* He thought of millions of particles of hail rushing, falling, thundering against the firestorm eating his mind, and there was a spit of steam, a flame that went out, a corner that grew cool . . . and he took his stand in that corner, thinking ice, thinking blocks and chunks and monuments of ice, edging them out to widen the circle of coolness and safety. Then the flames began to retreat, to slide back down the channels, and he sent ice after them, snuffing them, burying them in ice and chill waters.

When he opened his eyes, he was still on his knees, but he could think again, and the red surfaces had become normal again.

He will try again. You must be ready.

"Tell me *everything!* I can't go through this without knowing, I need help!"

You can help yourself. You have the strength. I gave you the spark.

. . . and the second derangement struck!

The air turned shaverasse and he held dripping chunks of unclean rova in his jowls, the taste making him weak with nausea. His pods withered and drew up into his shell and as the bones cracked he howled with strings of pain that came so fast they were almost one. He tried to scuttle away, but his eyes magnified the shatter of light that beat

against him. Facets of his eyes cracked and the juice began
to bubble out. The pain was unbelievable.

Fight him!

Stack rolled onto his back, sending out cilia to touch the
earth, and for an instant he realized he was seeing through
the eyes of another creature, another form of life he could
not even describe. But he was under an open sky and that
produced fear, he was surrounded by air that had become
deadly and *that* produced fear, he was going blind and *that*
produced fear, he was . . . he was a *man* . . . he fought
back against the feeling of being some other thing . . . he
was a *man* and he would not feel fear, he would stand.

He rolled over, withdrew his cilia, and struggled to lower
his pods. Broken bones grated and pain thundered through
his body. He forced himself to ignore it, and finally the
pods were down and he was breathing and he felt his head
reeling . . .

And when he opened his eyes he was Nathan Stack
again.

. . . and the third derangement struck:

Hopelessness.

Out of unending misery he came back to be Stack.

. . . and the fourth derangement struck:

Madness.

Out of raging lunacy he fought his way to be Stack.

. . . and the fifth derangement, and the sixth, and the
seventh, and the plagues, and the whirlwinds, and the pools
of evil, and the reduction in size and accompanying fall
forever through sub-microscopic hells, and the things that
fed on him from inside, and the twentieth, and the fortieth,
and the sound of his voice screaming for release, and the
voice of Snake always beside him, whispering *Fight him!*

Finally it stopped.

Quickly, now.

Snake took Stack by the hand and half-dragging him
they raced to the great palace of light and glass on the
slope, shining brightly under the star pinnacle, and they
passed under an arch of shining metal into the ascension
hall. The portal sealed behind them.

There were tremors in the walls. The inlaid floors of jewels began to rumble and tremble. Bits of high and faraway ceilings began to drop. Quaking, the palace gave one hideous shudder and collapsed around them.

Now, Snake said. *Now you will know everything!*

And everything forgot to fall. Frozen in mid-air, the wreckage of the palace hung suspended above them. Even the air ceased to swirl. Time stood still. The movement of the Earth was halted. Everything held utterly immobile as Nathan Stack was permitted to understand all.

19

Multiple Choice (Counts for ½ your final grade.)

1. **God is:**

    A. **An invisible spirit with a long beard.**
    B. **A small dog dead in a hole.**
    C. **Everyman.**
    D. **The Wizard of Oz.**

2. **Nietzsche wrote "God is dead." By this did he mean:**

    A. **Life is pointless.**
    B. **Belief in supreme deities has waned.**
    C. **There never was a God to begin with.**
    D. **Thou art God.**

3. **Ecology is another name for:**

    A. **Mother love.**
    B. **Enlightened self-interest.**
    C. **A good health salad with Granola.**
    D. **God.**

4. **Which of these phrases most typifies the profoundest love:**

    A. **Don't leave me with strangers.**
    B. **I love you.**

C. God is love.
D. Use the needle.

5. Which of these powers do we usually associate with God:

A. Power.
B. Love.
C. Humanity.
D. Docility.

20

None of the above.

Starlight shone in the eyes of the Deathbird and its passage through the night cast a shadow on the Moon.

21

Nathan Stack raised his hands and around them the air was still as the palace fell crashing. They were untouched. *Now you know all there is to know,* Snake said, sinking to one knee as though worshipping. There was no one there to worship but Nathan Stack.

"Was he always mad?"

From the first.

"Then those who gave our world to him were mad, and your race was mad to allow it."

Snake had no answer.

"Perhaps it was supposed to be like this," Stack said.

He reached down and lifted Snake to his feet, and he touched the shadow creature's head. "Friend," he said.

Snake's race was incapable of tears. He said, *I have waited longer than you can know for that word.*

"I'm sorry it comes at the end."

Perhaps it was supposed to be like this.

Then there was a swirling of air, a scintillance in the

ruined palace, and the owner of the mountain, the owner of the ruined Earth came to them in a burning bush.

AGAIN, SNAKE? AGAIN YOU ANNOY ME?

The time for toys is ended.

NATHAN STACK YOU BRING TO STOP ME? *I* SAY WHEN THE TIME IS ENDED. *I* SAY, AS I'VE ALWAYS SAID.

Then, to Nathan Stack:

GO AWAY. FIND A PLACE TO HIDE UNTIL I COME FOR YOU.

Stack ignored the burning bush. He waved his hand and the cone of safety in which they stood vanished. "Let's find him, first, then I know what to do."

The Deathbird sharpened its talons on the night wind and sailed down through emptiness toward the cinder of the Earth.

22

Nathan Stack had once contracted pneumonia. He had lain on the operating table as the surgeon made the small incision in the chest wall. Had he not been stubborn, had he not continued working around the clock while the pneumonic infection developed into empyema, he would never have had to go under the knife, even for an operation as safe as a thoractomy. But he was a Stack, and so he lay on the operating table as the rubber tube was inserted into the chest cavity to drain off the pus in the pleural cavity, and heard someone speak his name.

NATHAN STACK.

He heard it, from far off, across an Arctic vastness; heard it echoing over and over, down an endless corridor; as the knife sliced.

NATHAN STACK.

He remembered Lilith, with hair the color of dark wine. He remembered taking hours to die beneath a rock slide as his hunting companions in the pack ripped apart the remains of the bear and ignored his grunted moans for help.

He remembered the impact of the crossbow bolt as it ripped through his hauberk and split his chest and he died at Agincourt. He remembered the icy water of the Ohio as it closed over his head and the flatboat disappearing without his mates noticing his loss. He remembered the mustard gas that ate his lungs and trying to crawl toward a farmhouse near Verdun. He remembered looking directly into the flash of the bomb and feeling the flesh of his face melt away. He remembered Snake coming to him in the board room and husking him like corn from his body. He remembered sleeping in the molten core of the Earth for a quarter of a million years.

Across the dead centuries he heard his mother pleading with him to set her free, to end her pain. *Use the needle.* Her voice mingled with the voice of the Earth crying out in endless pain at her flesh that had been ripped away, at her rivers turned to arteries of dust, at her rolling hills and green fields slagged to greenglass and ashes. The voices of his mother and the mother that was Earth became one, and mingled to become Snake's voice telling him he was the one man in the world—the last man in the world—who could end the terminal case the Earth had become.

Use the needle. Put the suffering Earth out of its misery. *It belongs to you now.*

Nathan Stack was secure in the power he contained. A power that far outstripped that of gods or Snakes or mad creators who stuck pins in their creations, who broke their toys.

YOU CAN'T. I WON'T LET YOU.

Nathan Stack walked around the burning bush crackling impotently in rage. He looked at it almost pityingly, remembering the Wizard of Oz with his great and ominous disembodied head floating in mist and lightning, and the poor little man behind the curtain turning the dials to create the effects. Stack walked around the effect, knowing he had more power than this sad, poor thing that had held his race in thrall since before Lilith had been taken from him.

He went in search of the mad one who capitalized his name.

23

Zarathustra descended alone from the mountains, encountering no one. But when he came into the forest, all at once there stood before him an old man who had left his holy cottage to look for roots in the woods. And thus spoke the old man to Zarathustra.

"No stranger to me is this wanderer: many years ago he passed this way. Zarathustra he was called, but he has changed. At that time you carried your ashes to the mountains; would you now carry your fire into the valleys? Do you not fear to be punished as an arsonist?

"Zarathustra has changed, Zarathustra has become a child, Zarathustra is an awakened one; what do you now want among the sleepers? You lived in your solitude as in the sea, and the sea carried you. Alas, would you now climb ashore? Alas, would you again drag your own body?"

Zarathustra answered: "I love man."

"Why," asked the saint, "did I go into the forest and the desert? Was it not because I loved man all-too-much? Now I love God; man I love not. Man is for me too imperfect a thing. Love of man would kill me."

"And what is the saint doing in the forest?" asked Zarathustra.

The saint answered: "I make songs and sing them; and when I make songs, I laugh, cry, and hum: thus I praise God. With singing, crying, laughing, and humming, I praise the god who is my god. But what do you bring us as a gift?"

When Zarathustra had heard these words he bade the saint farewell and said: "What could I have to give you? But let me go quickly lest I take something from you!" And thus they separated, the old one and the man, laughing as two boys laugh.

But when Zarathustra was alone he spoke thus to his heart: "Could it be possible? This old saint in the forest had not yet heard anything of this, that *God is dead!*"

24

Stack found the mad one wandering in the forest of final moments. He was an old, tired man, and Stack knew with a wave of his hand he could end it for this god in a moment. But what was the reason for it? It was even too late for revenge. It had been too late from the start. So he let the old one go his way, wandering in the forest mumbling to himself, I WON'T LET YOU DO IT, in the voice of a cranky child; mumbling pathetically, OH, PLEASE, I DON'T WANT TO GO TO BED YET. I'M NOT YET DONE PLAYING.

And Stack came back to Snake, who had served his function and protected Stack until Stack had learned that he was more powerful than the God he'd worshipped all through the history of men. He came back to Snake and their hands touched and the bond of friendship was sealed at last, at the end.

Then they worked together and Nathan Stack used the needle with a wave of his hands, and the Earth could not sigh with relief as its endless pain was ended . . . but it did sigh, and it settled in upon itself, and the molten core went out, and the winds died, and from high above them Stack heard the fulfillment of Snake's final act; he heard the descent of the Deathbird.

"What was your name?" Stack asked his friend.

Dira.

And the Deathbird settled down across the tired shape of the Earth, and it spread its wings wide, and brought them over and down, and enfolded the Earth as a mother enfolds her weary child. Dira settled down on the amethyst floor of the dark-shrouded palace, and closed his single eye with gratitude. To sleep at last, at the end.

All this, as Nathan Stack stood watching. He was the last, at the end, and because he had come to own—if even for a few moments—that which could have been his from the start, had he but known, he did not sleep but stood and watched. Knowing at last, at the end, that he had loved and done no wrong.

25

The Deathbird closed its wings over the Earth until at last, at the end, there was only the great bird crouched over the dead cinder. Then the Deathbird raised its head to the star-filled sky and repeated the sigh of loss the Earth had felt at the end. Then its eyes closed, it tucked its head carefully under its wing, and all was night.

Far away, the stars waited for the cry of the Deathbird to reach them so final moments could be observed at last, at the end, for the race of men.

26

THIS IS FOR MARK TWAIN

Of Mist,
and Grass,
and Sand

Vonda N. McIntyre

Vonda N. McIntyre, one of sf's better new
writers, gives us here another character named
Snake, and again (not entirely coincidentally)
this Snake is a force for good who is feared.
The setting may be another planet, a far-future Earth, or perhaps an alternate time-
stream, but the story is clearly about the problems of scientific knowledge—and the kind of
person who must use such knowledge.

The little boy was frightened. Gently, Snake touched his
hot forehead. Behind her, three adults stood close together,
watching, suspicious, afraid to show their concern with
more than narrow lines around their eyes. They feared
Snake as much as they feared their only child's death. In
the dimness of the tent, the flickering lamplights gave no
reassurance.

The child watched with eyes so dark the pupils were not visible, so dull that Snake herself feared for his life. She stroked his hair. It was long and very pale, a striking color against his dark skin, dry and irregular for several inches near the scalp. Had Snake been with these people months ago, she would have known the child was growing ill.

"Bring my case, please," Snake said.

The child's parents started at her soft voice. Perhaps they had expected the screech of a bright jay, or the hissing of a shining serpent. This was the first time Snake had spoken in their presence. She had only watched, when the three of them had come to observe her from a distance and whisper about her occupation and her youth; she had only listened, and then nodded, when finally they came to ask her help. Perhaps they had thought she was mute.

The fair-haired younger man lifted her leather case. He held the satchel away from his body, leaning to hand it to her, breathing shallowly with nostrils flared against the faint smell of musk in the dry desert air. Snake had almost accustomed herself to the kind of uneasiness he showed; she had already seen it often.

When Snake reached out, the young man jerked back and dropped the case. Snake lunged and barely caught it, gently set it on the felt floor, and glanced at him with reproach. His husband and his wife came forward and touched him to ease his fear. "He was bitten once," the dark and handsome woman said. "He almost died." Her tone was not of apology, but of justification.

"I'm sorry," the younger man said. "It's—" He gestured toward her; he was trembling, and trying visibly to control the reactions of his fear. Snake glanced down, to her shoulder, where she had been unconsciously aware of the slight weight and movement. A tiny serpent, thin as the finger of a baby, slid himself around her neck to show his narrow head below her short black curls. He probed the air with his trident tongue in a leisurely manner, out, up and down, in, to savor the taste of the smells. "It's only Grass," Snake said. "He cannot harm you." If he were bigger, he might frighten; his color was pale green, but the scales around his mouth were red, as if he had just feasted as a mammal eats, by tearing. He was, in fact, much neater.

The child whimpered. He cut off the sound of pain; perhaps he had been told that Snake, too, would be offended by crying. She only felt sorry that his people refused themselves such a simple way of easing fear. She turned from the adults, regretting their terror of her but unwilling to spend the time it would take to convince them their reactions were unjustified. "It's all right," she said to the little boy. "Grass is smooth, and dry, and soft, and if I left him to guard you, even death could not reach your bedside." Grass poured himself into her narrow, dirty hand, and she extended him toward the child. "Gently." He reached out and touched the sleek scales with one fingertip. Snake could sense the effort of even such a simple motion, yet the boy almost smiled.

"What are you called?"

He looked quickly toward his parents, and finally they nodded. "Stavin," he whispered. He had no strength or breath for speaking.

"I am Snake, Stavin, and in a little while, in the morning, I must hurt you. You may feel a quick pain, and your body will ache for several days, but you will be better afterwards."

He stared at her solemnly. Snake saw that though he understood and feared what she might do, he was less afraid than if she had lied to him. The pain must have increased greatly as his illness became more apparent, but it seemed that others had only reassured him, and hoped the disease would disappear or kill him quickly.

Snake put Grass on the boy's pillow and pulled her case nearer. The lock opened at her touch. The adults still could only fear her; they had had neither time nor reason to discover any trust. The wife was old enough that they might never have another child, and Snake could tell by their eyes, their covert touching, their concern, that they loved this one very much. They must, to come to Snake in this country.

It was night, and cooling. Sluggish, Sand slid out of the

case, moving his head, moving his tongue, smelling, tasting, detecting the warmths of bodies.

"Is that——?" The older husband's voice was low, and wise, but terrified, and Sand sensed the fear. He drew back into striking position and sounded his rattle softly. Snake spoke, moving her hand, and extended her arm. The pit viper relaxed and flowed around and around her slender wrist to form black and tan bracelets. "No," she said. "Your child is too ill for Sand to help. I know it is hard, but please try to be calm. This is a fearful thing for you, but it is all I can do."

She had to annoy Mist to make her come out. Snake rapped on the bag, and finally poked her twice. Snake felt the vibration of sliding scales, and suddenly the albino cobra flung herself into the tent. She moved quickly, yet there seemed to be no end to her. She reared back and up. Her breath rushed out in a hiss. Her head rose well over a meter above the floor. She flared her wide hood. Behind her, the adults gasped, as if physically assaulted by the gaze of the tan spectacle design on the back of Mist's hood. Snake ignored the people and spoke to the great cobra, focusing her attention by her words. "Ah, thou. Furious creature. Lie down; 'tis time for thee to earn thy dinner. Speak to this child, and touch him. He is called Stavin." Slowly, Mist relaxed her hood and allowed Snake to touch her. Snake grasped her firmly behind the head, and held her so she looked at Stavin. The cobra's silver eyes picked up the yellow of the lamplight. "Stavin," Snake said, "Mist will only meet you now. I promise that this time she will touch you gently."

Still, Stavin shivered when Mist touched his thin chest. Snake did not release the serpent's head, but allowed her body to slide against the boy's. The cobra was four times longer than Stavin was tall. She curved herself in stark white loops across his swollen abdomen, extending herself, forcing her head toward the boy's face, straining against Snake's hands. Mist met Stavin's frightened stare with the gaze of lidless eyes. Snake allowed her a little closer.

Mist flicked out her tongue to taste the child.

The younger husband made a small, cut-off, frightened sound. Stavin flinched at it, and Mist drew back, opening her mouth, exposing her fangs, audibly thrusting her breath through her throat. Snake sat back on her heels, letting out her own breath. Sometimes, in other places, the kinfolk could stay while she worked. "You must leave," she said gently. "It's dangerous to frighten Mist."

"I won't—"

"I'm sorry. You must wait outside."

Perhaps the younger husband, perhaps even the wife, would have made the indefensible objections and asked the answerable questions, but the older man turned them and took their hands and led them away.

"I need a small animal," Snake said as he lifted the tent flap. "It must have fur, and it must be alive."

"One will be found," he said, and the three parents went into the glowing night. Snake could hear their footsteps in the sand outside.

Snake supported Mist in her lap and soothed her. The cobra wrapped herself around Snake's narrow waist, taking in her warmth. Hunger made the cobra even more nervous than usual, and she was hungry, as was Snake. Coming across the black sand desert, they had found sufficient water, but Snake's traps were unsuccessful. The season was summer, the weather was hot, and many of the furry tidbits Sand and Mist preferred were estivating. When the serpents missed their regular meal, Snake began a fast as well.

She saw with regret that Stavin was more frightened now. "I am sorry to send your parents away," she said. "They can come back soon."

His eyes glistened, but he held back the tears. "They said to do what you told me."

"I would have you cry, if you are able," Snake said. "It isn't such a terrible thing." But Stavin seemed not to understand, and Snake did not press him; she knew that his people taught themselves to resist a difficult land by refusing to cry, refusing to mourn, refusing to laugh. They denied themselves grief, and allowed themselves little joy, but they survived.

Mist had calmed to sullenness. Snake unwrapped her from her waist and placed her on the pallet next to Stavin. As the cobra moved, Snake guided her head, feeling the tension of the striking muscles. "She will touch you with her tongue," she told Stavin. "It might tickle, but it will not hurt. She smells with it, as you do with your nose."

"With her tongue?"

Snake nodded, smiling, and Mist flicked out her tongue to caress Stavin's cheek. Stavin did not flinch; he watched, his child's delight in knowledge briefly overcoming pain. He lay perfectly still as Mist's long tongue brushed his cheeks, his eyes, his mouth. "She tastes the sickness," Snake said. Mist stopped fighting the restraint of her grasp, and drew back her head. Snake sat on her heels and released the cobra, who spiraled up her arm and laid herself across her shoulders.

"Go to sleep, Stavin," Snake said. "Try to trust me, and try not to fear the morning."

Stavin gazed at her for a few seconds, searching for truth in Snake's pale eyes. "Will Grass watch?"

She was startled by the question, or, rather, by the acceptance behind the question. She brushed his hair from his forehead and smiled a smile that was tears just beneath the surface. "Of course." She picked Grass up. "Thou wilt watch this child, and guard him." The snake lay quiet in her hand, and his eyes glittered black. She laid him gently on Stavin's pillow.

"Now sleep."

Stavin closed his eyes, and the life seemed to flow out of him. The alteration was so great that Snake reached out to touch him, then saw that he was breathing, slowly, shallowly. She tucked a blanket around him and stood up. The abrupt change in position dizzied her; she staggered and caught herself. Across her shoulders, Mist tensed.

Snake's eyes stung and her vision was over-sharp, fever-clear. The sound she imagined she heard swooped in closer. She steadied herself against hunger and exhaustion, bent slowly, and picked up the leather case. Mist touched her cheek with the tip of her tongue.

She pushed aside the tent-flap and felt relief that it was still night. She could stand the heat, but the brightness of the sun curled through her, burning. The moon must be full; though the clouds obscured everything, they diffused the light so the sky appeared gray from horizon to horizon. Beyond the tents, groups of formless shadows projected from the ground. Here, near the edge of the desert, enough water existed so clumps and patches of bush grew, providing shelter and sustenance for all manner of creatures. The black sand, which sparkled and blinded in the sunlight, at night was like a layer of soft soot. Snake stepped out of the tent, and the illusion of softness disappeared; her boots slid crunching into the sharp hard grains.

Stavin's family waited, sitting close together between the dark tents that clustered in a patch of sand from which the bushes had been ripped and burned. They looked at her silently, hoping with their eyes, showing no expression in their faces. A woman somewhat younger than Stavin's mother sat with them. She was dressed, as they were, in a long loose robe, but she wore the only adornment Snake had seen among these people: a leader's circle, hanging around her neck on a leather thong. She and the older husband were marked close kin by their similarities: sharp-cut planes of face, high cheekbones, his hair white and hers graying early from deep black, their eyes the dark brown best suited for survival in the sun. On the ground by their feet a small black animal jerked sporadically against a net, and infrequently gave a shrill weak cry.

"Stavin is asleep," Snake said. "Do not disturb him, but go to him if he wakes."

The wife and young husband rose and went inside, but the older man stopped before her. "Can you help him?"

"I hope we may. The tumor is advanced, but it seems solid." Her own voice sounded removed, slighly hollow, as if she were lying. "Mist will be ready in the morning." She still felt the need to give him reassurance, but she could think of none.

"My sister wished to speak with you," he said, and left them alone, without introduction, without elevating himself by saying that the tall woman was the leader of this group. Snake glanced back. but the tent-flap fell shut. She was feeling her exhaustion more deeply, and across her shoulders Mist was, for the first time, a weight she thought heavy.

"Are you all right?"

Snake turned. The woman moved toward her with a natural elegance made slightly awkward by advanced pregnancy. Snake had to look up to meet her gaze. She had small fine lines at the corners of her eyes, as if she laughed, sometimes, in secret. She smiled. but with concern. "You seem very tired. Shall I have someone make you a bed?"

"Not now," Snake said, "not yet. I won't sleep until afterward."

The leader searched her face, and Snake felt a kinship with her in their shared responsibility.

"I understand. I think. Is there anything we can give you? Do you need aid with your preparations?"

Snake found herself having to deal with the questions as if they were complex problems. She turned them in her tired mind, examined them. dissected them, and finally grasped their meanings. "My pony needs food and water—"

"It is taken care of."

"And I need someone to help me with Mist. Someone strong. But it's more important that they aren't afraid."

The leader nodded. "I would help you," she said. and smiled again, a little. "But I am a bit clumsy of late. I will find someone."

"Thank you."

Somber again. the older woman inclined her head and moved slowly toward a small group of tents. Snake watched her go, admiring her grace. She felt small and young and grubby in comparison.

Sand began to unwrap himself from her wrist. Feeling the anticipatory slide of scales on her skin. she caught him before he could drop to the ground. Sand lifted the upper half of his body from her hands. He flicked out his tongue, peering toward the little animal, feeling its body heat, smelling its fear. "I know thou art hungry," Snake said, "but that creature is not for thee." She put Sand in the case, lifted Mist from her shoulder, and let her coil herself in her dark compartment.

The small animal shrieked and struggled again when Snake's diffuse shadow passed over it. She bent and picked it up. The rapid series of terrified cries slowed and diminished and finally stopped as she stroked it. Finally it lay still, breathing hard, exhausted, staring up at her with yellow eyes. It had long hind legs and wide pointed ears, and its nose twitched at the serpent smell. Its soft black fur was marked off in skewed squares by the cords of the net.

"I am sorry to take your life," Snake told it. "But there will be no more fear, and I will not hurt you." She closed her hand gently around it and, stroking it, grasped its spine at the base of its skull. She pulled. once, quickly. It seemed to struggle, briefly, but it was already dead. It convulsed; its legs drew up against its body, and its toes curled and quivered. It seemed to stare up at her, even now. She freed its body from the net.

Snake chose a small vial from her belt pouch, pried open the animal's clenched jaws, and let a single drop of the vial's cloudy preparation fall into its mouth. Quickly she opened the satchel again and called Mist out. The cobra came slowly, slipping over the edge, hood closed, sliding in the sharp-grained sand. Her milky scales caught the thin light. She smelled the animal, flowed to it, touched it with her tongue. For a moment Snake was afraid she would refuse dead meat, but the body was still warm, still twitching reflexively, and she was very hungry. "A tidbit for thee," Snake spoke to the cobra: a habit of solitude. "To whet thy appetite." Mist nosed the beast, reared back, and struck, sinking her short fixed fings into the tiny body, biting again, pumping out her store of poison. She released it, took a better grip, and began to work her jaws around it; it would hardly distend her throat. When Mist lay quiet, digesting the small meal, Snake sat beside her and held her, waiting.

She heard footsteps in the coarse sand.

"I'm sent to help you."

He was a young man, despite a scatter of white in his black hair. He was taller than Snake, and not unattractive. His eyes were dark, and the sharp planes of his face were further hardened because his hair was pulled straight back and tied. His expression was neutral.

"Are you afraid?

"I will do as you tell me."

Though his form was obscured by his robe, his long fine hands showed strength.

"Then hold her body, and don't let her surprise you." Mist was beginning to twitch from the effects of the drugs Snake had put in the small animal. The cobra's eyes stared, unseeing.

"If it bites—"

"Hold, quickly!"

The young man reached, but he had hestitated too long. Mist writhed, lashing out, striking him in the face with her tail. He staggered back, at least as surprised as hurt. Snake kept a close grip behind Mist's jaws, and struggled to catch the rest of her as well. Mist was no constrictor, but she was smooth and strong and fast. Thrashing, she forced out her breath in a long hiss. She would have bitten anything she could reach. As Snake fought with her, she managed to squeeze the posison glands and force out the last drops of venom. They hung from Mist's fangs for a moment, catching light as jewels would; the force of the serpent's convulsions flung them away into the darkness. Snake struggled with the cobra, aided for once by the sand, on which Mist could get no purchase. Snake felt the young man behind her, grabbing for Mist's body and tail. The seizure stopped abruptly, and Mist lay limp in their hands.

"I am sorry—"

"Hold her," Snake said. "We have the night to go."

During Mist's second convulsion, the young man held her firmly and was of some real help. Afterward, Snake answered his interrupted question. "If she were making poison and she bit you, you would probably die. Even now her bite would make you ill. But unless you do something foolish. if she manages to bite. she will bite me."

"You would benefit my cousin little, if you were dead or dying."

"You misunderstand. Mist cannot kill me." She held out her hand so he could see the white scars of slashes and punctures. He stared at them. and looked into her eyes for a long moment, then looked away.

The bright spot in the clouds from which the light radiated moved westward in the sky: they held the cobra like a child. Snake found herself half-dozing. but Mist moved her head. dully attempting to evade restraint. and Snake woke herself abruptly. "I must not sleep." she said to the young man. "Talk to me. What are you called?"

As Stavin had, the young man hesitated. He seemed afraid of her. or of something. "My people," he said, "think it unwise to speak our names to strangers."

"If you consider me a witch you should not have asked my aid. I know no magic. and I claim none."

"It's not a superstition." he said. "Not as you might think. We're not afraid of being bewitched."

"I can't learn all the customs of all the people on this earth, so I keep my own. My custom is to address those I work with by name." Watching him, Snake tried to decipher his expression in the dim light.

"Our families know our names, and we exchange names with those we would marry."

Snake considered that custom. and thought it would fit badly on her. "No one else? Ever?"

"Well . . . a friend might know one's name."

"Ah," Snake said. "I see. I am still a stranger, and perhaps an enemy."

"A *friend* would know my name." the young man said again. "I would not offend you, but now you misunderstand. An acquaintance is not a friend. We value friendship highly."

"In this land one should be able to tell quickly if a person is worth calling 'friend.' "

"We take friends seldom. Friendship is a great commitment."

"It sounds like something to be feared."

He considered that possibility. "Perhaps it's the betrayal of friendship we fear. That is a very painful thing."

"Has anyone ever betrayed you?"

He glanced at her sharply, as if she had exceeded the limits of propriety. "No," he said, and his voice was as hard as his face. "No friend. I have no one I call friend."

His reaction startled Snake. "That's very sad," she said, and grew silent, trying to comprehend the deep stresses that could close people off so far, comparing her loneliness of necessity and theirs of choice. "Call me Snake," she said finally, "if you can bring yourself to pronounce it. Saying my name binds you to nothing."

The young man seemed about to speak; perhaps he thought again that he had offended her, perhaps he felt he should further defend his customs. But Mist began to twist in their hands, and they had to hold her to keep her from injuring herself. The cobra was slender for her length, but powerful, and the convulsions she went through were more severe than any she had ever had before. She thrashed in Snake's grasp, and almost pulled away. She tried to spread her hood, but Snake held her too tightly. She opened her mouth and hissed, but no poison dripped from her fangs.

She wrapped her tail around the young man's waist. He began to pull her and turn, to extricate himself from her coils.

"She's not a constrictor," Snake said. "She won't hurt you. Leave her—"

But it was too late; Mist relaxed suddenly and the young man lost his balance. Mist whipped herself away and lashed figures in the sand. Snake wrestled with her alone while the young man tried to hold her, but she curled herself around Snake and used the grip for leverage. She started to pull herself from Snake's hands. Snake threw them both backward into the sand; Mist rose above her, open-mouthed, furious, hissing. The young man lunged and grabbed her just beneath her hood. Mist struck at him, but

Snake, somehow, held her back. Together they deprived Mist of her hold and regained control of her. Snake struggled up, but Mist suddenly went quite still and lay almost rigid between them. They were both sweating; the young man was pale under his tan, and even Snake was trembling.

"We have a little while to rest," Snake said. She glanced at him and noticed the dark line on his cheek where, earlier, Mist's tail had slashed him. She reached up and touched it. "You'll have a bruise," she said. "But it will not scar."

"If it were true, that serpents sting with their tails. you would be restraining both the fangs and the stinger, and I'd be of little use."

"Tonight I'd need someone to keep me awake, whether or not they helped me with Mist." Fighting the cobra produced adrenalin, but now it ebbed, and her exhaustion and hunger were returning, stronger.

"Snake . . ."

"Yes?"

He smiled, quickly, half-embarrassed. "I was trying the pronunciation."

"Good enough."

"How long did it take you to cross the desert?"

"Not very long. Too long. Six days."

"How did you live?"

"There is water. We traveled at night, except yesterday, when I could find no shade."

"You carried all your food?"

She shrugged. "A little." And wished he would not speak of food.

"What's on the other side?"

"More sand, more bush, a little more water. A few groups of people, traders, the station I grew up and took my training in. And farther on, a mountain with a city inside."

"I would like to see a city. Someday."

"The desert can be crossed."

He said nothing, but Snake's memories of leaving home were recent enough that she could imagine his thoughts.

The next set of convulsions came, much sooner than Snake had expected. By their severity she gauged something of the stage of Stavin's illness, and wished it were morning. If she were to lose him, she would have it done, and grieve, and try to forget. The cobra would have battered herself to death against the sand if Snake and the young man had not been holding her. She suddenly went completely rigid, with her mouth clamped shut and her forked tongue dangling.

She stopped breathing.

"Hold her," Snake said. "Hold her head. Quickly, take her, and if she gets away, run. Take her! She won't strike at you now, she could only slash you by accident."

He hesitated only a moment, then grasped Mist behind the head. Snake ran, slipping in the deep sand, from the edge of the circle of tents to a place where bushes still grew. She broke off dry thorny branches that tore her scarred hands. Peripherally she noticed a mass of horned vipers, so ugly they seemed deformed, nesting beneath the clump of desiccated vegatation. They hissed at her; she ignored them. She found a narrow hollow stem and carried it back. Her hands bled from deep scratches.

Kneeling by Mist's head, she forced open the cobra's mouth and pushed the tube deep into her throat, through the air passage at the base of Mist's tongue. She bent close, took the tube in her mouth, and breathed gently into Mist's lungs.

She noticed: the young man's hands, holding the cobra as she had asked; his breathing, first a sharp gasp of surprise, then ragged; the sand scraping her elbows where she leaned; the cloying smell of the fluid seeping from Mist's fangs; her own dizziness, she thought from exhaustion, which she forced away by necessity and will.

Snake breathed, and breathed again, paused, and repeated, until Mist caught the rhythm and continued it unaided.

Snake sat back on her heels. "I think she'll be all right," she said. "I hope she will." She brushed the back of her hand across her forehead. The touch sparked pain: she jerked her hand down and agony slid along her bones, up her arm, across her shoulder, through her chest, enveloping her heart. Her balance turned on its edge. She fell, tried to catch herself but moved too slowly, fought nausea and vertigo and almost succeeded, until the pull of the earth seemed to slip away in pain and she was lost in darkness with nothing to take a bearing by.

She felt sand where it had scraped her cheek and her palms, but it was soft. "Snake, can I let go?" She thought the question must be for someone else, while at the same time she knew there was no one else to answer it, no one else to reply to her name. She felt hands on her, and they were gentle; she wanted to respond to them, but she was too tired. She needed sleep more, so she pushed them away. But they held her head and put dry leather to her lips and poured water into her throat. She coughed and choked and spat it out.

She pushed herself up on one elbow. As her sight cleared, she realized she was shaking. She felt as she had the first time she was snake-bit, before her immunities had completely developed. The young man knelt over her, his water flask in his hand. Mist, beyond him, crawled toward the darkness. Snake forgot the throbbing pain. "Mist!" She slapped the ground.

The young man flinched and turned, frightened; the serpent reared up, her head nearly at Snake's standing eye-level, her hood spread, swaying, watching, angry, ready to strike. She formed a wavering white line against black. Snake forced herself to rise, feeling as though she were fumbling with the control of some unfamiliar body. She almost fell again, but held herself steady. "Thou must not go to hunt now," she said. "There is work for thee to do." She held out her right hand to the side, a decoy, to draw Mist if she struck. Her hand was heavy with pain. Snake feared, not being bitten, but the loss of the contents of Mist's poison sacs. "Come here," she said. "Come here, and stay thy anger." She noticed blood flowing down between her fingers, and the fear she felt for Stavin was intensified. "Didst thou bite me, creature?" But the pain was wrong: poison would numb her, and the new serum only sting . . .

"No," the young man whispered from behind her.

Mist struck. The reflexes of long training took over. Snake's right hand jerked away, her left grabbed Mist as she brought her head back. The cobra writhed a moment, and relaxed. "Devious beast," Snake said. "For shame." She turned and let Mist crawl up her arm and over her shoulder, where she lay like the outline of an invisible cape and dragged her tail like the edge of a train.

"She did not bite me?"

"No," the young man said. His contained voice was touched with awe. "You should be dying. You should be curled around the agony, and your arm swollen purple. When you came back—" He gestured toward her hand. "It must have been a bush viper."

Snake remembered the coil of reptiles beneath the branches, and touched the blood on her hand. She wiped it away, revealing the double puncture of a snakebite among the scratches of the thorns. The wound was slightly swollen. "It needs cleaning," she said. "I shame myself by falling to it." The pain of it washed in gentle waves up her arm, burning no longer. She stood looking at the young man, looking around her, watching the landscape shift and change as her tired eyes tried to cope with the low light of setting moon and false dawn. "You held Mist well, and bravely," she said to the young man. "I thank you."

He lowered his gaze, almost bowing to her. He rose, and approached her. Snake put her hand gently on Mist's neck so she would not be alarmed.

"I would be honored," the young man said, "if you would call me Arevin."

"I would be pleased to."

Snake knelt down and held the winding white loops as Mist crawled slowly into her compartment. In a little while, when Mist had stabilized, by dawn, they could go to Stavin.

The tip of Mist's white tail slid out of sight. Snake closed the case and would have risen, but she could not stand. She had not quite shaken off the effects of the new venom. The flesh around the wound was red and tender, but the hemorrhaging would not spread. She stayed where she was, slumped, staring at her hand, creeping slowly in her mind toward what she needed to do, this time for herself.

"Let me help you. Please."

He touched her shoulder and helped her stand. "I'm sorry," she said. "I'm so in need of rest . . ."

"Let me wash your hand," Arevin said. "And then you can sleep. Tell me when to awaken you—"

"I can't sleep yet." She collected herself, straightened, tossed the damp curls of her short hair off her forehead. "I'm all right now. Have you any water?"

Arevin loosened his outer robe. Beneath it he wore a loincloth and a leather belt that carried several leather flasks and pouches. His body was lean and well-built, his legs long and muscular. The color of his skin was slightly lighter than the sun-darkened brown of his face. He brought out his water flask and reached for Snake's hand.

"No, Arevin. If the poison gets in any small scratch you might have, it could infect."

She sat down and sluiced lukewarm water over her hand. The water dripped pink to the ground and disappeared, leaving not even a damp spot visible. The wound bled a little more, but now it only ached. The poison was almost inactivated.

"I don't understand," Arevin said, "how it is that you're unhurt. My younger sister was bitten by a bush viper." He could not speak as uncaringly as he might have wished. "We could do nothing to save her—nothing we have would even lessen her pain."

Snake gave him his flask and rubbed salve from a vial in her belt pouch across the closing punctures. "It's a part of our preparation," she said. "We work with many kinds of serpents, so we must be immune to as many as possible." She shrugged. "The process is tedious and somewhat painful." She clenched her fist; the film held, and she was steady. She leaned toward Arevin and touched his abraded cheek again. "Yes . . ." She spread a thin layer of the salve across it. "That will help it heal."

"If you cannot sleep," Arevin said, "can you at least rest?"

"Yes," she said. "For a little while."

Snake sat next to Arevin, leaning against him, and they watched the sun turn the clouds to gold and flame and amber. The simple physical contact with another human being gave Snake pleasure, though she found it unsatisfying. Another time, another place, she might do something more, but not here, not now.

When the lower edge of the sun's bright smear rose above the horizon, Snake rose and teased Mist out of the case. She came slowly, weakly, and crawled across Snake's shoulders. Snake picked up the satchel, and she and Arevin walked together back to the small group of tents.

Stavin's parents waited, watching for her, just outside the entrance of their tent. They stood in a tight, defensive, silent group. For a moment Snake thought they had decided to send her away. Then, with regret and fear like hot iron in her mouth, she asked if Stavin had died. They shook their heads, and allowed her to enter.

Stavin lay as she had left him, still asleep. The adults followed her with their stares, and she could smell fear. Mist flicked out her tongue, growing nervous from the implied danger.

"I know you would stay," Snake said. "I know you would help, if you could, but there is nothing to be done by any person but me. Please go back outside."

They glanced at each other, and at Arevin, and she thought for a moment that they would refuse. Snake wanted to fall into the silence and sleep. "Come, cousins," Arevin said. "We are in her hands." He opened the tent-flap and motioned them out. Snake thanked him with nothing more than a glance, and he might almost have smiled. She turned toward Stavin, and knelt beside him. "Stavin—" She touched his forehead; it was very hot. She noticed that her hand was less steady than before. The slight touch awakened the child. "It's time," Snake said.

He blinked, coming out of some child's dream, seeing

her, slowly recognizing her. He did not look frightened. For that Snake was glad; for some other reason she could not identify she was uneasy.

"Will it hurt?"

"Does it hurt now?"

He hesitated, looked away, looked back. "Yes."

"It might hurt a little more. I hope not. Are you ready?"

"Can Grass stay?"

"Of course," she said.

And realized what was wrong.

"I'll come back in a moment." Her voice changed so much, she had pulled it so tight, that she could not help but frighten him. She left the tent, walking slowly, calmly, restraining herself. Outside, the parents told her by their faces what they feared.

"Where is Grass?" Arevin, his back to her, started at her tone. The younger husband made a small grieving sound, and could look at her no longer.

"We were afraid," the older husband said. "We thought it would bite the child."

"I thought it would. It was I. It crawled over his face, I could see its fangs—" The wife put her hands on the younger husband's shoulders, and he said no more.

"Where is he?" She wanted to scream; she did not.

They brought her a small open box. Snake took it and looked inside.

Grass lay cut almost in two, his entrails oozing from his body, half turned over, and as she watched, shaking, he writhed once, flicked his tongue out once, and in. Snake made some sound, too low in her throat to be a cry. She hoped his motions were only reflex, but she picked him up as gently as she could. She leaned down and touched her lips to the smooth green scales behind his head. She bit him quickly, sharply, at the base of the skull. His blood flowed cool and salty in her mouth. If he were not dead, she had killed him instantly.

She looked at the parents, and at Arevin; they were all pale, but she had no sympathy for their fear, and cared nothing for shared grief. "Such a small creature," she said,

"Such a small creature, who could only give pleasure and dreams." She watched them for a moment more, then turned toward the tent again.

"Wait—" She heard the older husband move up close behind her. He touched her shoulder; she shrugged away his hand. "We will give you anything you want," he said, "but leave the child alone."

She spun on him in a fury. "Should I kill Stavin for your stupidity?" He seemed about to try to hold her back. She jammed her shoulder hard into his stomach, and flung herself past the tent-flap. Inside, she kicked over the satchel. Abruptly awakened, and angry, Sand crawled out and coiled himself. When the younger husband and the wife tried to enter, Sand hissed and rattled with a violence Snake had never heard him use before. She did not even bother to look behind her. She ducked her head and wiped her tears on her sleeve before Stavin could see them. She knelt beside him.

"What's the matter?" He could not help but hear the voices outside the tent, and the running.

"Nothing, Stavin," Snake said. "Did you know we came across the desert?"

"No," he said with wonder.

"It was very hot, and none of us had anything to eat. Grass is hunting now. He was very hungry. Will you forgive him and let me begin? I will be here all the time."

He seemed so tired; he was disappointed, but he had no strength for arguing. "All right." His voice rustled like sand slipping through the fingers.

Snake lifted Mist from her shoulders, and pulled the blanket from Stavin's small body. The tumor pressed up beneath his rib cage, distorting his form, squeezing his vital organs, sucking nourishment from him for its own growth, poisoning him with its wastes. Holding Mist's head, Snake let her flow across him, touching and tasting him. She had to restrain the cobra to keep her from striking; the excitement had agitated her. When Sand used his rattle, the vibrations made her flinch. Snake stroked her, soothing her; trained and bred-in responses began to return, overcoming the natural instincts. Mist paused when her tongue flicked the skin above the tumor, and Snake released her.

The cobra reared, and struck, and bit as cobras bite, sinking her fangs their short length once, releasing, instantly biting again for a better purchase, holding on, chewing at her prey. Stavin cried out, but he did not move against Snake's restraining hands.

Mist expended the contents of her venom sacs into the child, and released him. She reared up, peered around, folded her hood, and slid across the mats in a perfectly straight line toward her dark close compartment.

"It's done, Stavin."

"Will I die now?"

"No," Snake said. "Not now. Not for many years, I hope." She took a vial of powder from her belt pouch. "Open your mouth." He complied, and she sprinkled the powder across his tongue. "That will help the ache." She spread a pad of cloth across the series of shallow puncture wounds, without wiping off the blood.

She turned from him.

"Snake? Are you going away?"

"I will not leave without saying goodbye. I promise."

The child lay back, closed his eyes, and let the drug take him.

Sand coiled quiescently on the dark matting. Snake patted the floor to call him. He moved toward her, and suffered himself to be replaced in the satchel. Snake closed it, and lifted it, and it still felt empty. She heard noises outside the tent. Stavin's parents and the people who had come to help them pulled open the tent-flap and peered inside, thrusting sticks in even before they looked.

Snake set down her leather case. "It's done."

They entered. Arevin was with them too; only he was empty-handed. "Snake—" He spoke through grief, pity, confusion, and Snake could not tell what he believed. He looked back. Stavin's mother was just behind him. He took her by the shoulder. "He would have died without her. Whatever happens now, he would have died."

She shook his hand away. "He might have lived. It might

have gone away. We—" She could speak no more for hiding tears.

Snake felt the people moving, surrounding her. Arevin took one step toward her and stopped, and she could see he wanted her to defend herself. "Can any of you cry?" she said. "Can any of you cry for me and my despair, or for them and their guilt, or for small things and their pain?" She felt tears slip down her cheeks.

They did not understand her; they were offended by her crying. They stood back, still afraid of her, but gathering themselves. She no longer needed the pose of calmness she had used to deceive the child. "Ah, you fools." Her voice sounded brittle. "Stavin—"

Light from the entrance struck them. "Let me pass." The people in front of Snake moved aside for their leader. She stopped in front of Snake, ignoring the satchel her foot almost touched. "Will Stavin live?" Her voice was quiet, calm, gentle.

"I cannot be certain," Snake said, "but I feel that he will."

"Leave us." The people understood Snake's words before they did their leader's; they looked around and lowered their weapons, and finally, one by one, they moved out of the tent. Arevin remained. Snake felt the strength that came from danger seeping from her. Her knees collapsed. She bent over the satchel with her face in her hands. The older woman knelt in front of her, before Snake could notice or prevent her. "Thank you," she said. "Thank you. I am so sorry . . ." She put her arms around Snake, and drew her toward her, and Arevin knelt beside them, and he embraced Snake too. Snake began to tremble again, and they held her while she cried.

Later she slept, exhausted, alone in the tent with Stavin, holding his hand. The people had caught small animals for Sand and Mist. They had given her food, and supplies, and sufficient water for her to bathe, though the last must have strained their resources.

When she awakened, Arevin lay sleeping nearby, his

robe open in the heat, a sheen of sweat across his chest and stomach. The sternness in his expression vanished when he slept; he looked exhausted and vulnerable. Snake almost woke him, but stopped, shook her head, and turned to Stavin.

She felt the tumor, and found that it had begun to dissolve and shrivel, dying, as Mist's changed poison affected it. Through her grief Snake felt a little joy. She smoothed Stavin's pale hair back from his face. "I would not lie to you again, little one," she whispered, "but I must leave soon. I cannot stay here." She wanted another three days' sleep, to finish fighting off the effects of the bush viper's poison, but she would sleep somewhere else. "Stavin?"

He half woke, slowly. "It doesn't hurt any more," he said.

"I am glad."

"Thank you . . ."

"Goodbye, Stavin. Will you remember later on that you woke up, and that I did stay to say goodbye?"

"Goodbye," he said, drifting off again. "Goodbye, Snake. Goodbye, Grass." He closed his eyes.

Snake picked up the satchel and stood gazing down at Arevin. He did not stir. Half grateful, half regretful, she left the tent.

Dusk approached with long, indistinct shadows; the camp was hot and quiet. She found her tiger-striped pony, tethered with food and water. New, full water-skins bulged on the ground next to the saddle, and desert robes lay across the pommel, though Snake had refused any payment. The tiger-pony whickered at her. She scratched his striped ears, saddled him, and strapped her gear on his back. Leading him, she started west, the way she had come.

"Snake—"

She took a breath, and turned back to Arevin. He was facing the sun; it turned his skin ruddy and his robe scarlet. His streaked hair flowed loose to his shoulders, gentling his face. "You must leave?"

"Yes."

"I hoped you would not leave before . . . I hoped you would stay, for a time . . ."

"If things were different, I might have stayed."

"They were frightened—"

"I told them Grass couldn't hurt them, but they saw his fangs and they didn't know he could only give dreams and ease dying."

"But can't you forgive them?"

"I can't face their guilt. What they did was my fault, Arevin. I didn't understand them until too late."

"You said it yourself, you can't know all the customs and all the fears."

"I'm crippled," she said. "Without Grass, if I can't heal a person, I cannot help at all. I must go home and face my teachers, and hope they'll forgive my stupidity. They seldom give the name I bear, but they gave it to me—and they'll be disappointed."

"Let me come with you."

She wanted to; she hesitated, and cursed herself for that weakness. "They may take Mist and Sand and cast me out, and you would be cast out too. Stay here, Arevin."

"It wouldn't matter."

"It would. After a while, we would hate each other. I don't know you, and you don't know me. We need calmness, and quiet, and time to understand each other well."

He came toward her, and put his arms around her, and they stood embracing for a moment. When he raised his head, there were tears on his cheeks. "Please come back," he said. "Whatever happens, please come back."

"I will try," Snake said. "Next spring, when the winds stop, look for me. The spring after that, if I do not come, forget me. Wherever I am, if I live, I will forget you."

"I will look for you," Arevin said, and he would promise no more.

Snake picked up her pony's lead, and started across the desert.

The Death of
Dr. Island

Gene Wolfe

Gene Wolfe, who wrote *The Fifth Head of Cerberus* in last year's anthology, returns with a novella about a strange boy who moved his head continually from side to side, as certain reptiles do, and of what happened between him and two others on a man-made satellite circling Jupiter. Its setting is skillfully evoked, but its psychology is even more interesting.

I have desired to go
   Where springs not fail,
To fields where flies no sharp and sided hail
   And a few lilies blow.

   And I have asked to be
   Where no storms come,
Where the green swell is in the heavens dumb,
   And out of the swing of the sea.
          —Gerard Manley Hopkins

A grain of sand, teetering on the brink of the pit, trembled and fell in; the ant lion at the bottom angrily flung it out again. For a moment there was quiet. Then the entire pit, and a square meter of sand around it, shifted drunkenly while two coconut palms bent to watch. The sand rose, pivoting at one edge, and the scarred head of a boy appeared—a stubble of brown hair threatened to erase the marks of the sutures; with dilated eyes hypnotically dark he paused, his neck just where the ant lion's had been; then, as though goaded from below, he vaulted up and onto the beach, turned, and kicked sand into the dark hatchway from which he had emerged. It slammed shut. The boy was about fourteen.

For a time he squatted, pushing the sand aside and trying to find the door. A few centimeters down, his hands met a gritty, solid material which, though neither concrete nor sandstone, shared the qualities of both—a sand-filled organic plastic. On it he scraped his fingers raw, but he could not locate the edges of the hatch.

Then he stood and looked about him, his head moving continually as the heads of certain reptiles do—back and forth, with no pauses at the terminations of the movements. He did this constantly, ceaselessly—always—and for that reason it will not often be described again, just as it will not be mentioned that he breathed. He did; and as he did, his head, like a rearing snake's, turned from side to side. The boy was thin, and naked as a frog.

Ahead of him the sand sloped gently down toward sapphire water; there were coconuts on the beach, and sea shells, and a scuttling crab that played with the finger-high edge of each dying wave. Behind him there were only palms and sand for a long distance, the palms growing ever closer together as they moved away from the water until the forest of their columniated trunks seemed architectural; like some palace maze becoming as it progressed more and more draped with creepers and lianas with green, scarlet and yellow leaves, the palms interspersed with bamboo and deciduous trees dotted with flaming orchids until almost at the limit of his sight the whole ended in a spangled wall whose predominant color was black-green.

The boy walked toward the beach, then down the beach until he stood in knee-deep water as warm as blood. He dipped his fingers and tasted it—it was fresh, with no hint of the disinfectants to which he was accustomed. He waded out again and sat on the sand about five meters up from the high-water mark, and after ten minutes, during which he heard no sound but the wind and the murmuring of the surf, he threw back his head and began to scream. His screaming was high-pitched, and each breath ended in a gibbering, ululant note, after which came the hollow, iron gasp of the next indrawn breath. On one occasion he had screamed in this way, without cessation, for fourteen hours and twenty-two minutes, at the end of which a nursing nun with an exemplary record stretching back seventeen years had administered an injection without the permission of the attending physician.

After a time the boy paused—not because he was tired, but in order to listen better. There was, still, only the sound of the wind in the palm fronds and the murmuring surf, yet he felt that he had heard a voice. The boy could be quiet as well as noisy, and he was quiet now, his left hand sifting white sand as clean as salt between its fingers while his right tossed tiny pebbles like beachglass beads into the surf.

"*Hear me,*" said the surf. "*Hear me. Hear me.*"

"I hear you," the boy said.

"Good," said the surf, and it faintly echoed itself: "*Good, good, good.*"

The boy shrugged.

"What shall I call you?" asked the surf.

"My name is Nicholas Kenneth de Vore."

"Nick, *Nick . . . Nick?*"

The boy stood, and turning his back on the sea, walked inland. When he was out of sight of the water he found a coconut palm growing sloped and angled, leaning and weaving among its companions like the plume of an ascending jet blown by the wind. After feeling its rough exterior with both hands, the boy began to climb; he was inexpert and climbed slowly and a little clumsily, but his body was light and he was strong. In time he reached the top, and disturbed the little brown plush monkeys there, who fled chattering into other palms, leaving him to nestle alone among the stems of the fronds and the green coconuts. "I am here also," said a voice from the palm.

"Ah," said the boy, who was watching the tossing, sapphire sky far over his head.

"I will call you Nicholas."

The boy said, "I can see the sea."

"Do you know my name?"

The boy did not reply. Under him the long, long stem of the twisted palm swayed faintly.

"My friends all call me Dr. Island."

"I will not call you that," the boy said.

"You mean that you are not my friend."

A gull screamed.

"But you see, I take you for my friend. You may say that I am not yours, but I say that you are mine. I like you, Nicholas, and I will treat you as a friend."

"Are you a machine or a person or a committee?" the boy asked.

"I am all those things and more. I am the spirit of this island, the tutelary genius."

"Bullshit."

"Now that we have met, would you rather I leave you alone?"

Again the boy did not reply.

"You may wish to be alone with your thoughts. I would like to say that we have made much more progress today than I anticipated. I feel that we will get along together very well."

After fifteen minutes or more, the boy asked, "Where does the light come from?" There was no answer. The boy waited for a time, then climbed back down the trunk, dropping the last five meters and rolling as he hit in the soft sand.

He walked to the beach again and stood staring out at the

water. Far off he could see it curving up and up, the distant combers breaking in white foam until the sea became white-flecked sky. To his left and his right the beach curved away, bending almost infinitesimally until it disappeared. He began to walk, then saw, almost at the point where perception was lost, a human figure. He broke into a run; a moment later, he halted and turned around. Far ahead another walker, almost invisible, strode the beach; Nicholas ignored him; he found a coconut and tried to open it, then threw it aside and walked on. From time to time fish jumped, and occasionally he saw a wheeling sea bird dive. The light grew dimmer. He was aware that he had not eaten for some time, but he was not in the strict sense hungry—or rather, he enjoyed his hunger now in the same way that he might, at another time, have gashed his arm to watch himself bleed. Once he said, "Dr. Island!" loudly as he passed a coconut palm, and then later began to chant "Dr. Island, Dr. Island, Dr. Island" as he walked until the words had lost all meaning. He swam in the sea as he had been taught to swim in the great quartanary treatment tanks on Callisto to improve his coordination, and spluttered and snorted until he learned to deal with the waves. When it was so dark he could see only the white sand and the white foam of the breakers, he drank from the sea and fell asleep on the beach, the right side of his taut, ugly face relaxing first, so that it seemed asleep even while the left eye was open and staring; his head rolling from side to side; the left corner of his mouth preserving, like a death mask, his characteristic expression—angry, remote, tinged with that inhuman quality which is found nowhere but in certain human faces.

When he woke it was not yet light, but the night was fading to a gentle gray. Headless, the palms stood like tall ghosts up and down the beach, their tops lost in fog and the lingering dark. He was cold. His hands rubbed his sides; he danced on the sand and sprinted down the edge of the lapping water in an effort to get warm; ahead of him a pinpoint of red light became a fire, and he slowed.

A man who looked about twenty-five crouched over the fire. Tangled black hair hung over this man's shoulders, and he had a sparse beard; otherwise he was as naked as Nicholas himself. His eyes were dark, and large and empty, like the ends of broken pipes; he poked at his fire, and the smell of roasting fish came with the smoke. For a time Nicholas stood at a distance, watching.

Saliva ran from a corner of the man's mouth, and he wiped it away with one hand, leaving a smear of ash on his face. Nicholas edged closer until he stood on the opposite side of the fire. The fish had been wrapped in broad leaves and mud, and lay in the center of the coals. "I'm Nicholas," Nicholas said. "Who are you?" The young man did not look at him, had never looked at him.

"Hey, I'd like a piece of your fish. Not much. All right?"

The young man raised his head, looking not at Nicholas but at some point far beyond him; he dropped his eyes again. Nicholas smiled. The smile emphasized the disjointed quality of his expression, his mouth's uneven curve.

"Just a little piece? Is it about done?" Nicholas crouched, imitating the young man, and as though this were a signal, the young man sprang for him across the fire. Nicholas jumped backward, but the jump was too late—the young man's body struck his and sent him sprawling on the sand; fingers clawed for his throat. Screaming, Nicholas rolled free, into the water; the young man splashed after him; Nicholas dove.

He swam underwater, his belly almost grazing the wave-rippled sand until he found deeper water; then he surfaced, gasping for breath, and saw the young man, who saw him as well. He dove again, this time surfacing far off, in deep water. Treading water, he could see the fire on the beach, and the young man when he returned to it, stamping out of the sea in the early light. Nicholas then swam until he was five hundred meters or more down the beach, then waded in to shore and began walking back toward the fire.

The young man saw him when he was still some distance off, but he continued to sit, eating pink-tinted tidbits from his fish, watching Nicholas. "What's the matter?" Nicholas said while he was still a safe distance away. "Are you mad at me?"

From the forest, birds warned, "Be careful, Nicholas."

"I won't hurt you," the young man said. He stood up, wiping his oily hands on his chest, and gestured toward the fish at his feet. "You want some?"

Nicholas nodded, smiling his crippled smile.

"Come then."

Nicholas waited, hoping the young man would move away from the fish, but he did not; neither did he smile in return.

"Nicholas," the little waves at his feet whispered, "this is Ignacio."

"Listen," Nicholas said, "is it really all right for me to have some?"

Ignacio nodded, unsmiling.

Cautiously Nicholas came forward; as he was bending to pick up the fish, Ignacio's strong hands took him; he tried to wrench free but was thrown down, Ignacio on top of him. "Please!" he yelled. "Please!" Tears started into his eyes. He tried to yell again, but he had no breath; the tongue was being forced, thicker than his wrist, from his throat.

Then Ignacio let go and struck him in the face with his clenched fist. Nicholas had been slapped and pummeled before, had been beaten, had fought, sometimes savagely, with other boys; but he had never been struck by a man as men fight. Ignacio hit him again and his lips gushed blood.

He lay a long time on the sand beside the dying fire. Consciousness returned slowly; he blinked, drifted back into the dark, blinked again. His mouth was full of blood, and when at last he spit it out onto the sand, it seemed a soft flesh, dark and polymerized in strange shapes; his left cheek was hugely swollen, and he could scarcely see out of his left eye. After a time he crawled to the water; a long time after that, he left it and walked shakily back to the ashes of the fire. Ignacio was gone, and there was nothing left of the fish but bones.

"Ignacio is gone," Dr. Island said with lips of waves. Nicholas sat on the sand, cross-legged.

"You handled him very well."

"You saw us fight?"

"I saw you; I see everything, Nicholas."

"This is the worse place," Nicholas said; he was talking to his lap.

"What do you mean by that?"

"I've been in bad places before—places where they hit you or squirted big hoses of ice water that knocked you down. But not where they would let someone else—"

"Another patient?" asked a wheeling gull.

"—do it."

"You were lucky, Nicholas. Ignacio is homicidal."

"You could have stopped him."

"No, I could not. All this world is my eye, Nicholas, my ear and my tongue; but I have no hands."

"I thought you did all this."

"Men did all this."

"I mean, I thought you kept it going."

"It keeps itself going, and you—all the people here—direct it."

Nicholas looked at the water. "What makes the waves?"

"The wind and the tide."

"Are we on Earth?"

"Would you feel more comfortable on Earth?"

"I've never been there; I'd like to know."

"I am more like Earth than Earth now is, Nicholas. If you were to take the best of all the best beaches of Earth, and clear them of all the poisons and all the dirt of the last three centuries, you would have me."

"But this isn't Earth?"

There was no answer. Nicholas walked around the ashes of the fire until he found Ignacio's footprints. He was no tracker, but the depressions in the soft beach sand required none; he followed them, his head swaying from side to side as he walked, like the sensor of a mine detector.

For several kilometers Ignacio's trail kept to the beach; then, abruptly, the footprints swerved, wandered among the coconut palms, and at last were lost on the firmer soil inland. Nicholas lifted his head and shouted, "Ignacio? Ignacio!" After a moment he heard a stick snap, and the sound of someone pushing aside leafy branches. He waited.

"Mum?"

A girl was coming toward him, stepping out of the thicker growth of the interior. She was pretty, though too thin, and appeared to be about nineteen; her hair was blond where it had been most exposed to sunlight, darker elsewhere. "You've scratched yourself," Nicholas said. "You're bleeding."

"I thought you were my mother," the girl said. She was a head taller than Nicholas. "Been fighting, haven't you. Have you come to get me?"

Nicholas had been in similar conversations before and normally would have preferred to ignore the remark, but he was lonely now. He said, "Do you want to go home?"

"Well, I think I should, you know."

"But do you want to?"

"My mum always says if you've got something on the stove you don't want to burn—she's quite a good cook. She really is. Do you like cabbage with bacon?"

"Have you got anything to eat?"

"Not now. I had a thing a while ago."

"What kind of thing?"

"A bird." The girl made a vague little gesture, not looking at Nicholas. "I'm a memory that has swallowed a bird."

"Do you want to walk down by the water?" They were moving in the direction of the beach already.

"I was just going to get a drink. You're a nice tot."

Nicholas did not like being called a "tot." He said, "I set fire to places."

"You won't set fire to this place; it's been nice the last couple of days, but when everyone is sad, it rains."

Nicholas was silent for a time. When they reached the sea, the girl dropped to her knees and bent forward to drink, her long hair falling over her face until the ends trailed in the water, her nipples, then half of each breast, in the water. "Not there," Nicholas said. "It's sandy, because it washes the beach so close. Come on out here." He waded out into the sea until the lapping waves nearly reached his armpits, then bent his head and drank.

"I never thought of that," the girl said. "Mum says I'm stupid. So does Dad. Do you think I'm stupid?"

Nicholas shook his head.

"What's your name?"

"Nicholas Kenneth de Vore. What's yours?"

"Diane. I'm going to call you Nicky. Do you mind?"

"I'll hurt you while you sleep," Nicholas said.

"You wouldn't."

"Yes I would. At St. John's where I used to be, it was zero G most of the time, and a girl there called me something I didn't like, and I got loose one night and came into her cubical while she was asleep and nulled her restraints, and then she floated around until she banged into something, and that woke her up and she tried to grab, and then that made her bounce all around inside and she broke two fingers and her nose and got blood all over. The attendants came, and one told me—they didn't know then I did it—when he came out his white suit was, like, polka-dot red all over because wherever the blood drops had touched him they soaked right in."

The girl smiled at him, dimpling her thin face. "How did they find out it was you?"

"I told someone and he told them."

"I bet you told them yourself."

"I bet I didn't!" Angry, he waded away, but when he had stalked a short way up the beach he sat down on the sand, his back toward her.

"I didn't mean to make you mad, Mr. de Vore."

"I'm not mad!"

She was not sure for a moment what he meant. She sat down beside and a trifle behind him, and began idly piling sand in her lap.

Dr. Island said, "I see you've met."

Nicholas turned, looking for the voice. "I thought you saw everything."

"Only the important things, and I have been busy on another part of myself. I am happy to see that you two know one another; do you find you interact well?"

Neither of them answered.

"You should be interacting with Ignacio; he needs you."

"We can't find him," Nichoals said.

"Down the beach to your left until you see the big stone, then turn inland. Above five hundred meters."

Nicholas stood up, and turning to his right, began to walk away. Diane followed him, trotting until she caught up.

"I don't like," Nicholas said, jerking a shoulder to indicate something behind him.

"Ignacio?"

"The doctor."

"Why do you move your head like that?"

"Didn't they tell you?"

"No one told me anything about you."

"They opened it up"—Nicholas touched his scars—"and took this knife and cut all the way through my corpus . . . corpus . . ."

"Corpus callosum," muttered a dry palm frond.

"—corpus callosum," finished Nicholas. "See, your brain is like a walnut inside. There are the two halves, and then right down in the middle a kind of thick connection of meat from one to the other. Well, they cut that."

"You're having a bit of fun with me, aren't you?"

"No, he isn't," a monkey who had come to the water line to look for shellfish told her. "His cerebrum has been surgically divided; it's in his file." It was a young monkey, with a trusting face full of small, ugly beauties.

Nicholas snapped, "It's in my head."

Diane said, "I'd think it would kill you, or make you an idiot or something."

"They say each half of me is about as smart as both of us were together. Anyway, this half is . . . the half . . . the *me* that talks."

"There are two of you now?"

"If you cut a worm in half and both parts are still alive, that's two, isn't it? What else would you call us? We can't ever come together again."

"But I'm talking to just one of you?"

"We both can hear you."

"Which one answers?"

Nicholas touched the right side of his chest with his right hand. "Me; I do. They told me it was the left side of my brain, that one has the speech centers, but it doesn't feel that way; the nerves cross over coming out, and it's just the right side of me, I talk. Both my ears hear for both of us, but out of each eye we only see half and half—I mean, I only see what's on the right of what I'm looking at, and the other side, I guess, only sees the left, so that's why I keep moving my head. I guess it's like being a little bit blind; you get used to it."

The girl was still thinking of his divided body. She said, "If you're only half, I don't see how you can walk."

"I can move the left side a little bit, and we're not mad at each other. We're not supposed to be able to come together at all, but we do: down through the legs and at the ends of the fingers and then back up. Only I can't talk with my other side because he can't, but he understands."

"Why did they do it?"

Behind them the monkey, who had been following them, said, "He had uncontrollable seizures."

"Did you?" the girl asked. She was watching a sea bird swooping low over the water and did not seem to care.

Nicholas picked up a shell and shied it at the monkey, who skipped out of the way. After half a minute's silence he said, "I had visions."

"Ooh, did you?"

"They didn't like that. They said I would fall down and jerk around horrible, and sometimes I guess I would hurt myself when I fell, and sometimes I'd bite my tongue and it would bleed. But that wasn't what it felt like to me; I wouldn't know about any of those things until afterward. To me it was like I had gone way far ahead, and I had to come back. I didn't want to."

The wind swayed Diane's hair, and she pushed it back from her face. "Did you see things that were going to happen?" she asked.

"Sometimes."

"Really? Did you?"

"Sometimes."

"Tell me about it. When you saw what was going to happen."

"I saw myself dead. I was all black and shrunk up like the dead stuff they cut off in the 'pontic gardens; and I was floating and turning, like in water but it wasn't water —just floating and turning out in space, in nothing. And there were lights on both sides of me, so both sides were bright but black, and I could see my teeth because the stuff"—he pulled at his cheeks—"had fallen off there, and they were really white."

"That hasn't happened yet."

"Not here."

"Tell me something you saw that happened."

"You mean, like somebody's sister was going to get married, don't you? That's what the girls where I was mostly wanted to know. Or were they going to go home; mostly it wasn't like that."

"But sometimes it was?"

"I guess."

"Tell me one."

Nicholas shook his head. "You wouldn't like it, and anyway it wasn't like that. Mostly it was lights like I never saw anyplace else, and voices like I never heard any other time, telling me things there aren't any words for; stuff like that, only now I can't ever go back. Listen, I wanted to ask you about Ignacio."

"He isn't anybody," the girl said.

"What do you mean, he isn't anybody? Is there anybody here besides you and me and Ignacio and Dr. Island?"

"Not that we can see or touch."

The monkey called, "There are other patients, but for the present, Nicholas, for your own well-being as well as theirs, it is best for you to remain by yourselves." It was a long sentence for a monkey.

"What's that about?"

"If I tell you, will you tell me about something you saw that really happened?"

"All right."

"Tell me first."

"There was this girl where I was—her name was Maya. They had, you know, boys' and girls' dorms, but you saw everybody in the rec room and the dining hall and so on, and she was in my psychodrama group." Her hair had been black, and shiny as the lacquered furniture in Dr. Hong's rooms, her skin white like the mother-of-pearl, her eyes long and narrow (making him think of cats' eyes) and darkly blue. She was fifteen, or so Nicholas believed— maybe sixteen. *"I'm going home,"* she told him. It was psychodrama, and he was her brother, younger than she, and she was already at home; but when she said this the floating ring of light that gave them the necessary separation from the small doctor-and-patient audience, ceased, by instant agreement, to be Maya's mother's living room and became a visting lounge. Nicholas/Jerry said: "Hey, that's great! Hey, I got a new bike—when you come home you want to ride it?"

Maureen/Maya's mother said, "Maya, don't. You'll run into something and break your teeth, and you know how much they cost."

"You don't want me to have any fun."

"We do, dear, but *nice* fun. A girl has to be so much more careful—oh, Maya, I wish I could make you understand, really, how careful a girl has to be."

Nobody said anything, so Nicholas/Jerry filled in with, "It has a three-bladed prop, and I'm going to tape streamers to them with little weights at the ends, an' when I go down old thirty-seven B passageway, look out, here comes that old coleslaw grater!"

"Like this," Maya said, and held her legs together and extended her arms, to make a three-bladed bike prop or a crucifix. She had thrown herself into a spin as she made the movement, and revolved slowly, stage center—red shorts, white blouse, red shorts, white blouse, red shorts, no shoes.

Diane asked, "And you saw that she was never going home, she was going to hospital instead, she was going to cut her wrist there, she was going to die?"

Nicholas nodded.

"Did you tell her?"

"Yes," Nicholas said. "No."

"Make up your mind. Didn't you tell her? Now, don't get mad."

"Is it telling, when the one you tell doesn't understand?"

Diane thought about that for a few steps while Nicholas dashed water on the hot bruises Ignacio had left upon his face. "If it was plain and clear and she ought to have understood—that's the trouble I have with my family."

"What is?"

"They won't say things—do you know what I mean? I just say look, just tell me, just tell me what I'm supposed to do, tell me what it is you want, but it's different all the time. My mother says, 'Diane, you ought to meet some boys, you can't go out with him, your father and I have never met him, we don't even know his family at all, Douglas, there's something I think you ought to know about Diane, she gets confused sometimes, we've had her to doctors, she's been in a hospital, try—' "

"Not to get her excited," Nicholas finished for her.

"Were you listening? I mean, are you from the Trojan Planets? Do you know my mother?"

"I only live in these places," Nicholas said, "that's for a long time. But you talk like other people."

"I feel better now that I'm with you; you're really nice. I wish you were older."

"I'm not sure I'm going to get much older."

"It's going to rain—feel it?"

Nicholas shook his head.

"Look." Diane jumped, bunnyrabbit-clumsy, three meters into the air. "See how high I can jump? That means people are sad and it's going to rain. I told you."

"No, you didn't."

"Yes, I did, Nicholas."

He waved the argument away, struck by a sudden thought. "You ever been to Callisto?"

The girl shook her head, and Nicholas said, "I have; that's where they did the operation. It's so big the gravity's mostly from natural mass, and it's all domed in, with a whole lot of air in it."

"So?"

"And when I was there it rained. There was a big trouble at one of the generating piles, and they shut it down and it got colder and colder until everybody in the hospital wore their blankets, just like Amerinds in books, and they locked the switches off on the heaters in the bathrooms, and the nurses and the comscreen told you all the time it wasn't dangerous, they were just rationing power to keep from blacking out the important stuff that was still running. And then it rained, just like on Earth. They said it got so cold the water condensed in the air, and it was like the whole hospital was right under a shower bath. Everybody on the top floor had to come down because it rained right on their beds, and for two nights I had a man in my room with me that had his arm cut off in a machine. But we couldn't jump any higher, and it got kind of dark."

"It doesn't always get dark here," Diane said. "Sometimes the rain sparkles. I think Dr. Island must do it to cheer everyone up."

"No," the waves explained, "or at least not in the way you mean, Diane."

Nicholas was hungry and started to ask them for something to eat, then turned his hunger in against itself, spat on the sand, and was still.

"It rains here when most of you are sad," the waves were saying, "because rain is a sad thing, to the human psyche. It is that, that sadness, perhaps because it recalls to unhappy people their own tears, that palliates melancholy."

Diane said, "Well, I know sometimes I feel better when it rains."

"That should help you to understand yourself. Most people are soothed when their environment is in harmony with their emotions, and anxious when it is not. An angry person becomes less angry in a red room, and unhappy people are only exasperated by sunshine and birdsong. Do you remember:

> "And, missing thee, I walk unseen
> On the dry smooth-shaven green
> To behold the wandering moon,
> Riding near her highest noon,
> Like one that had been led astray
> Through the heaven's wide pathless way?"

The girl shook her head.

Nicholas said, "No. Did somebody write that?" and then "You said you couldn't do anything."

The waves replied, "I can't—except talk to you."

"You make it rain."

"Your heart beats; I sense its pumping even as I speak—do you control the beating of your heart?"

"I can stop my breath."

"Can you stop your heart? Honestly, Nicholas?"

"I guess not."

"No more can I control the weather of my world, stop anyone from doing what he wishes, or feed you if you are hungry; with no need of volition on my part your emotions are monitored and averaged, and our weather responds. Calm and sunshine for tranquillity, rain for melancholy, storms for rage, and so on. This is what mankind has always wanted."

Diane asked, "What is?"

"That the environment should respond to human thought. That is the core of magic and the oldest dream of mankind; and here, on me, it is fact."

"So that we'll be well?"

Nicholas said angrily, "You're not sick!"

Dr. Island said, "So that some of you, at least, can return to society."

Nicholas threw a sea shell into the water as though to strike the mouth that spoke. "Why are we talking to this thing?"

"Wait, tot, I think it's interesting."

"Lies and lies."

Dr. Island said, "How do I lie, Nicholas?"

"You said it was magic—"

"No, I said that when humankind has dreamed of magic, the wish behind that dream has been the omnipotence of thought. Have you never wanted to be a magician, Nicholas, making palaces spring up overnight, or riding an enchanted horse of ebony to battle with the demons of the air?"

"I am a magician—I have preternatural powers, and before they cut us in two—"

Diane interrupted him. "You said you averaged emotions. When you made it rain."

"Yes."

"Doesn't that mean that if one person was really, terribly sad, he'd move the average so much he could make it rain all by himself? Or whatever? That doesn't seem fair."

The waves might have smiled. "That has never happened. But if it did, Diane, if one person felt such deep emotion, think how great her need would be. Don't you think we should answer it?"

Diane looked at Nicholas, but he was walking again, his head swinging, ignoring her as well as the voice of the waves. "Wait," she called. "You said I wasn't sick; I am, you know."

"No, you're not."

She hurried after him. "Everyone says so, and sometimes I'm so confused, and other times I'm boiling inside, just boiling. Mum says if you've got something on the stove you don't want to have burn, you just have to keep one finger on the handle of the pan and it won't, but I can't, I can't always find the handle or remember."

Without looking back the boy said, "Your mother is probably sick; maybe your father too, I don't know. But you're not. If they'd just let you alone you'd be all right. Why shouldn't you get upset, having to live with two crazy people?"

"Nicholas!" She grabbed his thin shoulders. "That's not true!"

"Yes, it is."

"I am sick. Everyone says so."

"I don't; so 'everyone' just means the ones that do—isn't that right? And if you don't either, that will be two; it can't be everyone then."

The girl called, "Doctor? Dr. Island?"

Nicholas said, "You aren't going to believe that, are you?"

"Dr. Island, is it true?"

"Is what true, Diane?"

"What he said. Am I sick?"

"Sickness—even physical illness—is relative, Diane; and complete health is an idealization, an abstraction, even if the other end of the scale is not."

"You know what I mean."

"You are not physically ill." A long, blue comber curled into a line of hissing spray reaching infinitely along the sea to their left and right. "As you said yourself a moment ago, you are sometimes confused, and sometimes disturbed."

"He said if it weren't for other people, if it weren't for my mother and father, I wouldn't have to be here."

"Diane . . ."

"Well, is that true or isn't it?"

"Most emotional illness would not exist, Diane, if it were possible in every case to separate oneself—in thought as well as circumstance—if only for a time."

"Separate oneself?"

"Did you ever think of going away, at least for a time?"

The girl nodded, then as though she were not certain Dr. Island could see her, said, "Often, I suppose; leaving the school and getting my own compartment somewhere—going to Achilles. Sometimes I wanted to so badly."

"Why didn't you?"

"They would have worried. And anyway, they would have found me, and made me come home."

"Would it have done any good if I—or a human doctor—had told them not to?"

When the girl said nothing Nicholas snapped, "You could have locked them up."

"They were functioning, Nicholas. They bought and sold: they worked, and paid their taxes—"

Diane said softly, "It wouldn't have done any good anyway. Nicholas; they are inside me."

"Diane was no longer functioning: she was failing every subject at the university she attended, and her presence in her classes, when she came, disturbed the instructors and the other students. You were not functioning either, and people of your own age were afraid of you."

"That's what counts with you, then. Functioning."

"If I were different from the world, would that help you when you got back into the world?"

"You are different." Nicholas kicked the sand. "Nobody ever saw a place like this."

"You mean that reality to you is metal corridors, rooms without windows, noise."

"Yes."

"That is the unreality, Nicholas. Most people have never had to endure such things. Even now, this—my beach, my sea, my trees—is more in harmony with most human lives than your metal corridors; and here, I am your social environment—what individuals call 'they.' You see, sometimes if we take people who are troubled back to something like me, to an idealized natural setting, it helps them."

"Come on," Nicholas told the girl. He took her arm, acutely conscious of being so much shorter than she.

"A question," murmured the waves. "If Diane's parents had been taken here instead of Diane, do you think it would have helped them?"

Nicholas did not reply.

"We have treatments for disturbed persons, Nicholas. But, at least for the time being, we have no treatment for disturbing persons." Diane and the boy had turned away, and the waves' hissing and slapping ceased to be speech. Gulls wheeled overhead, and once a red-and-yellow parrot fluttered from one palm to another. A monkey running on all fours like a little dog approached them, and Nicholas chased it, but it escaped.

"I'm going to take one of those things apart someday," he said, "and pull the wires out."

"Are we going to walk all the way 'round?" Diane asked. She might have been talking to herself.

"Can you do that?"

"Oh, you can't walk all around Dr. Island; it would be too long, and you can't get there anyway. But we could walk until we get back to where we started—we're probably more than halfway now."

"Are there other islands you can't see from here?"

The girl shook her head. "I don't think so; there's just this one big island in this satellite, and all the rest is water."

"Then if there's only the one island, we're going to have to walk all around it to get back to where we started. What are you laughing at?"

"Look down the beach, as far as you can. Never mind how it slips off to the side—pretend it's straight."

"I don't see anything."

"Don't you? Watch." Diane leaped into the air, six meters or more this time, and waved her arms.

"It looks like there's somebody ahead of us, way down the beach."

"Uh-huh. Now look behind."

"Okay, there's somebody there too. Come to think of it, I saw someone on the beach when I first got here. It seemed funny to see so far, but I guess I thought they were other patients. Now I see two people."

"They're us. That was probably yourself you saw the other time, too. There are just so many of us to each strip of beach, and Dr. Island only wants certain ones to mix. So the space bends around. When we get to one end of our strip and try to step over, we'll be at the other end."

"How did you find out?"

"Dr. Island told me about it when I first came here." The girl was silent for a moment, and her smile vanished. "Listen, Nicholas, do you want to see something really funny?"

Nicholas asked, "What?" As he spoke, a drop of rain struck his face.

"You'll see. Come on, though. We have to go into the middle instead of following the beach, and it will give us a chance to get under the trees and out of the rain."

When they had left the sand and the sound of the surf, and were walking on solid ground under green-leaved trees, Nicholas said, "Maybe we can find some fruit." They were so light now that he had to be careful not to bound into the air with each step. The rain fell slowly around them, in crystal spheres.

"Maybe," the girl said doubtfully. "Wait, let's stop here." She sat down where a huge tree sent twenty-meter wooden arches over dark, mossy ground. "Want to climb up there and see if you can find us something?"

"All right," Nicholas agreed. He jumped, and easily caught hold of a branch far above the girl's head. In a moment he was climbing in a green world, with the rain pattering all around him; he followed narrowing limbs into leafy wildernesses where the cool water ran from every twig he touched, and twice found the empty nests of birds, and once a slender snake, green as any leaf with a head as long as his thumb; but there was no fruit. "Nothing," he said, when he dropped down beside the girl once more.

"That's all right, we'll find something."

He said, "I hope so," and noticed that she was looking at him oddly, then realized that his left hand had lifted itself to touch her right breast. It dropped as he looked, and he felt his face grow hot. He said, "I'm sorry."

"That's all right."

"We like you. He—over there—he can't talk, you see. I guess I can't talk either."

"I think it's just you—in two pieces. I don't care."

"Thanks." He had picked up a leaf, dead and damp, and was tearing it to shreds; first his right hand tearing while the left held the leaf, then turnabout. "Where does the rain come from?" The dirty flakes clung to the fingers of both.

"Hmm?"

"Where does the rain come from? I mean, it isn't because it's colder here now, like on Callisto; it's because the gravity's turned down some way, isn't it?"

"From the sea. Don't you know how this place is built?"

Nicholas shook his head.

"Didn't they show it to you from the ship when you came? It's beautiful. They showed it to me—I just sat there and looked at it, and I wouldn't talk to them, and the nurse thought I wasn't paying any attention, but I heard everything. I just didn't want to talk to her. It wasn't any use."

"I know how you felt."

"But they didn't show it to you?"

"No, on my ship they kept me locked up because I burned some stuff. They thought I couldn't start a fire without an igniter, but if you have electricity in the wall sockets it's easy. They had a thing on me—you know?" He clasped his arms to his body to show how he had been restrained. "I bit one of them, too—I guess I didn't tell you that yet: I bite people. They locked me up, and for a long time I had nothing to do, and then I could feel us dock with something, and they came and got me and pulled me down a regular companionway for a long time, and it just seemed like a regular place. Then they stuck me full of Tranquil-C—I guess they didn't know it doesn't hardly work on me at all—with a pneumogun, and lifted a kind of door thing and shoved me up."

"Didn't they make you undress?"

"I already was. When they put the ties on me I did things in my clothes and they had to take them off me. It made them mad." He grinned unevenly. "Does Tranquil-C work on you? Or any of that other stuff?"

"I suppose they would, but then I never do the sort of thing you do anyway."

"Maybe you ought to."

"Sometimes they used to give me medication that was supposed to cheer me up; then I couldn't sleep, and I walked and walked, you know, and ran into things and made a lot of trouble for everyone; but what good does it do?"

Nicholas shrugged. "Not doing it doesn't do any good either—I mean, we're both here. My way, I know I've made them jump; they shoot that stuff in me and I'm not mad any more, but I know what it is and I just think what I would do if I *were* mad, and I do it, and when it wears off I'm glad I did."

"I think you're still angry somewhere, deep down."

Nicholas was already thinking of something else. "This island says Ignacio kills people." He paused. "What does it look like?"

"Ignacio?"

"No, I've seen him. Dr. Island."

"Oh, you mean when I was in the ship. The satellite's round of course, and all clear except where Dr. Island is, so that's a dark spot. The rest of it's temperglass, and from space you can't even see the water."

"That *is* the sea up there, isn't it?" Nicholas asked, trying to look up at it through the tree leaves and the rain. "I thought it was when I first came."

"Sure. It's like a glass ball, and we're inside, and the water's inside too, and just goes all around up the curve."

"That's why I could see so far out on the beach, isn't it? Instead of dropping down from you like on Callisto it bends up so you can see it."

The girl nodded. "And the water lets the light through, but filters out the ultraviolet. Besides, it gives us thermal mass, so we don't heat up too much when we're between the sun and the Bright Spot."

"Is that what keeps us warm? The Bright Spot?"

Diane nodded again. "We go around in ten hours, you see, and that holds us over it all the time."

"Why can't I see it, then? It ought to look like Sol does from the Belt, only bigger; but there's just a shimmer in the sky, even when it's not raining."

"The waves diffract the light and break up the image. You'd see the Focus, though, if the air weren't so clear. Do you know what the Focus is?"

Nicholas shook his head.

"We'll get to it pretty soon, after this rain stops. Then I'll tell you."

"I still don't understand about the rain."

Unexpectedly Diane giggled. "I just thought—do you know what I was supposed to be? While I was going to school?"

"Quiet," Nicholas said.

"No, silly. I mean what I was being trained to do, if I graduated and all that. I was going to be a teacher, with all those cameras on me and tots from everywhere watching and popping questions on the two-way. Jolly time. Now I'm doing it here, only there's no one but you."

"You mind?"

"No, I suppose I enjoy it." There was a black-and-blue mark on Diane's thigh, and she rubbed it pensively with one hand as she spoke. "Anyway, there are three ways to make gravity. Do you know them? Answer, clerk."

"Sure; acceleration, mass, and synthesis."

"That's right; motion and mass are both bendings of space, of course, which is why Zeno's paradox doesn't work out that way, and why masses move toward each other—what we call falling—or at least try to; and if they're held apart it produces the tension we perceive as a force and call weight and all that rot. So naturally if you bend the space direct, you synthesize a gravity effect, and that's what holds all that water up against the translucent shell—there's nothing like enough mass to do it by itself."

"You mean"—Nicholas held out his hand to catch a slow-moving globe of rain—"that this is water from the sea?"

"Right-o, up on top. Do you see, the temperature differences in the air make the winds, and the winds make the waves and surf you saw when we were walking along the shore. When the waves break they throw up these little drops, and if you watch you'll see that even when it's clear they go up a long way sometimes. Then if the gravity is less they can get away altogether, and if we were on the outside they'd fly off into space; but we aren't, we're inside, so all they can do is go across the center, more or less, until they hit the water again, or Dr. Island."

"Dr. Island said they had storms sometimes, when people got mad."

"Yes. Lots of wind, and so there's lots of rain too. Only the rain then is because the wind tears the tops off the waves, and you don't get light like you do in a normal rain."

"What makes so much wind?"

"I don't know. It happens somehow."

They sat in silence, Nicholas listening to the dripping of the leaves. He remembered then that they had spun the hospital module, finally, to get the little spheres of clotting blood out of the air; Maya's blood was building up on the grills of the purification intake ducts, spotting them black, and someone had been afraid they would decay there and smell. He had not been there when they did it, but he could imagine the droplets settling, like this, in the slow spin. The old psychodrama group had already been broken up, and when he saw Maureen or any of the others in the rec room they talked about Good Old Days. It had not seemed like Good Old Days then except that Maya had been there.

Diane said, "It's going to stop."

"It looks just as bad to me."

"No, it's going to stop—see, they're falling a little faster now, and I feel heavier."

Nicholas stood up. "You rested enough yet? You want to go on?"

"We'll get wet."

He shrugged.

"I don't want to get my hair wet, Nicholas. It'll be over in a minute."

He sat down again. "How long have you been here?"

"I'm not sure."

"Don't you count the days?"

"I lose track a lot."

"Longer than a week?"

"Nicholas, don't ask me, all right?"

"Isn't there anybody on this piece of Dr. Island except you and me and Ignacio?"

"I don't think there was anyone but Ignacio before you came."

"Who is he?"

She looked at him.

"Well, who is he? You know me—us—Nicholas Kenneth de Vore; and you're Diane who?"

"Phillips."

"And you're from the Trojan Panets, and I was from the Outer Belt, I guess, to start with. What about Ignacio? You talk to him sometimes, don't you? Who is he?"

"I don't know. He's important."

For an instant, Nicholas froze. "What does that mean?"

"Important." The girl was feeling her knees, running her hands back and forth across them.

"Maybe everybody's important."

"I know you're just a tot, Nicholas, but don't be so stupid. Come on, you wanted to go, let's go now. It's pretty well stopped." She stood, stretching her thin body, her arms over her head. "My knees are rough—you made me think of that. When I came here they were still so smooth, I think. I used to put a certain lotion on them. Because my Dad would feel them, and my hands and elbows too, and he'd say if they weren't smooth nobody'd every want me; Mum wouldn't say anything, but she'd be cross after, and they used to come and visit, and so I kept a bottle in my room and I used to put it on. Once I drank some."

Nicholas was silent.

"Aren't you going to ask me if I died?" She stepped ahead of him, pulling aside the dripping branches. "See here, I'm sorry I said you were stupid."

"I'm just thinking," Nicholas said. "I'm not mad at you. Do you really know anything about him?"

"No, but look at it." She gestured. "Look around you; someone *built* all this."

"You mean it cost a lot."

"It's automated, of course, but still . . . well, the other places where you were before—how much space was there for each patient? Take the total volume and divide it by the number of people there."

"Okay, this is a whole lot bigger, but maybe they think we're worth it."

"Nicholas . . ." She paused. "Nicholas, Ignacio is homicidal. Didn't Dr. Island tell you?"

"Yes."

"And you're fourteen and not very big for it, and I'm a girl. Who are they worried about?"

The look on Nicholas's face startled her.

After an hour or more of walking they came to it. It was a band of withered vegetation, brown and black and tumbling, and as straight as if it had been drawn with a ruler. "I was afraid it wasn't going to be here," Diane said. "It moves around whenever there's a storm. It might not have been in our sector any more at all."

Nicholas asked, "What is it?"

"The Focus. It's been all over, but mostly the plants grow back quickly when it's gone."

"It smells funny—like the kitchen in a place where they wanted me to work in the kitchen once."

"Vegetables rotting, that's what that is. What did you do?"

"Nothing—put detergent in the stuff they were cooking. What makes this?"

"The Bright Spot. See, when it's just about overhead the curve of the sky and the water up there make a lens. It isn't a very good lens—a lot of the light scatters. But enough is focused to do this. It wouldn't fry us if it came past right now, if that's what you're wondering, because it's not that hot. I've stood right in it, but you want to get out in a minute."

"I thought it was going to be about seeing ourselves down the beach."

Diane seated herself on the trunk of a fallen tree. "It was, really. The last time I was here it was further from the water, and I suppose it had been there a long time, because it had cleared out a lot of the dead stuff. The sides of the sector are nearer here, you see; the whole sector narrows down like a piece of pie. So you could look down the Focus either way and see yourself nearer than you could on the beach. It was almost as if you were in a big, big room, with a looking-glass on each wall, or as if you could stand behind yourself. I thought you might like it."

"I'm going to try it here," Nicholas announced, and he clambered up one of the dead trees while the girl waited below, but the dry limbs creaked and snapped beneath his feet, and he could not get high enough to see himself in either direction. When he dropped to the ground beside her again, he said, "There's nothing to eat here either, is there?"

"I haven't found anything."

"They—I mean, Dr. Island wouldn't just let us starve, would he?"

"I don't think he could do anything; that's the way this place is built. Sometimes you find things, and I've tried to catch fish, but I never could. A couple of times Ignacio gave me part of what he had, though; he's good at it. I bet you think I'm skinny, don't you? But I was a lot fatter when I came here."

"What are we going to do now?"

"Keep walking, I suppose, Nicholas. Maybe go back to the water."

"Do you think we'll find anything?"

From a decaying log, insect stridulations called, "Wait."

Nicholas asked, "Do *you* know where anything is?"

"Something for you to eat? Not at present. But I can show you something much more interesting, not far from here, than this clutter of dying trees. Would you like to see it?"

Diane said, "Don't go, Nicholas."

"What is it?"

"Diane, who calls this 'the Focus,' calls what I wish to show you 'the Point.' "

Nicholas asked Diane, "Why shouldn't I go?"

"I'm not going. I went there once anyway."

"I took her," Dr. Island said. "And I'll take you. I wouldn't take you if I didn't think it might help you."

"I don't think Diane liked it."

"Diane may not wish to be helped—help may be painful, and often people do not. But it is my business to help them if I can, whether or not they wish it."

"Suppose I don't want to go?"

"Then I cannot compel you; you know that. But you will be the only patient in this sector who has not seen it, Nicholas, as well as the youngest; both Diane and Ignacio have, and Ignacio goes there often."

"Is it dangerous?"

"No. Are you afraid?"

Nicholas looked questioningly at Diane. "What is it? What will I see?"

She had walked away while he was talking to Dr. Island, and was now sitting cross-legged on the ground about five meters from where Nicholas stood, staring at her hands. Nicholas repeated, "What will I see, Diane?" He did not think she would answer.

She said, "A glass. A mirror."

"Just a mirror?"

"You know how I told you to climb the tree here? The Point is where the edges come together. You can see yourself—like on the beach—but closer."

Nicholas was disappointed. "I've seen myself in mirrors lots of times."

Dr. Island, whose voice was now in the sighing of the dead leaves, whispered, "Did you have a mirror in your room, Nicholas, before you came here?"

"A steel one."

"So that you could not break it?"

"I guess so. I threw things at it sometimes, but it just got puckers in it." Remembering dimpled reflections, Nicholas laughed.

"You can't break this one either."

"It doesn't sound like it's worth going to see."

"I think it is."

"Diane, do you still think I shouldn't go?"

There was no reply. The girl sat staring at the ground in front of her. Nicholas walked over to look at her and found a tear had washed a damp trail down each thin cheek, but she did not move when he touched her. "She's catatonic, isn't she," he said.

A green limb just outside the Focus nodded. "Catatonic schizophrenia."

"I had a doctor once that said those names—like that. They didn't mean anything." (The doctor had been a therapy robot, but a human doctor gave more status. Robots' patients sat in doorless booths—two and a half hours a day for Nicholas: an hour and a half in the morning, an hour in the afternoon—and talked to something that appeared to be a small, friendly food freezer. Some people sat every day in silence, while others talked continually, and for such patients as these the attendants seldom troubled to turn the machines on.)

"He meant cause and treatment. He was correct."

Nicholas stood looking down at the girl's streaked, brown-blond head. "What *is* the cause? I mean for her."

"I don't know."

"And what's the treatment?"

"You are seeing it."

"Will it help her?"

"Probably not."

"Listen, she can hear you, don't you know that? She hears everything we say."

"If my answer disturbs you, Nicholas, I can change it. It will help her if she wants to be helped; if she insists on clasping her illness to her it will not."

"We ought to go away from here," Nicholas said uneasily.

"To your left you will see a little path, a very faint one. Between the twisted tree and the bush with the yellow flowers."

Nicholas nodded and began to walk, looking back at Diane several times. The flowers were butterflies, who fled in a cloud of color when he approached them, and he wondered if Dr. Island had known. When he had gone a hundred paces and was well away from the brown and rotting vegetation, he said, "She was sitting in the Focus."

"Yes."

"Is she still there?"

"Yes."

"What will happen when the Bright Spot comes?"

"Diane will become uncomfortable and move, if she is still there."

"Once in one of the places I was in there was a man who was like that, and they said he wouldn't get anything to eat if he didn't get up and get it, they weren't going to feed him with the nose tube any more; and they didn't, and he died. We told them about it and they wouldn't do anything and he starved to death right there, and when he was dead they rolled him off onto a stretcher and changed the bed and put somebody else there."

"I know, Nicholas. You told the doctors at St. John's about all that, and it is in your file; but think: well men have starved themselves—yes, to death—to protest what they felt were political injustices. Is it so surprising that your friend killed himself in the same way to protest what he felt as a psychic injustice?"

"He wasn't my friend. Listen, did you really mean it when you said the treatment she was getting here would help Diane if she wanted to be helped?"

"No."

Nicholas halted in mid-stride. "You didn't mean it? You don't think it's true?"

"No. I doubt that anything will help her."

"I don't think you ought to lie to us."

"Why not? If by chance you become well you will be released, and if you are released you will have to deal with your society, which will lie to you frequently. Here, where there are so few individuals, I must take the place of society. I have explained that."

"Is that what you are?"

"Society's surrogate? Of course. Who do you imagine built me? What else could I be?"

"The doctor."

"You have had many doctors, and so has she. Not one of them has benefited you much."

"I'm not sure you even want to help us."

"Do you wish to see what Diane calls 'the Point'?"

"I guess so."

"Then you must walk. You will not see it standing here."

Nicholas walked, thrusting aside leafy branches and dangling creepers wet with rain. The jungle smelled of the life of green thing; there were ants on the tree trunks, and dragonflies with hot, red bodies and wings as long as his hands. "Do you want to help us?" he asked after a time.

"My feelings toward you are ambivalent. But when you wish to be helped, I wish to help you."

The ground sloped gently upward, and as it rose became somewhat more clear, the big trees a trifle farther apart, the underbrush spent in grass and fern. Occasionally there were stone outcrops to be climbed, and clearings open to the tumbling sky. Nicholas asked, "Who made this trail?"

"Ignacio. He comes here often."

"He's not afraid, then? Diane's afraid."

"Ignacio is afraid too, but he comes."

"Diane says Ignacio is important."

"Yes."

"What do you mean by that? Is he important? More important than we are?"

"Do you remember that I told you I was the surrogate of society? What do you think society wants, Nicholas?"

"Everybody to do what it says."

"You mean conformity. Yes, there must be conformity, but something else too—consciousness."

"I don't want to hear about it."

"Without consciousness, which you may call sensitivity if you are careful not to allow yourself to be confused by the term, there is no progress. A century ago, Nicholas, mankind was suffocating on Earth; now it is suffocating again. About half of the people who have contributed substantially to the advance of humanity have shown signs of emotional disturbance."

"I told you, I don't want to hear about it. I asked you an easy question—is Ignacio more important than Diane and me—and you won't tell me. I've heard all this you're saying. I've heard it fifty, maybe a hundred times from everybody, and it's lies; it's the regular thing, and you've got it written down on a card somewhere to read out when anybody asks. Those people you talk about that went crazy, they went crazy because while they were 'advancing humanity,' or whatever you call it, people kicked them out of their rooms because they couldn't pay, and while they were getting thrown out you were making other people rich that had never done anything in their whole lives except think about how to get that way."

"Sometimes it is hard, Nicholas, to determine before the fact—or even at the time—just who should be honored."

"How do you know if you've never tried?"

"You asked if Ignacio was more important than Diane or yourself. I can only say that Ignacio seems to me to hold a brighter promise of a full recovery coupled with a substantial contribution to human progress."

"If he's so good, why did he crack up?"

"Many do, Nicholas. Even among the inner planets space is not a kind environment for mankind; and our space, trans-Martian space, is worse. Any young person here, anyone like yourself or Diane who would seem to have a better-than-average chance of adapting to the conditions we face, is precious."

"Or Ignacio."

"Yes, or Ignacio. Ignacio has a tested IQ of two hundred and ten, Nicholas. Diane's is one hundred and twenty. Your own is ninety-five."

"They never took mine."

"It's on your records, Nicholas."

"They tried to and I threw down the helmet and it broke; Sister Carmela—she was the nurse—just wrote down something on the paper and sent me back."

"I see. I will ask for a complete investigation of this, Nicholas."

"Sure."

"Don't you believe me?"

"I don't think you believed me."

"Nicholas, Nicholas . . ." The long tongues of grass now beginning to appear beneath the immense trees sighed. "Can't you see that a certain measure of trust between the two of us is essential?"

"Did you believe me?"

"Why do you ask? Suppose I were to say I did; would you believe that?"

"When you told me I had been reclassified."

"You would have to be retested, for which there are no facilities here."

"If you believed me, why did you say retested? I told you I haven't ever been tested at all—but anyway you could cross out the ninety-five."

"It is impossible for me to plan your therapy without some estimate of your intelligence, Nicholas, and I have nothing with which to replace it."

The ground was sloping up more sharply now, and in a clearing the boy halted and turned to look back at the leafy film, like algae over a pool, beneath which he had climbed, and at the sea beyond. To his right and left his view was still hemmed with foliage, and ahead of him a meadow on edge (like the square of sand through which he had come, though he did not think of that), dotted still with trees, stretched steeply toward an invisible summit. It seemed to him that under his feet the mountainside swayed ever so slightly. Abruptly he demanded of the wind, "Where's Ignacio?"

"Not here. Much closer to the beach."

"And Diane?"

"Where you left her. Do you enjoy the panorama?"

"It's pretty, but it feels like we're rocking."

"We are. I am moored to the temperglass exterior of our satellite by two hundred cables, but the tide and the currents none the less impart a slight motion to my body. Naturally this movement is magnified as you go higher."

"I thought you were fastened right onto the hull; if there's water under you, how do people get in and out?"

"I am linked to the main air lock by a communication tube. To you when you came, it probably seemed an ordinary companionway."

Nicholas nodded and turned his back on leaves and sea and began to climb again.

"You are in a beautiful spot, Nicholas; do you open your heart to beauty?" After waiting for an answer that did not come, the wind sang:

> "The mountain wooded to the peak, the lawns
> And winding glades high up like ways to Heaven,
> The slender coco's drooping crown of plumes,
> The lightning flash of insect and of bird,
> The lustre of the long convolvuluses
> That coil'd around the stately stems, and ran
> Ev'n to the limit of the land, the glows
> And glories of the broad belt of the world,
> All these he saw."

"Does this mean nothing to you, Nicholas?"

"You read a lot, don't you?"

"Often, when it is dark, everyone else is asleep and there is very little else for me to do."

"You talk like a woman; are you a woman?"

"How could I be a woman?"

"You know what I mean. Except, when you were talking mostly to Diane, you sounded more like a man."

"You haven't yet said you think me beautiful."

"You're an Easter egg."

"What do you mean by that, Nicholas?"

"Never mind." He saw the egg as it had hung in the air before him, shining with gold and covered with flowers.

"Eggs are dyed with pretty colors for Easter, and my colors are beautiful—is that what you mean, Nicholas?"

His mother had brought the egg on visiting day, but she could never have made it. Nicholas knew who must have made it. The gold was that very pure gold used for shielding delicate instruments; the clear flakes of crystallized carbon that dotted the egg's surface with tiny stars could only have come from a laboratory high-pressure furnace. How angry he must have been when she told him she was going to give it to him.

"It's pretty, isn't it, Nicky?"

It hung in the weightlessness between them, turning very slowly with the memory of her scented gloves.

"The flowers are meadowsweet, fraxinella, lily of the valley, and moss rose—though I wouldn't expect you to recognize them, darling." His mother had never been below the orbit of Mars, but she pretended to have spent her girlhood on Earth; each reference to the lie filled Nicholas with inexpressible fury and shame. The egg was about twenty centimeters long and it revolved, end over end, in some small fraction more than eight of the pulse beats he felt in his cheeks. Visiting time had twenty-three minutes to go.

"Aren't you going to look at it?"

"I can see it from here." He tried to make her understand. "I can see every part of it. The little red things are aluminum oxide crystals, right?"

"I mean, look *inside*, Nicky."

He saw then that there was a lens at one end, disguised as a dewdrop in the throat of an asphodel. Gently he took the egg in his hands, closed one eye, and looked. The light of the interior was not, as he had half expected, gold tinted, but brilliantly white, deriving from some concealed source. A world surely meant for Earth shone within, as though seen from below the orbit of the moon—indigo sea and emerald land. Rivers brown and clear as tea ran down long plains.

His mother said, "Isn't it pretty?"

Night hung at the corners in funereal purple, and sent long shadows like cold and lovely arms to caress the day; and while he watched and it fell, long-necked birds of so dark a pink that they were nearly red trailed stilt legs across the sky, their wings making crosses.

"They are called flamingos," Dr. Island said, following the direction of his eyes. "Isn't it a pretty word? For a pretty bird, but I don't think we'd like them as much if we called them sparrows, would we?"

His mother said, "I'm going to take it home and keep it for you. It's too nice to leave with a little boy, but if you ever come home again it will be waiting for you. On your dresser, beside your hairbrushes."

Nicholas said, "Words just mix you up."

"You shouldn't despise them, Nicholas. Besides having great beauty of their own, they are useful in reducing tension. You might benefit from that."

"You mean you talk yourself out of it."

"I mean that a person's ability to verbalize his feelings, if only to himself, may prevent them from destroying him. Evolution teaches us, Nicholas, that the original purpose of language was to ritualize men's threats and curses, his spells to compel the gods; communication came later. Words can be a safety valve."

Nicholas said, "I want to be a bomb; a bomb doesn't need a safety valve." To his mother, "Is that South America, Mama?"

"No, dear, India. The Malabar Coast on your left, the Coromandel Coast on your right, and Ceylon below." Words.

"A bomb destroys itself, Nicholas."

"A bomb doesn't care."

He was climbing resolutely now, his toes grabbing at tree roots and the soft, mossy soil; his physician was no longer the wind but a small brown monkey that followed a stone's throw behind him. "I hear someone coming," he said.

"Yes."

"Is it Ignacio?"

"No, it is Nicholas. You are close now."

"Close to the Point?"

"Yes."

He stopped and looked around him. The sounds he had heard, the naked feet padding on soft ground, stopped as well. Nothing seemed strange; the land still rose, and there were large trees, widely spaced, with moss growing in their deepest shade, grass where there was more light. "The three big trees," Nicholas said, "they're just alike. Is that how you know where we are?"

"Yes."

In his mind he called the one before him "Ceylon"; the others were "Coromandel" and "Malabar." He walked toward Ceylon, studying its massive, twisted limbs; a boy naked as himself walked out of the forest to his left, toward Malabar—this boy was not looking at Nicholas, who shouted and ran toward him.

The boy disappeared. Only Malabar, solid and real, stood before Nicholas; he ran to it, touched its rough bark with his hand, and then saw beyond it a fourth tree, similar too to the Ceylon tree, around which a boy peered with averted head. Nicholas watched him for a moment, then said, "I see."

"Do you?" the monkey chattered.

"It's like a mirror, only backwards. The light from the front of me goes out and hits the edge, and comes in the other side, only I can't see it because I'm not looking that way. What I see is the light from my back, sort of, because it comes back this way. When I ran, did I get turned around?"

"Yes, you ran out the left side of the segment, and of course returned immediately from the right."

"I'm not scared. It's kind of fun." He picked up a stick and threw it as hard as he could toward the Malabar tree. It vanished, whizzed over his head, vanished again, slapped the back of his legs. "Did this scare Diane?"

There was no answer. He strode farther, palely naked boys walking to his left and right, but always looking away from him, gradually coming closer.

"Don't go farther," Dr. Island said behind him. "It can be dangerous if you try to pass through the Point itself."

"I see it," Nicholas said. He saw three more trees, growing very close together, just ahead of him; their branches seemed strangely intertwined as they danced together in the wind, and beyond them there was nothing at all.

"You can't actually go through the Point," Dr. Island Monkey said. "The tree covers it."

"Then why did you warn me about it?" Limping and scarred, the boys to his right and left were no more than two meters away now; he had discovered that if he looked straight ahead he could sometimes glimpse their bruised profiles.

"That's far enough, Nicholas."

"I want to touch the tree."

He took another step, and another, then turned. The Malabar boy turned too, presenting his narrow back, on which the ribs and spine seemed welts. Nicholas reached out both arms and laid his hands on the thin shoulders, and as he did, felt other hands—the cool, unfeeling hands of a stranger, dry hands too small—touch his own shoulders and creep upward toward his neck.

"Nicholas!"

He jumped sidewise away from the tree and looked at his hands, his head swaying. "It wasn't me."

"Yes, it was, Nicholas," the monkey said.

"It was one of them."

"You are all of them."

In one quick motion Nicholas snatched up an arm-long section of fallen limb and hurled it at the monkey. It struck the little creature, knocking it down, but the monkey sprang up and fled on three legs. Nicholas sprinted after it.

He had nearly caught it when it darted to one side; as quickly, he turned toward the other, springing for the monkey he saw running toward him there. In an instant it was in his grip, feebly trying to bite. He slammed its head against the ground, then catching it by the ankles swung it against the Ceylon tree until at the third impact he heard the skull crack, and stopped.

He had expected wires, but there were none. Blood oozed from the battered little face, and the furry body was warm and limp in his hands. Leaves above his head said, "You haven't killed me, Nicholas. You never will."

"How does it work?" He was still searching for wires, tiny circuit cards holding micro-logic. He looked about for a sharp stone with which to open the monkey's body, but could find none.

"It is just a monkey," the leaves said. "If you had asked, I would have told you."

"How did you make him talk?" He dropped the monkey, stared at it for a moment, then kicked it. His fingers were bloody, and he wiped them on the leaves of the tree.

"Only my mind speaks to yours, Nicholas."

"Oh," he said. And then, "I've heard of that. I didn't think it would be like this. I thought it would be in my head."

"Your record shows no auditory halluncinations, but haven't you ever known someone who had them?"

"I knew a girl once . . ." He paused.

"Yes?"

"She twisted noises—you know?"

"Yes."

"Like, it would just be a service cart out in the corridor, but she'd hear the fan, and think . . ."

"What?"

"Oh, different things. That it was somebody talking, calling her."

"Hear them?"

"What?" He sat up in his bunk. "Maya?"

"They're coming after me."

"Maya?"

Dr. Island, through the leaves, said, "When I talk to you, Nicholas, your mind makes any sound you hear the vehicle for my thoughts' content. You may hear me softly in the patter of rain, or joyfully in the singing of a bird—but if I wished I could amplify what I say until every idea and suggestion I wished to give would be driven like a nail into your consciousness. Then you would do whatever I wished you to."

"I don't believe it," Nicholas said. "If you can do that, why don't you tell Diane not to be catatonic?"

"First, because she might retreat more deeply into her disease in an effort to escape me; and second, because ending her catatonia in that way would not remove its cause."

"And thirdly?"

"I did not say 'thirdly,' Nicholas."

"I thought I heard it—when two leaves touched."

"Thirdly, Nicholas, because both you and she have been

chosen for your effect on someone else; if I were to change her—or you—so abruptly, that effect would be lost." Dr. Island was a monkey again now, a new monkey that chattered from the protection of a tree twenty meters away. Nicholas threw a stick at him.

"The monkeys are only little animals, Nicholas; they like to follow people, and they chatter."

"I bet Ignacio kills them."

"No, he likes them; he only kills fish to eat."

Nicholas was suddenly aware of his hunger. He began to walk.

He found Ignacio on the beach, praying. For an hour or more, Nicholas hid behind the trunk of a palm watching him, but for a long time he could not decide to whom Ignacio prayed. He was kneeling just where the lacy edges of the breakers died, looking out toward the water; and from time to time he bowed, touching his forehead to the damp sand; then Nicholas could hear his voice, faintly, over the crashing and hissing of the waves. In general, Nicholas approved of prayer, having observed that those who prayed were usually more interesting companions than those who did not; but he had also noticed that though it made no difference what name the devotee gave the object of his devotions, it was important to discover how the god was conceived. Ignacio did not seem to be praying to Dr. Island— he would, Nicholas thought, have been facing the other way for that—and for a time he wondered if he were not praying to the waves. From his position behind him he followed Ignacio's line of vision out and out, wave upon wave into the bright, confused sky, up and up until at last it curved completely around and came to rest on Ignacio's back again; and then it occurred to him that Ignacio might be praying to himself. He left the palm trunk then and walked about halfway to the place where Ignacio knelt, and sat down. Above the sounds of the sea and the murmuring of Ignacio's voice hung a silence so immense and fragile that it seemed that at any moment the entire crystal satellite might ring like a gong.

After a time Nicholas felt his left side trembling. With his right hand he began to stroke it, running his fingers down his left arm, and from his left shoulder to the thigh. It worried him that his left side should be so frightened, and he wondered if perhaps that other half of his brain, from which he was forever severed, could hear what Ignacio was saying to the waves. He began to pray himself, so that the other (and perhaps Ignacio too) could hear, saying not quite beneath his breath, "Don't worry, don't be afraid, he's not going to hurt us, he's nice, and if he does we'll get him; we're only going to get something to eat, maybe he'll show us how to catch fish, I think he'll be nice this time." But he knew, or at least felt he knew, that Ignacio would not be nice this time.

Eventually Ignacio stood up; he did not turn to face Nicholas, but waded out to sea; then, as though he had known Nicholas was behind him all the time (though Nicholas was not sure he had been heard—perhaps, so he thought, Dr. Island had told Ignacio), he gestured to indicate that Nicholas should follow him.

The water was colder than he remembered, the sand coarse and gritty between his toes. He thought of what Dr. Island had told him—about floating—and that a part of her must be this sand, under the water, reaching out (how far?) into the sea; when she ended there would be nothing but the clear temperglass of the satellite itself, far down.

"Come," Ignacio said. "Can you swim?" Just as though he had forgotten the night before. Nicholas said yes, he could, wondering if Ignacio would look around at him when he spoke. He did not.

"And do you know why you are here?"

"You told me to come."

"Ignacio means *here*. Does this not remind you of any place you have seen before, little one?"

Nicholas thought of the crystal gong and the Easter egg, then of the micro-thin globes of perfumed vapor that, at home, were sometimes sent floating down the corridors at Christmas to explode in clean dust and a cold smell of pine forests when the children stuck them with their hopping-canes; but he said nothing.

Ignacio continued, "Let Ignacio tell you a story. Once there was a man—a boy, actually—on the Earth, who—"

Nicholas wondered why it was always men (most often doctors and clinical psychologists, in his experience) who wanted to tell you stories. Jesus, he recalled, was always telling everyone stories, and the Virgin Mary almost never, though a woman he had once known who thought she was the Virgin Mary had always been talking about her son. He thought Ignacio looked a little like Jesus. He tried to remember if his mother had ever told him stories when he was at home, and decided that she had not; she just turned on the comscreen to the cartoons.

"—wanted to—"

"—tell a story," Nicholas finished for him.

"How did you know?" Angry and surprised.

"It was you, wasn't it? And you want to tell one now."

"What you said was not what Ignacio would have said. He was going to tell you about a fish."

"Where is it?" Nicholas asked, thinking of the fish Ignacio had been eating the night before, and imagining another such fish, caught while he had been coming back, perhaps, from the Point, and now concealed somewhere waiting the fire. "Is it a big one?"

"It is gone now," Ignacio said, "but it was only as long as a man's hand. I caught it in the big river."

Huckleberry—"I know, the Mississippi; it was a catfish. Or a sunfish."—*Finn.*

"Possibly that is what you call them; for a time he was as the sun to a certain one." The light from nowhere danced on the water. "In any event he was kept on that table in the salon in the house where life was lived. In a tank, but not the old kind in which one sees the glass, with metal at the corner. But the new kind in which the glass is so strong, but very thin, and curved so that it does not reflect, and there are no corners, and a clever device holds the water clear." He dipped up a handful of sparkling water, still not meeting Nicholas's eyes. "As clear even as this, and there were no ripples, and so you could not see it at all. My fish floated in the center of my table above a few stones."

Nicholas asked, "Did you float on the river on a raft?"

"No, we had a little boat. Ignacio caught this fish in a net, of which he almost bit through the strands before he could be landed; he possessed wonderful teeth. There was no one in the house but him and the other, and the robots; but each morning someone would go to the pool in the patio and catch a goldfish for him. Ignacio would see this goldfish there when he came down for his breakfast, and would think, 'Brave goldfish, you have been cast to the monster, will you be the one to destroy him? Destroy him and you shall have his diamond house forever.' And then the fish, who had a little spot of red beneath his wonderful teeth, a spot like a cherry, would rush upon that young goldfish, and for an instant the water would be all clouded with blood."

"And then what?" Nicholas asked.

"And then the clever machine would make the water clear once more, and the fish would be floating above the stones as before, the fish with the wonderful teeth, and Ignacio would touch the little switch on the table, and ask for more bread, and more fruit."

"Are you hungry now?"

"No, I am tired and lazy now; if I pursue you I will not catch you, and if I catch you—through your own slowness and clumsiness—I will not kill you, and if I kill you I will not eat you."

Nicholas had begun to back away, and at the last words, realizing that they were a signal, he turned and began to run, splashing through the shallow water. Ignacio ran after him, much helped by his longer legs, his hair flying behind his dark young face, his square teeth—each white as a bone and as big as Nicholas' thumbnail—showing like spectators who lined the railings of his lips.

"Don't run, Nicholas," Dr. Island said with the voice of a wave. "It only makes him angry that you run." Nicholas did not answer, but cut to his left, up the beach and among the trunks of the palms, sprinting all the way because he had no way of knowing Ignacio was not right behind him, about to grab him by the neck. When he stopped it was in the thick jungle, among the boles of the hardwoods, where he leaned, out of breath, the thumping of his own heart the only sound in an atmosphere silent and unwaked as Earth's long, prehuman day. For a time he listened for any sound Ignacio might make searching for him; there was none. He drew a deep breath then and said, "Well, that's over," expecting Dr. Island to answer from somewhere; there was only the green hush.

The light was still bright and strong and nearly shadowless, but some interior sense told him the day was nearly over, and he noticed that such faint shades as he could see stretched long, horizontal distortions of their objects. He felt no hunger, but he had fasted before and knew on which side of hunger he stood; he was not as strong as he had been only a day past, and by this time next day he would probably be unable to outrun Ignacio. He should, he now realized, have eaten the monkey he had killed; but his stomach revolted at the thought of the raw flesh, and he did not know how he might build a fire, although Ignacio seemed to have done so the night before. Raw fish, even if he were able to catch a fish, would be as bad, or worse, than raw monkey; he remembered his effort to open a coconut—he had failed, but it was surely not impossible. His mind was hazy as to what a coconut might contain, but there had to be an edible core, because they were eaten in books. He decided to make a wide sweep through the jungle that would bring him back to the beach well away from Ignacio; he had several times seen coconuts lying in the sand under the trees.

He moved quietly, still a little afraid, trying to think of ways to open the coconut when he found it. He imagined himself standing before a large and raggedly faceted stone, holding the coconut in both hands. He raised it and smashed it down, but when it struck it was no longer a coconut but Maya's head; he heard her nose cartilage break with a distinct, rubbery snap. Her eyes, as blue as the sky above Madhya Pradesh, the sparkling blue sky of the egg, looked up at him, but he could no longer look into them, they retreated from his own, and it came to him quite suddenly that Lucifer, in falling, must have fallen up, into the fires and the coldness of space, never again to see the warm blues and browns and greens of Earth: *I was watching Satan fall as lightning from heaven.* He had heard that on tape somewhere, but he could not remember where. He had read that on Earth lightning did not come down from the clouds, but leaped up from the planetary surface toward them, never to return.

"Nicholas."

He listened, but did not hear his name again. Faintly water was babbling; had Dr. Island used that sound to speak to him? He walked toward it and found a little rill that threaded a way among the trees, and followed it. In a hundred steps it grew broader, slowed, and ended in a long blind pool under a dome of leaves. Diane was sitting on moss on the side opposite him; she looked up as she saw him, and smiled.

"Hello," he said.

"Hello, Nicholas. I thought I heard you. I wasn't mistaken after all, was I?"

"I didn't think I said anything." He tested the dark water with his foot and found that it was very cold.

"You gave a little gasp, I fancy. I heard it, and I said to myself, *that's Nicholas,* and I called you. Then I thought I might be wrong, or that it might be Ignacio."

"Ignacio was chasing me. Maybe he still is, but I think he's probably given up by now."

The girl nodded, looking into the dark waters of the pool, but did not seem to have heard him. He began to work his way around to her, climbing across the snakelike roots of the crowding trees. "Why does Ignacio want to kill me, Diane?"

"Sometimes he wants to kill me too," the girl said.

"But why?"

"I think he's a bit frightened of us. Have you ever talked to him, Nicholas?"

"Today I did a little. He told me a story about a pet fish he used to have."

"Ignacio grew up all alone; did he tell you that? On Earth. On a plantation in Brazil, way up the Amazon—Dr. Island told me."

"I thought it was crowded on Earth."

"The cities are crowded, and the countryside closest to the cities. But there are places where it's emptier than it used to be. Where Ignacio was, there would have been Red Indian hunters two or three hundred years ago; when he was there, there wasn't anyone, just the machines. Now he doesn't want to be looked at, doesn't want anyone around him."

Nicholas said slowly, "Dr. Island said lots of people wouldn't be sick if only there weren't other people around all the time. Remember that?"

"Only there are other people around all the time; that's how the world is."

"Not in Brazil, maybe," Nicholas said. He was trying to remember something about Brazil, but the only thing he could think of was a parrot singing in a straw hat from the comview cartoons; and then a turtle and a hedgehog that turned into armadillos for the love of God, Montressor. He said, "Why didn't he stay here?"

"Did I tell you about the bird, Nicholas?" She had been not-listening again.

"What bird?"

"I have a bird. Inside." She patted the flat stomach below her small breasts, and for a moment Nicholas thought she had really found food. "She sits in here. She has tangled a nest in my entrails, where she sits and tears at my breath with her beak. I look healthy to you, don't I? But inside I'm hollow and rotten and turning brown, dirt and old feathers, oozing away. Her beak will break through soon."

"Okay." Nicholas turned to go.

"I've been drinking water here, trying to drown her. I think I've swallowed so much I couldn't stand up now if I tried, but she isn't even wet, and do you know something, Nicholas? I've found out I'm not really me, I'm her."

Turning back Nicholas asked, "When was the last time you had anything to eat?"

"I don't know. Two, three days ago. Ignacio gave me something."

"I'm going to try to open a coconut. If I can I'll bring you back some."

When he reached the beach, Nicholas turned and walked slowly back in the direction of the dead fire, this time along the rim of dampened sand between the sea and the palms. He was thinking about machines.

There were hundreds of thousands, perhaps millions, of machines out beyond the belt, but few or none of the sophisticated servant robots of Earth—those were luxuries. Would Ignacio, in Brazil (whatever that was like), have had such luxuries? Nicholas thought not; those robots were almost like people, and living with them would be like living with people. Nicholas wished that he could speak Brazilian.

There had been the therapy robots at St. John's; Nicholas had not liked them, and he did not think Ignacio would have liked them either. If he had liked his therapy robot he probably would not have had to be sent here. He thought of the chipped and rusted old machine that had cleaned the corridors—Maya had called it Corradora, but no one else ever called it anything but *Hey!* It could not (or at least did not) speak, and Nicholas doubted that it had emotions, except possibly a sort of love of cleanness that did not extend to its own person. "You will understand," someone was saying inside his head, "that motives of all sorts can be divided into two sorts." A doctor? A therapy robot? It did not matter. "Extrinsic and intrinsic. An extrinsic motive has always some further end in view, and that end we call an intrinsic motive. Thus when we have reduced motivation to intrinsic motivation we have reduced it to its simplest parts. Take that machine over there."

What machine?

"Freud would have said that it was fixated at the latter anal stage, perhaps due to the care its builders exercised in seeing that the dirt it collects is not released again. Because of its fixation it is, as you see, obsessed with cleanliness and order; compulsive sweeping and scrubbing palliate its anxieties. It is a strength of Freud's theory, and not a weakness, that it serves to explain many of the activities of machines as well as the acts of persons."

Hello there, Corradora.

And hello, Ignacio.

My head, moving from side to side, must remind you of a radar scanner. My steps are measured, slow, and precise. I emit a scarcely audible humming as I walk, and my eyes are fixed, as I swing my head, not on you, Ignacio, but on the waves at the edge of sight, where they curve up into the sky. I stop ten meters short of you, and I stand.

You go, I follow, ten meters behind. What do I want? Nothing.

Yes, I will pick up the sticks, and I will follow—five meters behind.

"Break them, and put them on the fire. Not all of them, just a few."

Yes.

"Ignacio keeps the fire here burning all the time. Sometimes he takes the coals of fire from it to start others, but here, under the big palm log, he has a fire always. The rain does not strike it here. Always the fire. Do you know how he made it the first time? Reply to him!"

"No."

"No, *Patrão!*"

" 'No, *Patrão.*' "

"Ignacio stole it from the gods, from Poseidon. Now Poseidon is dead, lying at the bottom of the water. Which is the top. Would you like to see him?"

"If you wish it, *Patrão.*"

"It will soon be dark, and that is the time to fish; do you have a spear?"

"No, *Patrão.*"

"Then Ignacio will get you one."

Ignacio took a handful of the sticks and thrust the ends into the fire, blowing on them. After a moment Nicholas leaned over and blew too, until all the sticks were blazing.

"Now we must find you some bamboo, and there is some back here. Follow me."

The light, still nearly shadowless, was dimming now, so that it seemed to Nicholas that they walked on insubstantial soil, though he could feel it beneath his feet. Ignacio stalked ahead, holding up the burning sticks until the fire seemed about to die, then pointing the ends down, allowing it to lick upward toward his hand and come to life again. There was a gentle wind blowing out toward the sea, carrying away the sound of the surf and bringing a damp coolness; and when they had been walking for several minutes, Nicholas heard in it a faint, dry, almost rhythmic rattle.

Ignacio looked back at him and said, "The music. The big stems talking; hear it?"

They found a cane a little thinner than Nicholas's wrist and pilled the burning sticks around its base, then added more. When it fell, Ignacio burned through the upper end too, making a pole about as long as Nicholas was tall, and with the edge of a seashell scrapped the larger end to a point. "Now you are a fisherman," he said. Nicholas said, "Yes, *Patrão*," still careful not to meet his eyes.

"You are hungry?"

"Yes, *Patrão*."

"Then let me tell you something. Whatever you get is Ignacio's, you understand? And what he catches, that is his too. But when he has eaten what he wants, what is left is yours. Come on now, and Ignacio will teach you to fish or drown you."

Ignacio's own spear was buried in the sand not far from the fire; it was much bigger than the one he had made for Nicholas. With it held across his chest he went down to the water, wading until it was waist high, then swimming, not looking to see if Nicholas was following. Nicholas found that he could swim with the spear by putting all his effort into the motion of his legs, holding the spear in his left hand and stroking only occasionally with his right. "You breathe," he said softly, "and watch the spear," and after that he had only to allow his head to lift from time to time.

He had thought Ignacio would begin to look for fish as soon as they were well out from the beach, but the Brazilian continued to swim, slowly but steadily, until it seemed to Nicholas that they must be a kilometer or more from land. Suddenly, as though the lights in a room had responded to a switch, the dark sea around them became an opalescent blue. Ignacio stopped, treading water and using his spear to buoy himself.

"Here," he said. "Get them between yourself and the light."

Open-eyed, he bent his face to the water, raised it again to breathe deeply, and dove. Nicholas followed his example, floating belly-down with open eyes.

All the world of dancing glitter and dark island vanished as though he had plunged his face into a dream. Far, far below him Jupiter displayed its broad, striped disk, marred with the spreading Bright Spot where man-made silicone enzymes had stripped the hydrogen from methane for kindled fusion: a cancer and a burning infant sun. Between that sun and his eyes lay invisible a hundred thousand kilometers of space, and the temperglass shell of the satellite; hundreds of meters of illuminated water, and in it the spread body of Ignacio, dark against the light, still kicking downward, his spear a pencil line of blackness in his hand.

Involuntarily Nicholas' head came up, returning to the universe of sparkling waves, aware now that what he had called "night" was only the shadow cast by Dr. Island when Jupiter and the Bright Spot slid beneath her. That shadow line, indetectable in air, now lay sharp across the water behind him. He took breath and plunged.

Almost at once a fish darted somewhere below, and his left arm thrust the spear forward, but it was far out of reach. He swam after it, then saw another, larger, fish farther down and dove for that, passing Ignacio surfacing for air. The fish was too deep, and he had used up his oxygen; his lungs aching for air, he swam up, wanting to let go of his spear, then realizing at the last moment that he could, that it would only bob to the surface if he released it. His head broke water and he gasped, his heart thumping; water struck his face and he knew again, suddenly, as though they had ceased to exist while he was gone, the pulsebeat pounding of the waves.

Ignacio was waiting for him. He shouted, "This time you will come with Ignacio, and he will show you the dead sea god. Then we will fish."

Unable to speak, Nicholas nodded. He was allowed three more breaths; then Ignacio dove and Nicholas had to follow, kicking down until the pressure sang in his ears. Then through blue water he saw, looming at the edge of the light, a huge mass of metal anchored to the temperglass hull of the satellite itself; above it, hanging lifelessly like the stem of a great vine severed from the root, a cable twice as thick as a man's body; and on the bottom, sprawled beside the mighty anchor, a legged god that might have been a dead insect save that it was at least six meters long. Ignacio turned and looked back at Nicholas to see if he understood; he did not, but he nodded, and with the strength draining from his arms, surfaced again.

After Ignacio brought up the first fish, they took turns on the surface guarding their catch, and while the Bright Spot crept beneath the shelving rim of Dr. Island, they speared two more, one of them quite large. Then when Nicholas was so exhausted he could scarcely lift his arms, they made their way back to shore, and Ignacio showed him how to gut the fish with a thorn and the edge of a shell, and reclose them and pack them in mud and leaves to be roasted by the fire. After Ignacio had begun to eat the largest fish, Nicholas timidly drew out the smallest, and ate for the first time since coming to Dr. Island. Only when he had finished did he remember Diane.

He did not dare to take the last fish to her, but he looked covertly at Ignacio, and began edging away from the fire. The Brazilian seemed not to have noticed him. When he was well into the shadows he stood, backed a few steps, then—slowly, as his instincts warned him—walked away, not beginning to trot until the distance between them was nearly a hundred meters.

He found Diane sitting apathetic and silent at the margin of the cold pool, and had some difficulty persuading her to stand. At last he lifted her, his hands under her arms pressing against her thin ribs. Once on her feet she stood steadily enough, and followed him when he took her by the hand. He talked to her, knowing that although she gave no sign of hearing she heard him, and that the right words might wake her to response. "We went fishing—Ignacio showed me how. And he's got a fire, Diane, he got it from a kind of robot that was supposed to be fixing one of the cables that holds Dr. Island, I don't know how. Anyway, listen, we caught three big fish, and I ate one and Ignacio ate a great big one, and I don't think he'd mind if you had the other one, only say, 'Yes, *Patrão*,' and 'No, *Patrão*,' to him—he likes that, and he's only used to machines. You don't have to smile at him or anything—just look at the fire, that's what I do, just look at the fire."

To Ignacio, perhaps wisely, he at first said nothing at all, leading Diane to the place where he had been sitting himself a few minutes before and placing some scraps from his fish in her lap. When she did not eat he found a sliver of the tender, roasted flesh and thrust it into her mouth. Ignacio said, "Ignacio believed that one dead," and Nicholas answered, "No, *Patrão*."

"There is another fish. Give it to her."

Nicholas did, raking the gob of baked mud from the coals to crack with the heel of his hand, and peeling the broken and steaming fillets from the skin and bones to give to her when they had cooled enough to eat; after the fish had lain in her mouth for perhaps half a minute she began to chew and swallow, and after the third mouthful she fed herself, though without looking at either of them.

"Ignacio believed that one dead," Ignacio said again.

"No, *Patrão*," Nicholas answered, and then added, "Like you can see, she's alive."

"She is a pretty creature, with the firelight on her face —no?"

"Yes, *Patrão,* very pretty."

"But too thin." Ignacio moved around the fire until he was sitting almost beside Diane, then reached for the fish Nicholas had given her. Her hands closed on it, though she still did not look at him.

"You see, she knows us after all," Ignacio said. "We are not ghosts."

Nichols whispered urgently, "Let him have it."

Slowly Diane's fingers relaxed, but Ignacio did not take the fish. "I was only joking, little one," he said. "And I think not such a good joke after all." Then when she did not reply, he turned away from her, his eyes reaching out across the dark, tossing water for something Nicholas could not see.

"She likes you, *Patrão,*" Nicholas said. The words were like swallowing filth, but he thought of the bird ready to tear through Diane's skin, and Maya's blood soaking in little round dots in the white cloth, and continued. "She is only shy. It is better that way."

"You. What do you know?"

At least Ignacio was no longer looking at the sea. Nicholas said, "Isn't it true, *Patrão?*"

"Yes, it is true."

Diane was picking at the fish again, conveying tiny flakes to her mouth with delicate fingers; distinctly but almost absently she said, "Go, Nicholas."

He looked at Ignacio, but the Brazilian's eyes did not turn toward the girl, nor did he speak.

"Nicholas, go away. Please."

In a voice he hoped was pitched too low for Ignacio to hear, Nicholas said, "I'll see you in the morning. All right?"

Her head moved a fraction of a centimeter.

Once he was out of sight of the fire, one part of the beach was as good to sleep on as another; he wished he had taken a piece of wood from the fire to start one of his own and tried to cover his legs with sand to keep off the cool wind, but the sand fell away whenever he moved, and his legs and his left hand moved without vilotion on his part.

The surf, lapping at the rippled shore, said, "That was well done, Nicholas."

"I can feel you move," Nicholas said. "I don't think I ever could before except when I was high up."

"I doubt that you can now; my roll is less than one one-hundredth of a degree."

"Yes, I can. You wanted me to do that, didn't you? About Ignacio.

"Do you know what the Harlow effect is, Nicholas?"

Nicholas shook his head.

"About a hundred years ago Dr. Harlow experimented with monkeys who had been raised in complete isolation —no mothers, no other monkeys at all."

"Lucky monkeys."

"When the monkeys were mature he put them into cages with normal ones; they fought with any that came near them, and sometimes they killed them."

"Psychologists always put things in cages; did he ever think of turning them loose in the jungle instead?"

"No, Nicholas, though we have . . . Aren't you going to say anything?"

"I guess not."

"Dr. Harlow tried, you see, to get the isolate monkeys to breed—sex is the primary social function—but they wouldn't. Whenever another monkey of either sex approached they displayed aggressiveness, which the other monkeys returned. He cured them finally by introducing immature monkeys—monkey children—in place of the mature, socialized ones. These needed the isolate adults so badly that they kept on making approaches no matter how often or how violently they were rejected, and in the end they were accepted, and the isolates socialized. It's interesting to note that the founder of Christianity seems to have had an intuitive grasp of the principle—but it was almost two thousand years before it was demonstrated scientifically."

"I don't think it worked here," Nicholas said. "It was more complicated than that."

"Human beings are complicated monkeys, Nicholas."

"That's about the first time I ever heard you make a joke. You like not being human, don't you?"

"Of course. Wouldn't you?"

"I always thought I would, but now I'm not sure. You said that to help me, didn't you? I don't like that."

A wave higher than the others splashed chill foam over Nicholas's legs, and for a moment he wondered if this were Dr. Island's reply. Half a minute later another wave wet him, and another, and he moved farther up the beach to avoid them. The wind was stronger, but he slept despite it, and was awakened only for a moment by a flash of light from the direction from which he had come; he tried to guess what might have caused it, thought of Diane and Ignacio throwing the burning sticks into the air to see the arcs of fire, smiled—to sleepy now to be angry—and slept again.

Morning came cold and sullen; Nicholas ran up and down the beach, rubbing himself with his hands. A thin rain, or spume (it was hard to tell which), was blowing in the wind, clouding the light to gray radiance. He wondered if Diane and Ignacio would mind if he came back now and decided to wait, then thought of fishing so that he would have something to bring when he came; but the sea was very cold and the waves so high they tumbled him, wrenching his bamboo spear from his hand. Ignacio found him dripping with water, sitting with his back to a palm trunk and staring out toward the lifting curve of the sea.

"Hello, you," Ignacio said.

"Good morning, *Patrão.*"

Ignacio sat down. "What is your name? You told me, I think, when we first met, but I have forgotten. I am sorry."

"Nicholas."

"Yes."

"*Patrão,* I am very cold. Would it be possible for us to go to your fire?"

"My name is Ignacio; call me that."

Nicholas nodded, frightened.

"But we cannot go to my fire, because the fire is out."

"Can't you make another one, *Patrão?*"

"You do not trust me, do you? I do not blame you. No, I cannot make another—you may use what I had, if you wish, and make one after I have gone. I came only to say goodbye."

"You're leaving?"

The wind in the palm fronds said, "Ignacio is much better now. He will be going to another place, Nicholas."

"A hospital?"

"Yes, a hospital, but I don't think he will have to stay there long."

"But . . . " Nicholas tried to think of something appropriate. At St. John's and the other places where he had been confined, when people left, they simply left, and usually were hardly spoken of once it was learned that they were going and thus were already tainted by whatever it was that froze the smiles and dried the tears of those outside. At last he said, "Thanks for teaching me how to fish."

"That was all right," Ignacio said. He stood up and put a hand on Nicholas's shoulder, then turned away. Four meters to his left the damp sand was beginning to lift and crack. While Nicholas watched, it opened on a brightly lit companionway walled with white. Ignacio pushed his curly black hair back from his eyes and went down, and the sand closed with a thump.

"He won't be coming back, will he?" Nicholas said.

"No."

"He said I could use his stuff to start another fire, but I don't even know what it is."

Dr. Island did not answer. Nicholas got up and began to walk back to where the fire had been, thinking about Diane and wondering if she was hungry; he was hungry himself.

He found her beside the dead fire. Her chest had been burned away, and lying close by, near the hole in the sand where Ignacio must have kept it hidden, was a bulky nuclear welder. The power pack was too heavy for Nicholas to lift, but he picked up the welding gun on its short cord and touched the trigger, producing a two-meter plasma discharge which he played along the sand until Diane's body was ash. By the time he had finished the wind was whipping the palms and sending stinging rain into his eyes, but he collected a supply of wood and built another fire, bigger and bigger until it roared like a forge in the wind. "He killed her!" he shouted to the waves.

"YES." Dr. Island's voice was big and wild.

"You said he was better."

"HE IS," howled the wind. "YOU KILLED THE MONKEY THAT WANTED TO PLAY WITH YOU, NICHOLAS—AS I BELIEVED IGNACIO WOULD EVENTUALLY KILL YOU, WHO ARE SO EASILY HATED, SO DIFFERENT FROM WHAT IT IS THOUGHT A BOY SHOULD BE. BUT KILLING THE MONKEY HELPED YOU, REMEMBER? MADE YOU BETTER. IGNACIO WAS FRIGHTENED BY WOMEN; NOW HE KNOWS THAT THEY ARE REALLY VERY WEAK, AND HE HAS ACTED UPON CERTAIN FANTASIES AND FINDS THEM BITTER."

"You're rocking," Nicholas said. "Am I doing that?"

"YOUR THOUGHT."

A palm snapped in the storm; instead of falling, it flew crashing among the others, its fronded head catching the wind like a sail. "I'm killing you," Nicholas said. "Destroying you." The left side of his face was so contorted with grief and rage that he could scarcely speak.

Dr. Island heaved beneath his feet. "NO."

"One of your cables is already broken—I saw that. Maybe more than one. You'll pull loose. I'm turning this world, isn't that right? The attitude rockets are tuned to my emotions, and they're spinning us around, and the slippage is the wind and the high sea, and when you come loose nothing will balance any more."

"NO."

"What's the stress on your cables? Don't you know?"

"THEY ARE VERY STRONG."

"What kind of talk is that? You ought to say something like: 'The D-twelve cable tension is twenty-billion kilograms' force. WARNING! WARNING! Expected time to failure is ninety-seven seconds! WARNING!' *Don't you even know how a machine is supposed to talk?*" Nicholas was screaming now, and every wave reached farther up the beach than the last, so that the bases of the most seaward palms were awash.

"GET BACK, NICHOLAS. FIND HIGHER GROUND. GO INTO THE JUNGLE." It was the crashing waves themselves that spoke.

"I won't."

A long serpent of water reached for the fire, which hissed and sputtered.

"GET BACK!"

"I won't!"

A second wave came, striking Nicholas calf-high and nearly entinguishing the fire.

"ALL THIS WILL BE UNDER WATER SOON. GET BACK!"

Nicholas picked up some of the still-burning sticks and tried to carry them, but the wind blew them out as soon as he lifted them from the fire. He tugged at the welder, but it was too heavy for him to life.

"GET BACK!"

He went into the jungle, where the trees lashed themselves to leafy rubbish in the wind and broken branches flew through the air like debris from an explosion; for a while he heard Diane's voice crying in the wind; it became Maya's, then his mother's or Sister Carmela's, and a hundred others; in time the wind grew less, and he could no longer feel the ground rocking. He felt tired. He said, "I didn't kill you after all, did I?" but there was no answer. On the beach, when he returned to it, he found the welder half buried in sand. No trace of Diane's ashes, nor of his fire. He gathered more wood and built another, lighting it with the welder.

"Now," he said. He scooped aside the sand around the welder until he reached the rough understone beneath it, and turned the flame of the welder on that; it blackened and bubbled.

"No," Dr. Island said.

"Yes." He was bending intently over the flame, both hands locked on the welder's trigger.

"Nicholas, stop that." When he did not reply, "Look behind you." There was a splashing louder than the crashing of the waves, and a groaning of metal. He whirled and saw the great, beetle-like robot Ignacio had shown him on the sea floor. Tiny shellfish clung to its metal skin, and water, faintly green, still poured from its body. Before he could turn the welding gun toward it, it shot forward hands like clamps and wrenched it from him. All up and down the beach similar machines were smoothing the sand and repairing the damage of the storm.

"That thing was dead," Nicholas said. "Ignacio killed it."

It picked up the power pack, shook it clean of sand, and turning, stalked back toward the sea.

"That is what Ignacio believed, and it was better that he believed so."

"And you said you couldn't do anything, you had no hands."

"I also told you that I would treat you as society will when you are released, that that was my nature. After that, did you still believe all I told you? Nicholas, you are upset now because Diane is dead—"

"You could have protected her!"

"—but by dying she made someone else—someone very important—well. Her prognosis was bad; she really wanted only death, and this was the death I chose for her. You could call it the death of Dr. Island, a death that would help someone else. Now you are alone, but soon there will be more patients in this segment, and you will help them, too—if you can—and perhaps they will help you. Do you understand?"

"No," Nicholas said. He flung himself down on the sand. The wind had dropped, but it was raining hard. He thought of the vision he had once had, and of describing it to Diane the day before, "This isn't ending the way I thought," he whispered. It was only a squeak of sound far down in his throat. "Nothing ever turns out right."

The waves, the wind, the rustling palm fronds and the

pattering rain, the monkeys who had come down to the beach to search for food washed ashore, answered, "Go away—go back—don't move."

Nicholas pressed his scarred head against his knees, rocking back and forth.

"Don't move."

For a long time he sat still while the rain lashed his shoulders and the dripping monkeys frolicked and fought around him. When at last he lifted his face, there was in it some element of personality which had been only potentially present before, and with this an emptiness and an expression of surprise. His lips moved, and the sounds were the sounds made by a deaf-mute who tries to speak.

"Nicholas is gone," the waves said. "Nicholas, who was the right side of your body, the left half of your brain, I have forced into catatonia; for the remainder of your life he will be to you only what you once were to him—or less. Do you understand?"

The boy nodded.

"We will call you Kenneth, silent one. And if Nicholas tries to come again, Kenneth, you must drive him back—or return to what you have been."

The boy nodded a second time, and a moment afterward began to collect sticks for the dying fire. As though to themselves the waves chanted:

> "Seas are wild tonight . . .
> Stretching over Sado island
> Silent clouds of stars."

There was no reply.

The Ones Who Walk Away from Omelas

(Variations on a Theme by William James)

Ursula K. Le Guin

Herewith, a short, haunting piece by the author of *The Left Hand of Darkness*: a tale of the utopian city called Omelas, where all is beauty and sanity—except for the inhabitant of a dark cell beneath the city. In a curious way, this narrative reminds me of the fictions of Jorge Luis Borges—a comparison not to be made lightly.

With a clamor of bells that set the swallows soaring, the Festival of Summer came to the city Omelas, bright-towered by the sea. The rigging of the boats in harbor sparkled with flags. In the streets between houses with red roofs and painted walls, between old moss-grown gardens and under avenues of trees, past great parks and public buildings, processions moved. Some were decorous: old people in long stiff robes of mauve and gray, grave master workmen, quiet, merry women carrying their babies and chatting as they walked. In other streets the music beat faster, a shimmering of gong and tambourine, and the people went dancing, the procession was a dance. Children dodged in and out, their high calls rising like the swallows' crossing flights over the music and the singing. All the processions wound toward the north side of the city, where on the great watermeadow called the Green Fields boys and girls, naked in the bright air, with mudstained feet and ankles and long, lithe arms, exercised their restive horses before the race. The horses wore no gear at all but a halter without bit. Their manes were braided with streamers of silver, gold, and green. They blew out their nostrils and pranced and boasted to one another; they were vastly excited, the horse being the only animal who had adopted our ceremonies as his own. Far off to the north and west the mountains stood up half-encircling Omelas on her bay. The air of morning was so clear that the snow still crowning the Eighteen Peaks burned with white-gold fire across the miles of sunlit air, under the dark blue of the sky. There was just enough wind to make the banners that marked the race course snap and flutter now and then. In the silence of the broad green meadows one could hear the music winding through the city streets, farther and nearer and ever approaching, a cheerful faint sweetness of the air that from time to time trembled and gathered together and broke out into the great joyous clanging of the bells.

Joyous! How is one to tell about joy? How describe the citizens of Omelas?

They were not simple folk, you see, though they were happy. But we do not say the words of cheer much any more. All smiles have become archaic. Given a description such as this one tends to make certain assumptions. Given a description such as this one tends to look next for the King, mounted on a splendid stallion and surrounded by his noble knights, or perhaps in a golden litter borne by great-muscled slaves. But there was no king. They did not use swords, or keep slaves. They were not barbarians. I do not know the rules and laws of their society, but I suspect that they were singularly few. As they did without monarchy and slavery, so they also got on without the stock exchange, the advertisement, the secret police, and the bomb. Yet I repeat that these were not simple folk, not dulcet shepherds, noble savages, bland utopians. They were not less complex than we. The trouble is that we have a bad habit, encouraged by pedants and sophisticates, of considering happiness as something rather stupid. Only pain is intellectual, only evil interesting. This is the treason of the artist: a refusal to admit the banality of evil and the terrible boredom of pain. If you can't lick 'em, join 'em. If it hurts, repeat it. But to praise despair is to condemn delight, to embrace violence is to lose hold of everything else. We have almost lost hold; we can no longer describe a happy man, nor make any celebration of joy. How can I tell you about the people of Omelas? They were not naive and happy children—though their children were, in fact, happy. They were mature, intelligent, passionate adults whose lives were not wretched. O miracle! But I wish I could describe it better. I wish I could convince you. Omelas sounds in my words like a city in a fairytale, long ago and far away, once upon a time. Perhaps it would be best if you imagined it as your own fancy bids, assuming it will rise to the occasion, for certainly I cannot suit you all. For instance, how about technology? I think that there would be no cars or helicopters in and above the streets; this follows from the fact that the people of Omelas are happy people. Happiness is based on a just discrimination of what is necessary, what is neither necessary nor destructive, and what is destructive. In the middle category, however—that of the unnecessary but undestructive, that of comfort, luxury, exuberance, etc.—they could perfectly well have central heating, subway trains, washing machines, and all kinds of marvelous devices not yet invented here, floating lightsources, fuelless power, a cure for the common cold. Or they could have none of that: it doesn't matter. As you like it. I incline to think that people from towns up and down the coast have been coming in to Omelas during the last days before the Festival on very fast little trains and double-decked trams, and that the train station of Omelas is actually the handsomest building in town, though plainer than the magnificent Farmers Market. But even granted trains, I fear that Omelas so far strikes some of you as goody-goody. Smiles, bells, parades, horses, bleh. If so, please add an orgy. If an orgy would help, don't hesitate. Let us not, however, have temples from which issue beautiful nude priests and priestesses already half in ecstasy and ready to copulate with whosoever, man or woman, lover or stranger, desires union with the deep godhead of the blood, although that was my first idea. But really it would be better not to have any temples in Omelas—at least, not manned temples. Religion yes, clergy no. Surely the beautiful nudes can just wander about, offering themselves like divine soufflés to the hunger of the needy and the rapture of the flesh. Let them join the processions. Let tambourines be struck above the copulations, and the glory of desire be proclaimed upon the gongs, and (a not unimportant point) let the offspring of these delightful rituals be beloved and looked after by all. One thing I know there is none of in Omelas is guilt. But what else should there be? I thought at first there were no drugs, but that is puritanical. For those who like it, the faint insistent sweetness of *drooz* may perfume the ways of the city, *drooz* which first brings a great lightness and brilliance to the mind and limbs, and then after some hours a dreamy languor, and wonderful visions at last of the very arcana and inmost secrets of the Universe, as well as exciting the pleasure of sex beyond all belief; and it is not habit-forming. For more modest tastes I think there ought to be beer. What else, what else belongs in the joyous city? The sense of victory, surely, the celebration of courage. But as we did without clergy, let us do without soldiers. The joy built upon successful slaughter is not the right kind of joy; it will not do; it is fearful and it is trivial. A boundless and generous contentment, a magnanimous triumph felt not against some outer enemy but in communion with the finest and fairest in the souls of all men everywhere and the splendor of the world's summer: this is what swells the hearts of the people of Omelas, and the victory they celebrate is that of life. I really don't think many of them need to take *drooz*.

Most of the processions have reached the Green Fields by now. A marvelous smell of cooking goes forth from the red and blue tents of the provisioners. The faces of small children are amiably sticky; in the benign gray beard of a man a couple of crumbs of rich pastry are entangled. The youths and girls have mounted their horses and are beginning to group around the starting line of the course. An old woman, small, fat, and laughing, is passing out flowers from a basket, and tall young men wear her flowers in their shining hair. A child of nine or ten sits at the edge of the crowd, alone, playing on a wooden flute. People pause to listen, and they smile, but they do not speak to him, for he never ceases playing and never sees them, his dark eyes wholly rapt in the sweet, thin magic of the tune.

He finishes, and slowly lowers his hands holding the wooden flute.

As if that little private silence were the signal, all at once a trumpet sounds from the pavilion near the starting line: imperious, melancholy, piercing. The horses rear on their slender legs, and some of them neigh in answer. Sober-faced, the young riders stroke the horses' necks and soothe them, whispering, "Quiet, quiet, there my beauty, my hope . . ." They begin to form in rank along the starting line. The crowds along the race course are like a field of grass and flowers in the wind. The Festival of Summer has begun.

Do you believe? Do you accept the festival, the city, the joy? No? Then let me describe one more thing.

In a basement under one of the beautiful public buildings of Omelas, or perhaps in the cellar of one of its spacious private homes, there is a room. It has one locked door, and no window. A little light seeps in dustily between cracks in the boards, secondhand from a cobwebbed window somewhere across the cellar. In one corner of the little room a couple of mops, with stiff, clotted, foul-smelling heads, stand near a rusty bucket. The floor is dirt, a little damp to the touch, as cellar dirt usually is. The room is about three paces long and two wide: a mere broom closet or disused toolroom. In the room a child is sitting. It might be a boy or a girl. It looks about six, but actually is nearly ten. It is feebleminded. Perhaps it was born defective, or perhaps it has become imbecile through fear, malnutrition, and neglect. It picks its nose and occasionally fumbles vaguely with its toes or genitals, as it sits hunched in the corner farthest from the bucket and the two mops. It is afraid of the mops. It finds them horrible. It shuts its eyes, but it knows the mops are still standing there; and the door is locked; and nobody will come. The door is always locked, and nobody ever comes, except that sometimes—the child has no understanding of time or interval—sometimes the door rattles terribly and opens, and a person, or several people, are there. One of them may come in and kick the child to make it stand up. The others never come close, but peer in at it with frightened, disgusted eyes. The food bowl and the water jug are hastily filled, the door is locked, the eyes disappear. The people at the door never say anything, but the child, who has not always lived in the toolroom, and can remember sunlight and its mother's voice, sometimes speaks. "I will be good," it says. "Please let me out. I will be good!" They never answer. The child used to scream for help at night, and cry a good deal, but now it only makes a kind of whining, "eh-haa, eh-haa," and it speaks less and less often. It is so thin there are no calves to its legs; its belly protrudes; it lives on a half-bowl of cornmeal and grease a day. It is naked. Its buttocks and thighs are a mass of festered sores, as it sits in its own excrement continually.

They all know it is there, all the people of Omelas. Some of them have come to see it, others are content merely to know it is there. They all know that it has to be there. Some of them understand why, and some do not, but they all understand that their happiness, the beauty of their city, the tenderness of their friendships, the health of their children, the wisdom of their scholars, the skill of their makers, even the abundance of their harvest and the kindly weathers of their skies, depend wholly on this child's abominable misery.

This is usually explained to children when they are between eight and twelve, whenever they seem capable of understanding; and most of those who come to see the child are young people, though often enough an adult comes, or comes back, to see the child. No matter how well the matter has been explained to them, these young spectators are always shocked and sickened at the sight. They feel disgust, which they had thought themselves superior to. They feel anger, outrage, impotence, despite all the explanations. They would like to do something for the child. But there is nothing they can do. If the child were brought up into the sunlight out of that vile place, if it were cleaned and fed and comforted, that would be a good thing, indeed; but if it were done, in that day and hour all the prosperity and beauty and delight of Omelas would wither and be destroyed. Those are the terms. To exchange all the goodness and grace of every life in Omelas for that single, small improvement: to throw away the happiness of thousands for the chance of the happiness of one: that would be to let guilt within the walls indeed.

The terms are strict and absolute; there may not even be a kind word spoken to the child.

Often the young people go home in tears, or in a tearless rage, when they have seen the child and faced this terrible paradox. They may brood over it for weeks or years. But as time goes on they begin to realize that even if the child could be released, it would not get much good of its freedom: a little vague pleasure of warmth and food, no doubt, but little more. It is too degraded and imbecile to know any real joy. It has been afraid too long ever to be free of fear. Its habits are too uncouth for it to respond to humane treatment. Indeed after so long it would probably be wretched without walls about it to protect it, and darkness for its eyes, and its own excrement to sit in. Their tears at the bitter injustice dry when they begin to perceive the terrible justice of reality, and to accept it. Yet it is their tears and anger, the trying of their generosity and the acceptance of their helplessness, which are perhaps the true source of the splendor of their lives. Theirs is no vapid, irresponsible happiness. They know that they, like the child, are not free. They know compassion. It is the existence of the child, and their knowledge of its existence, that makes possible the nobility of their architecture, the poignancy of their music, the profundity of their science. It is because of the child that they are so gentle with children. They know that if the wretched one were not there sniveling in the dark, the other one, the flute player, could make no joyful music as the young riders line up in their beauty for the race in the sunlight of the first morning of summer.

Now do you believe in them? Are they not more credible? But there is one more thing to tell, and this is quite incredible.

At times one of the adolescent girls or boys who go to see the child does not go home to weep or rage, does not, in fact, go home at all. Sometimes also a man or woman much older falls silent for a day or two, and then leaves home. These people go out into the street, and walk down the street alone. They keep walking, and walk straight out of the city of Omelas, through the beautiful gates. They keep walking across the farmlands of Omelas. Each one goes alone, youth or girl, man or woman. Night falls; the traveler must pass down village streets, between the houses with yellow-lit windows, and on out into the darkness of the fields. Each alone, they go west or north, toward the mountains. They go on. They leave Omelas, they walk ahead into the darkness, and they do not come back. The place they go toward is a place even less imaginable to most of us than the city of happiness. I cannot describe it at all. It is possible that it does not exist. But they seem to know where they are going, the ones who walk away from Omelas.

Sketches Among the Ruins of My Mind

Philip José Farmer

Philip José Farmer is one of the premier idea-
men of current science fiction, and his imagination is in full force in this fascinating long
story about a world whose people are being
robbed of their memories four days at a time.
It develops logically, inexorably, all the way to
an ending that, in retrospect, should not be
surprising.

I

June 1, 1980

It is now 11:00 P.M., and I am afraid to go to bed. I am
not alone. The whole world is afraid of sleep.

This morning I got up at 6:30 A.M., as I do every Wednesday. While I shaved and showered, I considered the case of the state of Illinois against Joseph Lankers, accused of murder. It was beginning to stink as if it were a three-day-old fish. My star witness would undoubtedly be charged with perjury.

I dressed, went downstairs, and kissed Carole good morning. She poured me a cup of coffee and said, "The paper's late."

That put me in a bad temper. I need both coffee and the morning newspaper to get me started.

Twice during breakfast, I left the table to look outside. Neither paper nor newsboy had appeared.

At seven, Carole went upstairs to wake up Mike and Tom, aged ten and eight respectively. Saturdays and Sundays they rise early even though I'd like them to stay in bed so their horsing around won't wake me. School days they have to be dragged out.

The third time I looked out of the door, Joe Gale, the paperboy, was next door. My paper lay on the stoop.

I felt disorientated, as if I'd walked into the wrong courtroom or the judge had given my client, a shoplifter, a life sentence. I was out of phase with the world. This couldn't be Sunday. So what was the Sunday issue, bright in its covering of the colored comic section, doing there? Today was Wednesday.

I stepped out to pick it up and saw old Mrs. Douglas, my neighbor to the left. She was looking at the front page of her paper as if she could not believe it.

The world rearranged itself into the correct lines of polarization. My thin panic dwindled into nothing. I thought, the *Star* has really goofed this time. That's what comes from depending so much on a computer to put it together. One little short circuit, and Wednesday's paper comes out in Sunday's format.

The *Star*'s night shift must have decided to let it go through; it was too late for them to rectify the error.

I said, "Good morning, Mrs. Douglas! Tell me, what day is it?"

"The twenty-eighth of May," she said. "I think . . ."

I walked out into the yard and shouted after Joe. Reluctantly, he wheeled his bike around.

"What is this?" I said, shaking the paper at him. "Did the *Star* screw up?"

"I don't know, Mr. Franham," he said. "None of us knows, honest to God."

By "us" he must have meant the other boys he met in the morning at the paper drop.

"We all thought it was Wednesday. That's why I'm late. We couldn't understand what was happening, so we talked a long time and then Bill Ambers called the office. Gates, he's the circulation manager, was just as bongo as we was."

"Were," I said.

"What?" he said.

"We *were,* not *was,* just as bongo, whatever that means," I said.

"For God's sake, Mr. Franham, who cares!" he said.

"Some of us still do," I said. "All right, what did Gates say?"

"He was upset as hell," Joe said. "He said heads were gonna roll. The night staff had fallen asleep for a couple of hours, and some joker had diddled up the computers, or . . ."

"That's all it is?" I said. I felt relieved.

When I went inside, I got out the papers for the last four days from the cycler. I sat down on the sofa and scanned them.

I didn't remember reading them. I didn't remember the past four days at all!

Wednesday's headline was: MYSTERIOUS OBJECT ORBITS EARTH.

I did remember Tuesday's articles, which stated that the big round object was heading for a point between the Earth and the moon. It had been detected three weeks ago when it was passing through the so-called asteroid belt. It was at that time traveling approximately 57,000 kilometers per hour, relative to the sun. Then it had slowed down, had changed course several times, and it became obvious that, unless it changed course again, it was going to come near earth.

By the time it was eleven million miles away, the radars had defined its size and shape, though not its material composition. It was perfectly spherical and exactly half a kilometer in diameter. It did not reflect much light. Since it had altered its path so often, it had to be artificial. Strange hands, or strange somethings, had built it.

I remembered the panic and the many wild articles in the papers and magazines and the TV specials made overnight to discuss its implications.

It had failed to make any response whatever to the radio and laser signals sent from Earth. Many scientists said that it probably contained no living passengers. It had to be of interstellar origin. The sentient beings of some planet circling some star had sent it out equipped with automatic equipment of some sort. No being could live long enough to travel between the stars. It would take over four years to get from the nearest star to Earth even if the object could travel at the speed of light, and that was impossible. Even one-sixteenth the speed of light seemed incredible because of the vast energy requirements. No, this thing had been launched with only electromechanical devices as passengers, had attained its top speed, turned off its power, and coasted until it came within the outer reaches of our solar system.

According to the experts, it must be unable to land on Earth because of its size and weight. It was probably just a surveying vessel, and after it had taken some photographs and made some radar/laser sweeps, it would proceed to wherever it was supposed to go, probably back to an orbit around its home planet.

II

Last Wednesday night, the president had told us that we had nothing to fear. And he'd tried to end on an optimistic note. At least, that's what Wednesday's paper said. The beings who had sent The Ball must be more advanced than we, and they must have many good things to give us. And we might be able to make beneficial contributions to them. Like what? I thought.

Some photographs of The Ball, taken from one of the manned orbiting laboratories, were on the second page. It looked just like a giant black billiard ball. One TV comic had suggested that the other side might bear a big white 8. I may have thought that this was funny last Wednesday, but I didn't think so now. It seemed highly probable to me that The Ball was connected with the four-days' loss of memory. How, I had no idea.

I turned on the 7:30 news channels, but they weren't much help except in telling us that the same thing had happened to everybody all over the world. Even those in the deepest diamond mines or submarines had been affected. The president was in conference, but he'd be making a statement over the networks sometime today. Meantime, it was known that no radiation of any sort had been detected emanating from The Ball. There was no evidence whatsoever that the object had caused the loss of memory. Or, as the jargon-crazy casters were already calling it, "memloss."

I'm a lawyer, and I like to think logically, not only about what has happened but what might happen. So I extrapolated on the basis of what little evidence, or data, there was.

On the first of June, a Sunday, we woke up with all memory of May 31 back through May 28 completely gone. We had thought that yesterday was the twenty-seventh and that this morning was that of the twenty-eighth.

If The Ball had caused this, why had it only taken four days of our memory? I didn't know. Nobody knew. But perhaps The Ball, its devices, that is, were limited in scope. Perhaps they couldn't strip off more than four days of memory at a time from everybody on Earth.

Postulate that this is the case. Then, what if the same thing happens tomorrow? We'll wake up tommorrow, June 2, with all memory of yesterday, June 1, and three more days of May, the twenty-seventh through the twenty-fifth, gone. Eight days in one solid stretch.

And if this ghastly thing should occur the following day, June 3, we'll lose another four days. All memory of June 2 will have disappeared. With it will go the memory of three more days, from May twenty-fourth through the twenty-second. Twelve days in all from June 2 backward!

And the next day? June 3 lost, too, along with May 21 through May 19. Sixteen days of a total blank. And the next day? And the next?

No, it's too hideous, and too fantastic, to think about.

While we were watching TV, Carole and the boys besieged me with questions. She was frantic. The boys seemed to be enjoying the mystery. They'd awakened expecting to go to school, and now they were having a holiday.

To all their questions, I said, "I don't know. Nobody knows."

I wasn't going to frighten them with my extrapolations. Besides, I didn't believe them myself.

"You'd better call up your office and tell them you can't come in today," Carole said. "Surely Judge Payne'll call off the session today."

"Carole, it's Sunday, not Wednesday, remember?" I said.

She cried for a minute. After she'd wiped away the tears, she said, "That's just it! I *don't* remember! My God, what's happening?"

The newscasters also reported that the White House was flooded with telegrams and phone calls demanding that rockets with H-bomb warheads be launched against The Ball. The specials, which came on after the news, were devoted to The Ball. These had various authorities, scientists, military men, ministers, and a few science fiction authors. None of them radiated confidence, but they were all temperate in their approach to the problem. I suppose they had been picked for their level-headedness. The networks had screened out the hotheads and the crackpots. They didn't want to be generating any more hysteria.

But Anel Robertson, a fundamentalist faith healer with a powerful radio/TV station of his own, had already declared that The Ball was a judgment of God on a sinful planet. It was The Destroying Angel. I knew that because Mrs. Douglas, no fanatic but certainly a zealot, had phoned me and told me to dial him in. Robertson had been speaking for an hour, she said, and he was going to talk all day.

She sounded frightened, and yet, beneath the fear, was a note of joy. Obviously, she didn't think that she was going to be among the goats when the last days arrived. She'd be right in there with the whitest of the sheep. My curiosity finally overcame my repugnance for Robertson. I dialed the correct number but got nothing except a pattern. Later today, I found out his station had been shut down for some infraction of FCC regulations. At least, that was the explanation given on the news, but I suspected that the government regarded him as a hysteria monger.

At eleven, Carole reminded me that it was Sunday and that if we didn't hurry, we'd miss church.

The Forrest Hill Presbyterian has a good attendance, but its huge parking lot has always been adequate. This morning, we had to park two blocks up the street and walk to church. Every seat was filled. We had to stand in the anteroom near the front door. The crowd stank of fear. Their faces were pale and set; their eyes, big. The air conditioning labored unsuccessfully to carry away the heat and humidity of the packed and sweating bodies. The choir was loud but quavering; their "Rock of Ages" was crumbling.

Dr. Boynton would have prepared his sermon on Saturday afternoon, as he always did. But today he spoke impromptu. Perhaps, he said, this loss of memory *had* been caused by The Ball. Perhaps there were living beings in it who had taken four days away from us, not as a hostile move but merely to demonstrate their immense powers. There was no reason to anticipate that we would suffer another loss of memory. These beings mere wanted to show us that we were hopelessly inferior in science and that we could not launch a successful attack against them.

"What the hell's he doing?" I thought. "Is he trying to scare us to death?"

Boynton hastened then to say that beings with such powers, of such obvious advancement, would not, could not, be hostile. They would be on too high an ethical plane for such evil things as war, unless they were attacked, of course. They would regard us as beings who had not yet progressed to their level but had the potentiality, the God-given potentiality, to be brought up to a high level. He was sure that, when they made contact with us, they would tell us that all was for the best.

They would tell us that we must, like it or not, become true Christians. At least, we must all, Buddhists, Moslems and so forth, become Christian in spirit, whatever our religion or lack thereof. They would teach us how to live as brothers and sisters, how to be happy, how to truly love. Assuredly, God had sent The Ball, since nothing happened without His knowledge and consent. He had sent these beings, whoever they were, not as Destroying Angels but as Sharers of Peace, Love and Prosperity.

That last, with the big P, seemed to settle down most of the congregation. Boynton had not forgotten that most of his flock were of the big-business and professional classes. Nor had he forgotten that, inscribed on the arch above the church entrance was, THEY SHALL PROSPER WHO LOVE THEE.

III

We poured out into a bright warm June afternoon. I looked up into the sky but could see no Ball, of course. The news media had said that, despite its great distance from Earth, it was circling Earth every sixty-five minutes. It wasn't in a free fall orbit. It was applying continuous power to keep it on its path, although there were no detectable emanations of energy from it.

The memory loss had occurred all over the world between 1:00 A.M. and 2:00 A.M. Central Standard Time.

Those who were not already asleep fell asleep for a minimum of an hour. This had, of course, caused hundreds of thousands of accidents. Planes not on automatic pilot had crashed, trains had collided or been derailed, ships had sunk, and more than two hundred thousand had been killed or seriously injured. At least a million vehicle drivers and passengers had been injured. The ambulance and hospital services had found it impossible to handle the situation. The fact that their personnel had been asleep for at least an hour and that it had taken them some time to recover from their confusion on awakening had aggravated the situation considerably. Many had died who might have lived if immediate service had been available.

There were many fires, too, the largest of which were still raging in Tokyo, Athens, Naples, Harlem, and Baltimore.

I thought, Would beings on a high ethical plane have put us to sleep knowing that so many people would be killed and badly hurt?

One curious item was about two rangers who had been thinning a herd of elephants in Kenya. While sleeping, they had been trampled to death. Whatever it is that's causing this, it's very specific. Only human beings are affected.

The optimism, which Boynton had given us in the church, melted in the sun. Many must have been thinking, as I was, that if Boynton's words were prophetic, we were helpless. Whatever the things in The Ball, whether living or mechanical, decided to do for us, or to us, we were no longer masters of our own fate. Some of them must have been thinking about what the technologically superior whites had done to various aboriginal cultures. All in the name of progress and God.

But this would be, must be, different, I thought. Boynton must be right. Surely such an advanced people would not be as we were. Even we are not what we were in the bad old days. We have learned.

But then an advanced technology does not necessarily accompany an advanced ethics.

"Or whatever," I murmured.

"What did you say, dear?" Carole said.

I said, "Nothing," and shook her hand off my arm. She had clung to it tightly all through the services, as if *I* were the rock of the ages. I walked over to Judge Payne, who's sixty years old but looked this morning as if he were eighty. The many broken veins on his face were red, but underneath them was a grayishness.

I said hello and then asked him if things would be normal tomorrow. He didn't seem to know what I was getting at, so I said, "The trial will start on time tomorrow?"

"Oh, yes, the trial," he said. "Of course, Mark."

He laughed whinnyingly and said, "Provided that we all haven't forgotten today when we wake up tomorrow."

That seemed incredible, and I told him so.

"It's not law school that makes good lawyers," he said. "It's experience. And experience tells us that the same damned thing, with some trifling variations, occurs over and over, day after day. So what makes you think this evil thing won't happen again? And if it does, how're you going to learn from it when you can't remember it?"

I had no logical argument, and he didn't want to talk any more. He grabbed his wife by the arm, and they waded through the crowd as if they thought they were going to step in a sinkhole and drown in a sea of bodies.

This evening, I decided to record on tape what's happened today. Now I lay me down to sleep, I pray the Lord my memory to keep, if I forget while I sleep . . .

Most of the rest of today, I've spent before the TV. Carole wasted hours trying to get through the lines to her friends for phone conversations. Three-fourths of the time, she got a busy signal. There were bulletins on the TV asking people not to use the phone except for emergencies, but she paid no attention to it until about eight o'clock. A TV bulletin, for the sixth time in an hour, asked that the lines be kept open. About twenty fires had broken out over the town, and the firemen couldn't be informed of them because of the tie-up. Calls to hospitals had been similarly blocked.

I told Carole to knock it off, and we quarreled. Our

suppressed hysteria broke loose, and the boys retreated upstairs to their room behind a closed door. Eventually, Carole started crying and threw herself into my arms, and then I cried. We kissed and made up. The boys came down looking as if we had failed them, which we had. For them, it was no longer a fun-adventure from some science-fiction story.

Mike said, "Dad, could you help me go over my arithmetic lessons?"

I didn't feel like it, but I wanted to make it up to him for that savage scene. I said sure and then, when I saw what he had to do, I said, "But all this? What's the matter with your teacher? I never saw so much . . ."

I stopped. Of course, he had forgotten all he'd learned in the last three days of school. He had to do his lessons all over again.

This took us until eleven, though we might have gone faster if I hadn't insisted on watching the news every half-hour for at least ten minutes. A full thirty minutes were used listening to the president, who came on at 9:30. He had nothing to add to what the newsmen had said except that, within thirty days, The Ball would be completely dealt with—one way or another. If it didn't make some response to our signals within two days, then we would send up a four-man expedition, which would explore The Ball.

If it can get inside, I thought.

If, however, The Ball should commit any more hostile acts, then the United States would immediately launch, in conjunction with other nations, rockets armed with H-bombs.

Meanwhile, would we all join the president in an interdenominational prayer?

We certainly would.

At eleven, we put the kids to bed. Tom went to sleep before we were out of the room. But about half an hour later, as I passed their door, I heard a low voice from the TV. I didn't say anything to Mike, even if he did have to go to school next day.

At twelve, I made the first part of this tape.

But here it is, one minute to one o'clock in the morning. If the same thing happens tonight as happened yesterday, then the nightside hemisphere will be affected first. People in the time zone which bisects the South and North Atlantic oceans and covers the eastern half of Greenland, will fall asleep. Just in case it does happen again, all airplanes have been grounded. Right now, the TV is showing the bridge and the salon of the trans-Atlantic liner *Pax*. Its five o'clock there, but the salon is crowded. The passengers are wearing party hats and confetti, and balloons are floating everywhere. I don't know what they could be celebrating. The captain said a little while ago that the ship's on automatic, but he doesn't expect a repetition of last night. The interviewer said that the governments of the dayside nations have not been successful keeping people home. We've been getting shots from everywhere, the sirens are wailing all over the world, but, except for the totalitarian nations, the streets of the daytime world are filled with cars. The damned fools just didn't believe it would happen again.

Back to the bridge and the salon of the ship. My God! They *are* falling asleep!

The announcers are repeating warnings. Everybody lie down so they won't get hurt by falling. Make sure all home appliances, which might cause fires, are turned off. And so on and so on.

I'm sitting in a chair with a tilted back. Carole is on the sofa.

Now I'm on the sofa. Carole just said she wanted to be holding on to me when this horrible thing comes.

The announcers are getting hysterical. In a few minutes, New York will be hit. The eastern half of South America is under. The central section is going under.

IV

True date: June 2, 1980. Subjective date: May 25, 1980

My God! How many times have I said, "My God!" in the last two days?

I awoke on the sofa beside Carole and Mike. The clock indicated three in the morning. Chris Turner was on the TV. I didn't know what he was talking about. All I could understand was that he was trying to reassure his viewers that everything was all right and that everything would be explained shortly.

What was I doing on the sofa? I'd gone to bed about eleven the night of May 24, a Saturday. Carole and I had had a little quarrel because I'd spent all day working on the Lankers case, and she said that I'd promised to take her to see *Nova Express*. And so I had—if I finished work before eight, which I obviously had not done. So what were we doing on the sofa, where had Mike come from, and what did Turner mean by saying that today was June 2?

The tape recorder was on the table near me, but it didn't occur to me to turn it on.

I shook Carole awake, and we confusedly asked each other what had happened. Finally, Turner's insistent voice got our attention, and he explained the situation for about the fifth time so far. Later, he said that an alarm clock placed by his ear had awakened him at two-thirty.

Carole made some coffee, and we drank four cups apiece. We talked wildly, with occasional breaks to listen to Turner, before we became half-convinced that we had indeed lost all memory of the last eight days. Mike slept on through it, and finally I carried him up to his bed. His TV was still on. Nate Frobisher, Mike's favorite spieler, was talking hysterically. I turned him off and went back downstairs. I figured out later that Mike had gotten scared and come downstairs to sit with us.

Dawn found us rereading the papers from May 24 through June 1. It was like getting news from Mars. Carole took a tranquilizer to quiet herself down, but I preferred Wild Turkey. After she'd seen me down six ounces, Carole said I should lay off the bourbon. I wouldn't be fit to go to work. I told her that if she thought anybody'd be working today, she was out of her mind.

At seven, I went out to pick up the paper. It wasn't there. At a quarter to eight, Joe delivered it. I tried to talk to him, but he wouldn't stop. All he said, as he pedaled away, was, "It ain't Saturday!"

I went back in. The entire front page was devoted to The Ball and this morning's events up to four o'clock. Part of the paper had been set up before one o'clock. According to a notice at the bottom of the page, the staff had awakened about three. It took them an hour to straighten themselves out, and then they'd gotten together the latest news and made up the front page and some of section C. They'd have never made it when they did if it wasn't for the computer, which printed justified lines from voice input.

Despite what I'd said earlier, I decided to go to work. First, I had to straighten the boys out. At ten, they went off to school. It seemed to me that it was useless for them to do so. But they were eager to talk with their classmates about this situation. To tell the truth, I wanted to get down to the office and the courthouse for the same reason. I wanted to talk this over with my colleagues. Staying home all day with Carole seemed a waste of time. We just kept saying the same thing over and over again.

Carole didn't want me to leave. She was too frightened to stay home by herself. Both our parents are dead, but she does have a sister who lives in Hannah, a small town nearby. I told her it'd do her good to get out of the house. And I just had to get to the courthouse. I couldn't find out what was happening there because the phone lines were tied up.

When I went outside to get into my car, Carole ran down after me. Her long blonde hair was straggling; she had big bags under her eyes; she looked like a witch.

"Mark! Mark!" she said.

I took my finger off the starter button and said, "What is it?"

"I know you'll think I'm crazy, Mark," she said. "But I'm about to fall apart!"

"Who isn't?" I said.

"Mark," she said, "what if I go out to my sister's and then forget how to get back? What if I forgot *you?*"

"This thing only happens at night," I said.

"So far!" she screamed. "So far!"

"Honey," I said, "I'll be home early. I promise. If you don't want to go, stay here. Go over and talk to Mrs. Knight. I see her looking out her window. She'll talk your leg off all day."

I didn't tell her to visit any of her close friends, because she didn't have any. Her best friend had died of cancer last year, and two others with whom she was familiar had moved away.

"If you do go to your sister's," I said, "make a note on a map reminding you where you live and stick it on top of the dashboard, where you can see it."

"You son of a bitch," she said. "It isn't funny!"

"I'm not being funny," I said. "I got a feeling . . ."

"What about?" she said.

"Well, we'll be making notes to ourselves soon. If this keeps up," I said.

I thought I was kidding then. Thinking about it later today I see that that is the only way to get orientated in the morning. Well, not the only way, but it'll have to be the way to get started when you wake up. Put a note where you can't overlook it, and it'll tell you to turn on a recording, which will, in turn, summarize the situation. Then you turn on the TV and get some more information.

I might as well have stayed home. Only half of the courthouse personnel showed up, and they were hopelessly inefficient. Judge Payne wasn't there and never will be. He'd had a fatal stroke at six that morning while listening to the TV. Walter Barbindale, my partner, said that the judge probably would have had a stroke sometime in the near future, anyway. But this situation must certainly have hastened it.

"The stock market's about hit bottom," he said. "One more day of this, and we'll have another worldwide depression. Nineteen twenty-nine won't hold a candle to it. And I can't even get through to my broker to tell him to sell everything."

"If everybody sells, then the market *will* crash," I said.

"Are you hanging onto your stocks?" he said.

"I've been too busy to even think about it," I said. "You might say I forgot."

"That isn't funny," he said.

"That's what my wife said," I answered. "But I'm not trying to be funny, though God knows I could use a good laugh. Well, what're we going to do about Lankers?"

"I went over some of the records," he said. "We haven't got a chance. I tell you, it was a shock finding out, for the second time, mind you, though I don't remember the first, that our star witness is in jail on a perjury charge."

Since all was chaos in the courthouse, it wasn't much use trying to find out who the judge would be for the new trial for Lankers. To tell the truth, I didn't much care. There were far more important things to worry about than the fate of an undoubtedly guilty murderer.

I went to Grover's Rover Bar, which is a block from the courthouse. As an aside, for my reference or for whoever might be listening to this someday, why am I telling myself things I know perfectly well, like the location of Grover's? Maybe it's because I think I might forget them some day.

Grover's, at least, I remembered well, as I should, since I'd been going there ever since it was built, five years ago. The air was thick with tobacco and pot smoke and the odors of pot, beer and booze. And noisy. Everybody was talking fast and loud, which is to be expected in a place filled with members of the legal profession. I bellied up to the bar and bought the D.A. a shot of Wild Turkey. We talked about what we'd done that morning, and then he told me he had to release two burglars that day. They'd been caught and jailed two days before. The arresting officers had, of course, filed their reports. But that wasn't going to be enough when the trial came up. Neither the burglars nor the victims and the officers remembered a thing about the case.

"Also," the D.A. said, "at two-ten this morning, the police got a call from the Black Shadow Tavern on Washington Street. They didn't get there until three-thirty because they were too disorientated to do anything for an hour or more. When they did get to the tavern, they found a dead man. He'd been beaten badly and then stabbed in the stomach. Nobody remembered anything, of course. But from what we could piece together, the dead man must've gotten into a drunken brawl with a person or persons unknown shortly before 1:00 A.M. Thirty people must've witnessed the murder. So we have a murderer or murderers walking the streets today who don't even remember the killing or anything leading up to it."

"They might know they're guilty if they'd been planning it for a long time," I said.

He grinned and said, "But he, or they, won't be telling anybody. No one except the corpse had blood on him nor did anybody have bruised knuckles. Two were arrested for carrying saps, but so what? They'll be out soon, and nobody, but nobody, can prove they used the saps. The knife was still half-sticking in the deceased's belly, and his efforts to pull it out destroyed any fingerprints."

V

We talked and drank a lot, and suddenly it was 6:00 P.M. I was in no condition to drive and had sense enough to know it. I tried calling Carole to come down and get me, but I couldn't get through. At 6:30 and 7:00, I tried again without success. I decided to take a taxi. But after another drink, I tried again and this time got through.

"Where've you been?" she said. "I called your office, but nobody answered. I was thinking about calling the police."

"As if they haven't got enough to do," I said. "When did *you* get home?"

"You're slurring," she said coldly.

I repeated the question.

"Two hours ago," she said.

"The lines were tied up," I said. "I tried."

"You knew how scared I was, and you didn't even care," she said.

"Can I help it if the D.A. insisted on conducting business at the Rover?" I said. "Besides, I was trying to forget."

"Forget what?" she said.

"Whatever it was I forgot," I said.

"You ass!" she screamed. "Take a taxi!"

The phone clicked off.

She didn't make a scene when I got home. She'd decided to play it cool because of the kids, I suppose. She was drinking gin and tonic when I entered, and she said, in a level voice, "*You*'ll have some coffee. And after a while you can listen to the tape you made yesterday. It's interesting, but spooky."

"What tape?" I said.

"Mike was fooling around with it," she said. "And he found out you'd recorded what happened yesterday."

"That kid!" I said. "He's always snooping around. I told him to leave my stuff alone. Can't a man have any privacy around here?"

"Well, don't say anything to him," she said. "He's upset as it is. Anyway, it's a good thing he did turn it on. Otherwise, you'd have forgotten all about it. I think you should make a daily record."

"So you think it'll happen again?" I said.

She burst into tears. After a moment, I put my arms around her. I felt like crying, too. But she pushed me away, saying, "You stink of rotten whiskey!"

"That's because it's mostly bar whiskey," I said. "I can't afford Wild Turkey at three dollars a shot."

I drank four cups of black coffee and munched on some shrimp dip. As an aside, I can't really afford that, either, since I only make forty-five thousand dollars a year.

When we went to bed, we went to bed. Afterward, Carole said, "I'm sorry, darling, but my heart wasn't really in it."

"That wasn't all," I said.

"You've got a dirty mind," she said. "What I meant was I couldn't stop thinking, even while we were doing it, that it wasn't any good doing it. We won't remember it tomorrow, I thought."

"How many do we really remember?" I said. "Sufficient unto the day is the, uh, good thereof."

"It's a good thing you didn't try to fulfill your childhood dream of becoming a preacher," she said. "You're a born shyster. You'd have made a lousy minister."

"Look," I said, "I remember the especially good ones. And I'll never forget our honeymoon. But we need sleep. We haven't had any to speak of for twenty-four hours. Let's hit the hay and forget everything until tomorrow. In which case . . ."

She stared at me and then said, "Poor dear, no wonder you're so belligerently flippant! It's a defense against fear!"

I slammed my fist into my palm and shouted, "I know! I know! For God's sake, how long is this going on?"

I went into the bathroom. The face in the mirror looked as if it were trying to flirt with me. The left eye wouldn't stop winking.

When I returned to the bedroom, Carole reminded me that I'd not made today's recording. I didn't want to do it because I was so tired. But the possibility of losing another day's memory spurred me. No, not another day, I thought. If this occurs tomorrow, I'll lose another four days. Tomorrow and the three preceding May 25. I'll wake up June 3 and think it's the morning of the twenty-second.

I'm making this downstairs in my study. I wouldn't want Carole to hear some of my comments.

Until tomorrow then. It's not tomorrow but yesterday that won't come. I'll make a note to myself and stick it in a corner of the case which holds my glasses.

VI

True date: June 3, 1980

I woke up thinking that today was my birthday, May 22. I rolled over, saw the piece of paper half-stuck from my glasses case, put on my glasses and read the note.

It didn't enlighten me. I didn't remember writing the

note. And why should I go downstairs and turn on the re-corder? But I did so.

As I listened to the machine, my heart thudded as if it were a judge's gavel. My voice kept fading in and out. Was I going to faint?

And so half of today was wasted trying to regain twelve days in my mind. I didn't go to the office, and the kids went to school late. And what about the kids in school on the dayside of Earth? If they sleep during their geometry class, say, then they have to go through that class again on the same day. And that shoves the schedule forward, or is it backward, for that day. And then there's the time work-ers will lose on their jobs. They have to make it up, which means they get out an hour later. Only it takes more than an hour to recover from the confusion and get oriented. What a mess it has been! What a mess it'll be if this keeps on!

At eleven, Carole and I were straightened out enough to go to the supermarket. It was Tuesday, but Carole wanted me to be with her, so I tried to phone in and tell my secre-tary I'd be absent. The lines were tied up, and I doubt that she was at work. So I said to hell with it.

Our supermarket usually opens at eight. Not today. We had to stand in a long line, which kept getting longer. The doors opened at twelve. The manager, clerks and boys had had just as much trouble as we did unconfusing themselves, of course. Some didn't show at all. And some of the trucks which were to bring fresh stores never appeared.

By the time Carole and I got inside, those ahead of us had cleaned out half the supplies. They had the same idea we had. Load up now so there wouldn't be any standing in line so many times. The fresh milk was all gone, and the powdered milk shelf had one box left. I started for it but some teen-ager beat me to it. I felt like hitting him, but I didn't, of course.

The prices for everything were being upped by a fourth even as we shopped. Some of the stuff was being marked upward once more while we stood in line at the checkout counter. From the time we entered the line until we pushed out three overflowing carts, four hours had passed.

While Carole put away the groceries, I drove to another supermarket. The line there was a block long; it would be emptied and closed up before I ever got to its doors.

The next two supermarkets and a corner grocery store were just as hopeless. And the three liquor stores I went to were no better. The fourth only had about thirty men in line, so I tried that. When I got inside, all the beer was gone, which didn't bother me any, but the only hard stuff left was a fifth of rotgut. I drank it when I went to college because I couldn't afford anything better. I put the terrible stuff and a half-gallon of cheap muscatel on the counter. Anything was better than nothing, even though the prices had been doubled.

I started to make out the check, but the clerk said, "Sorry, sir. Cash only."

"What?" I said.

"Haven't you heard, sir?" he said. "The banks were closed at 2:00 P.M. today."

"The banks are closed?" I said. I sounded stupid even to myself.

"Yes, sir," he said. "By the federal government. It's only temporary, sir, at least, that's what the TV said. They'll be reopened after the stock market mess is cleared up."

"But . . ." I said.

"It's destructed," he said.

"Destroyed," I said automatically. "You mean, it's another Black Friday?"

"It's Tuesday today," he said.

"You're too young to know the reference," I said. And too uneducated, too, I thought.

"The president is going to set up a rationing system," he said. "For the Interim. And price controls, too. Turner said so on TV an hour ago. The president is going to lay it all out at six tonight."

When I came home, I found Carole in front of the TV. She was pale and wide-eyed.

"There's going to be another depression!" she said. "Oh, Mark, what are we going to do?"

"I don't know," I said. "I'm not the president, you know." And I slumped down onto the sofa. I had lost my flippancy.

Neither of us, having been born in 1945, knew what a Depression, with a big capital D, was; that is, we hadn't experienced it personally. But we'd heard our parents, who were kids when it happened, talk about it. Carole's parents had gotten along, though they didn't live well, but my father used to tell me about days when he had nothing but stale bread and turnips to eat and was happy to get them.

The president's TV speech was mostly about the depression, which he claimed would be temporary. At the end of half an hour of optimistic talk, he revealed why he thought the situation wouldn't last. The federal government wasn't going to wait for the sentients in The Ball—if there were any there—to communicate with us. Obviously, The Ball was hostile. So the survey expedition had been canceled. Tomorrow, the USA, the USSR, France, West Germany, Israel, India, Japan and China would send up an armada of rockets tipped with H-bombs. The orbits and the order of battle were determined this morning by computers; one after the other, the missiles would zero in until The Ball was completely destroyed. It would be over-kill with a vengeance.

"That ought to bring up the stock market!" I said.

And so, after I've finished recording, to bed. Tomorrow, we'll follow our instructions on the notes, relisten to the tapes, reread certain sections of the newspapers and await the news on the TV. To hell with going to the courthouse; nobody's going to be there anyway.

Oh, yes. With all this confusion and excitement, everybody, myself included, forgot that today was my birthday. Wait a minute! It's *not* my birthday.!

True date: June 5, 1980. Subjective date: May 16, 1980

I woke up mad at Carole because of our argument the

previous day. Not that of June 4, of course, but our brawl of May 15. We'd been at a party given by the Burlingtons, where I met a beautiful young artist, Roberta Gardner. Carole thought I was paying too much attention to her because she looked like Myrna. Maybe I was. On the other hand, I really was interested in her paintings. It seemed to me that she had a genuine talent. When we got home, Carole tore into me, accused me of still being in love with Myrna. My protests did no good whatsoever. Finally, I told her we might as well get a divorce if she couldn't forgive and forget. She ran crying out of the room and slept on the sofa downstairs.

I don't remember what reconciled us, of course, but we must have worked it out, otherwise we wouldn't still be married.

Anyway, I woke up determined to see a divorce lawyer today. I was sick about what Mike and Tom would have to go through. But it would be better for them to be spared our terrible quarrels. I can remember my reactions when I was an adolescent and overheard my parents fighting. It was a relief, though a sad one, when they separated.

Thinking this, I reached for my glasses. And I found the note. And so another voyage into confusion, disbelief and horror.

Now that the panic has eased off somewhat, May 18 is back in the saddle—somewhat. Carole and I are, in a sense, still in that day, and things are a bit cool.

It's 1:00 P.M. now. We just watched the first rockets take off. Ten of them, one after the other.

It's 1:35 P.M. Via satellite, we watched the Japanese missiles.

We just heard that the Chinese and Russian rockets are being launched. When the other nations send theirs up, there will be thirty-seven in all.

No news at 12:30 A.M., June 5. In this case, no news must be bad news. But what could have happened? The newscasters won't say; they just talk around the subject.

VII

True date: June 6, 1980. Subjective date: May 13, 1980

My records say that this morning was just like the other four. Hell.

One o'clock. The president, looking like a sad old man, though he's only forty-four, reported the catastrophe. All thirty-seven rockets were blown up by their own H-bombs about three thousand miles from The Ball. We saw some photographs of them taken from the orbiting labs. They weren't very impressive. No mushroom clouds, of course, and not even much light.

The Ball has weapons we can't hope to match. And if it can activate our H-bombs out in space, it should be able to do the same to those on Earth's surface. My God! It could wipe out all life if it wished to do so!

Near the end of the speech, the president did throw out a line of hope. With a weak smile—he was trying desperately to give us his big vote-winning one—he said that all was not lost by any means. A new plan, called Project Toro, was being drawn up even as he spoke.

Toro was Spanish for bull, I thought, but I didn't say so. Carole and the kids wouldn't have thought it funny, and I didn't think it was so funny myself. Anyway, I thought, maybe it's a Japanese word meaning *victory* or *destruction* or something like that.

Toro, as it turned out, was the name of a small irregularly shaped asteroid about 2.413 kilometers long and 1.609 kilometers wide. Its peculiar orbit had been calculated in 1972 by an L. Danielsson of the Swedish Royal Institute of Technology and a W. H. Ip of the University of California at San Diego. Toro, the president said, was bound into a resonant orbit with the Earth. Each time Toro came near the Earth—"near" was sometimes 12.6 million miles—it got exactly enough energy or "kick" from the Earth to push it on around so that it would come back for another near passage.

But the orbit was unstable, which meant that both Earth and Venus take turns controlling the asteroid. For a few centuries, Earth governs Toro; then Venus takes over. Earth has controled Toro since A.D. 1580. Venus will take over in 2200. Earth grabs it again in 2350; Venus gets it back in 2800.

I was wondering what all this stuff about this celestial Ping-Pong game was about. Then the president said that it was possible to land rockets on Toro. In fact, the plan called for many shuttles to land there carrying parts of huge rocket motors, which would be assembled on Toro.

When the motors were erected on massive and deep stands, power would be applied to nudge Toro out of its orbit. This would require many trips by many rockets with cargoes of fuel and spare parts for the motors. The motors would burn out a number of times. Eventually, though, the asteroid would be placed in an orbit that would end in a direct collision with The Ball. Toro's millions of tons of hard rock and nickel-steel would destroy The Ball utterly, would turn it into pure energy.

"Yes," I said aloud, "but what's to keep The Ball from just changing its orbit? Its sensors will detect the asteroid; it'll change course; Toro will go on by it, like a train on a track."

This was the next point of the president's speech. The failure of the attack had revealed at least one item of information, or, rather, verified it. The radiation of the H-bombs had blocked off, disrupted all control and observation of the rockets by radar and laser. In their final approach, the rockets had gone in blind, as it were, unable to be regulated from Earth. But if the bombs did this to our sensors, they must be doing the same to The Ball's.

So, just before Toro's course is altered to send it into its final path, H-bombs will be set off all around The Ball. In effect, it will be enclosed in a sphere of radiation. It will have no sensor capabilities. Nor will The Ball *believe* that it will have to alter its orbit to dodge Toro. It will have calculated that Toro's orbit won't endanger it. After the radiation fills the space around it, it won't be able to *see* that Toro is being given a final series of nudges to push it into a collision course.

The project is going to require immense amounts of materials and manpower. The USA can't handle it alone; Toro is going to be a completely international job. What one nation can't provide, the other will.

The president ended with a few words about how Project Toro, plus the situation of memory loss, is going to bring about a radical revision of the economic setup. He's going to announce the outlines of the new structure—not just policy but structure—two days from now. It'll be designed, so he says, to restore prosperity and, not incidentally, rid society of many problems plaguing it since the industrial revolution.

"Yes, but how long will Project Toro take?" I said. "Oh, Lord, how long?"

Six years, the president said, as if he'd heard me. Perhaps longer.

Six years!

I didn't tell Carole what I could see coming. But she's no dummy. She could figure out some of the things that were bound to happen in six years, and none of them were good.

I never felt so hopeless in my life, and neither did she. But we do have each other, and so we clung tightly for a while. May 18 isn't forgotten, but it seems so unimportant. Mike and Tom cried, I suppose because they knew that this exhibition of love meant something terrible for all of us. Poor kids! They get upset by our hatreds and then become even more upset by our love.

When we realized what we were doing to them, we tried to be jolly. But we couldn't get them to smile.

True date: middle of 1981. Subjective date: middle of 1977

I'm writing this, since I couldn't get any new tapes today. The shortage is only temporary, I'm told. I could erase some of the old ones and use them, but it'd be like losing a vital part of myself. And God knows I've lost enough.

Old Mrs. Douglas next door is dead. Killed herself, according to my note on the calendar, April 2 of this year. I never would have thought she'd do it. She was such a strong fundamentalist, and these believe as strongly as the Roman Catholics that suicide is well-nigh unforgivable. I suspect that the double shock of her husband's death caused her to take her own life. April 2 of 1976 was the day he died. She had to be hospitalized because of shock and grief for two weeks after his death. Carole and I had her over to dinner a few times after she came home, and all she could talk about was her dead husband. So I presume that, as she traveled backward to the day of his death, the grief became daily more unbearable. She couldn't face the arrival of the day he died.

Hers is not the only empty house on the block. Jack Bridger killed his wife and his three kids and his mother-in-law and himself last month—according to my records. Nobody knows why, but I suspect that he couldn't stand seeing his three-year-old girl become no more than an idiot. She'd retrogressed to the day of her birth and perhaps beyond. She'd lost her language abilities and could no longer feed herself. Strangely, she could still walk, and her intelligence potential was high. She had the brain of a three-year-old, fully developed, but lacking all postbirth experience. It would have been better if she hadn't been able to walk. Confined to a cradle, she would at least not have had to be watched every minute.

Little Ann's fate is going to be Tom's. He talks like a five-year-old now. And Mike's fate . . . my fate . . . Carole's . . . God! We'll end up like Ann! I can't stand thinking about it.

Poor Carole. She has the toughest job. I'm away part of the day, but she has to take care of what are, in effect, a five-year-old and an eight-year-old, getting younger every day. There is no relief for her, since they're always home. All educational institutions, except for certain research laboratories, are closed.

The president says we're going to convert ninety percent of all industries to cybernation. In fact, anything that can be cybernated will be. They have to be. Almost everything, from the mines to the loading equipment to the railroads and trucks and the unloading equipment and the arrangement and dispersal of the final goods at central distribution points.

Are six years enough to do this?

And who's going to pay for this? Never mind, he says. Money is on its way out. The president is a goddamned radical. He's taking advantage of this situation to put over his own ideas, which he sure as hell never revealed during his campaign for election. Sometimes I wonder *who* put The Ball up there. But that idea is sheer paranoia. At least, this gigantic WPA project is giving work to those who are able to work. The rest are on, or going to be on, a minimum guaranteed income, and I mean minimum. But the president says that, in time, everybody will have all he needs, and more, in the way of food, housing, schooling, clothing, etc. *He* says! What if Project Toro doesn't work? And what if it does work? Are we then going to return to the old economy? Of course not! It'll be impossible to abandon everything we've worked on; the new establishment will see to that.

I tried to find out where Myrna lived. I'm making this record in my office, so Carole isn't going to get hold of it. I love her—Myrna, I mean—passionately. I hired her two weeks ago and fell headlong, burningly, in love with her. All this was in 1977, of course, but today, inside of *me, is* 1977.

Carole doesn't know about this, of course. According to the letters and notes from Myrna, which I should have destroyed but, thank God, never had the heart to do, Carole didn't find out about Myrna until two years later. At least, that's what this letter from Myrna says. She was away visiting her sister then and wrote to me in answer to my letter. A good thing, too, otherwise I wouldn't know what went on then.

My reason tells me to forget about Myrna. And so I will.

I've traveled backward in our affair, from our final bitter parting, to this state, when I was most in love with her. I know this because I've just reread the records of our relationship. It began deteriorating about six months before we split up, but I don't feel those emotions now, of course. And in two weeks I won't feel anything for her. If I don't refer to the records, I won't even know she ever existed.

This thought is intolerable. I have to find her, but I've had no success at all so far. In fourteen days, no, five, since every day ahead takes three more of the past, I'll have no drive to locate her. Because I won't know what I'm missing.

I don't hate Carole. I love her, but with a cool much-married love. Myrna makes me feel like a boy again. I burn exquisitely.

But where is Myrna?

True date: October 30, 1981

I ran into Brackwell Lee, the old mystery story writer today. Like most writers who haven't gone to work for the government propaganda office, he's in a bad way financially. He's surviving on his GMI, but for him there are no more first editions of rare books, new sports cars, Western Reserve or young girls. I stood him three shots of the rotgut which is the only whiskey now served at Grover's and listened to the funny stories he told to pay me for the drinks. But I also had to listen to his tales of woe.

Nobody buys fiction or, in fact, any long works of any kind anymore. Even if you're a speed reader and go through a whole novel is one day, you have to start all over again the next time you pick it up. TV writing, except for the propaganda shows, is no alternative. The same old shows are shown every day and enjoyed just as much as yesterday or last year. According to my records, I've seen the hilarious pilot movie of the "Soap Opera Blues" series fifty times.

When old Lee talked about how he had been dropped by the young girls, he got obnoxiously weepy. I told him that that didn't say much for him or the girls either. But if he didn't want to be hurt, why didn't he erase those records that noted his rejections?

He didn't want to do that, though he could give me no logical reason why he shouldn't.

"Listen," I said with a sudden drunken inspiration, "why don't you erase the old records and make some new ones? How you laid this and that beautiful young thing. Describe your conquests in detail. You'll think you're the greatest Casanova that ever lived."

"But that wouldn't be true!" he said.

"You, a writer of lies, say that?" I said. "Anyway, you wouldn't know that they weren't the truth."

"Yeah," he said, "but if I get all charged up and come barreling down here to pick up some tail, I'll be rejected and so'll be right back where I was."

"Leave a stern note to yourself to listen to them only late at night, say, an hour before The Ball puts all to sleep. That way, you won't ever get hurt."

George Palmer wandered in then. I asked him how things were doing.

"I'm up to here handling cases for kids who can't get drivers' licenses," he said. "It's true you can teach anybody how to drive in a day, but the lessons are forgotten the next day. Anyway, it's experience that makes a good driver, and . . . need I explain more? The kids have to have cars, so they drive them regardless. Hence, as you no doubt have forgotten, the traffic accidents and violations are going up and up."

"Is that right?" I said.

"Yeah. There aren't too many in the mornings, since most people don't go to work until noon. However, the new transit system should take care of that when we get it, sometime in 1984 or 5."

"What new transit system?" I said.

"It's been in the papers," he said. "I reread some of last week's this morning. The city of Los Angeles is equipped with a model system now, and it's working so well it's going to be extended throughout Los Angeles County. Eventually, every city of any size in the country'll have it. Nobody'll have to walk more than four blocks to get to a line. It'll cut air pollution by half and the traffic load by two-thirds. Of course, it'll be compulsory; you'll have to show cause to drive a car. And I hate to think about the mess *that's* going to be, the paper work, the pile-up in the courts and so forth. But after the way the government handled the L. A. riot, the rest of the country should get in line."

"How will the rest of the country know how the government handled it unless they're told?" I said.

"They'll be told. Every day," he said.

"Eventually, there won't be enough time in the day for the news channels to tell us all we'll need to know," I said. "And even if there were enough time, we'd have to spend all day watching TV. So who's going to get the work done?"

"Each person will have to develop his own viewing specialty," he said. "They'll just have to watch the news that concerns them and ignore the rest."

"And how can they do that if they won't know what concerns them until they've run through everything?" I said. "Day after day."

"I'll buy a drink," he said. "Liquor's good for one thing. It makes you forget what you're afraid not to forget."

VIII

True date: late 1982. Subjective date: late 1974

She came into my office, and I knew at once that she was going to be more than just another client. I'd been suffering all day from the "mirror syndrome," but the sight of her stabilized me. I forgot the thirty-seven-year-old face my twenty-nine-year-old mind had seen in the bathroom that morning. She is a beautiful woman, only twenty-seven. I had trouble at first listening to her story; all I wanted to do was to look at her. I finally understood that she wanted me to get her husband out of jail on a murder rap. It seemed he'd been in since 1976 (real time). She wanted me to get the case reopened, to use the new plea of rehabilitation by retrogression.

I was supposed to know that, but I had to take a quick look through my resumé before I could tell her what chance she had. Under RBR was the definition of the term and a notation that a number of people had been released because of it. The main idea behind it is that criminals are not the same people they were before they became criminals, if they have lost all memory of the crime. They've traveled backward to goodness, you might say. Of course, RBR doesn't apply to hardened criminals or to someone who'd planned a crime a long time before it was actually committed.

I asked her why she would want to help a man who had killed his mistress in a fit of rage when he'd found her cheating on him?

"I love him," she said.

And I love you, I thought.

She gave me some documents from the big rec bag she carried. I looked through them and said, "But you divorced him in 1977?"

"Yes, he's really my ex-husband," she said. "But I think of him now as my husband."

No need to ask her why.

"I'll study the case," I said. "You make a note to see me tomorrow. Meantime, how about a drink at the Rover bar so we can discuss our strategy?"

That's how it all started—again.

It wasn't until a week later, when I was going over some old recs, that I discovered it was *again*. It made no difference. I love her. I also love Carole, rather, *a* Carole. The one who married me six years ago, that is, six years ago in my memory.

But there is the other Carole, the one existing today, the poor miserable wretch who can't get out of the house until I come home. And I can't come home until late evening because I can't get started to work until about twelve noon. It's true that I could come home earlier than I do if it weren't for Myrna. I try. No use. I have to see Myrna.

I tell myself I'm a bastard, which I am, because Carole and the children need me very much. Tom is ten and acts as if he's two. Mike is a four-year-old in a twelve-year-old body. I come home from Myrna to bedlam every day, according to my records, and every day must be like today.

That I feel both guilt and shame doesn't help. I become enraged; I try to suppress my anger, which is born out of my desperation and helplessness and guilt and shame. But it comes boiling out, and then bedlam becomes hell.

I tell myself that Carole and the kids need a tower of strength now. One who can be calm and reassuring and, above all, loving. One who can handle the thousand tedious and aggravating problems that infest every household in this world of diminishing memory. In short, a hero. Because the real heroes, and heroines, are those who deal heroically with the everyday cares of life, though God knows they've been multiplied enormously. It's not the guy who kills a dragon once in his lifetime and then retires that's a hero. It's the guy who kills cockroaches and rats every day, day after day, and doesn't rest on his laurels until he's an old man, if then.

What am I talking about? Maybe I could handle the problems if it weren't for this memory loss. I can't adjust because I can't ever get used to it. My whole being, body and mind, must get the same high-voltage jolt every morning.

The insurance companies have canceled all policies for anybody under twelve. The government's contemplated taking over these policies but has decided against it. It will, however, pay for the burials, since this service is necessary. I don't really think that many children are being "accidentally" killed because of the insurance money. Most fatalities are obviously just results of neglect or parents going berserk.

I'm getting away from Myrna, trying to, anyway, because I wish to forget my guilt. I love her, but if I didn't see her tomorrow, I'd forget her. But I *will* see her tomorrow. My notes will make sure of that. And each day is, for me, love at first sight. It's a wonderful feeling, and I wish it could go on forever.

If I just had the guts to destroy all reference to her tonight. But I won't. The thought of losing her makes me panic.

IX

True date: middle of 1984. Subjective date: middle of 1968

I was surprised that I woke up so early.

Yesterday, Carole and I had been married at noon. We'd driven up to this classy motel near Lake Geneva. We'd spent most of our time in bed after we got there, naturally, though we did get up for dinner and champagne. We finally fell asleep about four in the morning. That was why I hadn't expected to wake up at dawn. I reached over to touch Carole, wondering if she would be too sleepy. But she wasn't there.

She's gone to the bathroom, I thought. I'll catch her on the way back.

Then I sat up, my heart beating as if it had suddenly discovered it was alive. The edges of the room got fuzzy, and then the fuzziness raced in toward me.

The dawn light was filtered by the blinds, but I had seen that the furniture was not familiar. I'd never been in this place before.

I sprang out of bed and did not, of course, notice the note sticking out of my glass case. Why should I? I didn't wear glasses then.

Bellowing, "Carole!" I ran down a long and utterly strange hall and past the bathroom door, which was open, and into the room at the other end of the hall. Inside it, I stopped. This was a kids' bedroom: bunks, pennants, slogans, photographs of two young boys, posters and blowups of faces I'd never seen, except one of Laurel and Hardy, some science fiction and Tolkien and Tarzan books, some school texts, and a large flat piece of equipment hanging on the wall. I would not have known that it was a TV set if its controls had not made its purpose obvious.

The bunks had not been slept in. The first rays of the sun fell on thick dust on a table.

I ran back down the hall, looked into the bathroom again, though I knew no one was there, saw dirty towels, underwear and socks heaped in a corner, and ran back to my bedroom. The blinds did not let enough light in, so I looked for a light switch on the wall. There wasn't any, though there was a small round plate of brass where the switch should have been. I touched it, and the ceiling lights came on.

Carole's side of the bed had not been slept in.

The mirror over the bureau caught me, drew me and held me. Who was this haggard old man staring out from my twenty-three-year-old self? I had gray hair, big bags under my eyes, thickening and sagging features, and a long scar on my right cheek.

After a while, still dazed and trembling, I picked up a book from the bureau and looked at it. At this close distance, I could just barely make out the title, and, when I opened it, the print was a blur.

I put the book down, *Be Your Own Handyman Around Your House,* and proceeded to go through the house from attic to basement. Several times, I whimpered, "Carole! Carole!" Finding no one, I left the house and walked to the house next door and beat on its door. No one answered; no lights came on inside.

I ran to the next house and tried to wake up the people in it. But there weren't any.

A woman in a house across the street shouted at me. I ran to her, babbling. She was about fifty years old and also hysterical. A moment later, a man her age appeared behind her. Neither listened to me; they kept asking me questions, the same questions I was asking them. Then I saw a black and white police car of a model unknown to me come around the corner half a block away. I ran toward it, then stopped. The car was so silent that I knew even in my panic that it was electrically powered. The two cops wore strange uniforms, charcoal gray with white helmets topped by red panaches. Their aluminum badges were in the shape of a spread eagle.

I found out later that the police throughout the country had been federalized. These two were on the night shift and so had had enough time to get reorientated. Even so, one had such a case of the shakes that the other told him to get back into the car and take it easy for a while.

After he got us calmed down, he asked us why we hadn't listened to our tapes.

"What tapes?" we said.

"Where's your bedroom?" he said to the couple.

They led him to it, and he turned on a machine on the bedside table.

"Good morning," a voice said. I recognized it as the husband's. "Don't panic. Stay in bed and listen to me. Listen to everything I say."

The rest was a resumé, by no means short, of the main events since the first day of memory loss. It ended by directing the two to a notebook that would tell them personal things they needed to know, such as where their jobs were, how they could get to them, where their area central distributing stores were, how to use their I.D. cards and so on.

The policeman said, "You have the rec set to turn on at 6:30, but you woke up before then. Happens a lot."

I went back, reluctantly, to the house I'd fled. It was mine, but I felt as if I were a stranger. I ran off my own recs twice. Then I put my glasses on and started to put together my life. The daily rerun of "Narrative of an Old-Young Man Shipwrecked on the Shoals of Time."

I didn't go any place today. Why should I? I had no job. Who needs a lawyer who isn't through law school yet? I did have, I found out, an application in for a position on the police force. The police force was getting bigger and bigger but at the same time was having a large turnover. My recs said that I was to appear at the City Hall for an interview tomorrow.

If I feel tomorrow as I do today, and I will, I probably won't be able to make myself go to the interview. I'm too grief-stricken to do anything but sit and stare or, now and then, get up and pace back and forth, like a sick leopard in a cage made by Time. Even the tranquilizers haven't helped me much.

I have lost my bride the day after we were married. And I love Carole deeply. We were going to live a long happy life and have two children. We would raise them in a house filled with love.

But the recs say that the oldest boy escaped from the house and was killed by a car and Carole, in a fit of anguish and despair, killed the youngest boy and then herself.

They're buried in Springdale Cemetary.

I can't feel a retroactive grief for those strangers called Mike and Tom.

But Carole, lovely laughing Carole, lives in my mind.

Oh, God, why don't I just erase all my recs? Then I'd not have to suffer remorse for all I've done or failed to do. I wouldn't know what a bastard I'd been.

Why don't I do it? Take the past and shed its heartbreaks and its guilts as a snake sheds its skin. Or as the legislature cancels old laws. Press a button, fill the wastebasket, and you're clean and easy again, innocent again. That's the logical thing to do, and I'm a lawyer, dedicated to logic.

Why not? Why not?

But I can't. Maybe I like to suffer. I've liked to inflict suffering, and according to what I understand, those who like to inflict, unconsciously hope to be inflicted upon.

No, that can't be it. At least, not all of it. My main reason for hanging on to the recs is that I don't want to lose my identity. A major part of me, a unique person, is not in the neurons of my mind, where it belongs, but in an electro-mechanical device or in tracings of lead or ink on paper. The protein, the flesh for which I owe, can't hang on to *me*.

I'm becoming less and less, dwindling away, like the wicked witch on whom Dorothy poured water. I'll become a puddle, a wailing voice of hopeless despair, and then . . . nothing.

God, haven't I suffered enough! I said I owe for the flesh and I'm down in Your books. Why do I have to struggle each day against becoming a dumb brute, a thing without memory? Why not rid myself of the struggle? Press the button, fill the wastebasket, discharge my grief in a chaos of magnetic lines and pulped paper?

Sufficient unto the day is the evil thereof.

I didn't realize, Lord, what that really meant.

X

I will marry Carole in three days. No, I would have. No, I did.

I remember reading a collection of Krazy Kat comic strips when I was twenty-one. One was captioned: COMA REIGNS. Coconing County was in the doldrums, comatose. Nobody, Krazy Kat, Ignatz Mouse, Officer Pupp, nobody had the energy to do anything. Mouse was too lazy even to think about hurling his brickbat. Strange how that sticks in my mind. Strange to think that it won't be long before it becomes forever unstuck.

Coma reigns today over the world.

Except for Project Toro, the TV says. And that is behind schedule. But the Earth, Ignatz Mouse, will not allow itself to forget that it must hurl the brickbat, the asteroid. But where Ignatz expressed his love, in a queer perverted fashion, by banging Kat in the back of the head with his brick, the world is expressing its hatred, and its desperation, by throwing Toro at The Ball.

I did manage today to go downtown to my appointment. I did it only to keep from going mad with grief. I was late, but Chief Moberly seemed to expect that I would be. Almost everybody is, he said. One reason for my tardiness was that I got lost. This residential area was nothing in 1968 but a forest out past the edge of town. I don't have a car, and the house is in the middle of the area, which has many winding streets. I do have a map of the area, which I forgot about. I kept going eastward and finally came to a main thoroughfare. This was Route 98, over which I've traveled many times since I was a child. But the road itself, and the houses along it, were strange. The private airport which should have been across the road was gone, replaced by a number of large industrial buildings.

A big sign near a roofed bench told me to wait there for the RTS bus. One would be along every ten minutes, the sign stated.

I waited an hour. The bus, when it came, was not the fully automated vehicle promised by the sign. It held a sleepy-looking driver and ten nervous passengers. The driver didn't ask me for money, so I didn't offer any. I sat down and watched him with an occasional look out of the window. He didn't have a steering wheel. When he wanted the bus to slow down or stop he pushed a lever forward. To speed it up, he pulled back on the lever. The bus was apparently following a single aluminum rail in the middle of the right-hand lane. My recs told me later that the automatic pilot and door-opening equipment had never been delivered and probably wouldn't be for some years—if ever. The grand plan of cybernating everything possible had failed. There aren't enough people who can provide the know-how or the man-hours. In fact, everything is going to hell.

The police chief, Adam Moberly, is fifty years old and looks as if he's sixty-five. He talked to me for about fifteen minutes and then had me put through a short physical and intelligence test. Three hours after I had walked into the station, I was sworn in. He suggested that I room with two other officers, one of whom was a sixty-year-old veteran, in the hotel across the street from the station. If I had company, I'd get over the morning disorientation more quickly. Besides, the policemen who lived in the central area of the city got preferential treatment in many things, including the rationed supplies.

I refused to move. I couldn't claim that my house was a

home to me, but I feel that it's a link to the past, I mean the future, no, I mean the past. Leaving it would be cutting out one more part of me.

True date: late 1984. Subjective date: early 1967

My mother died today. That is, as far as I'm concerned, she did. The days ahead of me are going to be full of anxiety and grief. She took a long time to die. She found out she had cancer two weeks after my father died. So I'll be voyaging backward in sorrow through my mother and then through my father, who was also sick for a long time.

Thank God I won't have to go through every day of that, though. Only a third of them. And these are the last words I'm going to record about their illnesses.

But how can I not record them unless I make a recording reminding me not to do so?

I found out from my recs how I'd gotten this big scar on my face. Myrna's ex-husband slashed me before I laid him out with a big ashtray. He was shipped off this time to a hospital for the criminally insane where he died a few months later in the fire that burned every prisoner in his building. I haven't the faintest idea what happened to Myrna after that. Apparently I decided not to record it.

I feel dead tired tonight, and, according to my recs, every night. It's no wonder, if every day is like today. Fires, murders, suicides, accidents and insane people. Babies up to fourteen years old abandoned. And a police department which is ninety percent composed, in effect, of raw rookies. The victims are taken to hospitals where the nurses are only half-trained, if that, and the doctors are mostly old geezers hauled out of retirement.

I'm going to bed soon even if it's only nine o'clock. I'm so exhausted that even Jayne Mansfield couldn't keep me awake. And I dread tomorrow. Besides the usual reasons for loathing it, I have one which I can hardly stand thinking about.

Tomorrow my memory will have slid past the day I met Carole. I won't remember her at all.

Why do I cry because I'll be relieved of a great sorrow?

XI

True date: 1986. Subjective date: 1962

I'm nuts about Jean, and I'm way down because I can't find her. According to my recs, she went to Canada in 1965. Why? We surely didn't fall in and then out of love? Our love would never die. Her parents must've moved to Canada. And so here we both are in 1962, in effect. Halfway in 1962, anyway. Amphibians of time. Is she thinking about me now? Is she unable to think about me, about anything, because she's dead or crazy? Tomorrow I'll start the official wheels grinding. The Canadian government should be able to find her through the International Information Computer Network, according to the recs. Meanwhile, I burn, though with a low flame. I'm so goddamn tired.

Even Marilyn Monroe couldn't get a rise out of me tonight. But Jean. Yeah, Jean. I see her as seventeen years old, tall, slim but full-busted, with creamy white skin and a high forehead and huge blue eyes and glossy black hair and the most kissable lips ever. And broadcasting sex waves so thick you can see them, like heat waves. Wow!

And so tired old Wow goes to bed.

February 6, 1987

While I was watching TV to get orientated this morning, a news flash interrupted the program. The president of the United States had died of a heart attack a few minutes before.

"My God!" I said. "Old Eisenhower is dead!"

But the picture of the president certainly wasn't that of Eisenhower. And the name was one I never heard, of course.

I can't feel bad for a guy I never knew.

I got to thinking about him, though. Was he as confused every morning as I was? Imagine a guy waking up, thinking he's a senator in Washington and then he finds he's the president? At least, he knows something about running the country. But it's no wonder the old pump conked out. The TV says we've had five prexies, mostly real old guys, in the last seven years. One was shot; one dived out of the White House window onto his head; two had heart attacks; one went crazy and almost caused a war, as if we didn't have grief enough, for crying out loud.

Even after the orientation, I really didn't get it. I guess I'm too dumb for anything to percolate through my dome.

A policeman called and told me I'd better get my ass down to work. I said I didn't feel up to it, besides, why would I want to be a cop? He said that if I didn't show, I might go to jail. So I showed.

True date: 1988. Subjective date: 1956

Here I am, eleven years old, going on ten.

In one way, that is. The other way, here I am forty-three and going on about sixty. At least, that's what my face looks like to me. Sixty.

This place is just like a prison except some of us get treated like trusties. According to the work chart, I leave through the big iron gates every day at twelve noon with a demolition crew. We tore down five partly burned houses today. The gang chief, old Rogers, says it's just WPA work, whatever that is. Anyway, one of the guys I work with kept looking more and more familiar. Suddenly, I felt like I was going to pass out. I put down my sledgehammer and walked over to him, and I said, "Aren't you Stinky Davis?"

He looked funny and then he said, "Jesus! You're Gabby! Gabby Franham!"

I didn't like his using the Lord's name in vain, but I guess he can be excused.

Nothing would've tasted good the way I felt, but the sandwiches we got for breakfast, lunch and supper tasted like they had a dash of oil in them. Engine oil, I mean. The head honcho, he's eighty if he's a day, says his recs tell him they're derived from petroleum. The oil is converted into a kind of protein and then flavoring and stuff is added. Oil-burgers, they call them.

Tonight, before lights-out, we watched the prez give a speech. He said that, within a month, Project Toro will be finished. One way or the other. And all this memory loss should stop. I can't quite get it even if I was briefed this morning. Men on the moon, unmanned ships on Venus and Mars, all since I was eleven years old. And The Black Ball, the thing from outer space. And now we're pushing asteroids around. Talk about your science fiction!

XII

September 4, 1988

Today's the day.

Actually, the big collision'll be tomorrow, ten minutes before 1:00 A.M. . . . but I think of it as today. Toro, going 150,000 miles an hour, will run head-on into The Ball. Maybe.

Here I am again, Mark Franham, recording just in case The Ball does dodge out of the way and I have to depend on my recs. It's 7:00 P.M. and after that raunchy supper of oilburgers, potato soup and canned carrots, fifty of us gathered around set No. 8. There's a couple of scientists talking now, discussing theories about just what The Ball is and why it's been taking our memories away from us. Old Doctor Charles Presley—any relation to Elvis?—thinks The Ball is some sort of unmanned survey ship. When it finds a planet inhabited by sentient life, sentient means intelligent, it takes specimens. Specimens of the mind, that is. It unpeels people's minds for days' worth at a time, because that's all it's capable of. But it can do it to billions of specimens. It's like it was reading our minds but destroying the mind at the same time. Presley said it was like some sort of Heisenberg principle of the mind. The Ball can't observe our memories closely without disturbing them.

This Ball, Presley says, takes our memories and stores them. And when it's through with us, sucked us dry, it'll take off for another planet circling some far-off star. Someday, it'll return to its home planet, and the scientists there will study the recordings of our minds.

The other scientist, Dr. Marbles—he's still got his, ha!

ha!—asked why any species advanced enough to be able to do this could be so callous? Surely, the extees must know what great damage they're doing to us. Wouldn't they be too ethical for this?

Doc Presley says maybe they think of us as animals, they are so far above us. Doc Marbles says that could be. But it could also be that whoever built The Ball have different brains than we do. Their mind-reading ray, or whatever it is, when used on themselves doesn't disturb the memory patterns. But we're different. The extees don't know this, of course. Not now, anyway. When The Ball goes home, and the extees read our minds, they'll be shocked at what they've done to us. But it'll be too late then.

Presley and Marbles got into an argument about how the extees would be able to interpret their recordings. How could they translate our languages when they have no references—I mean, referents? How're they going to translate *chair and recs* and *rock and roll* and *yucky* and so on when they don't have anybody to tell them their meanings. Marbles said they wouldn't have just words; they'd have mental images to associate with the words. And so on. Some of the stuff they spouted I didn't understand at all.

I do know one thing, though, and I'm sure those big-domes do, too. But they wouldn't be allowed to say it over TV because we'd be even more gloomy and hopeless-feeling. That is, what if right now the computers in The Ball are translating our languages, reading our minds, as they're recorded? Then they know all about Project Toro. They'll be ready for the asteroid, destroy it if they have the weapons to do it, or, if they haven't, they'll just move The Ball into a different orbit.

I'm not going to say anything to the other guys about this. Why make them feel worse?

It's ten o'clock now. According to regulations posted up all over the place, it's time to go to bed. But nobody is. Not tonight. You don't sleep when the End of the World may be coming up.

I wish my Mom and Dad were here. I cried this morning when I found they weren't in this dump, and I asked the chief where they were. He said they were working in a city nearby, but they'd be visiting me soon. I think he lied.

Stinky saw me crying, but he didn't say anything. Why should he? I'll bet he's shed a few when he thought nobody was looking, too.

Twelve o'clock. Midnight. Less than an hour to go. Then, the big smash! Or, I hate to think about it, the big flop. We won't be able to see it directly because the skies are cloudy over most of North America. But we've got a system worked out so we can see it on TV. If there's a gigantic flash when the Toro and The Ball collide, that is.

What if there isn't? Then we'll soon be just like those grown-up kids, some of them twenty years old, that they keep locked up in the big building in the northwest corner of this place. Saying nothing but Da Da or Ma Ma, drooling, filling their diapers. If they got diapers, because old Rogers says he heard, today, of course, they don't wear nothing. The nurses come in once a day and hose them and the place down. The nurses don't have time to change and wash diapers and give personal baths. They got enough to do just spoon-feeding them.

Three and a half more hours to go, and I'll be just like them. Unless, before then, I flip, and they put me in that building old Rogers calls the puzzle factory. They're all completely out of their skulls, he says, and even if memloss stops tonight, they won't change any.

Old Rogers says there's fifty million less people in the United States than there were in 1980, according to the recs. And a good thing, too, he says, because it's all we can do to feed what we got.

Come on, Toro! You're our last chance!

If Toro doesn't make it, I'll kill myself! I will! I'm not going to let myself become an idiot. Anyway, by the time I do become one, there won't be enough food to go around for those that do have their minds. I'll be starving to death. I'd rather get it over with now than go through that.

God'll forgive me.

God, You know I want to be a minister of the gospel when I grow up and that I want to help people. I'll marry a good woman, and we'll have children that'll be brought up right. And we'll thank You every day for the good things of life and battle the bad things.

Love, that's what I got, Lord. Love for You and love for Your people. So don't make me hate You. Guide Toro right into The Ball, and get us started on the right path again.

I wish Mom and Dad were here.

Twelve-thirty. In twenty minutes, we'll know.

The TV says the H-bombs are still going off all around The Ball.

The TV says the people on the East Coast are falling asleep. The rays, or whatever The Ball uses, aren't being affected by the H-bomb radiation. But that doesn't mean that its sensors aren't. I pray to God that they are cut off.

Ten minutes to go. Toro's got twenty-five thousand miles to go. Our sensors can't tell whether or not The Ball's still on its original orbit. I hope it is; I hope it is! If it's changed its path, then we're through! Done! Finished! Wiped out!

Five minutes to go; twelve thousand five hundred miles to go.

I can see in my mind's eyes The Ball, almost half a mile in diameter, hurtling on its orbit, blind as a bat, I hope and pray, the bombs, the last of the five thousand bombs, flashing, and Toro, a mile and a half long, a mile wide, millions of tons of rock and nickel-steel, charging toward its destined spot.

If it *is* destined.

But space *is* big, and even the Ball and Toro are small compared to all that emptiness out there. What if the mathematics of the scientists are just a little off, or the rocket motors on Toro aren't working just like they're supposed to, and Toro just tears on by The Ball? It's got to meet The Ball at the exact time and place, it's just *got* to!

I wish the radars and lasers could see what's going on.

Maybe it's better they can't. If we knew that The Ball had changed course . . . but this way we still got hope.

If Toro misses, I'll kill myself, I swear it.

Two minutes to go. One hundred and twenty seconds. The big room is silent except for kids like me praying or talking quietly into our recs or praying and talking and sobbing.

The TV says the bombs have quit exploding. No more flashes until Toro hits The Ball—if it does. Oh, God, let it hit, let it hit!

The unmanned satellites are going to open their camera lenses at the exact second of impact and take a quick shot. The cameras are encased in lead, the shutters are lead, and the equipment is special, mostly mechanical, not electrical, almost like a human eyeball. If the cameras see the big flash, they'll send an electrical impulse through circuits, also encased in lead, to a mechanism that'll shoot a big thin-shelled ball out. This is crammed with flashpowder, the same stuff photographers use, and mixed with oxygen pellets so the powder will ignite. There's to be three of the biggest flashes you ever saw. Three. Three for Victory.

If Toro misses, then only one flashball'll be set off.

Oh, Lord, don't let it happen!

Planes with automatic pilots'll be cruising above the clouds, and their equipment will see the flashes and transmit them to the ground TV equipment.

One minute to go.

Come on, God!

Don't let it happen, please don't let it happen, that some place way out there, some thousands of years from now, some weird-looking character reads this and finds out to his horror what his people have done to us. Will he feel bad about it? Lot of good that'll do. You, out there, I hate you! God, how I hate you!

Our Father which are in Heaven, fifteen seconds, Hallowed be Thy name, ten seconds, Thy will be done, five seconds, Thy will be done, but if it's thumbs down, God, why? Why? What did I ever do to you?

The screen's blank! Oh, my God, the screen's blank! What happened? Transmission trouble? Or they're afraid to tell us the truth?

It's on! It's on!

YAAAAAAY!

XIII

July 4, A.D. 2002

I may erase this. If I have any sense, I will. If I had any sense, I wouldn't make it in the first place.

Independence Day, and we're still under an iron rule. But old Dick the Dictator insists that when there's no longer a need for strict control, the Constitution will be restored, and we'll be a democracy again. He's ninety-five years old and can't last much longer. The vice-president is only eighty, but he's as tough an octogenarian as ever lived. And he's even more of a totalitarian than Dick. And when have men ever voluntarily relinquished power?

I'm one of the elite, so I don't have it so bad. Just being fifty-seven years old makes me a candidate for that class. In addition, I have my Ph.D. in education and I'm a part-time minister. I don't know why I say part-time, since there aren't any full-time ministers outside of the executives of the North American Council of Churches. The People can't afford full-time divines. Everybody has to work at least ten hours a day. But I'm better off than many. I've been eating fresh beef and pork for three years now. I have a nice house I don't have to share with another family. The house isn't the one my recs say I once owned. The People took it over for back taxes. It did me no good to protest that property taxes had been canceled during The Interim. That, say the People, ended when The Ball was destroyed.

But how could I pay taxes on it when I was only eleven years old, in effect?

I went out this afternoon, it being a holiday, with Leona to Springdale. We put flowers on her parents' and sisters'

graves, none of whom she remembers, and on my parents'
and Carole's and the children's graves, whom I know only
through the recs. I prayed for the forgiveness of Carole and
the boys.

Near Carole's grave was Stinky Davis's. Poor fellow, he
went berserk the night The Ball was destroyed and had to
be put in a padded cell. Still mad, he died five years later.

I sometimes wonder why I didn't go mad, too. The daily
shocks and jars of memloss should have made everyone fall
apart. But a certain number of us were very tough, tougher
than we deserved. Even so, the day-to-day attack by alarm
syndromes did its damage. I'm sure that years of life were
cut off the hardiest of us. We're the shattered generation.
And this is bad for the younger ones, who'll have no older
people to lead them in the next ten years or so.

Or is it such a bad thing?

At least, those who were in their early twenties or
younger when The Ball was smashed are coming along
fine. Leona herself was twenty then. She became one of my
students in high school. She's thirty-five physically but only
fifteen in what the kids call "intage" or internal age. But
since education goes faster for adults, and all those human-
ities courses have been eliminated, she graduated from high
school last June. She still wants to be a doctor of medicine,
and God knows we need M.D.'s. She'll be forty-two before
she gets her degree. We're planning on having two children, the maximum allowed, and it's going to be tough
raising them while she's in school. But God will see us
through.

As we were leaving the cemetery, Margie Oleander, a
very pretty girl of twenty-five, approached us. She asked
me if she could speak privately to me. Leona didn't like
that, but I told her that Margie probably wanted to talk to
me about her grades in my geometry class.

Margie did talk somewhat about her troubles with her
lessons. But then she began to ask some questions about
the political system. Yes, I'd better erase this, and if it
weren't for old habits, I'd not be doing this now.

After a few minutes, I became uneasy. She sounded as if she were trying to get me to show some resentment about the current situation.

Is she an agent provocateur or was she testing me for potential membership in the underground?

Whatever she was doing, she was in dangerous waters. So was I. I told her to ask her political philosophy teacher for answers. She said she'd read the textbook, which is provided by the government. I muttered something about, "Render unto Caesar what is Caesar's," and walked away.

But she came after me and asked if I could talk to her in my office tomorrow. I hesitated and then said I would.

I wonder if I would have agreed if she weren't so beautiful?

When we got home, Leona made a scene. She accused me of chasing after the younger girls because she was too old to stimulate me. I told her that I was no senile King David, which she should be well aware of, and she said she's listened to my recs and she knew what kind of man I was. I told her I'd learned from my mistakes. I've gone over the recs of the missing years many times.

"Yes," she said, "you know about them intellectually. But you don't *feel* them!"

Which is true.

I'm outside now and looking up into the night. Up there, out there, loose atoms and molecules float around, cold and alone, debris of the memory records of The Ball, atoms and molecules of what were once incredibly complex patterns, the memories of thirty-two years of the lives of four and a half billion human beings. Forever lost, except in the mind of One.

Oh, Lord, I started all over again as an eleven-year-old. Don't let me make the same mistakes again.

You've given us tomorrow again, but we've very little past to guide us.

Tomorrow I'll be very cool and very professional with Margie. Not too much, of course, since there should be a certain warmth between teacher and pupil.

If only she did not remind me of . . . whom?

But that's impossible. I can remember nothing from The Interim. Absolutely nothing.

But what if there are different kinds of memory?

The Women
Men Don't See

James Tiptree, Jr.

Like any branch of literature, science fiction
reflects the trends of current thinking. Last
year Joanna Russ won a Nebula Award for a
feminist story called *When It Changed*; this
year James Tiptree, Jr., offers a male viewpoint on the same subject. As you might expect, other than in the basic theme, there's
very little similarity between the two stories.

I see her first while the Mexicana 727 is barreling down to
Cozumel Island. I come out of the can and lurch into her
seat, saying "Sorry," at a double female blur. The near blur
nods quietly. The younger one in the window seat goes on
looking out. I continue down the aisle, registering nothing.
Zero. I never would have looked at them or thought of
them again.

Cozumel airport is the usual mix of panicky Yanks
dressed for the sand pile and calm Mexicans dressed for

333

lunch at the Presidente. I am a used-up Yank dressed for serious fishing; I extract my rods and duffel from the riot and hike across the field to find my charter pilot. One Captain Estéban has contracted to deliver me to the bonefish flat of Bélise three hundred kilometers down the coast.

Captain Estéban turns out to be four feet nine of mahogany Maya *puro*. He is also in a somber Maya snit. He tells me my Cessna is grounded somewhere and his Bonanza is booked to take a party to Chetumal.

Well, Chetumal is south; can he take me along and go on to Bélise after he drops them? Gloomily he concedes the possibility—*if* the other party permits, and *if* there are not too many *equipajes*.

The Chetumal party approaches. It's the woman and her young companion—daughter?—neatly picking their way across the gravel and yucca apron. Their Ventura two-suiters, like themselves, are small, plain and neutral-colored. No problem. When the captain asks if I may ride along, the mother says mildly "Of course," without looking at me.

I think that's when my inner tilt-detector sends up its first faint click. How come this woman has already looked me over carefully enough to accept on her plane? I disregard it. Paranoia hasn't been useful in my business for years, but the habit is hard to break.

As we clamber into the Bonanza, I see the girl has what could be an attractive body if there was any spark at all. There isn't. Captain Estéban folds a serape to sit on so he can see over the cowling and runs a meticulous checkdown. And then we're up and trundling over the turquoise Jello of the Caribbean into a stiff south wind.

The coast on our right is the territory of Quintana Roo. If you haven't seen Yucatan, imagine the world's biggest absolutely flat green-grey rug. An empty-looking land. We pass the white ruin of Tulum and the gash of the road to Chichen Itza, a half-dozen coconut plantations, and then nothing but reef and low scrub jungle all the way to the horizon, just about the way the conquistadores saw it four centuries back.

Long strings of cumulus are racing at us, shadowing the

coast. I have gathered that part of our pilot's gloom concerns the weather. A cold front is dying on the henequen fields of Mérida to the west, and the south wind has piled up a string of coastal storms: what they call *llovisnas*. Estéban detours methodically around a couple of small thunderheads. The Bonanza jinks, and I look back with a vague notion of reassuring the women. They are calmly intent on what can be seen of Yucatan. Well, they were offered the copilot's view, but they turned it down. Too shy?

Another *llovisna* puffs up ahead. Estéban takes the Bonanza upstairs, rising in his seat to sight his course. I relax for the first time in too long, savoring the latitudes between me and my desk, the week of fishing ahead. Our captain's classic Maya profile attracts my gaze: forehead sloping back from his predatory nose, lips and jaw stepping back below it. If his slant eyes had been any more crossed, he couldn't have made his license. That's a handsome combination, believe it or not. On the little Maya chicks in their minishifts with iridescent gloop on those cockeyes, it's also highly erotic. Nothing like the oriental doll thing; these people have stone bones. Captain Estéban's old grandmother could probably tow the Bonanza . . .

I'm snapped awake by the cabin hitting my ear. Estéban is barking into his headset over a drumming racket of hail; the windows are dark grey.

One important noise is missing—the motor. I realize Estéban is fighting a dead plane. Thirty-six hundred; we've lost two thousand feet!

He slaps tank switches as the storm throws us around; I catch something about *gasolina* in a snarl that shows his big teeth. The Bonanza reels down. As he reaches for an overhead toggle, I see the fuel gauges are high. Maybe a clogged gravity feed line; I've heard of dirty gas down here. He drops the set. It's a million to one nobody can read us through the storm at this range anyway. Twenty-five hundred—going down.

His electric feed pump seems to have cut in: the motor explodes—quits—explodes—and quits again for good. We are suddenly out of the bottom of the clouds. Below us is a long white line almost hidden by rain: The reef. But there isn't any beach behind it, only a big meandering bay with a few mangrove flats—and it's coming up at us fast.

This is going to be bad, I tell myself with great unoriginality. The women behind me haven't made a sound. I look back and see they're braced down with their coats by their heads. With a stalling speed around eighty, all this isn't much use, but I wedge myself in.

Estéban yells some more into his set, flying a falling plane. He is doing one jesus job, too—as the water rushes up at us he dives into a hair-raising turn and hangs us into the wind—with a long pale ridge of sandbar in front of our nose.

Where in hell he found it I'll never know. The Bonanza mushes down, and we belly-hit with a tremendous tearing crash—bounce—hit again—and everything slews wildly as we flat-spin into the mangroves at the end of the bar. Crash! Clang! The plane is wrapping itself into a mound of strangler fig with one wing up. The crashing quits with us all in one piece. And no fire. Fantastic.

Captain Estéban prys open his door, which is now in the roof. Behind me a woman is repeating quietly. "Mother. Mother." I climb up the floor and find the girl trying to free herself from her mother's embrace. The woman's eyes are closed. Then she opens them and suddenly lets go, sane as soap. Estéban starts hauling them out. I grab the Bonanza's aid kit and scramble out after them into brilliant sun and wind. The storm that hit us is already vanishing up the coast.

"Great landing, Captain."

"Oh, yes! It was beautiful." The women are shaky, but no hysteria. Estéban is surveying the scenery with the expression his ancestors used on the Spaniards.

If you've been in one of these things, you know the slow-motion inanity that goes on. Euphoria, first. We straggle down the fig tree and out onto the sandbar in the roaring hot wind, noting without alarm that there's nothing but miles of crystalline water on all sides. It's only a foot or so deep, and the bottom is the olive color of silt. The distant shore around us is all flat mangrove swamp, totally uninhabitable.

"Bahia Espiritu Santo." Estéban confirms my guess that we're down in that huge water wilderness. I always wanted to fish it.

"What's all that smoke?" The girl is pointing at the plumes blowing around the horizon.

"Alligator hunters," says Estéban. Maya poachers have left burn-offs in the swamps. It occurs to me that any signal fires we make aren't going to be too conspicuous. And I now note that our plane is well-buried in the mound of fig. Hard to see it from the air.

Just as the question of how the hell we get out of here surfaces in my head, the older woman asks composedly, "If they didn't hear you, Captain, when will they start looking for us? Tomorrow?"

"Correct," Estéban agrees dourly. I recall that air-sea rescue is fairly informal here. Like, keep an eye open for Mario, his mother says he hasn't been home all week.

It dawns on me we may be here quite some while.

Furthermore, the diesel-truck noise on our left is the Caribbean piling back into the mouth of the bay. The wind is pushing it at us, and the bare bottoms on the mangroves show that our bar is covered at high tide. I recall seeing a full moon this morning in—believe it, St. Louis—which means maximal tides. Well, we can climb up in the plane. But what about drinking water?

There's a small splat! behind me. The older woman has sampled the bay. She shakes her head, smiling ruefully. It's the first real expression on either of them; I take it as the signal for introductions. When I say I'm Don Fenton from St. Louis, she tells me their name is Parsons, from Bethesda, Maryland. She says it so nicely I don't at first notice we aren't being given first names. We all compliment Captain Estéban again.

His left eye is swelled shut, an inconvenience beneath his attention as a Maya, but Mrs. Parsons spots the way he's bracing his elbow in his ribs.

"You're hurt, Captain."

"Roto—I think is broken." He's embarrassed at being in pain. We get him to peel off his Jaime shirt, revealing a nasty bruise in his superb dark-bay torso.

"Is there tape in that kit, Mr. Fenton? I've had a little first-aid training."

She begins to deal competently and very impersonally with the tape. Miss Parsons and I wander to the end of the bar and have a conversation which I am later to recall acutely.

"Roseate spoonbills," I tell her as three pink birds flap away.

"They're beautiful," she says in her tiny voice. They both have tiny voices. "He's a Mayan Indian, isn't he? The pilot, I mean."

"Right. The real thing, straight out of the Bonampak murals. Have you seen Chichén and Uxmal?"

"Yes. We were in Mérida. We're going to Tikal in Guatemala . . . I mean, we were."

"You'll get there." It occurs to me the girl needs cheering up. "Have they told you that Maya mothers used to tie a board on the infant's forehead to get that slant? They also hung a ball of tallow over its nose to make the eyes cross. It was considered aristocratic."

She smiles and takes another peek at Estéban. "People seem different in Yucatan," she says thoughtfully. "Not like the Indians around Mexico City. More, I don't know, independent."

"Comes from never having been conquered. Mayas got massacred and chased a lot, but nobody ever really flattened them. I bet you didn't know that the last Mexican-Maya war ended with a negotiated truce in nineteen thirty-five?"

"No!" Then she says seriously, "I like that."

"So do I."

"The water is really rising very fast," says Mrs. Parsons gently from behind us.

It is, and so is another *llovisna*. We climb back into the Bonanza. I try to rig my parka for a rain catcher, which blows loose as the storm hits fast and furious. We sort a couple of malt bars and my bottle of Jack Daniels out of the jumble in the cabin and make ourselves reasonably comfortable. The Parsons take a sip of whiskey each, Estéban and I considerably more. The Bonanza begins to bump soggily. Estéban makes an ancient one-eyed Maya face at the water seeping into his cabin and goes to sleep. We all nap.

When the water goes down, the euphoria has gone with it, and we're very, very thirsty. It's also damn near sunset. I get to work with a bait-casting rod and some treble hooks and manage to foul-hook four small mullets. Estéban and the women tie the Bonanza's midget life raft out in the mangroves to catch rain. The wind is parching hot. No planes go by.

Finally another shower comes over and yields us six ounces of water apiece. When the sunset envelops the world in golden smoke, we squat on the sandbar to eat wet raw mullet and Instant Breakfast crumbs. The women are now in shorts, neat but definitely not sexy.

"I never realized how refreshing raw fish is," Mrs. Parsons says pleasantly. Her daughter chuckles, also pleasantly. She's on Mamma's far side away from Estéban and me. I have Mrs. Parsons figured now: Mother Hen protecting only chick from male predators. That's all right with me. I came here to fish.

But something is irritating me. The damn women haven't complained once, you understand. Not a peep, not a quaver, no personal manifestations whatever. They're like something out of a manual.

"You really seem at home in the wilderness, Mrs. Parsons. You do much camping?"

"Oh goodness no." Diffident laugh. "Not since my girl scout days. Oh, look—are those man-of-war birds?"

Answer a question with a question. I wait while the frigate birds sail nobly into the sunset.

"Bethesda. Would I be wrong in guessing you work for Uncle Sam?"

"Why, yes. You must be very familiar with Washington, Mr. Fenton. Does your work bring you there often?"

Anywhere but on our sandbar the little ploy would have worked. My hunter's gene twitches.

"Which agency are you with?"

She gives up gracefully. "Oh, just GSA records. I'm a librarian."

Of course, I know her now, all the Mrs. Parsonses in records divisions, accounting sections, research branches, personnel and administration offices. Tell Mrs. Parsons we need a recap on the external service contracts for fiscal '73. So Yucatan is on the tours now? Pity . . . I offer her the tired little joke. "You know where the bodies are buried."

She smiles deprecatingly and stands up. "It does get dark quickly, doesn't it?"

Time to get back into the plane.

A flock of ibis are circling us, evidently accustomed to roosting in our fig tree. Estéban produces a machete and a Maya string hammock. He proceeds to sling it between tree and plane, refusing help. His machete stroke is noticeably tentative.

The Parsons are taking a pee behind the tail vane. I hear one of them slip and squeal faintly. When they come back over the hull, Mrs. Parsons asks, "Might we sleep in the hammock, Captain?"

Estéban splits an unbelieving grin. I protest about rain and mosquitoes.

"Oh, we have insect repellent and we do enjoy fresh air."

The air is rushing by about force five and colder by the minute.

"We have our raincoats," the girl adds cheerfully.

Well, okay, ladies. We dangerous males retire inside the damp cabin. Through the wind I hear the women laugh softly now and then, apparently cozy in their chilly ibis roost. A private insanity, I decide. I know myself for the least threatening of men; my non-charisma has been in fact an asset jobwise, over the years. Are they having fantasies about Estéban? Or maybe they really are fresh-air nuts . . . Sleep comes for me in invisible diesels roaring by on the reef outside.

We emerge dry-mouthed into a vast windy salmon sunrise. A diamond chip of sun breaks out of the sea and promptly submerges in cloud. I go to work with the rod and some mullet bait while two showers detour around us. Breakfast is a strip of wet barracuda apiece.

The Parsons continue stoic and helpful. Under Estéban's direction they set up a section of cowling for a gasoline flare in case we hear a plane, but nothing goes over except one unseen jet droning toward Panama. The wind howls, hot and dry and full of coral dust. So are we.

"They look first in the sea," Estéban remarks. His aristocratic frontal slope is beaded with sweat; Mrs. Parsons watches him concernedly. I watch the cloud blanket tearing by above, getting higher and dryer and thicker. While that lasts nobody is going to find us, and the water business is now unfunny.

Finally I borrow Esteban's machete and hack a long light pole. "There's a stream coming in there, I saw it from the plane. Can't be more than two, three miles."

"I'm afraid the raft's torn." Mrs. Parsons shows me the cracks in the orange plastic; irritatingly, it's a Delaware label.

"All right," I hear myself announce. "The tide's going down. If we cut the good end of that air tube, I can haul water back in it. I've waded flats before."

Even to me it sounds crazy.

"Stay by plane," Estéban says. He's right, of course. He's also clearing running a fever. I look at the overcast and taste grit and old barracuda. The hell with the manual.

When I start cutting up the raft, Estéban tells me to take the serape. "You stay one night." He's right about that, too; I'll have to wait out the tide.

"I'll come with you," says Mrs. Parsons calmly.

I simply stare at her. What new madness has got into Mother Hen? Does she imagine Estéban is too battered to be functional? While I'm being astounded, my eyes take in that fact that Mrs. Parsons is now quite rosy around the knees, with her hair loose and a sunburn starting on her nose. A trim, in fact a very neat shading-forty.

"Look, that stuff is horrible going. Mud up to your ears and water over your head."

"I'm really quite fit and I swim a great deal. I'll try to keep up. Two would be much safer, Mr. Fenton, and we can bring more water."

She's serious. Well, I'm about as fit as a marshmallow at this time of winter, and I can't pretend I'm depressed by the idea of company. So be it.

"Let me show Miss Parsons how to work this rod."

Miss Parsons is even rosier and more windblown, and she's not clumsy with my tackle. A good girl, Miss Parsons, in her nothing way. We cut another staff and get some gear together. At the last minute Estéban shows how sick he feels: he offers me the machete. I thank him, but, no; I'm used to my Wirkkala knife. We tie some air into the plastic tube for a float and set out along the sandiest looking line.

Estéban raises one dark palm. *"Buen viaje."* Miss Parsons has hugged her mother and gone to cast from the mangrove. She waves. We wave.

An hour later we're barely out of waving distance. The going is purely god-awful. The sand keeps dissolving into silt you can't walk on or swim through, and the bottom is spiked with dead mangrove spears. We flounder from one pothole to the next, scaring up rays and turtles and hoping to God we don't kick a moray eel. Where we're not soaked in slime, we're desiccated, and we smell like the Old Cretaceous.

Mrs. Parsons keeps up doggedly. I only have to pull her out once. When I do so, I notice the sandbar is now out of sight.

Finally we reach the gap in the mangrove line I thought was the creek. It turns out to open into another arm of the bay, with more mangroves ahead. And the tide is coming in.

"I've had the world's lousiest idea."

Mrs. Parsons only says mildly, "It's so different from the view from the plane."

I revise my opinion of the girl scouts, and we plow on past the mangroves toward the smoky haze that has to be shore. The sun is setting in our faces, making it hard to see. Ibises and herons fly up around us, and once a big permit spooks ahead, his fin cutting a rooster tail. We fall into more potholes. The flashlights get soaked. I am having fantasies of the mangrove as universal obstacle; it's hard to recall I ever walked down a street, for instance, without stumbling over or under or through mangrove roots. And the sun is dropping, down, down.

Suddenly we hit a ledge and fall over it into a cold flow.

"The stream! It's fresh water!"

We guzzle and gargle and douse our heads; it's the best drink I remember. "Oh my, oh my—!" Mrs. Parsons is laughing right out loud.

"That dark place over to the right looks like real land."

We flounder across the flow and follow a hard shelf, which turns into solid bank and rises over our heads. Shortly there's a break beside a clump of spiny bromels, and we scramble up and flop down at the top, dripping and stinking. Out of sheer reflex my arm goes around my companion's shoulder—but Mrs. Parsons isn't there; she's up on her knees peering at the burnt-over plain around us.

"Its so good to see land one can walk on!" The tone is too innocent. *Noli me tangere.*

"Don't try it." I'm exasperated; the muddy little woman, what does she think? "That ground out there is a crust of ashes over muck, and it's full of stubs. You can go in over your knees."

"It seems firm here."

"We're in an alligator nursery. That was the slide we came up. Don't worry, by how the old lady's doubtless on her way to be made into handbags."

"What a shame."

"I better set a line down in the stream while I can still see."

I slide back down and rig a string of hooks that may get us breakfast. When I get back Mrs. Parsons is wringing muck out of the serape.

"I'm glad you warned me, Mr. Fenton. It *is* treacherous."

"Yeah." I'm over my irritation; God knows I don't want to *tangere* Mrs. Parsons, even if I weren't beat down to mush. "In its quiet way, Yucatan is a tough place to get around in. You can see why the Mayas built roads. Speaking of which—look!"

The last of the sunset is silhouetting a small square shape a couple of kilometers inland: a Maya *ruina* with a fig tree growing out of it.

"Lot of those around. People think they were guard towers."

"What a deserted-feeling land."

"Let's hope it's deserted by mosquitoes."

We slump down in the 'gator nursery and share the last malt bar, watching the stars slide in and out of the blowing clouds. The bugs aren't too bad; maybe the burn did them in. And it isn't hot any more, either—in fact, it's not even warm, wet as we are. Mrs. Parsons continues tranquilly interested in Yucatan and unmistakably uninterested in togetherness.

Just as I'm beginning to get aggressive notions about how we're going to spend the night if she expects me to give her the serape, she stands up, scuffs at a couple of hummocks and says, "I expect this is as good a place as any, isn't it, Mr. Fenton?"

With which she spreads out the raft bag for a pillow and lies down on her side in the dirt with exactly half the serape over her and the other corner folded neatly open. Her small back is toward me.

The demonstration is so convincing that I'm halfway under my share of serape before the preposterousness of it stops me.

"By the way. My name is Don."

"Oh, of course." Her voice is graciousness itself. "I'm Ruth."

I get in not quite touching her, and we lie there like two fish on a plate, exposed to the stars and smelling the smoke in the wind and feeling things underneath us. It is absolutely the most intimately awkward moment I've had in years.

The woman doesn't mean one thing to me, but the obtrusive recessiveness of her, the defiance of her little rump eight inches from my fly—for two pesos I'd have those shorts down and introduce myself. If I were twenty years younger. If I wasn't so bushed . . . But the twenty years and the exhaustion are there, and it comes to me wryly that Mrs. Ruth Parsons has judged things to a nicety. If I *were* twenty years younger, she wouldn't be here. Like the butterfish that float around a logy barracuda, only to vanish away the instant his intent changes, Mrs. Parsons knows her little shorts are safe. Those firmly filled little shorts, so close . . .

A warm nerve stirs in my groin—and just as it does I become aware of a silent emptiness beside me. Mrs. Parsons is imperceptibly inching away. Did my breathing change? Whatever, I'm perfectly sure that if my hand reached, she'd be elsewhere—probably announcing her intentions to take a dip. The twenty years bring a chuckle to my throat, and I relax.

"Good night, Ruth."

"Good night, Don."

And believe it or not, we sleep, while the armadas of the wind roar overhead.

Light wakes me—a cold white glare.

My first thought is 'gator hunters. Best to manifest ourselves as *turistas* as fast as possible. I scramble up, noting that Ruth has dived under the bromel clump.

"Quien estas? A secorro! Help, *senores!"*

No answer except the light goes out, leaving me blind.

I yell some more in a couple of languages. It stays dark. There's a vague scrabbling, whistling sound somewhere in the burn-off. Liking everything less by the minute, I try a speech about our plane having crashed and we need help.

A very narrow pencil of light flicks over us and snaps off.

"Eh-ep," says a blurry voice and something metallic twitters. They for sure aren't locals. I'm getting unpleasant ideas.

"Yes, help!"

Something goes crackle-crackle whish-whish, and all sounds fade away.

"What the holy hell!" I stumble toward where they were.

"Look." Ruth whispers behind me. "Over by the ruin."

I look and catch a multiple flicker which winks out fast.

"A camp?"

And I take two more blind strides; my legs goes down through the crust, and a spike spears me just where you stick the knife in to unjoint a drumstick. By the pain that goes through my bladder I recognize that my trick kneecap has caught it.

For instant basket case you can't beat kneecaps. First you discover your knee doesn't bend any more, so you try putting some weight on it, and a bayonet goes up your spine and unhinges your jaw. Little grains of gristle have got into the sensitive bearing surface. The knee tries to buckle and can't, and mercifully you fall down.

Ruth helps me back to the serape.

"What a fool, what a god-forgotten imbecile—"

"Not at all, Don. It was perfectly natural." We strike matches; her fingers push mine aside, exploring. "I think it's in place, but it's swelling fast. I'll lay a wet handkerchief on it. We'll have to wait for morning to check the cut. Were they poachers, do you think?"

"Probably," I lie. What I think they were is smugglers.

She comes back with a soaked bandanna and drapes it on. "We must have frightened them. That light . . . it seemed so bright."

"Some hunting party. People do crazy things around here."

'Perhaps they'll come back in the morning."

"Could be."

Ruth pulls up the wet serape, and we say goodnight again. Neither of us are mentioning how we're going to get back to the plane without help.

I lie staring south where Alpha Centauri is blinking in and out of the overcast and cursing myself for the sweet mess I've made. My first idea is giving way to an even less pleasing one.

Smuggling, around here, is a couple of guys in an outboard meeting a shrimp boat by the reef. They don't light up the sky or have some kind of swamp buggy that goes whoosh. Plus a big camp . . . paramilitary-type equipment?

I've seen a report of Guévarista infiltrators operating on the British Honduran border, which is about a hundred kilometers—sixty miles—south of here. Right under those clouds. If that's what looked us over, I'll be more than happy if they don't come back . . .

I wake up in pelting rain, alone. My first move confirms that my leg is as expected—a giant misplaced erection bulging out of my shorts. I raise up painfully to see Ruth standing by the bromels, looking over the bay. Solid wet nimbus is pouring out of the south.

"No planes today."

"Oh, good morning, Don. Should we look at that cut now?"

"It's minimal." In fact the skin is hardly broken, and no deep puncture. Totally out of proportion to the havoc inside.

"Well, they have water to drink," Ruth says tranquilly. "Maybe those hunters will come back. I'll go see if we have a fish—that is, can I help you in any way, Don?"

Very tactful. I emit an ungracious negative, and she goes off about her private concerns.

They certainly are private, too; when I recover from my own sanitary efforts, she's still away. Finally I hear splashing.

"It's a big fish!" More splashing. Then she climbs up the bank with a three-pound mangrove snapper—and something else.

It isn't until after the messy work of filleting the fish that I begin to notice.

She's making a smudge of chaff and twigs to singe the fillets, small hands very quick, tension in that female upper lip. The rain has eased off for the moment; we're sluicing

wet but warm enough. Ruth brings me my fish on a mangrove skewer and sits back on her heels with an odd
breathy sigh.

"Aren't you joining me?"

"Oh, of course." She gets a strip and picks at it, saying
quickly, "We either have too much salt or too little, don't
we? I should fetch some brine." Her eyes are roving from
nothing to noplace.

"Good thought." I hear another sigh and decide the girl
scouts need an assist. "Your daughter mentioned you've
come from Mérida. Seen much of Mexico?

"Not really. Last year we went to Mazatlan and
Cuernavaca . . ." She puts the fish down, frowning.

"And you're going to see Tikál. Going to Bonampak
too?"

"No." Suddenly she jumps up brushing rain off her face.
"I'll bring you some water, Don."

She ducks down the slide, and after a fair while comes
back with a full bromel stalk.

"Thanks." She's standing above me, staring restlessly
round the horizon."

"Ruth, I hate to say it, but those guys are not coming
back and it's probably just as well. Whatever they were up
to, we looked like trouble. The most they'll do is tell someone we're here. That'll take a day or two to get around,
we'll be back at the plane by then."

"I'm sure you're right, Don." She wanders over to the
smudge fire.

"And quit fretting about your daughter. She's a big girl."

"Oh, I'm sure Althea's all right . . . They have plenty
of water now." Her fingers drum on her thigh. It's raining
again.

"Come on, Ruth. Sit down. Tell me about Althea. Is she
still in college?"

She gives that sighing little laugh and sits. "Althea got
her degree last year. She's in computer programming."

"Good for her. And you, what do you do for GSA?"

"I'm in Foreign Procurement Archives." She smiles mechanically, but her breathing is shallow. "It's very interesting."

"I know a Jack Wittig in Contracts, maybe you know him?"

It sounds pretty absurd, there in the 'gator slide.

"Oh, I've met Mr. Wittig. I'm sure he wouldn't remember me."

"Why not?"

"I'm not very memorable."

Her voice is purely factual. She's perfectly right, of course. Who was that woman, Mrs. Jannings, Janny, who coped with my per diem for years? Competent, agreeable, impersonal. She had a sick father or something. But dammit, Ruth is a lot younger and better-looking. Comparatively speaking.

"Maybe Mrs. Parsons doesn't want to be memorable."

She makes a vague sound, and I suddenly realize Ruth isn't listening to me at all. Her hands are clenched around her knees, she's staring inland at the ruin.

"Ruth, I tell you our friends with the light are in the next county by now. Forget it, we don't need them."

Her eyes come back to me as if she'd forgotten I was there, and she nods slowly. It seems to be too much effort to speak. Suddenly she cocks her head and jumps up again.

"I'll go look at the line, Don. I thought I heard something—" She's gone like a rabbit.

While she's away I try getting up onto my good leg and the staff. The pain is sickening; knees seem to have some kind of hot line to the stomach. I take a couple of hops to test whether the Demerol I have in my belt would get me walking. As I do so, Ruth comes up the bank with a fish flapping in her hands.

"Oh, no, Don! *No!*" She actually clasps the snapper to her breast.

"The water will take some of my weight. I'd like to give it a try."

"You mustn't!" Ruth says quite violent and instantly modulates down. "Look at the bay, Don. One can't see a thing."

I teeter there, tasting bile and looking at the mingled curtains of sun and rain driving across the water. She's right, thank God. Even with two good legs we could get into trouble out there.

"I guess one more night won't kill us."

I let her collapse me back onto the gritty plastic, and she positively bustles around, finding me a chunk to lean on, stretching the serape on both staffs to keep rain off me, bringing another drink, grubbing for dry tinder.

"I'll make us a real bonfire as soon as it lets up, Don. They'll see our smoke, they'll know we're all right. We just have to wait." Cheery smile. "Is there any way we can make you more comfortable?"

Holy Saint Sterculius: playing house in a mud puddle. For a fatuous moment I wonder if Mrs. Parsons has designs on me. And then she lets out another sigh and sinks back onto her heels with that listening look. Unconsciously her rump wiggles a little. My ear picks up the operative word: *wait*.

Ruth Parsons is waiting. In fact, she acts as if she's waiting so hard it's killing her. For what? For someone to get us out of here, what else? . . . But why was she so horrified when I got up to try to leave? Why all this tension?

My paranoia stirs. I grab it by the collar and start idly checking back. Up to when whoever it was showed up last night, Mrs. Parson was, I guess, normal. Calm and sensible, anyway. Now's she's humming like a high wire. And she seems to want to stay here and wait. Just as an intellectual pastime, why?

Could she have intended to come here? No way. Where she planned to be was Chetumal, which is on the border. Come to think, Chetumal is an odd way round to Tikál. Let's say the scenario was that she's meeting somebody in Chetumal. Somebody who's part of an organization. So now her contact in Chetumal knows she's overdue. And when those types appeared last night, something suggests to her that they're part of the same organization. And she hopes they'll put one and one together and come back for her?

"May I have the knife, Don? I'll clean the fish."

Rather slowly I pass the knife, kicking my subconscious. Such a decent ordinary little woman, a good girl scout. My trouble is that I've bumped into too many professional agilities under the careful sterotypes. *I'm not very memorable. . .*

What's in Foreign Procurement Archives? Wittig handles classified contracts. Lots of money stuff; foreign currency negotiations, commodity price schedules, some industrial technology. Or—just as a hypothesis—it could be as simple as a wad of bills back in that modest beige Ventura, to be exchanged for a packet from say, Costa Rica. If she were a courier, they'd want to get at the plane. And then what about me and maybe Estéban? Even hypothetically, not good.

I watch her hacking at the fish, forehead knotted with effort, teeth in her lip. Mrs. Ruth Parsons of Bethesda, this thrumming, private woman. How crazy can I get? *They'll see our smoke . . .*

"Here's your knife, Don. I washed it. Does the leg hurt very badly?"

I blink away the fantasies and see a scared little woman in a mangrove swamp.

"Sit down, rest. You've been going all out."

She sits obediently, like a kid in a dentist chair.

"You're stewing about Althea. And she's probably worried about you. We'll get back tomorrow under our own steam, Ruth."

"Honestly I'm not worried at all, Don." The smile fades; she nibbles her lip, frowning out at the bay.

"You know, Ruth, you surprised me when you offered to come along. Not that I don't appreciate it. But I rather thought you'd be concerned about leaving Althea. Alone with our good pilot, I mean. Or was it only me?"

This gets her attention at last.

"I believe Captain Estéban is a very fine type of man."

The words surprise me a little. Isn't the correct line more like "I trust Althea," or even, indignantly, "Althea is a good girl"?

"He's a man. Althea seemed to think he was interesting."

She goes on staring at the bay. And then I notice her tongue flick out and lick that prehensile upper lip. There's a flush that isn't sunburn around her ears and throat too, and one hand is gently rubbing her thigh. What's she seeing, out there in the flats?

Oho.

Captain Estéban's mahogany arms clasping Miss Althea Parsons' pearly body. Captain Estéban's archaic nostrils snuffling in Miss Parsons' tender neck. Captain Estéban's copper buttocks pumping into Althea's creamy upturned bottom . . . The hammock, very bouncy. Mayas know all about it.

Well, well. So Mother Hen has her little quirks.

I feel fairly silly and more than a little irritated. *Now* I find out. But even vicarious lust has much to recommend it, here in the mud and rain. I settle back, recalling that Miss Althea the computer programmer had waved good-bye very composedly. Was she sending her mother to flounder across the bay with me so she can get programmed in Maya? The memory of Honduran mahogany logs drifting in and out of the opalescent sand comes to me. Just as I am about to suggest that Mrs. Parsons might care to share my rain shelter, she remarks serenely, "The Mayas seem to be a very fine type of people. I believe you said so to Althea."

The implications fall on me with the rain. *Type.* As in breeding, bloodline, sire. Am I supposed to have certified Estéban not only as a stud but as a genetic donor?

"Ruth, are you telling me you're prepared to accept a half-Indian grandchild?"

"Why, Don, that's up to Althea, you know."

Looking at the mother, I guess it is. Oh, for mahogany gonads.

Ruth has gone back to listening to the wind, but I'm not about to let her off that easy. Not after all that *noli me tangere* jazz.

"What will Althea's father think?"

Her face snaps around at me, genuinely startled.

"Althea's father?" Complicated semismile. "He won't mind."

"He'll accept it too, eh?" I see her shake her head as if a fly were bothering her, and add with a cripple's malice: "Your husband must be a very fine type of a man."

Ruth looks at me, pushing her wet hair back abruptly. I have the impression that mousy Mrs. Parsons is roaring out of control, but her voice is quiet.

"There isn't any Mr. Parsons, Don. There never was. Althea's father was a Danish medical student . . . I believe he has gained considerable prominence."

"Oh." Something warns me not to say I'm sorry. "You mean he doesn't know about Althea?"

"No." She smiles, her eyes bright and cuckoo.

"Seems like a rough deal for her."

"I grew up quite happily under the same circumstances."

Bang, I'm dead. Well, well, well. A mad image blooms in my mind: generations of solitary Parsons women selecting sires, making impregnation trips. Well, I hear the world is moving their way.

"I better look at the fish line."

She leaves. The glow fades. *No.* Just no, no contact. Good-bye, Captain Estéban. My leg is very uncomfortable. The hell with Mrs. Parsons' long-distance orgasm.

We don't talk much after that, which seems to suit Ruth. The odd day drags by. Squall after squall blows over us. Ruth singes up some more fillets, but the rain drowns her smudge; it seems to pour hardest just as the sun's about to show.

Finally she comes to sit under my sagging serape, but there's no warmth there. I doze, aware of her getting up now and then to look around. My subconscious notes that she's still twitchy. I tell my subconscious to knock it off.

Presently I wake up to find her penciling on the water-soaked pages of a little notepad.

"What's that, a shopping list for alligators?"

Automatic polite laugh. "Oh, just an address. In case we —I'm being silly, Don."

"Hey." I sit up, wincing. "Ruth, quit fretting. I mean it. We'll all be out of this soon. You'll have a great story to tell."

She doesn't look up. "Yes . . . I guess we will."

"Come on, we're doing fine. There isn't any real danger here, you know. Unless you're allergic to fish?"

Another good-little-girl laugh, but there's a shiver in it. "Sometimes I think I'd like to go . . . really far away."

To keep her talking I say the first thing in my head.

"Tell me, Ruth. I'm curious why you would settle for that kind of lonely life, there in Washington? I mean, a woman like you —"

"Should get married?" She gives a shaky sigh, pushing the notebook back in her wet pocket.

"Why not? It's the normal source of companionship. Don't tell me you're trying to be some kind of professional man-hater."

"Lesbian, you mean?" Her laugh sounds better. "With my security rating? No, I'm not."

"Well, then. Whatever trauma you went through, these things don't last forever. You can't hate all men."

The smile is back. "Oh, there wasn't any trauma, Don, and I *don't* hate men. That would be as silly as—as hating the weather." She glances wryly at the blowing rain.

"I think you have a grudge. You're even spooky of me."

Smooth as a mouse bite she says, "I'd love to hear about your family, Don?"

Touché. I give her the edited version of how I don't have one any more, and she says she's sorry, how sad. And we chat about what a good life a single person really has, and how she and her friends enjoy plays and concerts and travel, and one of them is head cashier for Ringling Brothers, how about that?

But it's coming out jerkier and jerkier like a bad tape, with her eyes going round the horizon in the pauses and her face listening for something that isn't my voice. What's wrong with her? Well, what's wrong with any furtively unconventional middle-aged woman with an empty bed. And a security clearance. An old habit of mind remards unkindly that Mrs. Parsons represents what is known as the classic penetration target.

"—so much more opportunity now." Her voice trails off.

"Hurrah for women's lib, eh?"

"The lib?" Impatiently she leans forward and tugs the serape straight. "Oh, that's doomed."

The apocalyptic word jars my attention.

"What do you mean, doomed?"

She glances at me as if I weren't hanging straight either and says vaguely, "Oh . . ."

"Come on, why doomed? Didn't they get that equal rights bill?"

Long hesitation. When she speaks again her voice is different.

"Women have no rights, Don, except what men allow us. Men are more aggressive and powerful, and they run the world. When the next real crisis upsets them, our so-called rights will vanish like—like that smoke. We'll be back where we always were: property. And whatever has gone wrong will be blamed on our freedom, like the fall of Rome was. You'll see."

Now all this is delivered in a grey tone of total conviction. The last time I heard that tone, the speaker was explaining why he had to keep his file drawers full of dead pigeons.

"Oh, come on. You and your friends are the backbone of the system; if you quit, the country would come to a screeching halt before lunch."

No answering smile.

"That's fantasy." Her voice is still quiet. "Women don't work that way. We're a —a toothless world." She looks around as if she wanted to stop talking. "What women do is survive. We live by ones and twos in the chinks of your world-machine."

"Sounds like a guerrilla operation." I'm not really joking, here in the 'gator den. In fact, I'm wondering if I spent too much thought on mahogany logs.

"Guerrillas have something to hope for." Suddenly she

switches on the jolly smile. "Think of us opossums, Don. Did you know there are opossums living all over? Even in New York City."

I smile back with my neck prickling. I thought I was the paranoid one.

"Men and women aren't different species, Ruth. Women do everything men do."

"Do they?" Our eyes meet, but she seems to be seeing ghosts between us in the rain. She mutters something that could be "My Lai" and looks away. "All the endless wars . . ." Her voice is a whisper. "All the huge authoritarian organizations for doing unreal things. Men live to struggle against each other; we're just part of the battlefields. It'll never change unless you change the whole world. I dream sometimes of—of going away—" She checks and abruptly changes voice. "Forgive me, Don, it's so stupid saying all this."

"Men hate wars too, Ruth," I say as gently as I can.

"I know." She shrugs and climbs to her feet. "But that's your problem, isn't it?"

End of communication. Mrs. Ruth Parsons isn't even living in the same world with me.

I watch her move around restlessly, head turning toward the ruins. Alienation like that can add up to dead pigeons, which would be GSA's problem. It could also lead to believing some joker who's promising to change the whole world. Which could just probably be my problem if one of them was over in that camp last night, where she keeps looking. *Guerrillas have something to hope for . . . ?*

Nonsense. I try another position and see that the sky seems to be clearing as the sun sets. The wind is quieting down at last too. Insane to think this little woman is acting out some fantasy in this swamp. But that equipment last night was no fantasy; if those lads have some connection with her, I'll be in the way. You couldn't find a handier spot to dispose of a body. Maybe some Guévarista is a fine type of man?

Absurd. Sure. The only thing more absurd would be to come through the wars and get myself terminated by a mad librarian's boyfriend on a fishing trip.

A fish flops in the stream below us. Ruth spins around so fast she hits the serape. "I better start the fire," she says, her eyes still on the plain and her head cocked, listening.

All right, let's test.

"Expecting company?"

It rocks her. She freezes, and her eyes come swiveling around at me like a film take captioned Fright. I can see her decide to smile.

"Oh, one never can tell!" She laughs weirdly, the eyes not changed. "I'll get the—the kindling." She fairly scuttles into the brush.

Nobody, paranoid or not, could call *that* a normal reaction.

Ruth Parsons is either psycho or she's expecting something to happen—and it has nothing to do with me; I scared her pissless.

Well, she could be nuts. And I could be wrong, but there are some mistakes you only make once.

Reluctantly I unzip my body-belt, telling myself that if I think what I think, my only course is to take something for my leg and get as far as possible from Mrs. Ruth Parsons before whoever she's waiting for arrives.

In my belt also is a .32 caliber asset Ruth doesn't know about—and it's going to stay there. My longevity program leaves the shoot-outs to TV and stresses being somewhere else when the roof falls in. I can spend a perfectly safe and also perfectly horrible night out in one of those mangrove flats . . . am I insane?

At this moment Ruth stands up and stares blatantly inland with her hand shading her eyes. Then she tucks something into her pocket, buttons up, and tightens her belt.

That does it.

I dry-swallow two 100 mg tabs, which should get me ambulatory and still leave me wits to hide. Give it a few minutes. I make sure my compass and some hooks are in my own pocket and sit waiting while Ruth fusses with her smudge fire, sneaking looks away when she thinks I'm not watching.

The flat world around us is turning into an unearthly amber and violet light show as the first numbness seeps into my leg. Ruth has crawled under the bromels for more dry stuff; I can see her foot. Okay. I reach for my staff.

Suddenly the foot jerks, and Ruth yells—or rather, her throat makes that *Uh-uh-hhh* that means pure horror. The foot disappears in a rattle of bromel stalks.

I lunge upright on the crutch and look over the bank at a frozen scene.

Ruth is crouching sideways on the ledge, clutching her stomach. They are about a yard below, floating on the river in a skiff. While I was making up my stupid mind, her friends have glided right under my ass. There are three of them.

They are tall and white. I try to see them as men in some kind of white jumpsuits. The one nearest the bank is stretching out a long white arm toward Ruth. She jerks and scuttles further away.

The arm stretches after her. It stretches and stretches. It stretches two yards and stays hanging in air. Small black things are wiggling from its tip.

I look where their faces should be and see black hollow dishes with vertical stripes. The stripes move slowly . . .

There is no more possibility of their being human—or anything else I've ever seen. What has Ruth conjured up?

The scene is totally silent. I blink, blink—this cannot be real. The two in the far end of the skiff are writhing those arms around an apparatus on a tripod. A weapon? Suddenly I hear the same blurry voice I heard in the night.

"Guh-give," it groans. "G-give . . ."

Dear God, it's real, whatever it is. I'm terrified. My mind is trying not to form a word.

And Ruth—Jesus, of course—Ruth is terrified too; she's edging along the bank away from them, gaping at the monsters in the skiff, who are obviously nobody's friends.

She's hugging something to her body. Why doesn't she get over the bank and circle back behind me?

"G-g-give." That wheeze is coming from the tripod. "Pee-eeze give." The skiff is moving upstream below Ruth, following her. The arm undulates out at her again, its black digits looping. Ruth scrambles to the top of the bank.

"Ruth!" My voice cracks. "Ruth, get over here behind me!"

She doesn't look at me, only keeps sidling farther away. My terror detonates into anger.

"Come back here!" With my free hand I'm working the .32 out of my belt. The sun has gone down.

She doesn't turn but straightens up warily, still hugging the thing. I see her mouth working. Is she actually trying to *talk* to them?

"Please . . ." She swallows. "Please speak to me. I need your help."

"RUTH!!"

At this moment the nearest white monster whips into a great S-curve and sails right onto the bank at her, eight feet of snowy rippling horror.

And I shoot Ruth.

I don't know that for a minute— I've yanked the gun up so fast that my staff slips and dumps me as I fire. I stagger up, hearing Ruth scream "No! No! No!"

The creature is back down by his boat, and Ruth is still farther away, clutching herself. Blood is running down her elbow.

"Stop it, Don! They aren't attacking you!"

"For God's sake! Don't be a fool, I can't help you if you won't get away from them!"

No reply. Nobody moves. No sound except the drone of a jet passing far above. In the darkening stream below me the three white figures shift uneasily; I get the impression of radar dishes focusing. The word spells itself in my head: *Aliens.*

Extraterrestrials.

What do I do, call the President? Capture them single-handed with my peashooter? . . . I'm alone in the arse end of nowhere with one leg and my brain cuddled in meperidine hydrochloride.

"Prrr-eese," their machine blurs again. "Wa-wat hep . . ."

"Our plane fell down," Ruth says in a very distinct, eerie voice. She points up at the jet, out towards the bay. "My —my child is there. Please take us *there* in your boat."

Dear God. While she's gesturing, I get a look at the thing she's hugging in her wounded arm. It's metallic, like a big glimmering distributor head. What—?

Wait a minute. This morning: when she was gone so long, she could have found that thing. Something they left behind. Or dropped. And she hid it, not telling me. That's why she kept going under that bromel clump—she was peeking at it. Waiting. And the owners came back and caught her. They want it. She's trying to bargain, by God.

"—Water," Ruth is pointing again. "Take us. Me. And him."

The black faces turn toward me, blind and horrible. Later on I may be grateful for that "us." Not now.

"Throw your gun away, Don. They'll take us back." Her voice is weak.

"Like hell I will. You—who are you? What are you doing here?"

"Oh God, does it matter? He's frightened," she cries to them. "Can you understand?"

She's as alien as they, there in the twilight. The beings in the skiff are twittering among themselves. Their box starts to moan.

"Ss-stu-dens," I make out. "S-stu-ding . . . not—huh-arm-ing . . . w-we . . . buh . . ." It fades into garble and then says, "G-give . . . we . . . g-go . . ."

Peace-loving cultural-exchange students—on the interstellar level now. Oh, no.

"Bring that thing here, Ruth—right now!"

But she's starting down the bank toward them saying, "Take me."

"Wait! You need a tourniquet on that arm."

"I know. Please put the gun down, Don."

She's actually at the skiff, right by them. They aren't moving.

"Jesus Christ." Slowly, reluctantly I drop the .32. When I start down the slide, I find I'm floating; adrenaline and Demerol are a bad mix.

The skiff comes gliding toward me, Ruth in the bow clutching the thing and her arm. The aliens stay in the stern behind their tripod, away from me. I note the skiff is camouflaged tan and green. The world around us is deep shadowy blue.

"Don, bring the water bag!"

As I'm dragging down the plastic bag, it occurs to me that Ruth really is cracking up, the water isn't needed now. But my own brain seems to have gone into overload. All I can focus on is a long white rubbery arm with black worms clutching the far end of the orange tube, helping me fill it. This isn't happening.

"Can you get in, Don?" As I hoist my numb legs up, two long white pipes reach for me. No you don't. I kick and tumble in beside Ruth. She moves away.

A creaky hum starts up. It's coming from a wedge in the center of the skiff. And we're in motion, sliding toward dark mangrove files.

I stare mindlessly at the wedge. Alien technological secrets? I can't see any, the power source is under that triangular cover, about two feet long. The gadgets on the tripod are equally cryptic, except that one has a big lens. Their light?

As we hit the open bay the hum rises and we start planing faster and faster still. Thirty knots? Hard to judge in the dark. Their hull seems to be a modified trihedral much like ours, with a remarkable absence of slap. Say twenty-two feet. Schemes of capturing it swirl in my mind: I'll need Estéban.

Suddenly a huge flood of white light fans out over us from the tripod, blotting out the aliens in the stern. I see Ruth pulling at a belt around her arm, still hugging the gizmo.

"I'll tie that for you."

"It's all right."

The alien device is twinkling or phosphorescing slightly. I lean over to look, whispering, "Give that to me, I'll pass it to Estéban."

"No!" She scoots away, almost over the side. "It's theirs, they need it!"

"What? Are you crazy?" I'm so taken aback by this idiocy I literally stammer. "We have to, we—"

"They haven't hurt us. I'm sure they could." Her eyes are watching me with feral intensity; in the light her face has a lunatic look. Numb as I am, I realize that the wretched woman is poised to throw herself over the side if I move. With the alien thing.

"I think they're gentle," she mutters.

"For Christ's sake, Ruth, they're *aliens!*"

"I'm used to it," she says absently. "There's the island! Stop! Stop here!"

The skiff slows, turning. A mound of foliage is tiny in the light. Metal glints—the plane.

"Althea! Althea! Are you all right?"

Yells, movement on the plane. The water is high, we're floating over the bar. The aliens are keeping us in the lead with the light hiding them. I see one pale figure splashing toward us and a dark one behind, coming more slowly. Estéban must be puzzled by that light.

"Mr. Fenton is hurt, Althea. These people brought us back with the water. Are you all right?"

"A-okay." Althea flounders up, peering excitedly. "You all right? Whew, that light!" Automatically I start handing her the idiotic water bag.

"Leave that for the captain," Ruth says sharply. "Althea, can you climb in the boat? Quickly, it's important."

"Coming!"

"No, no!" I protest, but the skiff tilts as Althea swarms in. The aliens twitter, and their voice box starts groaning. "Gu-give . . . now . . . give . . ."

"que llega?" Estéban's face appears beside me, squinting fiercely into the light.

"Grab it, get it from her—that thing she has—" but

Ruth's voice rides over mine. "Captain, lift Mr. Fenton out of the boat. He's hurt his leg. Hurry, please."

"Goddamn it, wait!" I shout, but an arm has grabbed my middle. When a Maya boosts you, you go. I hear Althea saying, "Mother, your arm!" and fall onto Estéban. We stagger around in water up to my waist; I can't feel my feet at all.

When I get steady, the boat is yards away, the two women head-to-head, murmuring.

"Get them!" I tug loose from Estéban and flounder forward. Ruth stands up in the boat facing the invisible aliens.

"Take us with you. Please. We want to go with you, away from here."

"Ruth! Estéban, get that boat!" I lunge and lose my feet again. The aliens are chirruping madly behind their light.

"Please take us. We don't mind what your planet is like; we'll learn—we'll do anything! We won't cause any trouble. Please. Oh please." The skiff is drifting farther away.

"Ruth! Althea! Are you crazy, wait—" But I can only shuffle nightmarelike in the ooze, hearing that damn voice box wheeze, "N-not come . . . more . . . not come . . ." Althea's face turns to it, open-mouthed grin.

"Yes, we understand," Ruth cries. "We don't want to come back. Please take us with you!"

I shout and Estéban splashes past me shouting too, something about radio.

"Yes-s-s" groans the voice.

Ruth sits down suddenly, clutching Althea. At that moment Estéban grabs the edge of the skiff beside her.

"Hold them, Estéban! Don't let her go."

He gives me one slit-eyed glance over his shoulder, and I recognize his total uninvolvement. He's had a good look at that camouflage paint and the absence of fishing gear. I make a desperate rush and slip again. When I come up Ruth is saying, "We're going with these people, Captain. Please take your money out of my purse, it's in the plane. And give this to Mr. Fenton."

She passes him something small; the notebook. He takes it slowly.

"Estéban! Don't!"

He has released the skiff.

"Thank you so much," Ruth says as they float apart. Her voice is shaky; she raises it. "There won't be any trouble, Don. Please send the cable. It's to a friend of mine, she'll take care of everything." Then she adds the craziest touch of the entire night. "She's a grand person; she's director of nursing training at N.I.H."

As the skiff drifts I hear Althea add something that sounds like "Right on."

Sweet Jesus . . . Next minute the humming has started; the light is receding fast. The last I see of Mrs. Ruth Parsons and Miss Althea Parsons is two small shadows against that light, like two opossums. The light snaps off, the hum deepens—and they're going, going, gone away.

In the dark water beside me Estéban is instructing everybody in general to *chingarse* themselves.

"Friends, or something," I tell him lamely. "She seemed to want to go with them."

He is pointedly silent, hauling me back to the plane. He knows what could be around here better than I do, and Mayas have their own longevity program. His condition seems improved. As we get in I notice the hammock has been repositioned.

In the night—of which I remember little—the wind changes. And at seven-thirty next morning a Cessna buzzes the sandbar under cloudless skies.

By noon we're back in Cozumel. Captain Estéban accepts his fees and departs laconically for his insurance wars. I leave the Parsons' bags with the Caribe agent, who couldn't care less. The cable goes to a Mrs. Priscilla Hayes Smith also of Bethesda. I take myself to a medico and by three P.M. I'm sitting on the Cabañas terrace with a fat leg and a double margarita, trying to believe the whole thing.

The cable said, *Althea and I taking extraordinary opportunity for travel. Gone several years. Please take charge our affairs. Love, Ruth.*

She'd written it that afternoon, you understand.

I order another double, wishing to hell I'd gotten a good look at that gizmo. Did it have a label, Made by Betelgeusians? No matter how weird it was, *how* could a person be crazy enough to imagine—?

Not only that but to hope, to plan? I'd like to go . . . really far away . . . That's what she was doing, all day. Waiting, hoping, figuring how to get Althea. To go sight unseen to an alien world . . .

With the third margharita I try a joke about alienated women, but my heart's not in it. And I'm certain there won't be any bother, any trouble at all. Two human women, one of them possibly pregnant, have departed for, I guess, the stars; and the fabric of society will never show a ripple. I brood; do all Mrs. Parsons' friends hold themselves in readiness for any eventuality, including leaving Earth? And will Mrs. Parsons somehow one day contrive to send for Mrs. Priscilla Hayes Smith, that grand person?

I can only send for another cold one, musing on Althea. What suns will Captain Estéban's sloe-eyed offspring, if any, look upon? "Get in, Althea, we're taking off for Orion." "A-okay, Mother." Is that some system of upbringing? *We survive by ones and twos in the chinks of your world-machine . . . I'm used to aliens . . .* She'd meant every word. Insane. How could a woman choose to live among unknown monsters, to say good-bye to her home, her world?

As the margharitas take hold, the whole mad scenario melts down to the image of those two small shapes sitting side by side in the receding alien glare.

Two of our oppossums are missing.

Honorable Mentions—1973

F. M. BUSBY: "Pearsall's Return," *Worlds of If*, August.
"Road Map," *Clarion III*.

GEO. ALEC EFFINGER: "The Ghost Writer," *Universe 3*.

GORDON EKLUND: "Free City Blues," *Universe 3*.

WILLIAM HARRISON: "Roller Ball Murder," *Esquire*, September.

JOHN HOPKINS: "The Wires," *Penthouse*, April.

R. A. LAFFERTY: "Parthen," *Galaxy*, May.

VONDA N. MC INTYRE: "Wings," *The Alien Condition*.

WARD MOORE: "Frank Merriwell in the White House," *Galaxy*, July.

LARRY NIVEN: "The Alibi Machine," *Vertex*, June.
"The Defenseless Dead," *Ten Tomorrows*.

K. M. O'DONNELL: "City Lights, City Nights," *Future City*.

EDGAR PANGBORN: "The Freshman Angle," *Ten Tomorrows*.
"My Brother Leopold," *An Exaltation of Stars*.

FREDERIK POHL: "Some Joys Under the Star," *Galaxy*, November.

ROSS ROCKLYNNE: "Randy-Tandy Man," *Universe 3*.

PAMELA SARGENT: "Clone Sister," *Eros in Orbit*.

ROBERT SHECKLEY: "Welcome to the Standard Nightmare," *Nova 3*.

ROBERT SILVERBERG: "In the Group," *Eros in Orbit.*
"Many Mansions," *Universe 3.*
"Some Notes on the Predynastic Epoch," *Bad Moon Rising.*
NORMAN SPINRAD: "The National Pastime," *Nova 3.*
JAMES TIPTREE, JR.: "Love is the Plan the Plan is Death," *The Alien Condition.*
GENE WOLFE: "La Befana," *Galaxy,* January.
"Feather Tigers," *Edge,* Autumn/Winter.

MORE S-F
from
🅑🅑
BALLANTINE BOOKS

SUPERB S-F
from
🆎
BALLANTINE BOOKS

BB 27/75